The Rise of Gideon

By Stan Matthews

THE RISE OF GIDEON

iUniverse books may be ordered through booksellers or by contacting:

iUniverse
1663 Liberty Drive
Bloomington, IN 47403
www.iuniverse.com
1-800-Authors (1-800-288-4677)

ISBN: 978-1-4917-8562-1 (sc)
ISBN: 978-1-4917-8561-4 (e)

Library of Congress Control Number: 2016902468

Print information available on the last page.

iUniverse rev. date: 3/16/2016

Contents

Chapter One

Even then he looked scared. A frightened, chunky little man with darting eyes and a quick uneasy smile. He was no more than thirty when I saw him that first time.

"Good morning, ladies and gentlemen," he said as he adjusted his shirt's cuffs to the correct half inch below the sleeves of his immaculately pressed gray suit.

He announced his name: "Gideon Pratt." He snapped his last name again and I wondered if he expected his audience, my fellow classmates at Richland University, to applaud. He had a "You-like-me-don't-you?" look on his dark-featured face.

Ordinarily I would have given a new lecturer scant attention. After all, lecturers come and lecturers go, and while I remember many of my professors quite well, the instructors on the lower end of the academic ladder were a passing parade. They marched onto the stage of Bond Hall like drill masters ready to do battle with an unruly antagonistic platoon.

Gideon Pratt was different. Instead of waiting for us to stop talking he launched immediately into his lecture, which he was careful to announce was neither a defense nor an attack upon the Romantic poets, but rather a careful analysis. Actually, he aptly described the Romantic Movement as a complex revolt against intellectualism, a point I happened to agree with. Despite his promise, he did launch into an attack upon Byron as a "juvenile" and "completely lacking in discipline," and, since he was attacking a particular literary hero of mine, I resolved to argue with him about that on some other occasion.

On the whole, however, he seemed in good humor, despite his nervous, fidgety style, which I put down to opening-day shakes, natural to a new man on the faculty. Even his voice kept changing. First it was as smooth as cream, low and sonorous, persuasive. Then it was raspy, a scratchy file, snarling, venomous. At times he gripped the lectern as if to hold himself from flying off the stage. He kept looking up from his notes to scan us, perhaps anticipating that at any moment we might escape.

He removed his heavy black glasses, laid them down, picked them up, polished them, put them on. He was soaring to a climax on Keats when the bell rang, ending his lecture. Despite his nervousness, Gideon Pratt had enthralled me with his knowledge of the basic private details of each poet's life. Literature lectures had never been like this. I began to clap, unintentionally I suspect, until soon all in my row joined me, and then the entire class until the hall resounded to the applause.

Gideon stepped back a pace from the lectern, removed his glasses, thrust them into his breast pocket, bowed slightly, shyly, and gathered up his notes. Since I was in the first row, just below the stage, I could hear him say "Good morning, ladies and gentlemen." He dead-marched from the stage into the wings and was gone.

Gideon was always the same on that stage. Always nervous. Always roaring above his nervousness. As the weeks passed I thought he would get over being nervous, but he never did. He was scared, but what of? He had been a teacher for several years at Windom College in Clevcland before coming to our mid-west university. I put it down to the natural fact that this was his first year at a large school, and I would have been willing to let it go at that if, one day in late October, he had not left me a note in my mailbox. He asked me to meet him in his office.

I lunged up the stairs to the third floor of the Arts and Science Building, my knees shaking. I had no idea what he wanted. The only reason I had been summoned that I could think of was that I must have failed his last test and that I was about to be put on the carpet.

Rightaway he bobbed over from his desk and whacked me on the shoulder. "How's the newspaper business?" he asked. I was taking a minor journalism course at the time. It was something of a shock to learn that Gideon knew it. I mumbled about my ambition to be a reporter. Gideon battled a tumbling black forelock that was always falling over his right eye. "Great profession, journalism," he said. "Was a time I thought of becoming a newspaperman myself."

I thought of asking him why he hadn't, but that would have been impertinent. Still, I complimented him about taking an interest in my personal life. A copy of his book, *The Wronged Romantics*, was on his desk. It was required reading for his course. I picked it up and flicked the pages. "I like your book, Mr. Pratt," I said.

Smiling, he plucked off his glasses. He looked five years younger. He half closed his eyes. A dreamy look came over his moon-shaped face. "It's not the best book in the world, but it isn't the worst either," he said. He spoke as if addressing an unseen audience. His voice was as smooth as that of a professional television announcer. "I suppose you shouldn't expect appreciation, not in this world," he said dreamily.

"Well, some of those poets," I replied, catching on that flattery was in order, "they weren't appreciated, not in their own time."

Gideon put on his glasses. His face flushed. He ran a tissue over his forehead, wiping away a thin stream of sweat. He leaned across the desk. "You and I know, Mr. James, the agony it is to write."

"Of course, being a reporter, that isn't exactly being a *writer*."

Gideon pounded his desk. "Never say that! When you're in journalism you contribute something important."

"I meant," I protested, "there's a real difference between newspaper writing and real writing." I was attempting to ingratiate myself with him and it was coming off badly.

"I wonder," he said with a vague wave of his hand. "Sometimes I wonder." He swiveled about and gazed out the window, lost in some reverie.

I glanced around the room. Books lined two walls from floor to ceiling. Stacks of books cluttered his desk. I was looking for his collection of the Romantics when he said "Books, books. The pain of life and the pleasure." He sighed and swiveled back again. He picked up a clutch of papers, dug into them and came up with a typed manuscript that I recognized as my latest treatise. He handed it to me. There was a large red *A* on it.

I suppose I stuttered something out of pure pleasure, because this was the first *A* he had ever given me.

"You deserve it, Mr. James," he said. "I wanted to see you about the paper because I happen to disagree with your main point, although I admit your argument is soundly presented." He said the topic I had chosen, the influence of Teresa Guiccioli on the poetry of Lord Byron, was interesting. "The question is," he said, "did Byron's romantic nature lead to his liaison with Teresa, or did Teresa give him romantic ideas which resulted in his greatest poems?"

I hedged. He had knifed into my thoughts about Byron as incisively as a surgeon knifes into a brain. He was saying that my essay had skirted the basic issue: cause and effect.

"I hope, Mr. James," Gideon went on, eyeing me with amusement, "that you don't presume there was something spiritual in Byron's attachment to Teresa."

"Well, he was romantic," I said weakly, a trembling throb assaulting my knees. "And think of the settings: Ravenna, Venice, Pisa."

"He was bored in Italy."

"But Teresa…he loved her!"

"He had dozens of women."

I am certain I blushed. I could feel it. "*We were entwined*," I quoted.

"He wrote the words to his sister," Gideon said dryly.

"He did?"

"Better check your research, Mr. James."

I took the paper, thanked him, and left. After that, because of his bold trafficking in my own nature, I tried to avoid him, but he was always asking me to come to see him for one reason or another. If it wasn't a paper he wanted to discuss, it was an examination to review. That was the subject of our interview in March. By then I had begun to take an interest in finding out what made Gideon Pratt tick. His platform brilliance, his insight into my own problems, which included a psychological block about admitting my own prejudices toward romanticism, while holding me at arm's length as far as getting to know him was concerned, intrigued me. I suppose I admired his ability to slice through layers of humbug concerning the private lives of the poets to reach the hard knurl of human failure that motivated each of them. Getting to know these poets was getting to know myself, and I didn't like what I was learning. To tell the truth, I was stumbling around for an excuse to get to know Gideon Pratt better, for by this time his personal attention, which I suspected was far beyond what he gave any other student in the class, had raised the nagging question of: "*Why me?*"

Gideon waved my ink-spotted examination paper. "This isn't up to your usual standard, Mr. James," he asserted dryly. "You have missed several important points." He slapped the paper on his desk. "Besides, the grammar is atrocious. And you want to be a journalist!"

I knew I was turning red. I stammered something about not having enough time to complete the test. He flung his glasses down. "Time! Wait until you go to work for a newspaper, if you ever make it."

I wasn't sure whether his anger was caused by disappointment in me or was alloyed with some secret motive. In any case, my dismay shook me. I had the usual student's prejudice against teacher's pets, but aside from that I considered myself one of Gideon's favorites, if not *the* favorite. Now he was attacking me, shunting me outside his coveted approval. The hurt was so physical that I had to turn my head away to wipe an incipient tear from my eye.

He asked me if I wanted to graduate in June, and I said of course I did. "Then buckle down!" he growled. I had one last chance, he said. That would be the final examination in May. If I didn't do better I would surely fail. Because I was majoring in English literature, his course was required. To fail would mean I wouldn't receive my degree.

I stood up. "Is that all, sir?"

He assumed a pose my father used to take when he lectured me for being a bad boy: leaning forward, elbows on his desk, hands clasped. "I'm being particularly hard on you for your own good, Mr. James. You want to be a newspaperman, be the best newspaperman you can. Your best, understand?"

I admitted that fraternity farewell parties had kept me from the books in recent weeks. I assured him that I would indeed "buckle down."

"Any plans for the summer?" he asked.

"Look for a job, I guess."

"Well, you want to be a reporter, don't you? Try the Morning Monitor? Ask to see Mr. Harper. He's the managing editor. He does the hiring."

"I don't know. I haven't any experience."

"Won't do any harm to apply, will it?'

"Well, I guess not."

Gideon Pratt let me go. He could flunk me if he wanted to, but I would never go through that hell again. He did summon me a couple of times

5

via his usual note in my mailbox, but I ignored him. We passed by in the halls, but I only nodded. Gideon Pratt had lifted me to the heights only to dash me to solid ground. Who was the real Gideon Pratt anyway? It took me several years to find out.

Chapter Two

I graduated in early June with the Class of 1964 after a report on my grades arrived in the mail. There it was! An *A* in Gideon's course. I didn't know whether to laugh or cry, whether to hate Gideon Pratt or love him. The final examination had not gone well. It was the toughest Gideon ever gave. I had come out dripping sweat, positive I had failed. But there it was on the impersonal report form: a big *A* branded forever on my past as an accolade for whatever it was I had meant to Gideon.

A few days later I went to the Monitor's downtown four-story building and told a receptionist that I wanted to apply for a newsroom job and could I see Mr. Harper. To my amazed delight, Harper gave me a job as a reporter in the Financial News Department. I labored over market statistics and grain reports, all the while hating it. I was getting nowhere as far as my writing ambition was concerned. Byron and the other Romantics now seemed utterly irrelevant. So did Gideon Pratt. What possible use were rolling cadences in reporting the market's seesaw action? Now my vocabulary was overloaded with clichés and I was sick every time I typed them. I was in a mood to tell all this to Gideon when he telephoned me and invited me to visit him at his home. The next Saturday I got off the bus near his modest frame house in suburban Melrose Park, one of those developments with circling streets on which the houses all look alike.

Gideon ran out the front door to greet me. "Art!" he cried out as he gripped my hand. I think it was the first time he had called me by my first name rather than "Mr. James." Now that I was an alumnus of Richland University, I thought, still rankling under the cloud of our last interview, he treated me as if we were old pals. The cloud quickly passed, however, as he guided me into the house and introduced me to his wife, Amy. She shook my hand warmly as I warmed to her. She was quite pretty, a perky woman with a brilliant smile and long brownish hair, done up in a bun at the back.

Right away, as Amy retired to the kitchen to prepare lunch with the family, Gideon led me into a nursery to meet his two children. Being an only child, I never had much to do with infants. I guess that is why I was taken aback when Debra, who was about two, insisted that I pick her up, reaching to me with her stubby arms. She hugged me, said "Big man" and then "I love you." Somewhat overcome and feeling awkward, I gave her a hug and handed her to a grinning Gideon. Then it was son Todd's turn. He was in a crib, lying on his back, gurgling as he fondled a yellow plastic duck. I tickled his stomach. Todd dribbled his pleasure.

Gideon lifted his son and kissed him hugely. "Who do you think he looks like?" he asked me, his eyes beaming.

"Oh, I think he looks like you, Mr. Pratt."

"They both look like me, darn it. It would be better if they looked like their mother."

At supper, after the children were quiet, we joined hands in a prayer circle, which Amy explained had been the custom with her large family in Cleveland. My parents practiced the same ritual. I felt at home. Amy told me her father had worked for years in a steel mill. She was one of seven children and had a hard time at college. By working part-time she made it through Windom College, where Gideon had been one of her teachers. She became a public school teacher after they were married and taught until she became pregnant with Debra She said she wanted to teach again as soon as the children were old enough to take care of themselves.

"No, you won't," Gideon said quietly.

I turned toward him to see if he was joking. He wasn't. He winked at me, as much as to let me know that he was boss in his family, even of Amy's career.

"We will see," was all Amy said. She was small enough to be termed petite and cute enough, in a rustic sort of way. I noticed that the bun was gone. Now her hair lay in a flat shingle, which made her look much older, offsetting the bright smile and bland straight gaze of her darkened eyes. She offered her left hand to Gideon to pet, an action so perfunctory that I presumed it was repeated at every meal.

Later, while Amy was doing the dishes, Gideon and I took chairs in the back yard, where high elms shaded the slanting western sun. He sat down heavily. The slatted chair creaked. He gestured toward the trim lawn and the surrounding beds of shadowed flowers.

"Isn't this something?" he said. "What more does a man need?"

Gideon told me that his father had owned Pratt Paper and Metal Company, which dealt in scrap. One day, in the company yard, a metal load fell from a magnet, breaking a leg. Gideon remembered his dad hauling himself up the stairs in his Cleveland Heights mansion. His father was killed several years later when one of his trucks backed up on him. That was after Gideon's mother died following a long illness. Gideon had been excluded from that room due to the nature of her illness, which he did not identify.

At this point Gideon faltered in his narrative. I hesitated to ask questions because he was looking off into the trees as if deep in thought. I was in no position to pry concerning the quality of his relationship with his parents, but I gathered from the unemotional way in which he related his father's injury and death that he was unaffected, whereas the memory of the illness and death of his mother was still painful.

While Gideon served in the Army in the Korean War. However, he said no more about his experience there than that he was glad to get home to Amy, who had been living alone in the Cleveland Heights house and saving his Army pay. They lived there for several years before buying their present house.

"My father's house was a white elephant," Gideon said. Just the same, I gained the impression that Gideon's father had left him a substantial inheritance, including ownership of Pratt Paper and Metal.

Suddenly Gideon turned his head to face me. "I've been watching for your byline, Art," he said. I was lost for a moment as to what to reply. I told him that it was the custom of my boss, the Monitor's financial news editor, not to give anyone a byline except himself. Gideon said he had "heard" that the Monitor's managing editor, Mr. Harper, was "a great guy." I had nothing to do with Harper, but my impression, from talking with a few Monitor reporters, confirmed that he was anything but a smiling uncle. In fact, Harper had the reputation as a rough, tough character whom it was best never to cross. Besides, Harper was a right-winger who used his weight to give right-wing groups columns of news space, as well as exercising some control over the editorial writers so that the Monitor was forever on the side of the far-right. Knowing what I did about Harper, I wasn't going to argue about him with Gideon. I was more interested in finding out what Gideon's interest in Harper was. But Gideon didn't pursue the subject. Instead, he changed again, with mercurial quickness, to ask "Art, you're *not* a member of the Newspaper Guild are you?"

"Yes, I am, why?"

Gideon pushed his chin up with his left hand while scrutinizing me as if examining a freak. What was Gideon up to? Was he merely prejudiced against labor unions?

"Did the Guild force you to join?"

"No coercion whatever," I said. I was both flattered and frustrated. Gideon seemed interested in me because I was a reporter, albeit a fledgling. I figured that his interest in me was geared to some private ambition of his own. I didn't dare ask him what that ambition was, although the question was on my tongue. He still impressed me as being afraid, because he did not pursue the subject of the Guild. Or was he merely being solicitous of a young guest's feelings? I couldn't understand his ambivalent nature, which made me feel at once both useful to him and a strain.

Amy came out and we talked generally for a while about Melrose Park and the nature of the community, which was a bedroom for rising young Richland businessmen (and women, Amy said). As an educator, Gideon was an exception in Melrose Park. However, he said the neighbors were fine and, politically, they got along nicely, since he shared many of their conservative political opinions. I steered him away from informing me what those opinions were by thanking him for the big *A*.

"You deserved it, Art," he said. He reached over and patted my shoulder. "Actually, and don't let this go to your head, I make it a practice never to tell my students things like this, you were the best student in my class."

I went away with the feeling that Gideon had been on the verge of asking me to do something for him but had backed off from asking it because he was, strangely, afraid to ask me. At one point something in me was urging me to come right out and ask *Is there anything I can do for you, Gideon?* I was cautious and I was growing suspicious. Why was he being so nice to me, Art James, just one of his many former students?

Chapter Three

No more than three days later I got a memo from the Monitor Managing Editor ordering me to report to his office. It was the first time since Harper hired me that I had been summoned. I received the memo in mid-afternoon, while I was in the midst of the stock market roundup, so I had a lot of time to think about what he wanted before I was required to report to him at six o'clock.

When I had applied for a job that summer I had in mind working for the city desk, covering any beat to which I might be assigned. However, the only job open was in the financial department. The cub reporter there had been drafted into the Army.

Now I was sweating out the hour until six. My stomach began twittering at the thought that at last I would be given the opportunity of proving what a great reporter I could be. There would surely be a raise to go with the promotion. Besides, I wasn't cut out for the financial beat. What I knew about stocks and bonds and the commodity market I had learned from Mr. Desmond, the financial editor, who was all smiles and kindness, eager to hold onto me, he said, but who was about as exciting to work for as Mr. Milquetoast.

At last the appointed hour arrived and I marched across my goal, the exciting city newsroom, to Harper's office, opened the door and peeped in.

"Ah, Art," he said, peering at me with his pale eyes. He was wearing an old-fashioned eyeshade, which he pushed high on his furrowed brow. He was sitting behind a wide gray metal desk, which was stacked high with piles of manuscripts and coils of Associate Press copy.

He started by asking me how long I had been with the Mirror and I replied, of course, "Only one month." Then he said I was about due for a raise and would ten more dollars a week be alright. I stammered something about the adequacy of the amount.

Harper folded his chubby hands under his equally chubby chin. He squinted at me.

"Mr. Pratt thinks you deserve it," he said.

If I hadn't been sitting down I would have fallen. A smile played tag around Harper's little mouth. "Mr. Pratt," he began, "thinks you'll be another John Gunther or Ernie Pyle, says your market analysis is better than Rowena Dobson's."

But I was lost, utterly confounded. Gideon hadn't indicated he knew Harper. He had said he "heard" that Harper was "a great guy." That Gideon should have put in a good word for me with my managing editor was almost beyond belief. I thanked Harper, because that was all there was to it, and I went out walking on air.

At my desk I tried putting together the financial words that were always a variation of yesterday's and of all the yesterdays before that. All I could think was: "Why me?" Why should Gideon make such a venture on my behalf? I dropped Gideon a note, thanking him for speaking to Harper. I added that if there was anything I could do for him, just call.

It took him only a week. Gideon was in the financial room before I knew he was there. "Hello Art," he said quietly behind my back. My fingers skittered on my typewriter's keys. I said, "Hi, Mr. Pratt," before I turned around. He sat down in Mr. Desmond's chair and told me to finish what I was writing, he could wait. "Mustn't hold up the presses," he said with such good humor that I banged out another few paragraphs just to please him. I yanked the copy from the machine, scribbled a 24-point head, slugged the copy, put it into a can and put the can into the pneumatic tube, where it went clattering off, like a bolt falling on a tin roof, to the composing room far above.

Gideon was taking in the details of the office, including the usual newspaper junk: stacks of bound Monitors, spiked clutches of wire copy. He shaded his eyes against the splotch of sun piercing the window facing Luke Street. "What kind of writing do you really want to do, Art?"

"Depth stuff," I said instantly. "News analysis. Commentary."

"You mean, write features, like Ed Lewis?"

Ed wrote a twice-a-week Monitor column titled *Neighborhood*.

"Sure, like Ed, only better, deeper," I said.

He went over to the window, looked down into the street, probably hearing the screech of horns and tires. His boxy shoulders were up. His thick neck vanished under his starched collar. He was wearing the suit he always wore when lecturing in Bond Hall. His black hair tumbled across his forehead.

"I might be able to help you get there, Art."

I jerked to a stop whatever it was I was doing. Already, for no reason I could think of, other than that he thought well of me as a student, he had gotten me a raise. Now he wanted to do something else for me. How lucky could I get, especially since Gideon had been revealed as a man who had influence with Harper.

"You've already done a lot for me, Mr. Pratt," I muttered.

"It was nothing. It just happened that Mr. Harper owed me a favor."

I wondered what Gideon might possibly have done for him that Harper would pay him back by raising my pay. Since I could hardly ask him that question I said that I appreciated his help and that I would like to get into the city newsroom one day.

Smiling with a friendly open grin like Puck, he tapped my shoulder and said "It could be arranged." I suppose it is a cliché, but I really was struck dumb. What could I say? I suppose I said something that didn't make sense because Gideon just said "Well?" At length I recovered enough to cough up a weak "Thank you!"

Gideon shrugged his shoulders. "You've got too much on the ball, Art, to be cooped up in this place." He waved his hand toward the narrow confines of the small office I was confined to.

"Nothing wrong with financial news," I said defensively. "Just lacks variety."

"Sure, and you want some excitement, don't you?" he asked. He came over and sat down on my desk.

"Now listen." He leaned down confidentially, his forehead creased, his deep voice oozing conspiratorial confidence. His black-rimmed glasses slid down his stubby nose. "I'm on to a hot story at the university," he said, "and I need someone I can trust to look into it and write it up in the way it should be written."

Gideon paused to see if I got the point. I did. He wanted a snow job on some person or persons. Either that or--it came to me in a flash--a blackball. Someone, maybe more than one, was in trouble at the university. Inside treatment was needed before a general reporter snooped out the news and gave it the works.

As he backed off a bit, Gideon said "You being a graduate of the university, loyal and all that, I thought you might do this for me."

He was offering me a free ride to somewhere. It had to be a big story for him to go to all the trouble of buttering me up with Harper. Just the same, I owed Gideon something. Because he proved he had influence he loomed even larger in my eyes as an important man. What was more, he was still the brilliant romanticist for whom only the facts mattered. I couldn't help thinking that, actually, he was a man after my own heart. Together we could go places. Maybe Gideon needed me even as I needed him. I said, as slowly and as softly as I could, breathing laboriously, "I wouldn't mind taking a crack at it."

Chapter Four

At three o'clock the next afternoon I was sitting on the steps outside the university's Arts and Science Building. I should have been in Gideon's office, but I had a lot to think about before keeping my appointment with him. I was about to go deeper into Gideon's debt. Or else I was to pay him back, I wasn't sure which. In either case, our relationship was unbalanced. It was no longer the teacher-student relationship. I had the feeling that I was deliberately setting myself up as Gideon's patsy. One thing kept me from rushing up the stairs: long ago I had determined to owe no one anything. I would make my own way in the world. Dad told me that was the only way to get ahead.

"The one sure way people have of getting their hooks into you," Dad would say, wagging a long bony finger at me, "is to give you something for nothing. Only it never is for nothing. Sooner or later, most likely sooner, they ask back what they gave, and that with interest."

I began pacing the broad concrete terrace. I asked myself if what I was getting into wasn't exactly what Dad warned me against. Gideon Pratt was offering me a free ride to somewhere. But where? I had to know. I had to find out. I swung open the heavy glass door and raced up the stairs to Gideon's den.

He bounced over and grabbed my hand. "Thank you for coming, Art," he said. "And thanks for being so prompt." This despite the fact that I had been ten minutes late. He edged onto his straight-back chair, a solid antique with bowed front legs. He folded his hands over his bulging paunch.

The room was full of sun, the air laden with settling dust. It smelled of stale sulphur, thick and sharp, like an extinguished match. Gideon looked me over as if he was a doctor seeking tell-tale spots. He laced his fingers. I wondered what he was waiting for. Surely he wasn't going to back out on me now! I could practically feel the story he was going to tell me. Visions of Page One bylines loomed. This was going to make my career.

"I wouldn't have called you up here, Art," Gideon began hesitantly, all the while shuffling papers on his desk, "if I wasn't sure of you. I know I can trust you. And you know you can trust me."

That was the very point: could Gideon be trusted? He was being deliberately coy, playing a cat-and-mouse game, but for what purpose? He appeared scared himself about what he was getting into.

After being silent for a few noticeable moments, I blurted out "Sure, Mr. Pratt, I'm ready any time you are."

Gideon straightened up. "I wish I had your confidence," he responded, linking his fingers tightly again. He took off his glasses. His eyes were misted over. Then: "These extremist tactics make me want to retch."

"Extremist tactics?" I asked. I suppose I was looking shocked, but I think I merely grimaced.

"Why, sure," Gideon said. "You know, of course, what I'm talking about."

"No I don't," I replied. And that's the truth. Of course I had heard the word *extremist* bandied about, but it hadn't meant anything special to me. Just a nonsensical political expression, I supposed.

"About the Communists," Gideon said. "The Communists on the campus."

"Students?" I asked.

"Faculty."

I honestly couldn't believe it. Faculty! My teachers?

"Seven of them," Gideon continued. "Members of a Communist cell."

I whistled. It could be a big story, a dirty story. The witch-hunt for Communists that had swept the United States in the 1950s had subsided, only to go underground in the 1960s, emerging occasionally in the form of disguised secret societies. A reporter had to be awfully sure of his ground before joining in the chase. I should have gotten out of there right then, but Gideon had not yet told me what role he wanted me to play. Besides, I was filled with curiosity about his own part in any move against the Reds. Why was a teacher of English literature getting mixed up in a witch-hunt?

Gideon handed me a piece of paper with the names of seven faculty members on it. "Of course you can't print the names," he said.

"I know the laws of libel," I told him. And I did. Our legal expert in journalism, Professor Montgomery, had told us, his great jaw jutting: "Just remember, your job as a reporter is not a hunting license. People have reputations you can hurt. Injure a reputation falsely and you can go to jail." If I went along with Gideon, wouldn't there be a chance of smearing innocent people?

Gideon suggested I memorize the names, because he intended to burn the list. I locked the names in my brain. They were all minor faculty, two of them assistant professors, the others holding the rank of instructor. Mainly they taught political and social sciences. Two were women. Taken together they made a motley crew. They came from all over the country. About the only thing they had in common was their areas of teaching.

I told Gideon that I couldn't do anything until I verified his charge against the seven.

He only smiled. "I can say you will corroborate my story," he said.

"No, don't, Mr. Pratt," I said, "It's better that I find sources myself."

That way, I thought, Gideon wouldn't be incriminated, because I was under the impression that while a reporter cannot be required to divulge his sources, a teacher might. It was a crazy reason, but at the time it was the only one I could think of that would stop Gideon from telling me more. I had to have time to think through the implications of this kind of reporting, and I couldn't do it with him urging me on. One thing I had to find out right away was Gideon's motive.

"Someone has to have the guts to do something," Gideon told me. "What you may not realize, Art, is the damage those damn Reds are doing. They're supposed to teach citizenship. What they teach is that the American system is rotten. Rotting." He slapped the arms of his chair. "Take their courses and you will find out."

I had taken a few courses taught by some of the seven. I told Gideon I couldn't remember hearing anything subversive.

He sprang up. His deep voice rose to fever pitch. "Ah, that's just the point. Young minds can't tell the difference. Those Reds, they're subtle. You were asked to examine American democracy, right? You found fault with basic American institutions, right? You were told that Russia was right, and we were wrong! Right?"

I tried to protest that he was painting them all black, when what they taught hadn't been nearly that simple. But Gideon was over near the window looking down on the quad. "We've got to get rid of those Reds, Art," he said. "You've got to help me."

"Of course I want to help you, Mr. Pratt," I responded sheepishly. Or to put it another dumb way, I suppose, was I being led like a sheep to the slaughter? I felt compelled to respond because he had put his request, or perhaps demand, on a personal basis. "I will do everything I can," I said weakly.

He turned toward me. His face was aflame. "Do this one thing for me, Art. I promise you won't regret it." He sat down in his swivel chair behind his littered desk. "Besides, you need this story, don't you?"

I had to admit it would be a break. It would also provide me with the opportunity to show Harper what I could do, and my promotion to the newsroom would surely follow. Still, the story had to be my own, not Gideon's. I wasn't about to ride to glory on Gideon's coattail. I asked him again why he was involved.

"When you get a story, Art," he said, "I'll tell you, and you won't by sorry."

Chapter Five

For two days I scoured the campus for Communists. I looked everywhere except under the rocks. I buttonholed students in the library, the cafeteria, the corridors of the Arts and Science Building. "Do you know of a Communist at Richland University?" Or "Did you ever meet a Communist here?" or "--well, anyone who even talked like a Communist--well, socialistic, against the U.S. government?"

Head-shaking and shoulder-shrugging was all I got. You would think that after an era when McCarthy had tried to convince the country there was a Red behind every tree who any patriot would be able to identify as a Communist, I was about to conclude that either everyone was too scared to talk or that Gideon's list was a fake. That's when I encountered Bill Hartley in the library stacks.

"Hi Bill," I called. "What do you know about Communism at Richland University?" I had known Bill for a couple of years, ever since he was a junior. Now he was doing postgraduate work for a master's in civil engineering. I was surprised to find him haunting the art books section.

"What! What kind of a question is that?" He gave me a wild popeyed stare as he crunched his narrow frame between two stacks of books as if he was trying to hide.

"Research," I replied. "You must have heard the rumor that Richland is crawling with Pinks."

Bill slapped his cheek with wide-open palm. "My God! What kind of a nut goes around asking that? Are you on a witch hunt?'

I told him I had merely heard the rumor and that my only interest was to determine the facts.

"I never heard of any Reds," he said, scratching his balding spot.

"It's common knowledge," I told him. "Everyone has heard about them."

Bill looked askance at me. "Art, are you pulling my leg? You want to get yourself in a mess of trouble?"

I quickly told Bill to forget it. I left him standing there looking after me with mouth agape. I had no alternative but to return to Gideon and confess failure.

Gideon winked. "I told you a student can't tell a Communist from a McCarthyite," he said. His smile mocked me, but it was a good-humored mocking, with the slight trace of a hidden secret in it, promising that he had something to tell me if I would only ask him. That was another thing I was beginning to learn about Gideon: he needed to be asked for help. He teased me with the promise of a big story, to say nothing of collaborating with him, and then waiting for me to come begging for more. I think he did it out of method rather than meanness. His method was to twist me and turn me to his purpose until my appetite was so whetted that I couldn't possibly refuse his next proposition. All this I was aware of, and thus I was entering into the conspiracy with eyes wide open. I offer no excuse of youth or innocence, because I was smart enough to realize that I could get burned in this venture. This was my chance. There was no way I was going to pass it up.

That's what I told myself while Gideon was on the phone arranging for me to see Professor Bentley at two o'clock. I knew that Burton Bentley led the campus conservatives, but he was no reactionary. Compared to what he later became you might say he was middle-road. At the time he was active in politics, but only as a committee member. He is today ambassador to the Gold Coast.

It wasn't difficult to figure out that Bentley must have been the instigator of the drive to oust the campus Communists. Gideon didn't rank high enough in the faculty to have the influence required for the job, which would have to involve the university's President Canning. Bentley certainly would have the required influence. He was the Arts and Science Department chairman and had been on the faculty for twenty years. But what motive could Bentley possibly have for instituting a campaign against the suspected Communists? I knew that back of every witch hunt was a political ambition. Was Bentley about to seek candidacy for political office? Several local offices were open: city councilman, even the mayoralty. Was it possible that Gideon had been recruited to aid Bentley's plans?

As soon as Gideon was off the phone, and had leaned back with a look of huge satisfaction, I told him what I surmised, and he said that was correct, and I had strengthened his faith in me as a man who knew the facts of life.

"But what I don't understand," I said, "is why you want to get involved with a man like Professor Bentley, who is obviously on the side of the right-wingers."

It had taken a lot for me to say that. Now it was out I realized I had committed myself to an interest in Gideon's higher goal. Riding along with Gideon to wherever he was going I might conceivably get a foot in the political door, where the real power lay.

"You're absolutely right," Gideon said. "Bentley is a right-winger. Why assume that I am too? Those Communists are a menace."

"Yeah, you told me," I said.

"We do understand one another, don't we, Art? We can go places together. Being a friend of Bentley's I can do great things for you. But perhaps you aren't interested?"

He laughed as he asked that one. He darn well knew what I wanted.

"I am interested," I said, clapping my hands for emphasis.

"All right then." Gideon leaned forward. "Let me tell you. Bentley wants to run for the Senate."

"State?"

"No. The top. Washington."

"Does he have a chance?"

"He'd have a good chance, Art. What he needs now is a name, in a hurry. The primaries are months away, but he's got to get known throughout the state. That's why he came to me."

"Because you discovered the existence of the Communist cell?"

"Right, Art. I started the investigation by writing a note to President Canning, just an inquiry, asking whether he approved of the cell's meetings. He never replied. Weeks later Bentley called me in, told me President Canning had talked with him about my letter, asked him to investigate, him and Professor Stoddard. So those two did some investigating and gave a report to Canning. Either Bentley or Stoddard will tell us about their report. I haven't seen it."

"Why not?"

"That's the way it's done, Art. Canning wants Bentley elected because Bentley could do a lot for the university, federal grants and all that. But he wants Bentley to get the glory." Gideon paused. "That means releasing the report to the Monitor, through you, Art. Then we'd wait for the public reaction." Gideon went silent, his gaze fixed on me. "Well, Art, how does that sound to you?"

"I'm not sure," I muttered. Suddenly I felt very tired, the tiredness that hits you when an exciting dream awakes you to the dawn's reality. What had I gotten myself into? I had dreamed of a byline, my first, one to be rewarded by promotion. The dream was fading. I awakened to reality. I was chained to Gideon now, for better or for worse. Gideon was waiting for my answer. I went for broke. "Sounds good to me," I said, the words choking me as they shot out of my dry mouth.

"Good," he exclaimed. "Now you know why Bentley needs a campaign manager."

I gasped. "I don't see how--"

Gideon laughed, a sharp chuckle. "Not you, Art. Me. But there would be a place for you in Bentley's staff if you want it."

If I wanted it! Now the prospect of a mere promotion to the newsroom of the Monitor paled to insignificance. To be part of an important political campaign in which I could help get a guy elected, even write his speeches, that would be perfect!

"When do I see Bentley?" I asked. Gideon held up two fingers. "I'm not saying I will write this story," I told him. "I want to get the facts. Then I will decide. And there's something else."

"What is it, Art?"

"You're sure all seven of those teachers are Communists?"

Gideon stood up and removed his glasses, revealing his commanding gaze. "I'm certain, Art. I don't have a single qualm about it. They deserve what they're going to get."

I wished I could have been that certain.

Chapter Six

Burton Bentley poised an elbow on the mantle and noisily lit his pipe. That his office in Athenia Hall had a fireplace indicated his high status. With its walnut paneled walls and thick maroon carpet one would have expected the room to be occupied by a tweedy type professor replete with shaggy mustache. Bentley was a surprise. He was the sleek type, black hair oiled and slick, high forehead, Italian silk suit, summer tan, tight little smile.

Bentley flicked the match, still lit, into the fireplace pit. He turned his attention to me. "Be sure to spell my last name with an extra e," he said. I had been taking notes in my semi-shorthand method, as fast as I could, but not fast enough to keep up with his staccato phrasing.

"Red cells," he rattled on, "are vestiges of the depression. Symbols of despair. Can't afford them any longer. Got to get rid of them because they corrupt. No place for them in higher education. They're closed societies. Secret. Corrupt. No room for the Reds to expand their thinking, change, emerge from their intellectual straightjacket, so to speak." Bentley waved his pipe, trailing a wake of smoke. "That's the trouble with them. Closed minds. Won't let the fresh air of freedom in. Cells. Good name for them."

He waited for me to catch up with him. I was sitting on a couch with my notebook grasped by my left hand. I was writing as fast as I could.

"Are you in favor of having Communists dismissed from the faculty?" I asked.

He bit hard on his pipe, clicking it between his large front teeth. He smiled as his thick black eyebrows soared up. Then he squinted at me quizzically. "Beside the point, Mr. James. Question is, how much harm have they done? University trustees will decide about dismissal. Out of my province. Point is, these people have to be identified. Put them under the spotlight, so to speak."

"But how can you be sure they're Communists, members of the Communist Party?"

Bentley loaded himself into his swivel chair. He tapped the gleaming surface of his big mahogany desk. "Beside the point," he said. "Break the cell, that's the job. No reason to persecute these folks. That's what they are. Soreheads. Not real Commies. Pink, perhaps. Socialists. They'll soon see they can't fool around with what's basic to our American way of life."

"And what's that?"

"Horse sense." He picked imagined lint from his silk suit. "The common ability of the ordinary American to smell a phony a mile away."

I had one more question. I pretended to be writing more notes. Actually, I was phrasing my question. Finally I had it.

"Doctor Bentley, do you think it is right to inform on your fellow faculty members?"

He took his time, knocked the ashes from his pipe, refilled if from a wooden humidor and slowly set the tobacco alight. "All depends," he said. "Ethics not my field. Practical matter of eliminating secret societies with political purposes. No place for 'em at a university. Contrary to democratic ideal. Anyway, I wouldn't use the word 'inform'. Full report to be made to President Canning."

I had to ask it. "Did Mr. Pratt start this? This investigation?"

Bentley coolly blew a puff of smoke. "Give credit to where credit is due, I say. Mr. Pratt had the courage to bring this cell to President Canning's attention."

"Directly?"

"Directly. The president appointed me and Professor Stoddard to make a full report, now completed and on the president's desk."

"Why professor Stoddard?" I asked.

"Well, everyone knows he's a rather rabid liberal. Gives the inquiry good balance, don't you think?"

"I'll note that." I wrote it down. Then, as Bentley stood up and I knew he wanted to end the interview, I stood up too and faced him for the crucial question.

"If the Monitor decides to print my story, will you object?" Of course I knew quite well that Bentley would have no objection, for the simple reason that he knew that Managing Editor Harper would send my report to him for approval before he would print it.

Bentley laughed, a melodious giggle. "Certainly not," he exclaimed. He laughed again. "Freedom of the press and all that, you know."

"And I may quote you?" I asked.

"Certainly. And Professor Stoddard too, I'm sure. I understand your interview with him has been arranged?"

"Mr. Pratt arranged it," I told him, but of course he would have already been informed about that by Gideon.

Bentley shook my hand firmly as he thanked me profusely. I got away as fast as courtesy allowed and set out down the corridor.

I knocked loudly on the door to Professor Stoddard's office. A raspy voice from within called out "The door's open." I entered gingerly upon a state of utter bedlam. Stoddard was madly throwing papers from his desk onto the floor.

"Dam it!" he yelled. "You'd think I could leave something on my desk and find it the next day. It's that cleaning guy, that what's-his-name, that's who it is. I've told him a hundred times don't touch anything--ah, here it is."

His back was to me now. He bent over his desk, his narrow rump high, his shaggy head dangling hair on the file that he was poring over. Papers and books and magazines littered the bare wood floor around the desk, which had enough paper on it to fill a couple of baskets. His arms pumped like pistons as he leafed through the pages in the file. Finally he turned and eyed me up and down. His disheveled brown hair fell over his snapping eyes. His shirt, open at the collar, fell in a roll over his waist.

"Well, don't just stand there," he said. "Sit down."

I looked around for a chair that wasn't piled high with papers and books. The only one that was vacant was the chair behind his desk.

"Sit!" he shouted. I obeyed him as he returned his attention to the file. He remained attentive to the task for a couple of minutes. "So you're the Monitor reporter," he said at last, not looking up. "What's your name again?"

"Arthur James. Most people call me Art."

"How the hell did you get mixed up in this asinine affair?"

I considered for a moment whether I should tell him to mind his own business, but that would have been risky. "Mr. Pratt," I told him as calmly as I could.

He clambered onto the edge of the desk, the file open in his hands. He turned to the second page, lowered his head until his blond spaded beard touched the paper. "Damn type is too small," he said. Then, suddenly: "You afraid, Art?" His high voice warbling, highly tuned, he added "That's an unfair question. I apologize. Don't answer. Gideon makes everyone afraid. You know why, Art?"

I mumbled. "Yes--well, no."

Stoddard eyed me sharply. "How old are you?"

"Twenty-three."

"And you're not afraid? No, I suppose you aren't. Not at twenty-three. Later you get scared. Like Gideon, you run scared. Sure, you don't act like it, but you try to scare everybody else. Because you're so damned scared yourself." He sniffed. His nostrils quivered. "Still," he continued, "you go ahead. You ask yourself, what's there to be scared of? The world to win and all that crap. Makes you stop and think, doesn't it?"

"Yes sir," I said firmly, feigning agreement.

He continued to rattle on at a speedy gait like a drunk at a racetrack. He lofted the file. "Do you know what I have here, Art? The report, authored jointly by that distinguished professor of all things historical, Burton Bentley, concerning that infamous group of seven, Communists all. You don't believe me? Here, take a look."

He handed the file to me. "And don't be so shocked, Art. I was ready for you. Well, almost. Bentley announced your impending arrival by telephone."

I took the file with shaking hands. The otherwise blank cover was labeled *Confidential*. I turned to the inside page. I read slowly, absorbing every word, for I knew I wouldn't be permitted to take the file with me. In a curious blend of terse diction and overblown phrases the report told of a discussion by the seven about, of all things, juvenile delinquency. I recognized Bentley's telegraphic style and Stoddard's literary touch. Details of the cell's discussion had obviously been written from memory rather than from notes. There were no verbatim quotes. It all sounded no more dangerous than the last meeting of my fraternity. Perhaps the emphasis on the necessity for greater state regulation of education offended Bentley, but hardly, it seemed to me, Stoddard.

"What do you think?" Stoddard asked.

"Tame," I said. "What's all the fuss about?"

"You're asking *me*?" Stoddard grabbed the file. "What we have here is going to ruin the lives of five men and two women. Ruin them! Do you think that's worth one man's glory?"

"You mean Mr. Pratt?"

"I say this in confidence, Art. Not for publication, okay?"

"Of course."

"Professor Bentley is involved in this because he wants to run for the U.S. Senate."

"Mr. Pratt told me about that. Does he have a chance?"

"Who knows, Art. Basically he's an honest man, but an opportunist. When President Canning tossed him Gideon's hot potato, Bentley recognized a good chance. Bentley is in this with Gideon now. Only God knows how it will all end."

"Your name is on this report too."

Stoddard turned, whacked a stack of books from a chair and sat down. "Command performance as far as I am concerned," he said. "Presidential orders. And, Art, was it Gideon got you interested in this imbroglio?"

"Mr. Pratt asked the Monitor's managing editor, Mr. Harper, to assign me to write the story."

"You don't say?" Stoddard drew a deep breath.

"Yes, sir."

Stoddard slapped his thigh. "Well, I'll be damned!" he exclaimed. "That means Gideon has joined the witch hunt himself. I would have thought he'd have more sense. Goes to prove just how scared he is."

"Maybe Mr. Pratt is a friend of Mr. Harper."

"There's something more to it than that, Art. I figure Gideon has joined the witch hunt as an active participant." He stroked his whiskers and peered at me intently. "Tell me, young fellow, what's in this for you?"

I began to squirm. Stoddard had my number. "Routine," I replied. "News is news."

"Like hell!" Stoddard crossed one leg over the other and pointed an accusing finger at me. "This is a witch hunt and you know it. What are you after, Art? Money? Fame? Fortune? A story like this will do your career a lot of good, won't it? Tell me, honestly, don't you feel a bit sick?"

If he had taken any approach other than the direct attack I would have confessed that I was indeed feeling sick. Despite his flamboyance I was attracted to his let's-lay-the-cards-on-the-table honesty. "I have a job to do," I said.

"Alright, if that's the way you want it," he answered through gritted teeth. "Only don't come crying to me when the hounds start nipping at your tail."

To my nervous surprise the palms of both my hands were tingling as a tense fear enslaved me. Somehow I knew that this was it: the time to forge ahead or turn back. Never in my life had I felt so certain that the door of opportunity was opening. But what was on the other side? I told myself: *Take it*. And I did. The portal opened wide. I made the deciding step into the unknown.

"What will happen to the seven teachers?" I asked Stoddard.

"What the hell do you expect? They will be kicked off the campus."

"Without a trial? But nobody has proved they're Communists!"

Stoddard tossed his mane of unruly hair. He rolled his eyes. "Lord protect us from the innocent!" he cried out. "These days, Art, just to be suspected is enough. Sure, maybe Gideon doesn't want anyone to get fired, but that's the trouble with a witch hunt. Once started, you can't stop it. A lot of good people are bound to end up on a burning stake."

I hesitated, then blurted out "Why did Mr. Pratt report it to the president?"

Stoddard tilted his chair. His beard upended. He gurgled with glee. "Ah, our friend Gideon is just getting started. Communists today, tomorrow who knows? One day that guy is going to rise to the top of the totem pole. Believe me, Art, there will be no stopping him. Stand aside or you will get hurt." He bent forward, his ragged brows lowered. "Stand aside, Art. Don't get involved in this. Believe me, you've got a two-edged broad-ax in your hands. It cuts both ways."

I was on my feet. "I know what I'm doing," I said as forcefully as I could. "I don't want to hurt anyone. And I'm certainly not going to let Gideon push me around."

Stoddard stood up. "Art, I'm warning you. That's exactly what Gideon is doing."

As I was leaving he began picking up books and papers from the floor and heaving them onto his desk. I caught myself mimicking the bearded professor. *What the hell do you expect, Art?*

What's it to *me*? Just seven teachers dismissed from the faculty because they discussed juvenile delinquency flavored with social solutions? Seven people condemned to bear the Communist tag forever because of one lowly instructor's lust for power? Sure, that was it. Gideon Pratt was looking out for Number One. He was on his way, off to a flying start. And there was Art James about to climb aboard the Pratt bandwagon, Stars and Stripes waving proudly as we rolled over seven lives.

"Got enough dope?" Gideon asked as I entered his office.

"Sure, enough to hang them all." I sat down. I was very tired. "I just can't see it, Mr. Pratt. I just can't see a story in this."

He smiled. There was a trace of a smirk in it. "What did Stoddard have to say?"

"I can't tell you that, Mr. Pratt."

"Reporter confidential, I suppose. Well, never mind." He adjusted his dark striped tie, then removed its pearl clip and replaced it. His glasses dropped down his nose. "I talked to Mr. Harper on the phone just now. He's eager to see your story."

His quick sly glance told me all I wanted to know. If he was afraid for his own skin he didn't show it.

Back at the office I banged out the story:

A Communist cell is in operation on the campus of Richland University, it was charged today by three members of the faculty. The charge was made in a report they filed with university President Canning.

Gideon Pratt, instructor in English literature, who first reported the alleged existence of the cell, told the Mirror that the cell had engaged in subversive activity designed to undermine the faith of students in the American system of government.

Allied with Pratt in the protest against Communist activity on the campus are Dr. Burton Bentley, professor of history, and Dr. Silenus Stoddard, professor of philosophy.

I went on for a column with paraphrases of the report, and brief biographies of Gideon, Bentley and Stoddard. I mentioned that Bentley was being seriously touted as a possible candidate for the U.S. Senate.

I snapped the final page from my typewriter. I edited it all the way through. A knot tightened around my stomach. Something was missing in the story. I read it again. My story was tight. I had stuck to the facts, at least as many as I had been told. I hadn't editorialized. I had been fair to the three faculty members responsible for revealing the Communist cell. Then it struck me: I had been fair to Gideon, Bentley and Stoddard, but had I been fair to the seven people accused? Everyone would wonder who the unnamed Communists were. A new guessing game would be the campus rage: Is so-and-so a Communist? Is such-and-such a member of the Communist cell?

Although I was a neophyte in the newspaper game, I knew enough theory to realize what a hornet's nest I would stir up. Fear would breed like mosquitoes in a swamp. Every teacher would fear being suspected of being a Communist. This would happen because my story presumed the guilt of the cell members. I had stepped beyond the boundaries of journalistic decency and ethical principle. Without intending harm I had balanced the scales against the suspected. I had done exactly what Professor Miner, that stooped old journalist, had warned against.

"As a reporter, caught up in the heat of the day's news," Miner told us, "you will be tempted to use your power to judge and condemn. Don't use it. That is a dangerous power, dangerous to those you write about, dangerous to you, dangerous to your freedom. Your role is to report the facts, all the facts, and don't forget the facts until you have them all."

What was missing in my story, I saw now, were the balancing facts concerning the cell itself. Was it really Communist? Some way I had to find out. I said a silent prayer of gratitude for Professor Miner's advice. From memory I wrote down the names of the five men and two women. I knew two of them, Clarence Ferguson and Karl Krautz. Mr. Ferguson taught me political science, but that was long ago, in my sophomore year. Mr. Krautz was a more recent acquaintance. He taught graphic arts in the journalism school. His paintings had been exhibited at several Richland galleries. Once he had a one-man show. He was a quiet fellow who never spoke of his Eastern European background. I decided that Krautz would be as good as any of the seven to interview.

I telephoned his home, spoke first to his wife, who had a slight accent, perhaps Swedish, and then to Mr. Krautz. He said he remembered me very well. I said I would like to see him. He invited me over without asking why.

Mr. Krautz's apartment on Richland's near-south side, not far from the university, was on the second floor rear of a brownstone dating from the 1890 era. Paintings, which I recognized from their style as Mr. Krautz's own, decorated the parlor walls. Not being a fan of modern art, I had never cared much for his work, but I had to admit his colors were brilliant. Favoring rectangles, he painted mostly in blotches rather than dribbles.

He bowed slightly as he motioned me in. "You are looking well, Art." His voice was precise, clipped. "You are working, are you not?"

As he helped me out of my coat I told him about my job at the Monitor. I looked around at his paintings. "A home-made gallery," I said. He thrust his thumbs, cowboy-style, into the pockets of his faded blue jeans. "That is very good of you to say, Art. If my paintings were good, they would sell." He smiled wryly at me, the leftward twisting of his mouth drawing sharp narrow lines on his taut dark skin. His black hair was combed straight forward, even above his small flat ears. "But you did not come to see my paintings," he said. The room was bare, except for a few canvas chairs. "Sit, sit," Mr. Krautz said. I squeezed into one of the chairs, which wobbled under me. "What is it I do for you, Art?" While his accent was faintly Germanic, it was the way he arranged his words that betrayed his foreign birth.

"Well--" I said, searching for a way to start. I began to wish I hadn't come. "There's a rumor about, just a rumor, mind you, nothing more, that some faculty people are getting together, that is, holding meetings of, well, a controversial nature."

He reached inside his sweater's turtle-neck for a pack of cigarettes. He offered one to me. I shook my head. He lit a cigarette and carefully stubbed out the match on a nearby tray. "What is this you say?"

"It's a Communist cell!" I blurted out.

He blew a stream of smoke. He drew his knees to his chest and leaned forward. "A cell? I do not understand. What is meaning of this word?"

"A secret unit. A group."

"And this, ah, group, you say is Communist?" He pronounced it "Com-you-neest."

"That's what I hear, Mr. Krautz."

"You say I am member of this group?"

"That's what they say."

He puffed the cigarette, which dangled from the back of his hand. "This group, you say, which one?"

"There's more than one?"

"If you say, Art. I do not know."

"Clarence Ferguson, he goes to this one."

Mr. Krautz laughed, a silent shaking of his slight body at first, then a toes-up, head-back chuckle. He rocked back and forth for a while, laughing. "You know what I laugh, Art? That funny man. Clarence." He snapped an opposed thumb and finger open and shut, imitating a goose. "Talk! He talk, talk, talk. Me? I sit, I say nothing. But what you say? Interesting. I learn much."

He was in such good humor, seemed so innocent of the import of my questions, that I hesitated to go on. I had always liked him. He gave me fair grades, as fair as I deserved. More than anything I admired his talent. But I had to go on. It was either that or leave him guessing what I was up to. That would have been even more cruel.

"Mr. Krautz, you came from Eastern Europe, didn't you?"

"Lietuva, what you say Lithuania."

"And that's part of Russia now?"

For a flashing second his face darkened, his narrow lips compressing. "You know that, Art. Why you ask that?"

"I'm sorry, Mr. Krautz. It was a stupid question."

He leaned forward, gripped his hands together around his knee. "No, you say good question. You think, I from Lithuania, I Communist?"

"No, no," I protested.

"I tell you, Art. I am no Communist. You do not know what it is like there. My family--"

"I know, Mr. Krautz. Russia occupied your country during the war."

"I leave Lithuania. I think we have Russia always. I go to Germany. I am in refugee camp. The Americans, they let me come to America. I am happy here. I am citizen now. American!"

I stood up. The canvas chair stuck with me. Mr. Krautz laughed. He reached over and pulled me off it. "I'm sorry to have bothered you, Mr. Krautz," I said.

He scrambled up. "This no bother, Art. I happy to see you. You do well, you say?"

"Very well," I answered.

"Wait, Art. I call wife. She painter too."

"No," I said. "I must go now. You know these newspaper deadlines."

"Ah yes," he said. "In Germany I work on refugee camp paper. We call it *Freedom*."

I said goodnight at the door. He shook my hand, firmly, warmly, as a friend.

At the Monitor office I inserted several paragraphs into my story. They summed up my personal belief that charges of Communism against the group were premature. I typed:

No evidence has been presented that any members
of the discussion group alleged to be a Communist cell
are or ever have been members of the Communist party
or any organization affiliated with or fronting for the
Communist Party.

I was editorializing, but I didn't care. I typed *By Arthur James* at the top of the story, not to insist on a byline, but because the story required it.

I delivered the story to Gideon the next day. He asked me to leave it with him, promising he would call me. For the rest of the day I fidgeted with my weekend roundup of stock market quotations. Several times I picked up the phone to call him. Each time I put the phone down. By ten o'clock that night my nerves were frazzled. Then, a few minutes after ten, he called and asked me to come to his office immediately. "We're having a meeting," he said. "We need you."

The meeting turned out to be a conference in Bentley's office. Stoddard had not been there and was not expected. "Has he seen my story?" I asked Gideon.

"No, and he won't," he answered. My story was spread out on a small table. Gideon concentrated upon eliminating a word here, adding a word there.

"I will talk to Professor Stoddard later," Bentley said as he touched my arm to get my attention. Now he was getting chummy. Something had been decided about me. "Silenus has a tough schedule," Bentley added.

"Professor Stoddard is on the apposing side, Art," Gideon said.

Now the collusion between Gideon and Bentley was clear. These two were using Stoddard as they were using me. "What about my story?" I asked impatiently.

Gideon handed it to me. My editorial comments and every mention of Stoddard had been eliminated.

"Professor Stoddard deserves credit," I protested.

"Doesn't want it," Bentley said. He shifted his gaze from Gideon to me and back again. "Just as well. Stoddard's soft. No stomach for this."

I had enough. "That goes for me too, Professor Bentley," I shouted as I shuffled the pages of my story into their proper order. "I won't play politics when the careers of seven teachers are at stake."

Gideon thumped the table. "That's just the point, Art. You have to expect casualties in this kind of fight. When Professor Bentley is elected senator he's going to battle for a law that will require every teacher to take a loyalty oath. That will eliminate problems such as this Communist cell."

I could see no logic in that argument and I said so. Bentley put his pipe in his pocket and folded his arms. "What Gideon means," he said, "is that we can do more by political action about the Communist menace than we can as teachers." He exchanged a nervous glance with Gideon. "However, if you have reservations about going along with us--"

"I have," I said. "Count me out."

Gideon reached for my story. I gave it to him. "But why, Art?" he asked.

"That," I said, "is something you will never understand."

"Too bad, Art." He fanned the air with my story. "This could have made you famous."

I stood up and moved toward the door. "Keep it as a souvenir," Mr. Pratt. At the door I turned. "I'm sorry, Professor Bentley."

Bentley waved me away. "I understand, son," he said.

Chapter Seven

I thought the whole affair was at an end as far as I was concerned. Gideon Pratt could get himself another boy. But that is where I had Gideon pegged all wrong. Gideon never gave up.

Thursday evening of the following week was like all other evenings: watch for last-minute financial news breaks on the AP and UP wires, write headlines for stories I considered important, and send them to the composing room. Between such jobs I did the daily running account on the stock market quotes, writing them up in big log books.

About nine o'clock the copy boy tossed the early Monitor edition on my desk.

I finished a column of figures before picking it up. The three-column headline at the top of Page One was like a slap in the face:

Red Cell Runs Openly at Richland U,
Professor Burton Bentley Charges

It was my story, as edited by Gideon and Bentley, without a byline. My stomach was doing gymnastics as I scanned the column. I turned to Page Four where the story was continued. I turned back to Page One. I was right: Gideon's name had been eliminated. Bentley got all the glory. One new paragraph had been inserted:

Professor Bentley recommended an investigation begin to determine the extent of Communist infiltration into the university, and that teachers found guilty of attending cell meetings be disciplined by university administrators. He declined to specify what kind of discipline he would then recommend to President Canning.

I thought of Mr. Krautz and the inquisition he faced. He may have heard the news on the radio already. Would he accuse me of betraying him?

As for the subtle reason why Gideon's name had been edited out of the story, I would think about that later. Meanwhile, I knew what I had to do.

I walked slowly through the vacated newsroom, consciously clicking my heels on the tiles. I stopped at Harper's office, drew a breath and banged open the door.

Harper was reading the paper. He looked up. His pale eyes were more piggish than ever. I stood before him, arms akimbo.

Smiling, bland, Harper pointed to my story. "Good job, Art," he said.

"Thanks."

He leaned back, swiveled around, and put his fat legs on the desk. "In fact, you did such a good job that I've decided to take a chance with you. What would you say to a city beat?"

My mind was aflame. "You knew, Mr. Harper, didn't you, that Bentley tore my story apart?"

"Take it easy, Art," he said, still grinning, his fat cheeks puffed. "How about the political beat? You'd like that, wouldn't you?"

"Mr. Harper, what in the hell made you think I would be your patsy, your's and Bentley's?"

Dropping his legs to the floor, he glared at me. "You can't talk to me like that!"

"Like hell I can't," I said. "That was *my* story. You let Bentley take it away from me. Bentley and Gideon Pratt."

"If you weren't such a kid," he said, baring his ugly teeth, "I'd throw you out." He smiled weakly. " I'll ignore what you said because this was your first experience in writing a political story. You're still too wet behind the ears to know that the treatment of your story was routine."

"Then you, you and Bentley, you planned this, this whole thing!"

He settled back in his chair. He wrapped his hands behind his neck. "Sure, kid. I thought you knew that. Now, what say we forget what you said? You're a damn fine writer. You've got the makings of a good political reporter. Don't give all that up on account of some personal pet peeve you've got against the folks at the university."

"Pet peeve!" I think I stamped my foot. "You call a conscience that bothers me because we're crucifying seven good teachers *a pet peeve?*" I rushed over and leaned on his desk. "Mr. Harper, give your damn political beat to some hypocrite who'd rather be some politician's private press agent than an honest man."

"James," said Harper evenly. His utter calm, his affable smile, his piggish eyes poking fun, was like a boy's when caught raiding the cookie jar. "James, I wouldn't give you the morgue."

"Mr. Harper, I wouldn't take City Hall."

"Then you can stay in the financial department forever."

I don't know how I managed to smile.

"That's where you're wrong, Mr. Harper. I'm not working for you anymore."

As I blasted out of his office my stomach felt like a hot sword was stuck in it. I would have enjoyed seeing the look on Harper's face, but I didn't have the nerve to turn around.

At my desk I gathered my personal stuff. Not much: a pica ruler, a pack of stale cigarettes. It wasn't the best job I ever had, but it was an experience. I have forgotten almost everything I ever learned about stocks and bonds, but I will never forget the surge of freedom and release I felt as I emerged from the Monitor building into the cold night air and looked up at the bright sky, blazing with a million stars.

I was unemployed for a week. I went over to the *Evening Star*. I walked into the managing editor's office and presented my resume, not including the story on Bentley. I was given the emergency and hospital beat, which required almost continuous phoning of a couple dozen hospitals and police stations and writing reports on minor accidents and thefts. I was grateful. I had taken another foot up the ladder. It wasn't much, but it was a start.

Meanwhile, both the Star and the Monitor ran the story about Bentley's resignation from the faculty of Richland University to contend for nomination as U.S. senator. Tucked way down in the story was the incidental information that Gideon Pratt had also resigned to become Bentley's campaign manager, except he wasn't called campaign manager. He was called *special assistant*. Now it was clear why Gideon's name had been dropped from my story. He had become Bentley's ghost.

The next day the Monitor came out with a story about the firing of five men and two women faculty members for engaging in activity detrimental to the purpose and objectives of Richland University. Once again the Monitor kindly refrained from naming the suspected teachers. Bentley's crocodile tears had been in vain. Even his publicized compassion for the seven was political pap.

Bentley was frequently in the news thereafter, always as the region's chief Communist hunter as he gave speeches around the state to promote his senatorial candidacy. What he did at Richland University, with Gideon's help, established his reputation as a fearless foe of the Reds. Editorials declared, seriously, he had even been willing to risk his teaching job to reveal the subversive influences that infected the university. In July he won nomination for senator and immediately launched his election campaign. He stumped the state from one end to the other. Gideon was with him everywhere, always the *campaign aide* in poses with Bentley in Indian feathers, Bentley petting dogs, Bentley kissing babies, Bentley visiting hospitals. It was revealed that Bentley had money. Actually, it was his wife who was loaded. She was the daughter of a railroad tycoon, Stephen R. Muelenberg. She was seen with her husband everywhere.

In the middle of an early November heat wave I visited the university to pick up some news. The Star had promoted me to the education beat, of all things. In the public relations office I asked what Professor Stoddard was doing. A girl told me that he had left the university to accept a position at Pythia University in New York City. Since the policy of Richland U was to announce only appointments, never resignations, I wrote to Stoddard and received the following reply:

Dear Art:

My departure from good old R.U. was subversive. Under the cloak of darkness, that is. I am alarmed anyone knows I left. Enclosed is some poop turned out by Pythia's publicity gal. Use it if you want to. When you get to Gotham be sure to look me up. The best. Silenus.

I wrote a paragraph about him and submitted it to the City Desk. The item was buried among the obituaries.

Bentley's campaign swung into high gear in mid-January, and from then on until the November elections he was seldom off Page One. I saw Gideon's hand in many of his press releases: a return visit to Richland University to address the annual alumni reunion, a personal endorsement by University President Canning, with a photograph showing Gideon at

Bentley's elbow. Every time I saw Gideon's picture I was reminded that I might have been there too.

Since Bentley's election in November, 1963, was a cinch I didn't even stay up to hear the concession statement of his opponent. The next day, however, I waded through pages of post-election news to find mention of Gideon Pratt. Would Bentley take him to Washington? I could not conceive of Gideon's failure to receive his reward. But that is exactly what happened, as Gideon himself told me when he appeared at my desk the next January, his heavy overcoat white with snow.

He was thinner. A certain lean hardness now coated his features. His eyes, whose blueness had surprised me, seemed deeply recessed, and thus darker. Deep lines slivered the flesh beneath his eyes. "How are you, Art?" While his voice had lost none of its edginess, it sounded softer, more secure. He sat down in a wooden chair beside my desk. "I was surprised to hear you had come over to the Star."

I was in the middle of a hot story on a Board of Education squabble over an American history textbook to which the Parent-Teachers Society objected on the grounds the book was tainted with Communism. Since my deadline was an hour away I set the story aside.

"I discovered the Monitor and I were incompatible," I told Gideon.

"They ran your story after all," Gideon said. The way he half-closed his eyes I knew he was looking for a jealous reaction.

"I couldn't care less," I said. "You got what you wanted."

He looked away toward the Copy Desk, where the copy editors circled the horseshoe. "It was interesting," he said.

"That's all it was to you, Gideon?" I asked.

He seemed intrigued by the Copy Desk. "Those men over there, I suppose they butcher the hell out of your stories?"

"No, not as much as you would think. They do catch the obvious typos and bad grammar. I don't mind the editing. Improves my stuff."

"You don't object to their changing what you write?"

"No," I replied. "I don't. Copy editors have a lot more experience than I have."

Gideon shrugged. He gave me a look of disbelief and disapproval. "You should be allowed to write what you like," he said.

Gideon's ignorance of the journalistic process by which news is written, edited and printed was so profound that I said no more on the subject. I asked "How do you like Washington?"

He picked up a pencil and started doodling on my scratch pad. "What makes you ask that?" he asked.

"Well, that's where you live, isn't it?"

"Not yet, Art. I live in New Jersey and work in Manhattan. Senator Bentley has a special reason for me to work there."

"New York!"

Gideon took a piece of paper from a pocket. "Here's a press release for you. I wrote it myself."

The release was on a printed form headed *Gibson Green Associates, Public Relations Counsel.* The story announced Gideon's appointment as vice-president of the firm.

"I was sure you were going to Washington."

"Preliminary assignment," he said. "Senator Bentley thought I would be more useful to him in New York."

"Doing what?"

He resumed the doodling, a series of circles. "Just what it says. Public relations. Chief account is the Educational Foundation of America."

"The one that gives scholarships to teachers?"

He looked surprised that I had heard of the Foundation. "Actually, it's a political job. The Foundation has a lot of contacts in Washington."

"I don't see the connection," I said, "but I suppose it's a step in the right direction."

He got my point, for he reacted with a smile. "You could have come with me," he said. "I'm on my way, Art."

"New York isn't Washington," I said.

"I'll make it, don't you worry."

I laughed. "I'm not worried, Mr. Pratt. I'm not worried about you in the least. Someone once told me there was no stopping you."

He used his pen to doodle a towering box. It could have been a skyscraper. "Well, I appreciate what you did for me, Art. I really do. When you get to New York be sure to drop in. I'll always be glad to see you. Maybe I'll be able to return a favor."

"Thanks," I said. "But I wouldn't count on it. I like it here."

"That's what I used to think," Gideon replied. "But circumstances change." He picked up the press release and began reading it, as if to make certain it contained no errors. "Can you use this?"

"Sure," I said. "Why not?"

"Maybe you could use my picture." He smiled. "Just happened to have one with me." He took an envelope from his pocket. It had a pack of photos in it. He gave me one.

"I'll submit the photo," I said. "I can't promise we will run it."

"Anything you can do will be very much appreciated." He stood up and put out his hand. I shook it. He almost broke my fingers. "Art. It's been a pleasure. Don't forget. Come see me in New York. Anytime." He looked at his watch. "Well, I've got to run. Lunch with Harper."

"Covering all the bases, Mr. Pratt?"

"See you, Art. Lots of luck." He waved to me as he headed toward the elevator.

"Same to you," I said, although he could not hear me. "You're going to need it."

Then, remembering, I took off after him, wading through the sea of desks. I caught him as the elevator door opened. "Say, Mr. Pratt, you heard that Professor Stoddard is in New York."

He shoved up his drooping eyeglasses. "Had lunch with him the other day," he said. He stepped into the elevator, waved, the door slid shut and he was gone.

For several years I heard no more of Gideon Pratt. Once or twice a year I was assigned to an event in which Senator Bentley was involved. Most of these local events took place at Richland University where Bentley had been made a trustee. Three years after this appointment he was given an honorary Doctor of Laws degree. A reception in his honor was held at the University Club. The press was invited. Johnny, my city editor, gave me the assignment.

Apart from the gray around his temples and the affectation of a pince-nez, Senator Bentley was little changed. He waved to me from the head table. After his brief speech in which he recalled his pride at being a professor at the university, he greeted me with a smooth handshake and asked me how I was doing.

"Fine, just fine, Senator," I replied.

"Glad to hear it, Art." He looked over my shoulder and waved at someone behind me.

"How is Mr. Pratt doing?" I asked Bentley.

"Remarkable job. First class."

"He's still with that public relations firm in New York?"

"Doing a swell job."

"Well, nice to see you again, Senator."

"Good to see you, Art. Lots of luck."

My job settled into routine: visiting the university public relations office and the Board of Education, covering leading Parent-Teachers meetings, reporting activities of the Teachers Union. I floated in and out of other beats, included the county court. I got a lot of bylines on feature stories, including a series on a county fair. I aged from being a cub reporter to become a journeyman, was elected secretary of our Newspaper Guild, went around with one girl reporter after another. Only bit by bit did I come to realize that I was in a rut. Thus it was a jolt to receive a letter from Gideon in which he told me the New York *Dispatch,* a morning newspaper, was looking for a reporter to cover education news. What the *Dispatch* wanted, he said, was a man with exactly my kind of experience.

It was the first time in years that Gideon had written. He was still vice-president of Gibson Green Associates and public relations counsel for the Educational Foundation of America. I wrote Gideon immediately that I was interested in the Dispatch job. I suppose every newspaperman outside New York had thought about trying his luck in the big city. I was no exception. Manhattan's towered pinnacles loomed, challenging me to scale their peaks. I wondered whatever happened to Gideon Pratt that he never made it to Washington.

I mailed my resume to the New York Dispatch. I was interviewed by a guy from a Richland employment agency. In a few days the managing editor of the Dispatch telephoned and offered me the job.

Chapter Eight

Gideon was waiting for me at New York's Grand Central Station. He was leaning against the Information counter, that round affair in the middle of the high vast hall through which passengers flowed quickly from inbound trains.

He was chunkier than ever, definitely stouter, although it was a trim stoutness clothed in Madison Avenue lapels and cuff-less trousers. I watched him for a moment before approaching him. A cigarette dangled between two fingers. He flicked the ash to the floor, never once placing the glowing cigarette to his lips. He suddenly straightened up as he saw me, shoulders square, hands gripping his ample waist. He dropped the cigarette to the floor and stamped on it. Then, feet firmly apart, legs stiff, back hunched, he waved to me.

"Art! Buddy boy!" He whacked my shoulder. "How are ya?" I towered over him. His forelock had vanished, his forehead line had receded considerably, but his hair was still a healthy black and combed the same way, straight back. There was a noticeable thickening of the jowls. His darker eyes were deeply underlined.

He grabbed my hand and pumped my arm. "Damn it, Art, it's great to see ya. How ya been?"

Besides the jovial expressions and slurring that his speech now contained, there was a stridency in his tone that, I thought, was more than due to adoption of the New York twang. He spoke fast, upending his words.

"Watcha know, buddy boy? Long time no see, eh? Boy, you look great, just great! Ah, but I can't wait to hear what you've been doin'. I want to know everything. Everything!"

I wondered whether this was really the Gideon Pratt I had known. He wanted to know about *me*! New York had done something to him or for him, I wasn't sure which. I was eager to find out. Was he still the scared lecturer I once knew? Had New York slaked his thirst to rise to the top of the heap, anybody's heap?

"You're looking great yourself, Gideon," I said. I was thirty years old. I figured I could call him by his first name. "And prosperous," I added.

He linked his arm in mine and pushed me through the crowd. "You ain't seen nothing, buddy boy. Nothin'! This town is loaded with dough. Just follow your old friend Gideon. He's going to show you what a real town is!"

Follow him? He was shoving me along as if we were escaping a fire. "What's the hurry?" I shouted at him over a loudspeaker announcement of a train to Richland, of all places.

"Who's hurrying? That's New York for you."

This new Gideon was a wonder. He checked my bag, tipped the attendant a dollar, raced me through the corridor, down a ramp, and pushed me into a taxi. "Press Gallery," he commanded the driver.

We sped down Madison Avenue. Gideon kept up a running commentary on the street scene. "Over there, CBS," he cried. "Now, there's Benton and Bowles--ah--Ogilvy's--now B-B-D-and-O. The biggest ad agencies in the world."

"Not even in Washington, I asked?"

He picked a bit of lint from his tan suit. "Well, that's different. Seat of government. But New York is where the power is."

His explosive excitement began to get to me. I wondered what New York had done to change my peacock professor into an unguided missile. The taxi had hardly stopped before Gideon had the door open and was on the sidewalk. "Let's go," he commanded as he gave the driver a bill, not waiting for the change.

He shoved me into the revolving door that came in behind me like a charging bull. I was practically flung into the restaurant lobby. The sudden gloom struck me blind. "Where is everybody?" I asked nobody in particular.

"Straight ahead of you, Art!" He poked his fist into the small of my back and pressed me, like a ball being pushed by a stick, to the rear of the room, then up a plush stairway to the second floor. While not as black as below, this room was still dark enough to make me feel my way along by the backs of chairs, all of them occupied by types as smartly dressed as Gideon. I looked for women. There were only two, both of them seated in a corner booth where a small lamp shed an ochre glow over a table.

"Our gals," said Gideon.

One of the women, the tallest, was shaded by a hat nearly two-feet wide. The next thing I noticed was the plunging decolletage of her sparkling red dress. The other woman had her back to me. She was hatless, her blond hair cut in a shingle, her plain pink dress high around the throat.

Gideon ushered me to the table. "Jo!" he cried. He took the glamour-gal's long-gloved left hand and pressed it between both of his own. "And Mary!" He nodded to the other woman, who sat opposite her and whom I saw now was much younger than Jo. Gideon grabbed my arm again as if I might run away.

"May I present my old newspaper friend, Art James," Gideon said. "Art, this is Jo Davis--*Miss* Josephine Davis. And Mary Wright."

"How do you do?" said Jo, her blackened lashes blinking. She smiled widely, revealing the whitest teeth I ever saw.

"Hello, Art," said Mary, hardly looking at me. She was pert rather than pretty, with small nose and mouth, but bright eyes surmounted by very blond brows. I tipped my hand to each of them.

I tipped my hand to each of them. "My pleasure," was the best I could manage.

"Well, sit down, Art, there beside Mary. That's it." Gideon slipped in beside Jo and took her hand again. "How are ya, Jo?"

Jo took her hand away from Gideon. As if not knowing what to do with it, she held it against her cheek. "That's our Gideon," she said to me. "Hasn't seen me for an hour and he asks me how am I doing."

Gideon picked up the menu, which was about two-feet high, it seemed to me, and had a gold string and tassel. "What's it going to be, boy and girls? Don't be shy. This is on my boss, old man Green. Business conference, entertain the press. Got to have good relations with the press, you know." He giggled at his joke.

"Don't pay any attention to him, Art," said Jo. "He's only this way ninety-nine percent of the time. He improves when he's sober."

Gideon playfully slapped her wrist. "I won't have you telling lies about me in front of an old friend."

Mary touched my right arm. I was surprised by this token of familiarity. I began to realize what I had been missing in Richland. "Mr. Pratt's really very dull," she said. "You should see him at the office."

"I forgot to tell you, Art," said Gideon. "Mary works for me. Gal Friday, receptionist, typist, stenographer. The whole bit. I'd be lost without her. So don't get any ideas about taking her away from me."

"Gideon!" cried Jo.

He patted her hand. "Now now, dear. Don't be jealous."

"He's incorrigible," said Jo.

"And Jo," said Gideon, "is *the* public relations director of the Educational Foundation of America." He leaned across the table and, in a whisper directed to me, intoned "She's actually my mistress."

"Gideon!" Jo exclaimed. She removed her huge hat, revealing her bright red hair. "He's married and has two kids."

"I know," I said. "I met them years ago. Charmers."

"Pay no attention to her, Art," Gideon retorted. "Nothing shocks her, not ever."

Jo patted her cheek again. I was still intrigued by the low cut of her dress, and its color, which kept getting a brighter red as my eyes adjusted to the gloom. I shivered, but I attributed that to the icy cold of the air-conditioning.

A waiter in a green corduroy jacket and a white napkin on his arm came over. He began filling our long-stem water glasses.

"How are you, Irving?" asked Gideon.

"Fine, Mr. Pratt. How's yourself?"

"Great, Irving. Just great. How's the wife?"

"Holding her own, Mr. Pratt. Thank you very much."

"How's the filet mignon today, Irving?"

Irving straightened to attention. "The way you like it, Mr. Pratt. Not too rare, not too well done."

"Irving, are you talking about filet mignon or women?"

"Yes, sir, Mr. Pratt. How about some Chianti? We got something special."

"Not too cold, not too hot, Irving."

"Yes sir, Mr. Pratt."

Jo groaned.

"Now," Gideon said as the waiter went off, "I want everybody to have a good time. And to start the party off I want to tell you about this friend of mine from the great city of Richland."

For ten minutes he told Jo and Mary things about me I hardly knew myself and lots that I had forgotten. He had my history down cold. He recited facts from when I was born and raised in Richland, the corporation law my dad practiced, the social status of my mother, including the fact she was an inveterate do-gooder belonging to everything from Cancer to Red Cross, my "excellent" record at Richland University, which caused me to smile to myself remembering my last official interview with him as a student, my scoop for the Monitor on the Communist cell at the university, my inside knowledge of the financial markets and my shoot-from-the-hip reporting on both politics and education, lower and higher, for the Star. He recalled stories I had forgotten, but which he obviously had read. I figured he must have a pretty thick file of clippings on me and was a regular reader of the Star.

"And now," Gideon went on, "Art is about to turn this town on its ear, because he's going to work for the Dispatch!"

The way he announced the name of the newspaper you would have thought it as great as the *Times*. In fact, the Dispatch was Manhattan's smallest daily newspaper.

Jo pressed Gideon's hand to make him stop talking. "I understand you are going to report education news, Art."

"Yes--"

"He's going to show those other education reporters what real education news is like," Gideon proclaimed. "Why, in Richland he turned out education stuff that made crime look like a Sunday school picnic."

I had no idea what he was talking about, but I admit I liked his approach. I swallowed a mouthful of iced water, which sobered me enough to realize that Gideon hadn't really changed. He was buttering me up for something, and it had to be a big one to be worth both women and filet mignon. I also began to wonder if he hadn't paved the way for me to come to New York just to get me to do him a favor. Jo was saying something to Gideon in a tone too low for me to hear. I grasped the opportunity to get better acquainted with Mary. "How do you like public relations?" I asked her.

Her eyes widened. She seemed to regard me with some awe and wonder. "It's fun working with Mr. Pratt," she said. "Actually I just do what he tells me to do. Mr. Green I like, very much."

"And Gideon?"

She made a quick motion with her hand on her lap. Jo was trying to catch my eye and when Jo did, she said "Gideon was saying this might be a good time to tell you about the Educational Foundation."

"I would like to learn all I can about it, Miss Davis."

She batted her dark eyelashes. "Do call me Jo, Art. Everyone does. I hope you will feel free to come to our public relations office anytime. We have a lot of good stories. Of course I will personally see to it that your name gets on our mailing list, not just for press releases, but our general publications as well."

"I appreciate that, Jo."

"They've got a terrific story," Gideon said. "What they're doing for the good of the teaching profession is terrific."

Jo restrained Gideon again in the same manner as before: by holding his hand. I wondered whether Gideon had been serious in saying that Jo was his mistress. "Of course Gideon is paid to say that," she said, "but I want you to have the opportunity to make up your own mind."

"What the Foundation does," Gideon said, "in a nutshell, is to help teachers get a master's degree."

"Our scholarships provide full tuition," Jo said rapidly, not allowing Gideon to get in another word.

"Where does the money come from?" I asked.

"Business, mainly," she answered. "Philanthropic foundations too. Gideon helps us raise the money by the publications he writes for us, and the publicity." She smiled at him. "He's very good at it, by the way."

Gideon was restless. "That's not the whole story, Jo," he said.

Jo gave him a sharp sidelong glance. "I realize that, Gideon, but it's about as much as Art wants to know right now. We needn't carry this conference idea too far."

"No, no," I said. "I don't mind. I want to learn."

"Alright then," Jo said to me. "But here come our steaks."

I liked her. She was openly friendly in the way she dealt with me. I was a newcomer to the big city, a hick by anyone's standards, but she treated me as if I were a favorite cousin long absent. It was interesting to watch Gideon and Jo struggle for control of our meeting. Gideon had gained in aggression what he had lost in academic dignity. Although he was outclassed by Jo, he seized every opportunity to grab the ball from her and run with it.

As we ate our steaks Gideon plied Jo with questions about her background. His performance was transparent; he did it to impress me with what a high-class woman he worked with. I felt sorry for Mary having to put up with his inverted way of boasting.

Gideon said "Jo, tell me how you got into public relations."

She had removed her gloves. She flicked her superbly manicured fingers in Gideon's direction in a gesture that meant, louder than words: *Stop making an ass of yourself.*

"Go on, tell him, Jo." Gideon appealed to me. "It's a terrific story, Art. You do want to hear it, don't you?'

I said "Sure, Jo. I'm interested. I really am."

Mary, who had been minding her own business all this time, surprised me by interjecting: "I would like to hear it too, Miss Davis." She looked fearfully at Gideon, with good cause, for Gideon was warning her with a knitting of his brows. Suddenly there was something about Gideon I noticed for the first time: he was not wearing glasses. Odd that I should have missed that. I peered more closely. The table light glinted off his eyes. He was wearing contact lenses.

"I can't let this steak get cold," Jo said. "It's delicious." Her mouth full, she nodded to Gideon. "You're too good to me, Gideon."

He was eating with just as much abandon as Jo. "Want to fatten you up," he told her. He seemed to have forgotten about the proposed story of Jo's life. It made me feel good to know there was someone in the world who could defeat Gideon Pratt. My elation was premature. Gideon turned his guns on poor Mary.

"My gal Friday here," he said, pointing his fork at her while she visibly cowered. "She has a terrific story too. Tell Art about yourself, Mary."

"Oh, for heaven's sake, Gideon!" Jo cried. "Leave the poor girl alone."

Gideon raised his hands in mock defense. "What did I say?"

I butted in. "I'm sure Mary has an interesting story too."

"Sad, very sad," said Gideon.

Mary knifed him with a slit-eyed look. "I don't think it's sad," she said evenly. "Lots of people are orphans."

"Don't let her kid you," Gideon said to me. "She's a poor lost waif. Her parents were killed in an automobile accident a few years ago." Gideon reached across the table and patted Mary's hand. "Poor kid. You should have seen her, Art, when she came to work for me. That was--how long's it been, Mary?"

"Four years," she muttered miserably, her voice almost inaudible.

"God, how time flies!" Gideon said loud enough for a couple on the next table to turn around to give him a disturbed look. "Has it really been four years? Well, she was the most forlorn little thing. I gave her a job just to shelter her from the storm, so to speak. Never talked. Never smiled. You didn't know that, did you, Mary?"

Poor kid, indeed! Mary was red to her scalp. I began to suspect that Gideon must be blind. How could he fail to see what he was doing to her?

Gideon continued to pursue Mary, yapping "But you straitened up fast, didn't you, kid? What a change! Cut her hair. Cast off the country rags. Blossomed into the rosy creature we see before us. She used to sit for hours hunting-and-pecking. *Never can find the p!*" He roared at himself, "heh, heh, heh!"

I smiled at Mary, trying to reassure her. Her head was down.

"You should see her now," Gideon continued without remorse. Fastest little typist you ever did see! A real pro. If she ever left me I'd be lost--lost!"

Jo gave Gideon a warning touch, but she had lost her control of him.

Gideon roared on, forgetting his meal, even as the waiter filled our wine glasses. Gideon wagged a finger at me. "You should have seen the first secretary I had. Wee bit of a thing. Ninety pounds. But what a dynamo! Mildred was her name. Hey, Mildred, I used to say. And darned if she wasn't at my desk in a split second. Timed her. Hey, Mildred! Fastest gal in New York, maybe the entire U.S.A. Fast other ways too. All the time the boys from Mad Av chasing her. Good for public relations, I used to say. She up and left me one day." He snapped his fingers. "Like that. Pregnant."

He paused to observe the effect. No one laughed. He plunged on. "What a town! Did I ever tell you, Art? No, I guess I didn't. How I rocked this town first week I arrived. Old man Green, he set me on this account he had then. Teachers Union. National Union of Teachers. Loaded with

Reds, Pinks, all shades. No safeguards at all. Let anybody in. Ex-teachers too. I told old man Green, let's get out of this one. He said, what for, their money isn't red, it's green, like everybody else's. I said, this isn't good for business. How can we get out of it, he asked. Contract's a contract. I said, get them to breach it. How? he asked. I said, I'll handle it." Gideon looked around, as if for spies. He whispered "Know how I did it, boy and girls? I put out a press release. Straight stuff. National Union of Teachers to hold annual meeting. Something like that. I spelled the name out in the lead. Every paragraph after that I didn't write 'the union.' I wrote the N-U-T-S. The publicity!" Gideon leaned back and tapped the table.

We were as quiet as editors. "What happened?" I asked.

Gideon picked up his glass. He twirled it around. "Oh, what's the difference? The firm got fired from the account, of course. And, just to ruin the story, that's what I wanted."

Mary, who had been listening open-mouthed, said "I don't think that was very nice." No one laughed. Mary turned to me. "Do you think so, Mr. James?"

"Nuts," Gideon said. "Who's for dessert?"

I shook my head. Jo and Mary shook theirs. Gideon was scanning the menu, which the alert Irving had brought over upon Gideon's signal. "The eclair royale is terrific," he said. "Bring four, Irving."

Jo shrugged her shoulders and winked at me. Irving began clearing the table. Gideon looked around the room, whose dark paneling shone with the reflected light of the table lamps. "Excuse me a minute, kiddos," he said.

He darted among the tables like a copy boy on the way to the top. At a table near the opposite wall he slapped a fellow on the shoulder. The man's shout of "Gideon!" rang across the room. The man waved to us. Jo waved back.

"Dick Doyle," Jo said to me. "You'll meet him sooner or later. He works for the H. Thomas Bronson advertising company. Want me to call him over?"

"Not now, Jo, if you don't mind," I said.

Mary called out, with a little wave, "Hi, Dick," although he could not possibly have heard her.

"That's Gideon for you," said Jo. "Always working."

"This adverting agency--" I ventured.

"H. Thomas Bronson?"

"Yes. What connection does it have with Gibson Green?"

"None, actually," Jo replied. "Except indirectly. H. Thomas Bronson prepares the advertising for the Educational Foundation. Maybe you've seen some of our ads on television or on billboards. *Education Is the Strength of the Nation.*"

I remembered having seen the billboards and car cards on buses in Richland. "Boy with a microscope," I said.

"They're the ones. Gideon thought up the slogan. Rather good, don't you think?"

"It has a certain roll to it," I said. "Also true."

Jo smiled. She had a certain way of smiling: her slightly protruding lips pouting, her eyes crinkling, that started me thinking that I wouldn't mind being alone with her for a while to find out more about her, if Gideon didn't have her sewed up. It also made me wonder why Mary was there. Then that became obvious too. Gideon was pairing me off with Mary. I suspected he had a motive for that.

"We also have newspaper and magazine ads, spots on radio and television, and free editorial material," Jo was saying. I watched the way Gideon was off to another table, shaking hands, slapping shoulders, and also kissing the cheeks of some women almost in a class with Jo.

"There are three-sheet posters at train stations too," Jo went on. Gideon was on his way back to us when he stopped three tables away. "Time and space for our advertising are donated by the media through the Advertising Association," she said. "So you see how dependent the Educational Foundation is upon the good will of American business and industry."

Jo stopped. She was watching Gideon. "I can't believe it," she said. "He's talking to George Rankin. He used to work for the Foundation. He was my boss. That Gideon! I'll kill him."

I leaned toward Mary. I caught a whiff of perfume. "Let's leave," I said.

"It's nothing," Mary said. She made no attempt to keep her voice down. "It's just that Mr. Rankin is working for Mr. Cotter now."

"Who?" I asked.

Mary put a finger to her lips. Gideon rejoined us. He sat down heavily, half out of breath. He raised his glass of wine. "Salud! Where's the éclairs?"

Jo rested her hand over her stomach. "Not for me, Gideon."

"You, Art? You, Mary?" He waved to Irving, who came over with a tray. He helped himself to an éclair that looked like a frozen hotdog covered with a brown sauce. He ate alone.

Jo was grim through all this. I figured she was boiling inside. Her long black eyelashes were lowered. Her fingers drummed the table. "Gideon!" He gave her an innocent look. "Did you have to?" She spoke through clenched teeth.

His mouth stuffed with whipped cream, Gideon snapped "Have to what?"

"I suppose you had to tell George Rankin I was here?"

"You're not invisible."

"I'll speak to you later."

"Tell me!" Gideon said harshly. "Tell me now!"

Jo looked at me as if I ought to share her exasperation, appealing to me with a sigh, raised eyebrows and a shrug of her surprisingly broad shoulders, signaling that Gideon was being particularly difficult that day. "You know perfectly well, Gideon, that you shouldn't be seen talking to George."

Gideon polished off the rest of his éclair. He wiped the excess chocolate from his lips. "Oh, hell, Jo. George means well."

Jo rolled her napkin into a ball and tossed it onto the table. "George *means* well? I don't care if he's an undercover agent for the FBI! He's Cotter's boy now, and we can't have anyone thinking there's the slightest link between Cotter and the Foundation." She waved her hands excitedly. I was amazed to see that Gideon was paying attention to her. He was actually listening, head cocked, eyes serious. "If anyone ever thought that because George was once Mr. Fletcher's assistant, that the Foundation has the slightest--"

"You're repeating yourself," Gideon said.

I raised my hand. "Who is Cotter? Who is Fletcher?"

"Cotter, the grapefruit king," Gideon said. He flung his arm behind Jo's chair. He was half-turned toward her. "I didn't mean any harm, Jo.

Anyway, he already knew you were here." The old whine was creeping into his voice. "I couldn't pass him by without saying hello, could I?"

Jo laced her fingers together. She twisted an emerald ring. "No, I suppose not. I haven't seen George in here--well, not since he left the Foundation. If he's going to come here we'll have to lunch somewhere else, that's all."

"Who is Fletcher?" I repeated.

Jo's eyes, I'm positive, were near overflowing. She blinked a few times and held it back. "Oh, Art, I'm sorry. This is an awful way to behave in front of a guest. Jo reached across the table to hold Mary's hands. "Dear, let's get together some day, just you and I. We can talk sensibly about this bear who causes us so much grief."

"What'd I do? What'd I say?" Gideon cried, hands flung high, looking at me for confirmation that he had done nothing to merit Jo's discipline.

"All I want to know is," I said, "who is Cotter and who is Fletcher?"

"I told you," said Gideon. "Cotter's the grapefruit king. Arch-foe of the Communists. Leader of the Cotterites. Don't tell me you've never heard of him?"

"Oh, him," I said. Harry M. Cotter, retired president and owner of the Cotter Grapefruit Company, was one of the ultra-conservative right-wingers stamping about the country, raising an alarm about Communism among teachers.

"Cotter himself," Gideon said. "Enemy of the people. Fearless foe of the friendless teacher."

"What Gideon means," Jo said, "is that Cotter is going about saying that some of the teachers who get our Foundation scholarships are Communists."

"Mr. Fletcher doesn't like it," Gideon said.

"Mr. Fletcher is president of the Foundation," Jo explained.

"That makes sense," I said. "I mean Mr. Fletcher couldn't *like* what Cotter is doing. You have to ignore nuts like Cotter."

"Ignore him?" Gideon almost yelled. "Ignore him! You hear that, Jo?" He leaned toward me, an elbow on the table. "I have news for you, buddy boy. In your job at the Dispatch you're going to have a lot to do with Harry M. Cotter."

"Speaking of the Dispatch," I said. "I have to get down there right away. What time is it?"

Jo looked at her wristwatch, which had little diamonds all around it. "Two."

"I'll just about make it," I said.

On the sidewalk, under the bright summer sun, I said goodbye to each of them. I paused by Mary's side. "See you soon, Mary," I said.

She smiled shyly, holding her little white purse in front of her, much as a child does. "Come see us," she said. "You will like Mr. Green."

I climbed into a taxi and waved to them. Gideon took Jo's arm, right there in front of Mary. He shoved her before him through the Madison Avenue swarm of secretaries and executives.

New York, I told myself, was my piece of cake.

Chapter Nine

Every few days after that Gideon telephoned to ask how I was doing. He always managed to slip in some piece of information about the Cotterites that he had picked up on his trips to St. Louis, Los Angeles, Dallas or wherever. The Educational Foundation, he told me, had assigned him to run around the country refuting Cotterite charges that five percent of American teachers were Communists.

"Spoke to this citizens education committee in Denver last night," he said. "Egghead liberals. They think this Cotterite movement is a passing phase, that it will blow over. How ignorant can you get? That's the trouble with those liberals. They talk, talk, never act. So what happens? The Cotterites walk in and capture two seats on the school board. Under their noses!"

Although small items about Cotterite activity kept popping up in the Dispatch, I didn't think about the movement too much. This sort of thing had been going on for a long time: teacher firings, banning books from school shelves, required adherence to certain study texts presumed to be *more American*. I suppose I was just too busy getting acquainted with my new job and the people with whom I worked to pay much attention to the Cotterites.

"In the New York newspaper pyramid in which the Times and the Herald Tribune are at the apex, the Dispatch is at the base," is the way Al Farmer, my city editor, put it one night over coffee.

"Everyone thinks we ought to die--or merge," Al said. His tough, hard eyes glinted. "But there's still life in this hungry old bear." He flipped open a copy of that night's Dispatch. The corner signal, *Flash Final*, was printed in a bilious green. The tabloid was slim that night, only twenty-four pages. "Yes sir, she raised me from a cub. A great old bear!"

I raised my cup of coffee. "Here's to her," I said.

"Don't," Al said. "Too much like a wake." He caressed the front page, smudging the 72-point black headline, *Scandal!* "Truth is the *News* doesn't want us," he went on. The way he smiled at the paper you would have thought he was admiring the faded but still warm face of a woman. He swiveled on the bar stool, buckling his long legs. "Did you ever watch a stand to see who buys the Dispatch? I swear they're all bearded. That's who we appeal to, the downtrodden and the forsaken, who shall inherit the earth."

"Then why don't we fold?" I asked.

"I'll show you," Al said. He sprang agilely from the stool. You would never had known he was nearly seventy, not from the way he barged out of the coffee bar. He was as tall as me, lean and hard.

Al took me via a rickety freight elevator, which howled and screeched in protest, to the sub-basement of the Dispatch building. We crossed the oily concrete floor, slick with the footsteps of five generations of pressmen, to the monster machine on which the Dispatch was ground out. The press was still. Several men, faces smudged black with ink, sat about on wooden platforms eating sandwiches out of wax paper bags. "Hi, Moe. Hello, Sid," Al said. The pressmen waved and smiled.

I almost ran to keep up with Al as he led me around the press, whose gears dripped thick black oil. "It's not the press," he said, "although, God bless her, she's kept us in business long past her time. It's those pressmen." The stygian heat made me sweat. Al raced on. "Non-union men. Free enterprise boys. Expelled from other printing plants. Sometimes I think they put out our four editions a day by the sheer power of their disgrace."

He leaped the stairs on the other side of the press two at a time. I breathed with relief in the cooler composing room. Linotype arms swung and shuttled. Molten lead bubbled in the hell pots. Al strode down the line between the typesetting machines. "Kept together with tape and baling wire," he said. "And look at this!" He pointed to a silvered rack. It contained two rows of battered wood type, each capital letter about two inches tall. "Stuff was delivered in those racks fifty years ago," Al told me. "Used for the Page One banner headline." A compositor was setting the word *Triumph!* on a block. "For the *final* final edition. You'll see that at least once a month. And there." He pointed to the word *Disaster!* set in the same type. "Good any day."

After that I had a lot more respect for the old bear. She might not be anything to look at but she had been a real fighter in her time. Perhaps, I thought, there was still some fight left in her.

With the help of the Teachers Union I ran down a report that a Long Island teacher had been fired because of suspected Communism. "Ah ha," I said to Charlie Aitkin, the union secretary, who also handled publicity, "the Cotterites!" I was at my desk talking to Charlie on the telephone. "No, the Guardians," Charlie said. "Same breed though. Teacher's name is Mrs. Knittle, Mrs. Garland Knittle. Here's her bio." I clamped on the headphone and began typing notes. "Taught at this same school, Brookwood, since 1929. Mostly early grades, looks like. Was social studies teacher, grade eight, when dismissed. Graduate, Newark, 1929; master's, Teachers College, Columbia, 1947, on scholarship from Educational Foundation of America."

"Oh, oh." I said.

"What's the matter, Art?"

"The Foundation won't like this one."

"Then ask the Foundation what they're going to do about Mrs. Knittle. This is one time when it should get off its fat ass and holler like hell."

"I'll look into it," I promised Charlie. I asked him for Mrs. Knittle's address and wrote it down. "Got a union statement, Charlie?" He did. I switched on the headphone and typed the statement Charlie dictated. The union claimed that Mrs. Knittle was framed by the Guardians in an obvious attempt to set the stage for capture of the Brookwood School Board.

I told Al about Mrs. Knittle. He said "Okay, Art. Be sure to get a statement from the Brookwood School principal. We've got to have both sides."

"Exactly," I answered.

The next afternoon I took the subway to the end of the line and then a bus beyond Queens to Brookwood, an elegant ancient town with arching elms and spacious lawns. Mrs. Knittle opened the door to her apartment, just a crack, and peeked out at me. A chain guarded the door. I introduced myself and she let me in.

She fingered the bun of her gray hair. "You didn't give me much time to fix up," she said. She ushered me into the sun-filled parlor, walking stiff-legged before me. The veins of her hands stood out, blue and puffy. She sat down on the sofa, fingering the white lace on the sofa's arm. "I'm glad you came, Mr. James. I was wondering when someone was going to do something for me. Mr. Aitkin said he told the newspapers about me, so I'm glad you're interested."

"I'll do what I can, Mrs. Knittle."

She sat, very stiff, her gnarled hands on the lap of her flowered dress. "It's not for myself," she said crisply. "They were going to retire me anyway. What I did, joining those groups, was to help others. Tell me, Mr. James, was that a crime?"

"No, it wasn't, Mrs. Knittle."

If the firm set of her jaw, the calm clearness of her eyes, were any criteria, Mrs. Knittle didn't realize what had happened to her, nor why. "Those groups you joined, Mrs. Knittle, you didn't know they were Communist-front groups?"

She looked startled, like a little girl told for the first time to stay away from lone men in parked cars. "You mean, like the Aid-to-Russia? Why, that was during the war, when the Russians were our allies."

"But it was cited by the Attorney General as a Communist-front group."

She toiled with a handkerchief, twisting it into a cord. "Well, I'm sure it wasn't then. At least I didn't know it."

"Did you tell that to the school board?"

"They never asked me."

"You didn't have a hearing?"

Mrs. Knittle shook her head. "No. You see, I wasn't actually fired. The School Board superintendent, he suggested that I retire, on account of my arthritis."

"Did you believe him?"

She unfolded the handkerchief and pressed it flat on her lap. "Well, yes. But then Mr. Aitkin, he came to see me."

"And he told you about the Guardians?"

"Of course I had heard of them. Some of them speak up at the Parent-Teacher Association meetings, but I never put much stock in what they say."

"What do they say?"

"The Guardians? Oh, they say we ought to be teaching more about how the Communists are trying to take over the government, things like that."

"And did you?"

Mrs. Knittle laughed heartily. "No, I didn't take over the government. Did I teach what they wanted? I've always taught the truth about the Communists, Mr. James, how the Communist Party was established in this country, the whole history of the movement, especially its international aspects."

"Then you were never a Communist yourself?"

She knotted her handkerchief again. She studied me for a moment, appearing suspicious and then laughed. I was relieved. "I should say not! Is that what you were told?"

"You mean by the School Board or the Guardians?"

"Both. I think. Mr. Blanchard, superintendent of the board, he's a Guardian."

I stood up. "What are your plans, Mrs. Knittle?"

She smiled proudly, her eyes crinkling. "Why, you know, I'm going to be so busy. The PTA wants me to give a talk. And my church women's group. About my experience with the Guardians. I'm going to fight back, you see." She struggled up and put out her hand. I shook it. Her grasp was strong, sure. "This is a fight, we're in, Mr. James. A fight to the finish!"

I thanked her. Before I left I got Blandford's address.

I was there in half an hour. Blandford marched toward me, straight as a printer's rule, big hand outthrust. His smart two-toned suit was expensively tailored to his tall angular frame.

"I hope I haven't kept you waiting, Mr. James," he said as he smiled. "This is one of those days when nothing seems to go right. Teachers down with the flu. Not enough substitutes. Contractor ran into marine clay on the annex to the south district school. And if that weren't enough, two textbook publishers are late on deliveries."

Blandford's voice was flavored with a tough combination of grittiness and hard-packed cadence, words running head-to-tail like a record run wild. He escorted me into his office, which gave a panoramic view of Brookwood's main intersection, where a revolving clock on a bank across the street told me, in quadruplicate, that it was four o'clock.

"Now, Mr. James, suppose you tell me what I can do for you."

While his manner exuded affability and a desire to please, his eyes remained cold and hard. The way he walked back and forth reminded me of the pacing lion in Richland Zoo.

I took the nearest chair. I decided on the oblique attack. "Is there a teacher shortage in Brookwood, Mr. Blandford?" I asked.

He stopped pacing and threw up his hands. "Shortage! We're running double shift in two schools, not because of lack of space, but because we simply can't find enough teachers. Same everywhere."

"In the face of this teacher shortage, then, what is your policy on teacher retirement?"

His hard thick lips shut like a trap. He frowned, lowering his massive eyebrows. His face darkened in the shadow. "We retire our teachers on a regular schedule on the July following the sixty-fifth birthday."

"But some teachers, for one reason or another, are retired early?"

"Of course. Sickness, mostly. Some choose to retire at age sixty-three. They have that option."

Blandford thrust his hands into his pants pockets. He went over to the window and looked into the street. His great shoulders slumped. "In the case of Mrs. Knittle," he said thickly, "there were extenuating circumstances."

I took out my notepad and pencil. "And those were?"

"The board's reasons are not of public concern, Mr. James." He turned around. When he saw me making notes he did a double-take. "That's off the record. Mrs. Knittle is sick, Mr. James. The board did her a kindness."

"Then it was a *forced* retirement?"

"Let's say she was asked to retire for the sake of her health."

"What about her teaching?"

His eyes flicked, ever so slightly. "There's been criticism of that, but the overriding concern--"

I put my notepad away. I stood up. "Let's cut out the smokescreen, Mr. Blandford. You and I know that Mrs. Knittle was fired because you, or the board, or both, suspect she's a Communist."

He smiled easily. "You can't print that, Mr. James."

"I can and I will, Mr. Blandford." I started toward the door. "Do you want to make a statement or don't you?"

"Mr. James!" I turned around. He plunged toward me, grabbed my arm. "Give me time to think!" He guided me toward my chair, then sat down behind his desk. He wrote a few words, then tossed his pencil down. "I can't do this on my own, Mr. James. I must consult the Woodland Board of Education."

"Send it to me at the Dispatch," I said.

"You're not being fair, Mr. James. You can hold your story until you get our statement, can't you?"

"If I have it by nine o'clock tonight, Mr. Blandford. You can call me."

He leaned back. He sighed heavily. "Is this some kind of a personal vendetta you're on?"

"You might call it that." I thought for a moment. I had backed Blandford into a corner. Now I had the advantage. I might never get the chance again to peel the hide off a witch hunter. "Are you a Guardian, Mr. Blandford?"

He snuffled, pinched his spade-like nose. "What if I am? What's that got to do with the Knittle case?"

I pursued him. "Didn't you personally order her to change her method of teaching, to stick to the new prescribed text, instead of allowing her pupils to investigate books on their own? Didn't you personally issue the order for her to stop her free-wheeling discussion groups and citizenship projects, and to report her lesson outlines to her principal?"

I was making all this up, but I knew enough about the general oppression of teachers to know the pattern. Blandford was impressed. He raised his eyebrows, turned down the corners of his mouth, crumpling his chin. "I don't know where you got your information, young man, but nothing was done in the case of Mrs. Knittle that didn't carry out board policy."

"Then you admit to a policy of teacher intimidation?"

He laughed, a nervous "He, he." He squashed the piece of paper on which he had begun his statement, lunged it into his wastebasket. "I advise you not to use that word, Mr. James. You could be in a lot of trouble if you do."

"From the Cotterites, Mr. Blandford?"

"Our group is called Guardians," he snapped.

"Then it is a Cotterite group?"

He looked at me as if he could have bitten off his tongue. Mouth agape, fingering his nose, tapping his foot, he began to puff as if he had just finished last in a race. "We stand firmly on the right of an individual to fight Communism wherever it appears," he said.

"Right out of the Cotterite *Black Book*," I told him.

"Preservation of the republic demands that Communist sympathizers be unmasked, that they be stripped of positions of power."

"Sure," I said, "like Mrs. Knittle."

Blandford peered at me as if a fog parted us. "Teachers are in a unique position to do incomparable harm to innocent minds. They lack the sophistication required to detect the insidious propaganda methods of the Communists."

"So teachers must be told how and what to teach?"

"Curricula must be prepared by experts alert to the Communist plot to overthrow governments by capturing control of young minds."

I stood up. "And that makes it right, of course, for the Guardians, the Cotterites, and every other extremist group, to assume all positions of power themselves, so *they* can tell everybody what to do? Turn off the record, Mr. Blandford."

He pursued me to the door. "Everywhere in the republic," he cried, "the Communists are moving into key spots, in government, business, labor, education."

"Turn it off," I said as I grabbed the knob. I slammed the door open. "You'd better call in your statement, Mr. Blandford, because tomorrow Brookwood will be a dirty word."

Back at the office I put in a call to Gideon. I figured I had better let him know, just to be fair, that an Educational Foundation protégé was the victim of a Cotterite stab-in-the-back. There was no answer at Gibson Green's. I phoned Gideon's home in Rosewood, New Jersey.

"How ya doin', buddy boy?" His cheerful, ingratiating voice warned me to watch my step. I told him about Mrs. Knittle.

"And you say this Mrs. Knittle got her master's degree on an Education Foundation scholarship?"

"Yes, that's confirmed by the Teachers Association."

I could hear the shouts of a child in the background. One of Gideon's two youngsters, I presumed. "Art, would you be willing to do me a favor?"

I knew what was coming. His voice was smooth, dripping with the we're-old-buddies syrup. "Could you hold your story for an hour, until I get there?" It was obvious he wanted me to refrain from any mention of the Foundation. It was a lot of years since Gideon had censored one of my stories. I wasn't about to let it happen again.

"It's too late to change anything," I said.

"You know me, Art. I wouldn't want to change a word of your story. It's just that I've had, well, a lot of experience in this Cotterite business that might be helpful. You wouldn't want to make any mistakes, would you?"

His pell-mell speech made my ear ring. "No, I sure as hell wouldn't want to make any mistakes," I said, although sarcasm was wasted on Gideon.

"That's what I thought. I have a hot tip about Cotter for you, if you could hold your story until I get there."

I told him to get over fast because my deadline was nine o'clock. As I hung up I felt a sensation on the nape of my neck, a tingling that warned me Gideon was up to his old tricks. He wanted something from me. To get it he was bringing me a gift. I wondered what he had wrapped up this time.

I finished typing the story and was about to type *30* at the end when Gideon charged across the newsroom, wading between the rows of reporters desks, slapping shoulders, shaking hands. "Hi ya, buddy boy," he said as he yanked up the chair beside my desk. "Got here as fast as I could." He reached for my story but I was quicker. I put my elbow on it. "Uh-uh. Not until you tell me your little secret." Viewing me with a kind of amused interest, as if he was analyzing me, Gideon said "If you would like to meet Harry Cotter, to interview him, I think I can arrange it."

This was something I hadn't bargained for: the opportunity to get a Cotter exclusive. Time magazine referred to Cotter as one of the most elusive figures, public or private, in the country. He never gave exclusive interviews, or interviews of any kind for that matter. Perhaps for this reason Cotter was something of a mystery. He was known better for his *Black Book*, the charges of treachery against the Supreme Court, the President and some President's cabinet members, rather than for his personal utterances. To get an interview with Cotter would be a scoop. That would mean a lot to any reporter getting started in New York.

"Just to meet Cotter, to see what he's like, even if I don't get a line--"

Gideon smiled. "One thing about your story on Mrs. Knittle, Art." I could see him coming at me for payment in advance. "You don't have to mention that she got a Foundation scholarship, do you?"

I was determined to make him fight a little for what he wanted. "I think it shows Mrs. Knittle was a darn good teacher," I said.

Gideon leaned forward to whisper "We both know that the charge against her is a phony. But why hurt the Foundation? You know what people will say. They'll say the Foundation must be a Communist-front organization."

I handed the story to him. He quickly found the biographical details about Mrs. Knittle. "No, no, this will never do, Art. The reference to the Foundation is irrelevant. What difference does it make that she got a Foundation scholarship?"

"As I said, in case you didn't hear me, Gideon, it shows she was recognized as a good teacher."

"Why give Cotter more ammunition to use against us?"

"Aren't you interested in defending Mrs. Knittle?"

Gideon brushed his hair back. The overhead lights glinted on his eye contacts. "Sure we are. But we can't get involved in every case of a teacher firing. We're after the big game, Cotter himself."

"And the Mrs. Knittles of this world can fend for themselves?"

Gideon poked my shoulder. "Come on, Art, for old time's sake."

"It is like old times, isn't it Gideon? When you cut the heart out of my story on the cell group at Richland University, remember?"

His eyes narrowed. "When do you want to see Cotter? Friday? He's coming to town, you know." Gideon told me that Cotter usually stayed at the Powers Hotel and the reason he was coming was to preside at a meeting of the Cotterite Board of Directors. "This is off the record, Art. Just between you and me."

"Will you arrange a meeting, Gideon? You won't let me down?"

"Sure, Art. You know me. Have I ever let you down?"

"Only you," I replied, "could ask a question like that."

I eliminated my story's reference to the Foundation scholarship. I told myself this was only a temporary compromise with Gideon. Still, my hand shook as I cut the offensive words. Brandon never called. My deadline neared. I typed in a final paragraph that made it clear that I was awaiting a statement from Brookwood Board of Education. I handed the story to Al at the city desk.

After Gideon left I decided that if I was going to meet Harry M. Cotter in the flesh I'd better find out a little more about him. As I passed through the back corridor on the way to the "morgue," a newspaper's name for its library, I had to stoop to keep my head from banging against the steam pipes. Max Jordan, the drama editor, called me into his cubicle office. He was a wizened little man with a cigarette drooping from his thin parched lips.

Max held up two tickets. "Art, how would you like to cover a play for me? I have two Broadway plays opening Thursday night. Can't get to both of them."

"Will it corrupt my morals?" I asked.

Max laughed. He had only half his teeth, and what he had were broken and yellow. "What morals? This is by Georgia Wilson. Called *Out of Eden*."

"What's it about?"

"School teacher in a Southern town. White trash."

"Anything like Wilson's other stuff?"

"Worse," Max said. "They gave it a tryout in St. Louis. Even the Protestants called for a boycott."

"I don't go for boycotts," I said.

Max lit a cigarette on the butt of another. "I have a better idea than boycotts. Working late Saturday nights I never go to church much, but I've been thinking about this idea for years. It's so simple, wonder it hasn't been tried before. Instead of calling things wrong, immoral, unethical, adjectives like that, call them unchristian. Think what that would mean. Even the ministers in St. Louis, they never called Wilson's play unchristian. They should have."

I thought about Max's idea on the way down the dark damp corridor. Calling everything you didn't like unchristian would get monotonous. Besides, would a Jew go around sayings things were un-jewish? Max was a moral man. I had to give him credit for that. His reviews cited the moral implications for what he saw. What Max was doing in telling me his idea was to suggest I follow his example. I put the pair of tickets in my pocket.

The morgue was a high-ceiling room with blinking fluorescent lights suspended low above the row on row of four-drawer wooden files. I went into the second aisle and halfway down pulled out a drawer. I picked through the fat brown-paper envelope. I extracted the one labeled *Harry M. Cotter.*

I opened the envelope on a black scored table by the far wall and dumped the dozens of newspaper clippings and papers. There was a mimeographed biography of Cotter. I read that first. Born on Chicago's Gold Coast, Cotter was raised there and at family homes on Cape Cod and Miami Beach. He attended private schools, went to Yale, was credited with serving the Army with distinction in World War One. His father was board chairman of Cotter Grapefruit Company until he died. Harry Cotter was forty-five then and president of the company. Apparently the job wasn't too demanding, for Cotter was quite a yachtsman, having entered the All-American several times. Also, he was a world traveler.

I waded through the newspaper and magazine clippings. There was an early sketch of Cotter's life, dated 1941, from *Business Today* in which Cotter was credited with saving the Florida grapefruit industry from economic disaster through stock manipulations, written just after the German attack on Russia, in which Cotter was cited for his service to the Aid-the-U.S.S.R.-Now-Committee, which struck me as an anomaly, considering Cotter's present anti-Communist activity; a full-blown *Look* profile by Mike O'Hara, and a reprint of it from *Saturday Digest*, which showed, in blunt language, the demagogic Cotter technique of implication-by-associations that charged the country's leaders, including the President himself, the Secretary of State, the Attorney General, and the Chief Justice of the Supreme Court, as servants of the Communist conspiracy; a satire, written in the form of a play, by an anonymous author and printed in a little magazine, *Inner Space*, which was circulated mainly among students at Columbia, New York, and Pythia universities. The play's hero was a man named Blech, who, in 2000 A.D., after the world had largely been destroyed in a thermonuclear holocaust and death-dealing radioactive winds swirled the globe, refused to take the last spacecraft to Mars until he was assured that no Communists lived there; and, finally, a scholarly analysis of Cotter's my-mind-is-made-up, don't-confuse-me-with-the facts mentality.

The byline on this last piece, *Silenus Stoddard*, leaped off the page. My old friend from Richland, Pythia University's philosophy professor, had gotten into the act.

I dug deeper into the pile. I found another report by Professor Stoddard, this one from the *Platonic Academy Journal*. It was entitled *Cotter's Red Year*. I read it slowly, hardly believing what I read.

After leaving the Army in the early twenties, Stoddard's article said, Cotter studied at Oxford for a year. A year later he enrolled at Moscow University. There he wrote a thesis on the nature of the "Socialist Experiment," or, in other words, the Communist revolution.

"The damned hypocrite!" I said aloud. I looked around. The morgue was quiet. I was the only one in the room. I copied a paragraph of Stoddard's text:

> *Peculiar to Cotter's psychology is his claim that his year*
> *of study in Moscow in 1922-23 gives him a certain authority*
> *as an expert on Communism today. He believes he knows*
> *Communism because he talked with a number of Marxist-*
> *Leninist idealists in the years when the Bolshevists were*
> *organizing their utopia. Cotter documented his faith in the*
> *ultimate triumph of the Revolution in a thesis he wrote as a*
> *requirement for a course in Russian history.*

Incredible! If Cotter had written something favorable to Communism, that would be enough to shoot his anti-Communism campaign full of holes! I wondered if Stoddard had a copy of Cotter's thesis.

I knew I was on to something. I began to have visions of a day-after-day Dispatch crusade against Cotter. Our circulation would soar. Our deficits would turn into profits. I might even be hailed as the Dispatch's savior.

Chapter Ten

My first impulse was to telephone Silenus Stoddard to ask him about Cotter's thesis. Right away I knew this would be the wrong move because of one unknown qualifier: what was the professor's relationship to Gideon? I had often wondered about the extent of Stoddard's involvement in the Communist cell case at Richland University. That was why I had hesitated about getting in touch with him since coming to New York. I still suspected that Stoddard had more to do with spring-boarding Bentley into the Senate than merely co-authoring the report to President Canning. If Gideon and Stoddard were still pals, I reasoned, it would be a natural step for Gideon to try to take over my discovery of the Moscow thesis and to promote it for his own ends. And, now that I was indebted to Gideon for an impending interview with Cotter, I didn't want to pile up another obligation.

Gideon, true to his word, had arranged for me to see Cotter. The appointment was set for three o'clock Friday afternoon. While Gideon wouldn't tell me how he did it, saying only when and where to meet Cotter, I guessed he had strong-armed George Rankin, the man at the Press Gallery restaurant whom Jo wanted to avoid. I promised Gideon again that I certainly would not tell anyone how I got the interview, and I didn't even tell Al Farmer, my city editor. I am by nature a pessimist, I suppose, and I was afraid something might happen to cancel the meeting. Either that or Cotter would order the whole thing kept off the record. It was better, I told myself, to present my story on a Cotter interview to Al as a pleasant surprise. If the whole deal failed to go through then Al would have nothing to be disappointed about.

During the next two days I wrote and rewrote a dozen times the questions I wanted to ask Cotter. I typed my questions on index cards. In addition, hour after hour, I labored on the Cotter file in the morgue, jamming into my brain every pertinent piece of information on Cotter I could find. I did this in the mornings, on my own time, to keep Al from getting suspicious. I emerged from the morgue on Thursday noon an expert on Cotter and the Cotterites. Or so I thought.

Max Jordan hailed me on my way back to the newsroom. He reminded me of the opening of *Out of Eden* that night and that my review had to be written for that night's final street edition. I checked with Al, who said he could spare me for a few hours. Blandford, the Brookwood school superintendent, called me late in the afternoon to cry loud and long about my story on Mrs. Knittle. However. his school board insisted on reviewing any statement to the press. "Too bad," I told him.

Charlie Aikin called to say he liked the headline on my story, which was: *Teachers Union Charges Rightists with Teacher Firing*. I asked him to keep me informed.

Meanwhile, Al showed me a carbon of a brief editorial that was to be run in the Dispatch that evening. It raked the Brookwood School Board over the coals for being unfair to teachers. It wasn't the first time I had received editorial support for a story, but it was the first time since I joined the Dispatch. I felt good about it.

To top off the afternoon, Gideon called to congratulate me on the story and to ask if I could come to his office to meet Mr. Green, who had some ideas he would like to explore with me. I began to feel something of a celebrity.

I walked to Gideon's office, crossing Time's Square, where an usher in a maroon uniform tried to coax people into a theater where a television quiz show was about to begin. He shoved a ticket at me. I shook my head.

Gideon's office was east of the Square in one of those narrow boxes set cheek-by-jowl in a block of similar boxes of varying height. At the seventh floor I exited from the elevator directly into the bright tiled lobby, and there was Mary, looking as scrubbed as a country girl at dawn, seated behind a glass-topped desk. "Hello, Mr. James. Mr. Pratt told me you were coming over. It's nice to see you again."

In a world where receptionists all looked alike Mary was a refreshing change. She wore little makeup, just a touch of lipstick, perhaps a pat or two of powder. She didn't need more than that, for her skin was, to be old-fashioned, peaches and cream. The high puffed sleeves of her pink organdy dress accentuated the whiteness of her arms.

"Mr. Pratt is in with Mr. Green right now," she said in that rather nasal singing voice I remembered so well from our first meeting at the Press Gallery. She invited me to sit down by her desk, and although there was an unfinished letter in her typewriter she seemed eager to talk.

I commented on the carnations in a cut-glass vase. "Courtesy of Mr. Pratt," she said. "Brings me a bunch every morning." I made a mental note to credit Gideon with being nice to fresh-faced blond secretaries.

For some reason, probably because I was feeling taken by Mary, who continued to regard me as if I were a TV idol, I stuffed my hand in my pocket and fingered the pair of tickets that Max Jordan gave me. Why not ask Mary to go to the play with me? I apologized for giving her such short notice.

"Not at all," she said. "I'd love to go. I love Georgia Wilson's plays."

Her frank smile and the way her eyes crinkled when she laughed threw me off my stride. I wasn't accustomed to having women whom I hardly knew accepting my invitations with alacrity. The thought did cross my mind that Gideon might object, for some crazy reason. But then, I thought, he might try to own me professionally but he certainly wasn't going to run my private life.

I said, "No point you're going home, Mary. How about dinner before the show?"

"I'd love it," she replied.

The door to Mr. Green's office creaked open. Gideon poured out. His eyes popping, he looked like an editor who has just been scooped. He gestured to me to join him and disappeared behind the door.

Mary shrugged. "It's like that some days," she said.

I followed into Green's office. Green came around his desk to shake my hand. His shock of white hair reached for the ceiling. "Mr. James," he said, emphasizing *mister*. "It's a pleasure to meet you, a real pleasure." His voice was like gravel on gravel.

I caught Gideon's look of pain, mouth grim, jaw set, which accompanied Green's explosive greeting. "Art has been a real help to me," Gideon said.

"I'm sure he has," Green said. "I'm sure he has." Green scrunched himself into his chair, which seemed a size too small for his well-upholstered torso. "I asked Gideon to invite you over, Mr. James, so we could discuss the Cotter affair."

I settled back in a padded armchair, one of several similar chairs which almost alone relieved the room's Spartan economy. Green's office was stripped for action, with steel-gray walls, battleship linoleum, and a big calendar with a picture of the skyscraper Chase Manhattan Bank on it, all contributing their military discipline.

Gideon turned sideways, apparently to avoid the glare from the big windows overlooking the street. "What Mr. Green means is--"

"Art knows what I mean," Green snapped. Gideon visibly shook under this reproof. Green wasn't a man to be pushed around. "Don't you, Art?"

"I can guess," I said. "You weren't too happy about my story on Mrs. Knittle."

A smile skittered around Green's stern mouth. His deep brown eyes warned me, however, that he didn't want to play games. "Gideon tells me you left out the references to the Foundation. I appreciate that. What I don't understand is why you let Cotter off so easy."

"I reported most of the facts I knew," I said.

"You knew Blandford is a Cotterite. Why didn't you report that?"

I slammed his desk. Green had no business questioning what I wrote. I was a free reporter, writing for a free press. His tactics resembled those of a press censor. "What do you want, Mr. Green? Get Blanchard to sue the Dispatch for libel?"

Green tapped his bony fingers together. He grinned. His eyes relaxed. He swiveled his chair. "Gideon, if you had half of Art's brains you'd have seen that."

I began to feel sorry for Gideon, who was looking aggrieved. "It was just an idea," he mumbled. "How about a statement from the Foundation?"

"Now I ask you," Green said, turning to me, his thick white eyebrows up, "what would you do with a guy who thinks another press handout is the cure-all for Cotterism, when what this cancer calls for is radical surgery--amputation?"

Gideon knotted his hands until his knuckles yellowed. "You might as well hear me out," he said to Green, who retained a pained expression, as if waiting for me to answer his despair. "My idea is to get the Foundation to reveal the facts about Cotter and the Cotterites. Not just the same old propaganda about how nasty he is to teachers. No!" Gideon's old force returned. He grabbed his chair's arms. His voice moved down to a cellar register. "The newspapers will be carrying stories all week about the Cotterite directors, right? The papers like side stories, comments by other groups, to set the record straight, right? Alright then, this is our chance to tell the truth about Cotter, the real truth." Gideon slapped his knee. "We can show that Cotter isn't the Elijah he thinks he is."

Green lit a pipe. A cloud of smoke spiraled over his head. "What the hell can be said about Cotter, pro or con, that hasn't been said a thousand times over? What are we going to hit Cotter with, another balloon filled with hot air about how he's shaking the foundations of democracy? It's been done, done to death."

The way Gideon smiled at me, taking me into his confidence, made me wonder if he knew I had uncovered Cotter's secret. "I was thinking about something personal, Mr. Green," Gideon said. "Something in Cotter's past."

Green's eyebrows shot up again. "Mud?"

"Muck. Black, filthy muck."

Posing to blow another column of smoke, Green observed Gideon with open-eyed approval. "Now you're talking my language," he said. "No doubt we could find *some* dirt in Cotter's life. However, Gideon, I don't think the Foundation would go for that type of campaign." Gideon squirmed.

I was itching to get into the conversation. I put my foot into it, literally, by stamping. "And why not?" I began. "What is so high and mighty about the Foundation that it won't stop to get its hands dirty? Mrs. Knittle gets fired. What do you do about it? Alright, I realize you're not the Foundation, but you represent it. You say the Foundation must not be associated with Mrs. Knittle. Well, let me tell you this, Mr. Green, unless and until the Foundation decides to get down into the arena and fight Cotter where the fight is going on, there are going to be a lot more Mrs. Knittles." I stopped. I was out of breath.

Green regarded me coolly. He sucked his pipe. "I agree with you," he said. "Mrs. Knittle is the issue. But let's remember this: Cotter's got a lot of friends, a lot of important friends, here in New York, in Washington, everywhere. In forty years of business he's garnered a lot of I.O.U.s, and now he's collecting. And one other thing. Some of Cotter's friends, even those who contribute to the Cotterite cause, also contribute to the Foundation."

Gideon brushed this off with a wave of his hand. "I'm aware of that. But I'm also aware that Cotter is up to something, something big, otherwise he wouldn't be holding a directors meeting in New York, where it's going to attract attention. That's not like Cotter. Especially his announcing the meeting in advance." Gideon glanced at me. "I think he's going to make some new charge, Art. For instance, that five percent of the American public school teachers are Communists, something like that." He paused for effect, eyeing Green sharply.

The effect on Green was nil. He showed about as much alarm as a lion at a lamb's bleat. "You heard that from George Rankin?" he asked Gideon.

"Let's say I hear things on the Avenue," Gideon replied with a smile of mistaken triumph. "The point is that Cotter is holding this meeting in New York for a reason. It could be he's decided to make a direct attack upon the Foundation, probably about the scholarship program supporting Communists. And don't forget that Cotter *knows* that Mrs. Knittle got a Foundation scholarship. I wonder why you haven't heard from Cotter yet, Art."

"You're right," I said. "Makes me wonder too." I told them that Brandford had failed to come through with a rebuttal defending the Brookwood board. "The reason may be that Cotter is saving Mrs. Knittle to blast the Cotterites into--whatever it is."

"Well, that's the kind of man we're fighting," Gideon said. "And this *is* a fight. A battle. You can't reason with Cotter. You've got to fight him with his own weapons. That's all he understands."

This was a new, militant Gideon Pratt. I admired his guts, bouncing back as he did following Green's slashing attack. I was beginning to gain a glimmer of the pressures Gideon worked under. He despised Green, and yet he didn't let this interfere with his performance. Gideon was durable. Still, I wondered just how much needling Gideon could take.

Green dismissed me with a hard handshake. I remarked to Gideon, when we were safely in Gideon's box of an office, that Green certainly didn't go out of his way to make friends with the press.

"That's his method," Gideon said. "Kick them when they're down."

Without windows, Gideon's office was dim, hot and stuffy. Gideon stood on a chair and felt the overhead grill. "Never enough air," he said.

"Who but an idiot would spend the best seven years of his life in this coffin?"

"Why do you put up with it?"

He shunted a stack of papers from one side of his desk to the other. "I'm damn well not going to put up with it much longer." He leaned back and clasped his hands behind his head. "I've got several irons in the fire right now. Red hot deals. One of these days I'm going to pull out. I don't need this job. I don't need Green."

"Can't say I appreciate Green myself," I said.

"Where would he be without me?" Gideon asked me. "Hell, I put the agency on its feet. Green doesn't know a thing about public relations."

The old egging curiosity got me again. I have to admit that I was envious of Gideon. I thought he had it made. Up there among the bigshots of Madison Avenue. A doll like Jo Davis to run around with. He was only temporarily stalled. He was still on his way to the top. I wondered why he had stayed with Gibson Green as long as he had. "You certainly have an important job, Gideon," I said, pouring it on. "And doing great things for the Foundation, I hear."

He leaped at the bait, leaning forward, tipping his chair. "The Foundation! That self-appointed spokesman for teachers? What do any of those fat asses over there know about public relations? Jo Davis excepted. What they don't realize is that we're in a war with Cotter. Yes! While Cotter snipes away at us, hauls up his big guns, they weep about maybe hurting the feelings of their rich supporters. They shake with fear. The self-righteous hypocrites! I ask for ammunition to fight Cotter. What do I get? A prissy directive, from the great pooh-bah Fletcher himself, to stop calling Cotter names. Isn't that sweet? Well, they don't know Gideon Pratt!"

Throughout this diatribe I kept wondering how I ever got the impression that Gideon was the smooth-as-silk Madison Avenue man. He really hadn't changed, not at all. He was still the same old Gideon, clamoring against bosses too stupid to appreciate him. I could almost see the wheels turning in his ambitious brain, clanking with distrust of the despised *them*. I didn't know whether to feel sorry for him or be afraid of him. I suppose I felt a bit of both.

"I don't see what there is to be afraid of, Gideon," I said. "About the Cotterites, I mean. Fear-mongers like Cotter, they come and go. Sooner or later they stew in their own sour juices."

Gideon pointed to a pile of papers on his desk. "See those! Stuff I've written about Cotter for the Foundation. They won't use a paragraph. You know why? Because they're too stupid to realize that Cotter is a new breed of cat. They can't see that Cotter believes every word he says. For instance, Cotter's line about the Commies preparing to take over the country. Cotter really believes that. He really believes that some day soon someone in the Kremlin will push a button and all the hidden Communists in American government, business, labor, education, will throw off their disguises, and we will wake up to find them all under Communist control. Why will that happen? Cotter says because we're asleep, and sometimes I believe that myself. We have blind faith that our institutions are so rock-bottom democratic that the Communists have more chance of taking over Heaven than the good old U.S.A. Sure, J. Edgar Hoover warns us all the time about the Communist master plot. But we aren't fooled, we tell ourselves. No right-thinking American will ever be taken in by a Communist."

Gideon began tossing his manuscripts into his wastebasket one sheet at a time. "That's Cotter's talking point," Gideon continued. "Americans generally, Cotter says, are like children when it comes to fighting Communism. What we need is a hard-headed breed of Communist-fighters who can be trusted to deal with the Communists on the only terms the Communists understand. I mean the terms of secrecy, the terms of private investigation. That's why Cotter set up his secret societies, like the Guardians. They publish no reports, hold no public gatherings. They meet in each other's homes, a few members at a time. They swear allegiance to Cotter, to the republic, to one another. On their jobs they watch and wait. They watch the people they work with. They listen for socialistic views, leftist attitudes, a word against the republic. They never call it democracy. They report suspects to leaders of their Cotterite society. You know what happens? One day a guy doesn't show up for work. He's been asked to resign. One more suspected Communist joins the unemployed. Another victory for Cotter. That's the pattern. Repeated thousands of times, all over the country."

"And that's what happened to Mrs. Knittle?"

Gideon dropped the last of the papers into the basket. "Sure," he said. "Sometimes the teachers don't know what hit them. Contract is not renewed, for specious reasons, such as incompetence. The point is, these teachers are blackmailed forever. I heard of one teacher in California who tried to get a job in seventy school districts and was turned down by all of them. So now he's digging ditches for the state. And all the while Cotter sheds crocodile tears about the teacher shortage. What he wants is for Charterites to move into the schools, not only as teachers, but in the PTAs, the school boards, administration. That's where the Cotterite takeover of education begins. And that's not the worst."

"You mean the book burnings?"

"They don't actually burn books. That would be too obvious, although it's been done. Cotterites set up committees to investigate the schools. They recommend, and get adopted, required studies on Communism. They don't like some of the current social studies textbooks. Too soft on Communism. So they get their favorite books adopted, written by extremists like themselves. Not that that is all bad. Sometimes teachers were afraid to teach about Communism, for fear of being suspected of promoting it. Now they can teach the subject. What's happened is, they've lost their former freedom to select books of their own choosing, books that deal realistically with the Communist ideology. While book burnings are passe, library shelves are gleaned of solid, conservative texts."

"How does Cotter do it?" I asked. "How does he get away with it?"

"Simple matter of totalitarian control," Gideon replied. "His control of his organization is absolute. Cotterite policy is Cotter's policy. They obey every command. Not democratic, from the civilian viewpoint, but effective. With Cotter the end does justify the means. So what if a few innocent people are hurt? Better that a few good fruit should spoil rather than the entire crop be rotted by the Communists."

"But that's tyranny!" I cried.

Gideon grimaced. "I don't particularly like pasting labels on anybody. Next thing you know the guy's popular, and where does that leave us?" He looked at his watch. "Five o'clock. Never work a minute overtime. Besides, I've got to see Jo."

"You don't call that working?"

Gideon grinned. "Don't you wish you had it so good?"

I showed him the tickets to *Out of Eden*. "I'm taking your Gal Friday."

He punched my shoulder. "Alright with me, buddy boy. Just remember she's just up from the country. Not used to the big city boys."

"I'm just up from the country myself," I said.

Gideon regarded me seriously, patted the wave in his hair. "Y'er right smart for a country feller," he said, mocking me. "You and I are going to make a great team, Art. Just as soon as I get my hands on some dirt about Cotter I'm going to start a campaign that'll make him wish he'd never heard of Moscow."

I was on my way out the door. I almost tripped. All this time I had been thinking how smart I was. On my own I had discovered that Cotter had been a student at Moscow University. Gideon knew it too! But then, of course, that fact must be common knowledge. What Gideon might not know was that Cotter had written a thesis. If I could get my hands on that before Gideon did! But perhaps Gideon was already on its trail. I told myself that I had better act fast. I began to regret accepting the assignment to cover *Out of Eden*. I should have been on my way to Silenus Goddard instead of taking Mary to dinner.

The sight of Mary, however, looking radiant and expectant, clasping her little black handbag, drove that selfish thought from my mind. Gideon came over. "Watch out for this guy," he told Mary. "Take it from his old pal, he's not to be trusted."

Mary and I walked down Seventh Avenue to Times Square. Although it was hardly dusk, the million lights blazed. Mary set a brisk pace. I hurried to keep up with her. That was one thing I had noticed about New Yorkers: they were always in a hurry. I asked Mary where she was from and when she said Chesterton I did a double take. Chesterton is south of Richland, where one summer I had fallen in love with Jenny Glen, a farmer's daughter. "Chesterton!"

"No one ever heard of it, but it's a nice place."

"Here's one who has heard of it." I told her about my assignment to cover the last fair ever held in Chesterton County and of the collusion between the fair directors and a Richland company that wanted to buy the fairgrounds for a new factory." Mary said she remembered going to the fair, but vaguely, because she was a young girl then. It made me feel old. Mary, I figured, was at least twenty-four.

We went into Jack Dempsey's. We were lucky. We got a table by a window where we could watch the crowds and the gathering twilight. But Times Square never got dark. I settled on the smoked salmon and Mary said that was fine with her. "Ever been here before?" I asked. She patted her lips with her napkin. "Once," she said, "with Mr. Doyle."

"The man from H. Charles Bronson, the one Gideon talked to at the Press Gallery?"

"That's him. He comes to the office to see Mr. Pratt."

"What is Doyle like?" I asked. She didn't appear to mind my rudeness. It was none of my business, really, but it suddenly seemed important.

"He's alright, I guess. Let's just say Mr. Doyle likes himself an awful lot."

"Egotistical?"

"A mile wide. He and Mr. Pratt, they have the worst fights."

"In the office?"

"Sometimes I think they can be heard on the street. I don't know which one is more aggressive."

"Or scared," I said.

Dimples popped into her cheeks. "You know, I would have said that too, if I was sure. Sometimes I think Mr. Pratt is scared, but then I ask myself, what's he scared of? He doesn't *act* scared. I mean he never lets anyone take advantage of him. Like with Mr. Green this afternoon. I could hear him, the wall is so thin. Mr. Pratt came right back with that idea of a smear campaign against Cotter."

"Often down, but never out," I said, remembering where we were. "Our golden boy."

"Mr. Pratt interests me," Mary said, "because he's so--so changeable."

"Ambivalent."

"That's the word. He's always nice to me. You saw the flowers. I tell myself that a man who brings me flowers every day can't be all bad. But the things I hear!"

"Mary, perhaps you shouldn't be telling me all this. After all, you work for him. He's your boss."

She surprised me by laughing heartily. "Don't be silly, Art." She touched my hand. "He's not my boss. Mr. Green is."

"But, you take dictation, don't you? You type his letters."

"Only for Mr. Green. Mr. Pratt types his own letters. Mails them too. Besides, he travels a lot. Hardly ever in his office. He works at the Foundation most often."

We had finished our main course. We settled for coffee. Mary was a dynamo. She showed no sign of being tired. Actually, she needed no encouragement from me. In a way, it wasn't right, but my reporter's instinct got the better of me. I wanted to learn all I could about Gideon Pratt.

"The things I hear," Mary rattled on. There was no stopping her and I had no desire to do so. "Like George Rankin calling him all the time. You heard what Miss Davis thinks of that, now that Rankin works for Cotter. George is a talker. He never calls but he has to have a nice long chat with me. You have to read between the lines, but George says things about Mr. Pratt like 'Where's that double-dealing boss of yours?' I tell him Mr. Pratt's gone for the day. 'And which side of the bread is he buttering today?' he says. I tell you, Mr. James, if Mr. Pratt only knew."

"I don't think Mr. Pratt would very much care," I said. "I'll bet he doesn't know you come from Chesterton."

"Well, he must know that. I wrote it on my application. But, come to think of it, he hasn't ever asked me about Chesterton. I mean, he's not like you. Right away you were interested in knowing about me."

"He's a married man. Maybe that makes a difference."

She shook her head slowly. A curl broke loose and danced on her high smooth forehead. "No. I don't think it's that. He brings me flowers, but after that he's all business. Mary, do this, or Mary, get me that. Never hardly looks at me."

"He certainly looks at Jo Davis."

"She's more his type, don't you think? I don't mean to be catty, but she has a certain made-up flashiness."

"I always thought it was opposites attracted," I said.

Mary looked away. I detected a slight reddening of her cheeks. "I think that's a myth. You have to have a lot in common."

"Like Gideon's attraction to Jo? They're alike, you say, and I agree with you. But it seems to me Jo has a lot more, shall I say--integrity."

Mary's eyes widened. "Oh, I didn't mean to imply that Mr. Pratt doesn't have integrity. He's loyal. Look how he lets Mr. Green treat him. I wouldn't go so far as to say he's happy."

"With Gideon, happiness is irrelevant."

"Maybe you're right," Mary said. "He's so busy all the time, going to conferences, making those trips around the country. I suppose he doesn't have time to be bored."

"No, that's not one of his vices."

Mary looked at her watch. "Oh my gosh," she said. "We better get out of here, Mr. James. We don't want to be late for the play."

"Please call me Art, Mary." She did. I took her hand as we safely crossed Times Square to the theater. Our reserved seats were in the second row, a privilege of the press. A few other drama editors obviously wondered why I was sitting in Max Jordan's seat.

The main set of *Out of Eden* was a rundown boarding house with a rotting verandah. There were only three characters: a tall man in a black suit who spent most of the evening leaning against a post; a woman in a skin-tight black dress; and a lean young fellow in glued-on jeans who was the star boarder. You can guess the rest.

Midway through the first act Mary's hand stole into mine. I held it for the remainder of the play. Her occasional tightening grip had an automatic, perfunctory performance to it, and seemed to be a substitute for "Ohs" and "Ahs" in rhythm to the early insinuations of *Out of Eden*. Thus punctuated, my memory of the play is a mixture of the misery caused by her movements and the mire of the magnolia-scented scene on the stage. I was miserable because I didn't want to leave Mary after the play, but knew I had to return to the Dispatch to write my review. I wondered if she wanted me to take her home, but of course she would have expected that in the natural course of things. During an intermission she told me she lived in a YWCA hotel, but I had to coax that information out of her. She seemed reluctant to admit she was well protected. That only served to make me more miserable, for I realized that I liked her a great deal. But then there was the difference in our ages. Still, she had held my hand. Perhaps she *was* mature for her age. She certainly was intelligent and New York hadn't turned her head. I decided to let things go their natural way. If anything was to come of this relationship, Mary was not the kind of girl who could be forced.

I saw her off in a cab. I sensed regret in her look and in her voice as she said she understood the cruel demands of a newspaperman's life. My regret was for the incompletion of the evening. *Out of Eden* ended with a question mark. However, I told myself, perhaps there would be another evening with Mary. Another time there would be a final statement, ending with an exclamation point!

Back at the Dispatch I dashed off the review. It came easily:

Quite apart from its infantile obsession with filth,
Out of Eden is a distorted slice of life. Revolting dialog,
piled deep line by dirty line, is guaranteed to turn the
stomic. What is Georgia Wilson, the author of the new
play that opened last night at the Old Virginia, trying to prove?

I paused and read what I had written, searching for an answer to my question. I resumed typing:

If he is attempting to show that life can be sordid,
he has succeeded magnificently. If, on the other hand,
he is seeking merely to give his audience an experience
similar to slumming, then he has also made a purposeful
achievement.

Only a few reporters were in the newsroom as I finished the review, which I delivered immediately to Max Jordan, who was busy writing his own review of the other opening play. He glanced over my review. He wrote my byline on it. "You certainly clobbered that one," he said.

"It's not too extreme?" I asked, eager for his approval.

"Watch the ads day after tomorrow. "How did you learn to praise with such faint condemnation?"

"I didn't praise it," I protested.

"Oh, but you did," Max said. His cigarette, barely an inch long, drooped on his sad lip. "Took me years to learn the trick. But you young fellows, you learn fast. I predict a great future for you as a reporter who can look both ways at once. There's getting to be a lot of you guys around."

"That's show business," I said as I stalked out.

Chapter Eleven

I was ushered to Cotter's suite in the Powers Hotel by Patricia Lawrence, who identified herself as "Mr. Cotter's private secretary." The way she said it, with the emphasis on the word *private*, I got the feeling she was on the defensive about being caught in Cotter's hideout. She explained that Cotter was in the next room, which I presumed was the bedroom, and would be with me in a moment.

She busied herself at a leather-topped desk, opening a pile of letters and sorting through a file of index cards packed with type. She worked systematically, neatly, her red-tipped fingers smoothing out the letters. Once in a while she looked over at me, smiling as if to reassure me that the wait would be worthwhile, and then returning with a nod of her blond head to her work. I guessed she was about forty, although her figure was as softly rounded as a girl's. Her features were on the small side, except for her chin, which jutted slightly, and there was a certain hardness in the lines about her mouth. I was sitting on a sofa when I heard Cotter's voice.

"Hello, Art."

I looked up from a magazine. Cotter flowed down on me with all his famous affability. I glanced over at the open door from the other room. He had emerged without a sound, padding across the carpet as quietly as an usher at a funeral.

As I grasped his proffered hand I was surprised to discover he was shorter than me, surprised because he gave the impression, in his frequent appearances on television, of being inches taller than he was. Besides, his innocent-looking pudginess, the sleek jowls, the bland smooth forehead and cheeks, the slick back-swept gray hair, the too-small nose, the round chin, the owl-like sparkling blue eyes beneath thin arched brows, all denied his harsh public image as an ogre who ate Communists for breakfast. I was also surprised by his use of my nickname.

"Good of you to come," he said in a voice buttered with good humor, another direct contrast to that hoarse public voice of doom which prophesied the destruction of the republic unless, as he put it, the present course of events was reversed. "Sorry to keep you waiting."

He glanced over at his secretary. "Miss Lawrence isn't much company, I'm afraid." He laughed in her direction as she looked up sheepishly. "I keep her too busy for that." He sat down beside me, hitching up the knees of his cuffed gray trousers and crossing his silk-clad ankles.

"You have some questions," he said. "Fire away."

He motioned to the sofa. We sat down together. I opened my notebook and poised my pencil. I laid the set of question cards on a cushion. I read the first question: "Mr. Cotter, have you ever been sympathetic to the Communist cause?"

He laughed, a weak chuckle. "You're a fighter, aren't you, Mark? Not many people would have the courage to ask me that question. Who put you up to it? Sam Marx?"

"My managing editor doesn't know I'm here."

"As far as *you* know," Cotter said. He went over to the window beside Miss Lawrence's desk. I knew he was looking through the rain at Fifth Avenue below. His shoulders were up and he rested his chin in one hand. "Pat, have you had any communication whatever from Mr. Marx?"

She shook her head, looking bewildered by all this. "Nothing, Mr. Cotter."

For a full minute Cotter stared out the window, his back still to me. He rested easily, his weight on one leg. Now the knot tightened on my stomach. I cursed myself for asking the question which tipped my hand. Subtlety was never one of my virtues.

Then Cotter did a strange thing. Not looking at me, his eyes intent on the object of his pursuit, he strode across the room to a closet and took out a cane. It was a straight mahogany-colored shaft, tipped by a white knob. Cotter returned, head down, to the window. As he stood there, stiffly now, he polished the cane's knob with one palm, gripped the shaft with the other. At last he turned slowly around. He sat on the windowsill's marble edge. Against the window glare his face was shadowed.

"Art, do you want to lay it on the line?" His hand throbbed on the cane. "By and large we've had a pretty fair press, but if you're going to

84

bring up that Moscow business you at least ought to realize you're playing the Communist game."

I tried not to look flustered, but my hands shook just the same. "All I'm interested in, Mr. Cotter, are the facts."

He pounded the cane's knob. "Are you? Cotter can play dirty too. Just remember that."

"I don't have anything to lose, Mr. Cotter."

A smile cut across his face. "You're just getting started in New York, Art. Already you have shown, with your story on Mrs. Knittle, a strong love for your country. Maybe my saying that doesn't make sense to you. It does to Cotter. You're independent, Art. Your own man. I like that. It shows you aren't going to be pushed around."

I had to squirm. The sofa lost its comfort. Cotter was using my kind of language against me and I didn't like it. I wanted to tell him to go to hell, but he went on remorselessly, the cane swiveling in little arcs.

Cotter peered at me. "Like millions of others in this country you've been fed a lot of leaking liberalism," he said, his voice still soft and imploring, as if he was an understanding father lecturing a foolish son. "What we need, what Cotter wants, are men behind him who aren't afraid of the truth. You know what I mean, Art. Cotter isn't your enemy. The Commies are. Put your service to our cause, the cause of Americanism, Art. Don't waste your real talent on a petty dispute with Cotter." He swung his cane so that it rolled down his outthrust fingers. "After all, the defense of the republic, the Constitution, is a cause much bigger than Cotter."

This was such a self-righteous plea to my loyalty as a citizen that for a moment I was quite taken by it. His voice was easy, his argument reasonable. Then I realized what he was doing to me: subverting my intention to get a clear statement regarding his Moscow experience. I almost laughed, he was so sure of himself, as if his voice, his soft and easy manner, would win me to his side. I began to get a glimmer of Cotter's appeal. His pose of humility, his appeal to character, his projection of candid honesty, his granite conviction. These were his stock-in-trade. I could understand how others groveled at the feet of such certainty.

"What about Moscow, Mr. Cotter?" I asked boldly.

He spun the cane viciously. "What are you trying to do to me, Art? Has Cotter done you harm?"

I stood up. Miss Lawrence was making notes on letters, pretending we weren't there. "I had a lot of questions, Mr. Cotter. But if you would prefer not to answer them--"

He came over and touched my arm with the cane. His eyes blinked merrily. His mouth worked up a smile. "Now, Art, I can't let you go without some news. I appreciate your coming up here. That's one thing Cotter does appreciate. Consideration of the press. I've had my differences with some, especially the so-called columnists who are not more than paid propagandists and Communist dupes, if the truth were known, but when I'm asked a fair question I always give a fair answer. But this stuff--" He nudged the question cards in my hand. "--this stuff I've answered a hundred times." He winked at me. "You know that, Art. Don't try to bluff Cotter. You didn't really expect me to answer those questions, did you?"

I tried to turn away but he grabbed my arm.

"Now, how about some real news, Art? Exclusive. Just for you." He went over to his secretary. "Miss Lawrence, would you mind?"

"Not at all, Mr. Cotter," she said, giving me a reproving glance. Her voice had a Southern roll to it. She went into the other room and closed the door.

Cotter guided me to the sofa. "Now, Art, here's the story." He told me that the Cotterite board of directors would consider holding a public rally in Madison Square Garden. This would be Cotter's own proposal. He said he realized the magnitude of the task of filling the Garden, but that an all-out advertising and publicity campaign would take care of that.

I asked whether he planned to make any new charges at the rally regarding Communist infiltrations. He merely smiled. "I can only say that the question you raised about the Brookwood School Board will not go unanswered."

"Then I can say that the issue of Communism in the schools will be raised?"

"That is substantially correct," he said.

I asked him a few more questions, to which he gave vague answers. The rally would be held later that fall, the exact date to be announced. I figured it would be late in November, sometime following the elections. It was an off year with only a few state and local contests. As for the rally program, that would also be decided by Cotter's directors.

He said goodbye in a mood as affable as when he greeted me. The cane was on the sofa as he shook my hand. "Great to see you, Art." He whacked my shoulder. "Good luck!"

When I reached Washington Square on my way to see Silenus Stoddard at Pythia University the clouds were breaking. I walked through the shadow of the Arch into the sun and back into the shadow. Around the Square old men playing checkers, beards and tattered coats flapping in the breeze, made their moves in silence. One, crowning a king, said only "Ah!"

Leaves fell from the pale elms. Rust ran on the iron fences. I thought of the paths of Richland University when long walks led to easy discussions under the trees. That was before the lightning shafts of dissent split the faculty. Now I was on my way to one of the men who had caused that split. I had not come very far, really.

From the west the soft wind swept the October leaves, all red and gold, in whorls about my feet. I shaded my eyes and looked up at the massive façade of the arch, beyond the shadow, beyond the shafts of sun, to the dark vault. There the misty air rose wraith-like from the stone wreaths and I thought of the victory over tyranny those wreaths represented and of the enshrinement of unnamed heroes.

Near the university two students loped by, he in bucks, she in clogs. Then a wind-breakered fellow, then a girl in a high-throated shapeless sweater, black skirt and black stockings, flat-footed in slippers. Another, hair cropped and capped by a beret.

Cut-stone laurel branches, flat leaves spreading like fat fingers from the stems, garlanded the entrance to Pythia's Main Hall. Above the arch's keystone was the draped figure of Pythia herself, seated precariously on her oracular tripod. She fondled the belt of knowledge (or was it chastity?) and leaned back on her stool like a tippler at a bar. Passing between the great bronze doors, I felt like Apollo about to slay the dragon, but meditating first in Delphi's sanctuary, the great vaulted Pythian foyer.

In his office on the twenty-first floor, Silenus Stoddard put out a hairy hand. His grip was steel hard. His ragged sand-colored beard waggled. "Would you like a drink?" he asked, his voice a high nasal.

He pulled out a drawer of his desk, then another. "Where in hell did I put it?" At last he found what he was looking for, a silver flask and two small glasses. "Say when," he said as he poured the liquor. One glass overflowed onto the desk's blotter.

"When," I said.

Stoddard raised his glass and sniffed. His nostrils quivered. "I only drink on the job," he said with a twinkle in his bright blue eyes. Drink up, my friend. Got to celebrate our reunion."

I swallowed a sip of the whisky, put down the glass. "I'd better take it easy, Professor."

He snorted again, a wheeze high in his sinuses. "Nonsense! You come seeking pearls of wisdom. You have dared to cross the bridge to Academe. You don't feel a bit dry?"

"Alright, Professor." I raised my glass.

"Call me Silenus." He pronounced it sigh-lean-us. He clinked his glass against mine. "Here's to the Abiezrites and all the good fellows of Manassah, and especially to Asher, Zebulus and Napthali!" He put down the glass half-empty.

"That's one thing *Who's Who* missed, Silenus, the fact that you're a Bible scholar."

Leaning back in his chair, Silenus put one foot on his cluttered desk. "So! You want to kick Cotter's ass, do you?"

A sharp ray of sunshine pierced the office. It was hard to believe I was so far above Washington Square. The sun glinted off the bright bindings of his books, which filled several shelves. I took out a volume of Nietzsche.

"What would Nietzsche do, Silenus?" I asked, holding up the German philosopher's book.

Silenus spat toward the open window, splattering the pane. "That idiot! Nietzsche would wait for Superman. What would Jefferson do, you should ask. What we need is action, Art. Action! What's that bastard Cotter up to now?"

I told Silenus what I had learned from Cotter himself about his plan for a Cotterite rally in Madison Square Garden. Silenus bared his teeth and hee-hawed. "Fear not, friend," he cried out. "The benches of the opposition will be filled. Our concrete campus cutups are in arms. In arms! Boil the tar! Pluck the feathers!"

With Cotter's guns about to thunder on the far right, I thought, the defense needed more than the tools of the mob.

"What in the world are you raving about, Silenus?"

He waved his arms wildly. "The clarion sounds! The fox hunt is on!"

"Silenus, I came here to get your help."

He leaned forward and peered at me as through a cloud. "Ah! That's what we need. Let us confer together, draw up the battle plan. A council. A council of war." He collapsed again. His beard waggled. "It may be too late, Art. What we need is a general to lead us. Me? I'm only an armchair strategist." He slapped the arm of his chair. "Guess what? Cotter is about to scale the ramparts of higher education!"

I sat down heavily. "The universities? The colleges?"

Silenus wiped his sweating forehead. Straight strands of hair drooped toward his flat equine nose. "Little children were not enough. Now Cotter wants to corrupt our youth." He squinted at me. "But in youth, friend, Cotter will meet his match, his equal in cunning. Now he will see the whites of the enemy's eyes, for youth is not afraid."

I went over to the window and raised it higher. Dark clouds, high and puffy, rolled over New York Bay. The sky glistened, freshened by rain. A few buses circled the Square, ready for their slow uptown journey. Washington Arch cast its magnet-shaped shadow over the Square.

Perhaps Silenus was right, I thought. Perhaps it was time for the liberals to be called to arms, to descend upon Cotter, the enemy dragon, while he slept in his camp, to frighten Cotter into thinking his enemy was legion.

Silenus was scratching his leg, but, drunk or sober, he was Cotter's enemy. Still, I wondered if Silenus could be trusted. I could not forget that in Richland he had worked with Gideon toward the elimination of the cell group. While he had dissociated himself from the results, the firing of seven faculty members, he had nevertheless compromised himself as far as I was concerned. However, Silenus might possess a copy of Cotter's thesis, which I had to have in order to prove that Cotter had been as much a dupe of the Communists as those he accused.

I decided to take the direct approach. I told Silenus what I had discovered about Cotter's experience in Moscow. "What you wrote in Richland," I said, turning away from the window, "shows you are an expert on Cotter."

He looked askance at me. "This must be my lucky day," he said. "I've already had one offer. From Gideon. What's yours?"

"Gideon! Don't tell me you're working for Gideon!"

"I'm considering it," he replied calmly, stroking his beard. "For pay, of course. Fifty an hour to be exact. Not bad for a philosophy professor, eh?"

"I don't think the Dispatch can afford--"

Silenus stopped scratching. "Forget it. I never charge the press. Gideon is a horse of a different color. Besides, his money comes direct from the Foundation."

"You didn't make a bargain with him?"

"Not yet. Something I can do for you, Art?"

I told Silenus I wanted to see Cotter's Moscow thesis. He sipped a little whiskey. "You swear you're not working for Gideon?"

"I'm working for the Dispatch," I replied firmly.

"I thought you might be working for Gideon," Silenus said, "because that's what Gideon wants. Cotter's thesis. You know what that thesis would do to Cotter?"

"Who cares?"

Silenus stroked his tangled beard. "You don't march lightly into character assassination."

"Has Cotter avoided character assassination?" I cried out. "Has he hesitated a minute before accusing someone of being a Communist?"

Silenus held up a hand. "Hold on a minute, Art. I'm on your side. I was thinking of the practical reasons against a personal assault on Cotter. For instance, it would give him the chance to cry foul ball. That would enable him to use another extremist tactic, that of playing the role of persecuted underdog."

"We've got to do *something*, Silenus."

The professor rolled the glass between his palms. "You don't need to convince me that Cotter is dangerous. He's a menace to the country. Beneath his disguise of decency what do we find? A demagogue. Beneath that benign countenance? A passion for power." He refilled his glass, this time not spilling a drop. "Let's remember one thing, Art, if we do decide to engage in a smear job against Cotter. Remember that when you have a tiger by the tail you have only three choices: kill him, cage him, or tame him."

"Let's tame him," I said firmly.

"That's the approach of the moderate. Alright, I'll help you." Silenus levered a stack of papers and extracted a copy of Cotter's *Black Book*, which, naturally, had a solid black cover. He flipped the pages. "You don't remember what people said about Hitler's *Mein Kampf* during the thirties, do you? No, of course you don't. You were too young. You may have read about it. Hitler told specifically what he was going to do. Take over Germany, unite the people, capture Europe. Some people didn't believe him. Yet that book was Hitler's exact blueprint. Same thing with the *Black Book*. It is Cotter's *Mein Kampf*."

I turned the book over, felt the smooth cover. I had read a good portion of it, but it was so jammed with the most unnerving diatribes about the danger of the Commies that I could never finish it. Silenus told me to turn to the section on education. "Read it," he commanded.

I read the introductory paragraph aloud: "Education, both public and private, is the key to community power. Strive always to warn the child, the youth, against the atheistic aims of Communism. Do this not only through formal educational systems, both lower and high, but also through informal methods in factory, office, school and campus. Where management refuses to authorize the organization of a Cotterite society, report his name to national headquarters. The name will be listed in future editions of our Bulletin."

"That should be clear enough," Silenus said.

"His chief weapon is blackmail."

"That's right," Silenus agreed. "Cotter says: cooperate and you won't have any trouble with Cotter. Don't cooperate and you get listed. Note the reference to the campus. We can't say he didn't warn us. He's after the colleges and universities now." He tossed a brochure at me. "Here, have a look at this."

Entitled *Are You Sending Your Child to a Communist School?*, the brochure warned parents that a startlingly large number of colleges and universities were "hotbeds of Communism" at which Communist teachers and administrators served the Communist conspiracy by indoctrinating students in methods of accommodating Americanism to Communist aims of world domination.

Silenus said one of his students gave him a brochure. The student received it from his parents. "It's a new kind of hate literature that is flooding the country," he said. "Not all from the Cotterites, but a great deal of it, more now than ever before. Which makes me believe that Cotter is getting ready to hit the universities like he's never hit them before."

"Did you tell Gideon this?"

"I did. That's why he hired me. I'm now special counsel to Gibson Green Associates."

"I thought you were only considering it."

"I decided to take the job. Just now I decided."

"And that means, I suppose, that to get anything from you I've got to go through Gideon?"

Silenus smoothed his mustache. "That's about the long and short of it. But I don't think you will have to wait. Gideon was hot on the trail of--"

"The Moscow thesis!"

"You guessed it."

"Do you have a copy?"

Silenus grinned. "I don't have a copy of the thesis, but I do have some notes on it. When I was writing that article for the Platonic Academy I did some research in the Pythia library, plowed through a raft of material and came across the thesis by chance. Apparently it was a copy that Cotter overlooked, because I discovered through discreet inquiries at a few other universities that their copies were missing. I checked with our library this afternoon. Now our copy is gone."

"Can I have a look at your notes?"

"That's up to Gideon." From the north window I could see the Empire State Building. Lights were spreading floor by high floor. Not far away was Cotter's hotel. Was Cotter there at that very moment, seated at his desk of power, plotting new ways to destroy freedom? "I don't see why I must play second fiddle to Gideon Pratt," I said.

Silenus reached for his glass. "Neither do I," he said. "But I always have, haven't I?" He invited me to drop into his apartment that evening. That was where he kept his notes on Cotter's Moscow thesis.

"Gideon will be there," Silenus said. "We'll have grand reunion, won't we?"

Chapter Twelve

As I sat before my typewriter fingering the keys, trying to think up a lead sufficient to Cotter's threat, I felt like David about to slay Goliath--I hoped. To get started I typed again and again *The quick brown fox jumped over the lazy dog*. They were all there. All twenty-six letters of the alphabet. Twenty-six keys. Keys that could unlock many doors: the door of achievement, leading to journalism's accolade, the Pulitzer Prize; the door of ambition, leading to promotion to rewrite and the copy desk; the door of destiny, leading to public recognition of my talent; the door of intention, leading to perfection of my writing skill; the door of desire, leading to an established reputation.

Suddenly I realized what was happening to me. I was beginning to lose my objectivity, without which a reporter is either a hack or a hatchet man. I suppose every newspaperman, at one time or another, dreams of being so famous that his very byline causes readers to plunk down coins by the millions to read what he has to say. There is a lot of plain humdrum work in being a newspaperman, despite the public impression created by *The Front Page* and other movies about exciting reporters. Perhaps that is why I could see Cotter as being my special story. He could be my whipping boy. With the liberal Dispatch behind me I could cry havoc forever. A regular column might follow, then syndication. I could see it: my name up there next to Lippman's. Well, why not? I had the keys. All I had to do was use them.

I let fly. I wrote in hopes of a Page One banner headline. The first word would have to be a zinger:

Fired with indignation, the grapefruit industry's gift
to Americanism, Harry M. Cotter, said here today

I looked around. My fellow reporters were at their desks. Fred Roberts was at the desk next to me. His fingers flew on his typewriter's keys. All two fingers. Fred was the fastest typest I ever saw. His red hair flopped as he jerked his head in motion with the carriage's flight. I wondered if he was working on a Page One story. I swore silently. Had I waited too long to get my story in? Had I wasted time with crazy Silenus?

that a Madison Square Garden rally of Cotterites
was definitely in the offing.

I hesitated. This was slanted reporting. The tone was definitely anti-Cotter. Well, I wasn't writing for the *Times*.

Refusing to answer persistent questions by this reporter,
Cotter would not say when such a rally would take place.

Now Fred was up and away to the city desk with his story. I glanced up at the big round clock on the wall above the copy desk. The fat black hands pointed to seven o'clock. Fifteen minutes to deadline. I knocked out the next paragraph:

Communism in the schools, Cotter said in an
exclusive interview, would be on the chopping
block at the rally. He added that he was consulting
with his New York leaders, who are backing his
one-night appearance at the Garden.

I jerked another set of copy paper into the machine. I yelled "Copy!" One of our two copy boys rushed to my desk. I handed him the story and he rushed it to the city editor. *Look at it, look at it, Al!* But Al was busy with something else. I typed furiously. I sent the sheets to Al one at a time. After he got the fourth sheet, he made the traditional throat-slitting gesture. He had enough. Still, I continued to write. Al might want more for later editions. I had just finished when my phone rang.

"It's your dime," I said.

"How are ya, buddy boy?"

I told Gideon I was feeling much better now that I had gotten even with Cotter.

"Great stuff, fella," Gideon said. "Say, if you aren't doing anything later on, how would you like to go over to Silenus' place with me?"

It was the first time I was one up on Gideon. Or was it? He said to wait for him, that he would pick me up.

Al called me over. He pointed to my story. "New approach for you, isn't it, Art?" He was referring to the way I slanted the story.

"Not too extreme?"

Al folded the last sheet of my story. He shouted for a copy boy, who took the story to the copy desk for editing and a headline. "Not too extreme for Cotter," he said. "For you maybe." He leaned back, his work finished for a while. "Aren't you afraid of what Cotter may do to you?"

"You mean, like being blackmailed? That would be a compliment."

"I mean threats, phone calls. You know."

I laughed. "One thing in my favor as a crusader for freedom of mankind," I said, "is that I'm not married. No wife they can scare half to death with midnight cross-burnings on the lawn."

"Have you thought of what they can do to your parents?"

I felt a chill on my spine. As a corporation lawyer, Dad was heavily involved with big Richland companies. "They wouldn't go that far, Al."

Al picked up a piece of AP wire copy. "Oh, no?"

The story was datelined Richland. President Canning of Richland University, the story said, had submitted his resignation in the face of rising right-wing pressure either to clean alleged Communists off the campus or hire an executive assistant who could do the job. His resignation, the story added, was under consideration.

"How the mighty have fallen," I said. I told Al how Canning had fired seven teachers for suspected Communism. "Shows you nobody's safe," I added.

Al adjusted his lanky frame to his chair. His lean face hardened. "That's right, Art. Not even reporters with good intentions."

"What can Cotter do to me?"

"Whatever he does to you he's going to do it to the Dispatch. But this is a helluva tough old bear. If Cotter starts anything to smear the Dispatch he's going to be one helluva sorry old man."

I laughed loudly. "The Dispatch is one helluva great newspaper," I said.

Al smiled his reserved shy smile. "We're in this together, Art. Cotter is going to wish he'd been born a liberal."

Back at my desk I pondered Al's statement. It was true. We largely inherit our liberal or conservative attitudes. That is not the same as a political inclination, although you do inherit that too, to a certain extent. And that was why, I realized, I was not involved in a political battle but in an ideological struggle. This fight cut across party lines and involved the very nature of the fabric of American life.

Al knew this as much as I did. He promised that the Dispatch stood behind me. Then why was I playing the lone wolf? This was Al's fight too. To keep my intentions about Cotter's Moscow thesis to myself was to credit myself with the lone ability to pierce Cotter's armor and to bring him down to defeat. What was I doing but using the Dispatch as a strategic hill from which to launch my personal attack? This was not fair to Al, nor very smart. Without Al, without the Dispatch, I was nothing, I could do nothing. I decided to tell Al everything, and I did, in a ten-minute conference punctuated by Al's bursts of desk-pounding and exclamations of "That's great, Art!" He was so enthusiastic about letting the public in on Cotter's secret life as a student in Moscow that it made me shiver a bit, knowing I had caused responsibility for Al and, surely, dispatch readers too.

"After you finish this job on the thesis," Al said, I want you to hightail it to Richland to cover the story of Canning's resignation, to find out if the Cotterites are behind that."

I told Al that I could probably go there in a couple of days. "Don't tell Gideon Pratt about it," Al said. "I have an idea that the only one he's working for is Gideon Pratt."

"In other words, you don't trust him?"

Al jabbed a pencil on a pad of paper. "Gideon's the kind of guy who always looks out for Number One. I'm not saying he doesn't have principles. But whose principles?"

"I'll be careful," I replied. "I know Gideon from way back."

"And don't think Gideon won't take advantage of that," Al said, his eyes hardening. "Gideon never forgets his friends. With Gideon that's not a compliment."

I was about to say Gideon is no friend of mine but thought better of it. As I returned to my desk I wondered exactly what Gideon meant to me. A friend? An acquaintance? He was neither, because our relationship had never gone as far as friendship. It was also more than the business relationship of a reporter to a public relations man. We were linked in a fight against a common enemy: Cotter. That made us fellow soldiers--buddies. I wondered if Cotter was really Gideon's enemy, or merely his current target on his long hard climb to wherever he was going.

Gideon burst through the newsroom like a reporter with a sure-fire scoop. He flicked a piece of paper on my desk and sat down. "Got a statement for you," he said with a triumphant glint, "from the Foundation."

"You mean from Gideon Pratt," I said dryly.

Far from mowing him down, this crack appeared to compliment him. "Of course I wrote it," he said, beaming. I wouldn't have been surprised if he had polished his nails on his lapel. He was wearing a brown corduroy jacket, which in itself was a surprise because it contrasted with his usual Madison Avenue uniform. I read the statement through:

America's teachers are on the front line of the battle
for people's minds. Conflicting ideologies in this battle
call for total understanding of the nature of this fray.
That is why teacher education is very important. Our
teachers must be kept up to date, receive the latest
information, benefit from the most profound thinking
available. to provide teachers with an opportunity for
continuing study in the meaning of democracy and the
nature of the ideological struggle which they are called
upon to interpret in the classroom. The Educational
Foundation of America has lent the resources of American
business and industry, the bastions of our free enterprise,
our way of life--

"That's a pile of crap," I told Gideon. "Who do you think you're writing for? Professors?"

Gideon clucked his tongue. "I thought it was pretty hard-hitting myself."

"It's the usual public relations crap," I went on. "When is the foundation going to wise up? Your stuff doesn't cause a dent in Cotter's armor. What we need right now is an outright charge by the foundation that Cotter is a prick and a bastard, that if he or the Cotterites interfere any more with the freedom of the teacher to teach the way she damn well pleases, that you're going to take Cotter to court?" I waved Gideon's *Statement* in his flaming face.

"On what charge?" he asked.

"On the charge that Cotter uses strong-armed tactics: coercion, threats, intimidation, slander, to influence school boards, colleges and universities.

He denies these officials the opportunity to do the job they are elected or appointed to do by deliberately creating an atmosphere of fear, prejudice, mistrust and suspicion. And if that's not enough--"

Gideon waved a limp hand. "Woa, buddy boy! How come all of a sudden you're such an evangelist for the left?"

I waved his paper at him again. "The hell with left or right. I'm talking about plain old American decency and fair play!"

Gideon leaned forward. "Don't make a federal case out of it," he whispered.

I looked around the newsroom. Fred and a couple of other reporters were staring at Gideon and me. Fred put a cautioning finger to his lips. He pointed a thumb toward the City Desk where Al was looking at me severely. It was against the rules to conduct an interview in the newsroom. I whispered to Gideon "Follow me." We used the stairway to the floor beneath us that housed the Circulation Department offices. A corner room housed a small room containing a coffee bar and several tables. The room was empty. We poured coffee for ourselves and sat down at a table.

Gideon displayed a look of injured innocence. "I did my best," Gideon said. "You don't know Fletcher. He runs the foundation as if it is a health charity. As if teachers are patients in need of treatment."

"I can't use your statement, Gideon," I said. "I need news."

"That's okay, Art. It is crap."

I calmed down. Reporters are supposed to be neutral. That was my problem. I admitted to Gideon that I found it difficult to be neutral as far as Cotter was concerned. "After all," I said, using the old cliché, "I'm only human."

"Well, I am too," Gideon said. "I can't get anywhere with the foundation. Every time I advise Fletcher to do something effective about the Cotterites he only says he'll consider it. Nothing happens. What do you think, Art?"

I began to get suspicious. Was he buttering me up in a deceitful way, or was there a real human being lurking somewhere in the depth of his soul? Gideon was hiding something and it was driving me crazy that I couldn't figure him out. "What about Cotter's rally in Madison Square Garden?" I asked. I kept a close eye on him. Gideon concentrated on his coffee while I waited for his reaction. I wasn't completely surprised when he told me he had "heard about it." But how? Silenus? I needed somebody to launch an attack upon Cotter or else my campaign would fizzle like a wet firecracker.

Gideon smiled at me as if I was an accomplice in an undercover crime investigation. Was this merely a game to Gideon? "What can the foundation do?" he asked me. "It is so monolithic you can't get it to make any sensible move. What are we going to hit Cotter with? A balloon of hot air? Trouble is, Cotter doesn't give any facts to knock down, only insinuations, vague charges. What you have to rely on, in the long run, is good old American horse sense."

"You've got to fight back, Gideon. It's not enough just to point with pride at the teachers."

On the way out I picked up a copy of the Dispatch. My story was inside under a two-column headline: *Cotterite Rally/ in the Garden?* My byline was intact.

It was raining again. Gideon and I hopped a cab and headed south of Washington Square to Silenus' apartment on the second floor of an ancient brownstone. There was a bar on the first floor of a building across the street. Its *Midas* neon sign blinked on and off.

We struggled up a long flight of stairs. Silenus, in a green bathrobe, his hair wild, greeted us. "I started working for you a half hour ago," he told Gideon. He ushered us into his parlor, a gaudy tasseled and paneled room with a bright orange sofa facing a six-foot-wide copy of Goya's painting, *Duchess of Alba*, the nude version. The duchess's eyes gleamed with invitation. On a stand on one side of the painting was a two-foot Aphrodite of Cyrene, headless and armless, and on the other side Michelangelo's *Dying Swan*.

Gideon went over to examine the art. He circled the Aphrodite, taking in every curve of her full buttocks and the pear-shaped Mount of Venus. He followed the sweeping lines of the Duchess from her toes to her pink-tipped melon breasts. Then he went over to the sofa and sat down beside me, eyes still focused on the Duchess.

I said, "How would you like to have that stuff, Gideon?"

Silenus, plumping himself down in a sack-like chair opposite us, said, "You have to be a bachelor, Gideon."

"This place looks like the Gaslight Club," Gideon said.

Silenus thrust his fingers through his newly-showered hair. "You've been to the Gaslight, Gideon? I didn't know you were the type."

I gave Silenus the Dispatch, open at my story on Cotter. "Good job," he said. "I'll read it later."

Gideon kept on looking at the Duchess. "Jo has a key," he said.

"Gideon means a key to the Gaslight," Silenus said. "Jo pays the bill."

"Be quiet, Silenus," said Gideon.

Silenus knew something about Gideon's relationship to Jo Davis that I didn't know. Curiosity is inbred, I suppose. Anyway, I was overcome with a desire to know exactly what that relationship was. Gideon was a man who took what he wanted when he wanted it. Still, I couldn't imagine Jo Davis going to bed with my scared little rabbit. For the first time I wished I could get inside Gideon's head, which says something about me, I suppose. Then it occurred to me that Silenus had referred to his apartment as a bachelor's lair, or something like that.

"I thought you were married, Silenus," I said.

The professor hitched up the bathrobe. He didn't appear to be wearing much of anything underneath. "She divorced me," Silenus said.

"Oh yes, in Richland," I said, recalling my encounters with him years ago at Richland University. "While Bentley was running hard to get the Senate nomination."

Silenus turned his attention to Gideon. "What's the pitch on Cotter?"

"You're the one who's on the mound, Silenus. Your pitch."

"Of course. The notes." Silenus dashed into another room.

Gideon stood up. "I'd better call my wife," he said. He told Amy that he was with me in Silenus' place. "See you tomorrow, honey," he said.

"Need a place to stay?" I asked.

"We'll be here half the night, Art. Silenus will find a comfy place for us."

"With the Duchess," I said, smirking.

"She'd look good at my house," he said with a stiff smile, "but Amy might object."

"Looking at the Duchess," I said, "reminds me, for obvious reasons, of Cotter's secretary. She's quite a doll."

Gideon suppressed his amusement. "She's forty-one," he said calmly. "I asked her."

"You didn't! You know her? Don't tell me you call her Patricia?" I paused. "Then you have met Cotter?"

Gideon grinned. "Only off stage."

"Anything going on between her and Cotter?"

Gideon made out as if he was shocked. "Why, Arthur James. You dirty old man. Don't be so old-fashioned. Everybody's doing it." He laughed heartily. "Seriously, Art, I got the go-ahead from Green today. He says, 'I don't care how you stop Cotter, just stop him.' He got the word from Fletcher, you see. Not by way of Jo, either. It's a complete turnabout for him, being president of the Foundation. Great man, Fletcher. You ought to meet him. I bet you didn't know that Fletcher and Cotter went to Yale together. Yep, nothing like old school ties to throttle a man's better instincts. That's just one of the reasons Fletcher has held back from lambasting Cotter. Plus the fact that the Foundation gets a whale of a lot of money from Cotter's pals." Gideon smirked, his lips curling. "That's why Fletcher uses Gibson Green. So Fletcher can use me as his hatchet man."

"Cotter's got a hard cane too, Gideon," I said. "He could whack *you* with it."

"Ironic, isn't it, buddy boy? I do the dirty work, Fletcher comes out smelling like a rose. But that's public relations for you. Be careful, Art, lest you get your head under the cane too."

Gideon's sidestepping of the issue of direct action by the Foundation began to make sense. Was I out on a limb? Gideon had been pushed to the very brink. We could hope for little public support from Fletcher. If the tide went against us Gideon would face Cotter's wrath alone. Or would he? Even Green would get off lightly, for Green had left to Gideon the choice of weapons. I wondered how Jo Davis fit into this sticky web on which I was also quickly being trapped.

"Seems to me," I said, "that Cotter is dealing from a stacked deck."

Gideon turned sideways to look at me. "What is Cotter really like, Art?"

"You've never met him? I presumed--"

"Saw him only briefly, that's all."

"At first you think Cotter is a sweet old gent," I said. "Then he starts getting tough, swinging that cane of his like a baton-twirler."

"A cane?" The blood drained from Gideon's face.

"He doesn't actually use it like a cane," I told him. "It's more like a club. Anyway, he swishes the damn thing--"

Gideon turned away. He looked toward the room into which Silenus had disappeared. "What's he doing?" he asked.

"You know these absent-minded professors," I answered. I went into the back room. Silenus, on hands and knees, was scrounging through masses of paper that littered the linoleum. "It's got to be here somewhere," he cried. "It's got to be here!"

I retreated to the sofa. Gideon was smiling at the Duchess. I snapped my fingers. His grin was almost sheepish. I told him that Silenus was ready for the psychiatric ward. Gideon laughed. "Can you imagine Silenus being a general in the Army? I'll bet he misplaced a division." I told Gideon that was news to me. "Sure," Gideon said. "He was a colonel when the war ended. He was retired as a major general."

At last Silenus came out holding a paper file. "Your weapon, Gideon," he said. He waved the papers at us. "The notes on Cotter's Moscow thesis."

Gideon and I leaped up. "Sit down, sit down," Silenus said. "You can't read my scrawl, so let me do the honors. Just a paragraph, to give you the gist of it." He sat down on a wooden footstool and faced Gideon and me on the sofa. He opened the file. He pursed his lips and stroked his beard as he turned the pages. "Here we are. Remember, this is Cotter, writing from Moscow in 1924."

He began to read, his voice triumphant, as if he were Columbus proclaiming his discoveries to Isabella: "'Communism marched upon the stage of world history to offer new hope for all mankind.'" Silenus jabbed a pointed finger at us. "Get this: 'Where else but in the Soviet republic could emerge such a masterful answer to chronic economic depression of the masses?'"

He turned the page. "I'll skip a bit here. This next part should be read to the directors of the Cotter Grapefruit Company. 'While the West has relied on the pendulum swing of time to correct declining production and employment, the Soviets have courageously sought to provide stability through controls exercised by consumers'."

Gideon slapped his knee. "That will sell a lot of oranges!"

I joined in the laughter. It was almost too good to be true. I could see the headline: *HYPOCRISY!*

"Let's not get hysterical," Silenus said. He took a deep breath. "Listen: 'While the social program of Communism is still in its first years of implementation, there are signs already that Communism is spelling a life of hope for millions who heretofore have been deprived of opportunity to attain a level of living which those in the West take for granted.'" Silenus looked up. He was botching the job of controlling his giggles. "Hah! Now what do you think?"

I was laughing so much the tears started. "No more, I can't stand it."

But Silenus read on, his cheeks puffed, his teeth gritted. "And next: 'To Lenin and his associates must go the credit, in this writer's view, for the alleviation of oppression and the granting to the people a great measure of control over their own destiny.'" Silenus closed the file. "Now I know what happened to the original copies of the thesis. Cotter ate them."

"It's enough to bury him," I said amidst my choking laughter.

For an hour we discussed the various uses to which we could put Cotter's own words. I held out for running them in the Dispatch a piece at a time, perhaps hinting at its existence the first day, quoting a few paragraphs the next, a few more after that. Silenus was the perfect neutral. It didn't matter much to him what we did with his notes, he said, although he was inclined to favor my suggestion, since by dragging the story out over a week or so he would continue on Gibson Green's payroll and thereby make a mint. He let it be known that at fifty dollars an hour Gibson Green was getting a bargain.

I suggested we turn the whole thing over to Jo Davis and ask her to get the Foundation to release the text, thus assuming the responsibility for leading the attack on Cotter, and thus making the Foundation the target for the kickbacks that were sure to follow. Gideon was against that. There wasn't a chance, he said, that Fletcher, the Foundation president, would agree to my plan. And Gibson Green had no authority to do the job on Fletcher's behalf. I ended the argument by saying that all such conjectures were premature, since such potential bombs had to be approved by Mr. Marx, my managing editor.

"Marx!" Silenus exclaimed.

"His first name isn't Karl," I said. "It isn't Groucho either."

"Then it is spelled M-A-R-X?" I nodded. "Wait until Cotter reads this. He will spell it with a K."

That set us off on another tangent. I defended the Dispatch as the only New York newspaper with the guts to start a campaign against Cotter, and I pointed out that not even the *News* had carried an item on Mrs. Knittle. I flapped the copy of that night's Dispatch, I pointed to the headline on my story. "That's the kind of guts Mr. Marx has," I said. Gideon huffed a bit about the Dispatch trying to pass the buck to the Foundation, but at last he came around to my view. He agreed to rely upon Mr. Marx's judgment.

"What choice do you have?" I asked.

"Just remember," Gideon said, pounding the sofa, "you wouldn't have a chance at this story, Art, if it weren't for me."

"Which brings up a nice point, Gideon." I was ready to tell him to forget the whole thing. "What makes you think you own the Moscow thesis notes? Just because you're paying Silenus? That's for advice." I turned to Silenus. "What if I got you a thousand for the notes, Silenus? We could shake the Foundation off our backs."

Silenus twisted uneasily. He tightened the bathrobe's belt. "Just a minute, Art. I'm not climbing onto anybody's bandwagon. I'm not selling the notes to anyone. Not to Gibson Green. Not to the Dispatch."

Gideon leaned so far forward he almost fell off the sofa. I thought he was going to crawl. "Come on, Silenus," he said. "I just want to borrow the notes. If it's having your name involved, forget it. I won't even tell Green where I got them."

"No."

"No what?"

Silenus was loading the notes back into the filing cover. "I will give copies of the notes to both of you. You can do whatever the hell you want with them. But, remember, you need verification. After all, we don't have a copy of the thesis. My notes are, legally, only hearsay. Anybody could say I faked them. Cotter could sue for libel. Forget it. Find the original, if you can. Gideon, you'll get my bill for tonight." He slammed the file on the floor.

Gideon was silent. He was trying to appear relaxed, even as he gripped an arm of the sofa. "Think of it this way, Silenus," he said. "If Cotter was taken in by the Communists when he was in his twenties, what right does he have to speak against them in his sixties?"

"Plenty of Communists have recanted," Silenus replied miserably. "Youth has its foibles, makes mistakes."

"Oh, stop it, Silenus," Gideon said. "If there's anything I can't stand it's a fence sitter."

Silenus cringed. He slowly eased himself up from the stool. He hovered over Gideon. "Always the complete pragmatist, aren't you, Gideon?"

Gideon laughed. "Don't blame me, Silenus. I'm following orders."

I was too tired to figure out who had won this engagement. The more Gideon attacked, the more Silenus backed away. My yawning caught Silenus' attention. "Fine host I am," he said. "My God, it's after one o'clock. And I have an eight o'clock class."

Gideon didn't flinch. "The notes, Silenus."

That stopped Silenus, who was on his way to the other room. He swung around, his mouth contorted. "You want me to type them *now?*"

"Green--" Gideon cowered under Silenus' stare. "Okay. Later, Silenus."

"Get your own bedding," Silenus muttered as he entered his bedroom.

I was nonplussed. "I've slept here before, Art," Gideon said. No need for you to leave now. It's too late." We tossed a coin. I got the sofa. Gideon got the Murphy bed that dropped from the wall opposite the windows. Gideon found the bedding in a closet near the apartment's entrance.

When the lights were out, the only sound was that of typing from Silenus' bedroom. I had a hard time adjusting my height to the confines of the sofa. I lay back with my hands under my head thinking about the strange turn of events in which the decision had been no decision, but rather a state of limbo in which I would have to wait for the real decision to be made by others in the morning. What bothered me most was Silenus' reluctance to grab hold of the axe which I wanted to wield against Cotter. As for Gideon, he displayed a temper that reached for but never quite succeeded in obtaining command. It occurred to me there was in Gideon's surliness toward Silenus something of the attitude I had observed in certain privates in the Richland Army R.O.T.C. toward our officers. Could it be that Gideon's was a private's animosity toward a hated commander? That was something else about Gideon Pratt that required investigation if I was ever to find out what made Gideon the frightened man he was.

"Are you asleep, Art?'

His voice, low, meek, startled me. "No, Gideon."

"I want to apologize for the way I behaved."

"That's alright," I said. I yawned loudly. I could stand his belligerence but I couldn't stand his fawning.

"I realize you want to see the thesis plastered all over the front page."

"A piece at a time."

"But we'll have to wait and see. You need patience to be a public relations man."

Only Gideon would believe he had patience. "Sure, Gideon."

"How would you like to get into the public relations racket?"

"You could fix it for me, I suppose."

"Big money in it," he said. "If you know the right people."

"Put in a good word for me, Gideon."

"Nothing like it, Art. Not for excitement, anyway."

I yawned again. I thought he had taken the hint, for he said nothing more, but the next thing I knew a light flashed against my closed lids.

"What are you doing? Gideon!"

He was standing in front of the Duchess, his hand on the chain of a small lamp that hung over the painting. Quickly he pulled the chain. The room was plunged into darkness.

"What a woman!" Gideon said as he returned to bed.

I closed my eyes against the blue blinks of the Midas sign. *Crazy professor*, I thought. *Crazy public relations man. Alba--where was that?-- quite a guy, that Goya--duchess for a mistress--whatever happened to the duke?*

Chapter Thirteen

The day dawned bright and clear. I went to the window. I breathed deeply. The cool air felt good. The street was quiet, deserted. I hoped that this day, begun calmly, would end the same way.

Gideon, folded like a corkscrew on the Murphy bed, stirred. He asked what time it was. I told him. He staggered up and stumbled to the bathroom.

After I dressed I found Silenus puttering in the kitchen. He was still in his bathrobe. His long hair stood up wildly. He served us coffee, very black, and toast. He gave Gideon and I carbon copies of the Moscow thesis notes. We went our separate ways, he to Gibson Green's, I to the Dispatch.

Standing before the Dispatch building, I looked up at the crumbling façade. Weathered stone blocks projected, spaced by deep crevasses where mortar had eroded away. The broad street-level windows mirrored the scene in the street: three rows of taxis and buses crawling uptown. This was the face of the Dispatch: antique Roman, bold and free. At once secure and unsafe: the security of a noble institution, the danger of cracking foundation. The building was the image of the newspaper itself: tumbledown caricature. I wondered if the Dispatch had the strength for the battle in which I was about to involve her. Still, she was an old bear, as Al said, and had engaged many enemies. And, perhaps, like the bear, she was wily enough to outdo Cotter's parrying thrusts.

The newsroom was empty. The edges of the room were blanked by shadows. I sat before my typewriter. The keys blurred. Now, before starting my story on Cotter's thesis, I had a chance to turn back. If I went ahead I would be alone. I had little faith that the Educational Foundation of America would rescue me if I faltered in my charge. Once this series of stories was begun I was committed to see them through until the end, whatever that might be.

It was not that the Foundation lacked courage. I have made many mistakes, but never that of attributing human qualities to impersonal institutions. The Foundation was nothing in itself, only a set of ideals, principles, inert. I was not fooled by Gideon's press releases, which spoke of the Foundation as if it was a person. "It" had integrity, strength, conviction, significance. "It" had concern, sympathy, wisdom, compassion, and, above all, a distinct service to perform. Words. Nothing but words. The Foundation was nothing. It was powerless to defend me, incapable of making the charge against Cotter that I was about to make. I alone would bear the brunt of Cotter's counterattack.

So be it, I said to myself. I started typing:

Harry M. Cotter, leader of right-wing elements
in the forefront of the current hunt for Communists
among school teachers and other U.S. educators, at
one time was enamored by the Communist cause, it
was revealed here today.

I summarized the facts of Cotter's experience in Moscow. I paraphrased passages from Silenus' notes on Cotter's thesis. I promised that more would be revealed in succeeding issues of the Dispatch. I deposited the story into the *IN* box on Al's desk, then locked my copy of the notes in one of my desk's drawers.

For a long while I sat at my desk in the quiet and darkness. I had a strange urge to phone someone, anyone, to hear a friendly voice, to obtain assurance that what I had done couldn't be helped. I asked myself if I wasn't an instrument, not essentially different from the telephone itself, a useful tool of communication. That was what it meant to be a reporter, wasn't it? To receive a message and pass it on to the person for whom it was intended: that inchoate mass for whose welfare I cared, for whose benefit I wrote.

I unlocked the drawer and took out the notes. I looked at them blankly for a full minute as a slow determination, a flood of stubbornness, filled me. The fact was clear: Harry M. Cotter, the champion of the anti-Communist cause, had written, in his youth, a treatise friendly to the emerging conspiracy. It had proved that Cotter had viewed the Reds "through rose-colored glasses." Well, it was the truth. Then what did I have to fear? I could play this story out for days. Day after day the story could be built up.

I would start a hot public debate in which Cotter's true motives would be inspected by the blazing spotlight of public alarm. Besides, played out to its proper length, the story would cause the Dispatch's circulation to soar. We would score a clear scoop over the competition. Surely the Dispatch's concern and courage would be worth a story in *Time*. I would be hailed as the St. George who took up the sword against the dragon and vanquished Cotter, the enemy of the people.

I was lifted from this reverie by the ringing of my phone.

"Art, this is Josephine Davis."

I told her I wasn't surprised to hear from her. Gideon probably told her everything.

"Would it be possible for you to come over and see me? I mean, right away?" Her voice had a sharp anxious edge to it.

I looked around the newsroom, now beginning to receive some stray light filtered through the grimy windows. Not even the morgue could have been more silent. "Sure," I told her.

At Times Square I boarded the shuttle to Grand Central. The train started off right away. I sat down beside two boys, one of them white, who were talking freely about the racial situation in Harlem. I glanced the length of the car-card advertisements, looking for the one put up by the Foundation. I spotted it over the door. Under a picture of a boy holding a microscope was the slogan *Education: The Strength of the Nation*. Embedded in the art was the name of the Foundation. In its simplicity the poster symbolized the nationwide cry for an emphasis on science which would help keep us ahead of the Russians. Even the slogan had a military touch. I could almost see Gideon's hand in the phrasing.

From Grand Central I ascended the stairway and hustled to Madison Avenue, walked south two blocks through the morning crowds to the skyscraper that housed the Education Foundation. Jo's office was on the ninth floor. I ran the gauntlet of gilt-edged portraits of past Foundation presidents, each elegantly clothed, the Brooks Brothers pride of his era. The last painting before the end of the corridor was Fletcher's. He looked like Mount McKinley, snow-capped, craggy. You could almost feel the icy wind blowing from that imperious brow. I turned left and opened the door on which the words *Office of Public Information* were lettered in gold. A brunet with upended black lashes swept me at a glance. She motioned me to the white leather sofa, dialed a number, spoke softly, returned to her typing. For a philanthropic outfit, I thought, the Foundation had posh. Even the white floor tile had gold in it. I was deep in the latest issue of *Life* when the brunet sang, "You may go in now, Mr. James."

From the reception room a door led to an inner corridor and there Jo met me. "Hi, Art," she called as she came toward me, her tall slim figure swaying slightly, her long red hair tossing on her broad shoulders. She extended her hand. I grasped it, feeling its soft smoothness and the long slow caress of her nails. I wondered why she seemed so much younger than the first time I met her in the Press Gallery restaurant. Surprisingly, she seemed no older than me. I felt a sudden surge of interest in her, seeing her not as Gideon's part-time girlfriend, but for what she seemed in her own right, a bright warm woman allowing me to hold her hand a moment longer than was socially correct under the circumstances. I glanced away. Behind glass panels girls were working row on row at desks precisely aligned by rank and file. Jo beckoned to me to follow her, and as I did I watched the way her dress, a straight sheath, deep rust, clung to her, creasing over her smooth hips. Her legs tapered to perfection down to her black shining spike-heeled shoes.

"Here we are," Jo said over her shoulder in a full-breathed voice like a commercial for *My Sin* perfume. She opened a door to an office whose wide windows framed the Empire State Building to the south. A mist veiled the towering shaft. "It is a sensational view, isn't it?" Jo said.

I turned around to look at her. "You are," I said.

She folded her arms. She continued to look at me boldly. "We've got a lot to talk about," she said. "Let's get down to business."

She walked in a cocoon of sweet incense. She sat behind a teak desk, above which hung a framed print of Picasso's ugly *Urchin*. I commented on the print and others by Klee which were scattered around the bright yellow walls.

"They're in fashion," she said in an offhand way.

I scrubbed my toes into the deep sepia carpet. "Soft," I said. "Tell me, Jo, when can I move in with you?"

She batted her darkened eyelashes at me. "Why, Mr. James!"

"I'm sorry," I said lamely.

"You'd look good in an office like this, Art." She leaned against her desk, her elbows on it. She was smiling, her gray-green eyes sparkling. I was convinced she was serious. "Have you ever thought of working in public relations?"

"Someone else asked me that very same thing not long ago. Yesterday, as a matter of fact."

"Gideon?"

"He said there was nothing like it for excitement."

"That's not true, Art. It has its headaches, the same as any other job. But if you ever want to get into public relations, I'll be glad to recommend you."

I told her I appreciated that, but I wouldn't be ready to move for a while, since I had just joined the Dispatch.

"Nevertheless," she said, "you have to think of your future. Especially since the Dispatch--"

I knew what she was thinking. The Dispatch might fold any day. When a newspaper's end comes, the next morning you're on the street. "I'll let you know," I said. "And thanks."

She held my gaze a moment and then looked up at the Picasso. "Mother wanted me to be an artist," she said.

I sat down in a plump red chair opposite her desk. "Oh?' This was such a personal turn in her conversation that I began to nurse an idea that she was interested in me on more than the professional level.

"Yes," she said, neither seeking nor seeming to require encouragement on my part. "Mother insisted I had talent and so she sent me to Saturday classes at the Museum. After I finished Bryn Mawr. My father could afford it because he's really quite well off. I studied fine arts at Pythia. Yes! I believed then that art was a matter of expressing one's soul! I did some painting, some sculpture." She had been looking past me out the window, but now she fixed me with a bold glance. "Have you ever been in a class where they have a nude woman model?"

I shook my head.

"There was this goateed little professor," she went on, tossing her hair, "who kept asking me if I wanted to earn a little extra money modeling. He always looked at me as if I was already naked. Made me feel as if long-legged animals were crawling over me, I tell you. Anyway, I got the rudiments of advertising art. I was all for commercialism, because I was cured of soul-expression by the starving garret types in the Village whose idea of a swell evening was to squat on the floor of some coffee joint smelling of pot and having my eardrums split by tom-toms."

She smoothed back her hair. "Anyway, Father thought it was time I either got married or got a job, although Mother was all for me giving vent to my pent-up emotions by painting abstractions for the next forty years. On Father's money, of course. Either I stayed in the Village and became as beat as my New World classmates, or I take the plunge and looked for a job. I couldn't fancy myself winding up as some bearded existentialist's pad-mate, so I went home and got dressed. I mean I left all my decent clothes at home in Bronxville while I was living in this god-awful coldwater flat with three other girls, and if there was one thing I never needed there it was a cocktail dress. You have to see me in turtle-neck sweater and jeans, also sans paint."

I tried to imagine Jo Davis among the Pythia students I had seen in Washington Square. It was impossible to imagine. She was so much the Madison Avenue type. "It's hard to picture," I said.

Jo lit a cigarette. She blew the smoke to one side. "Anyway, I started the rounds of the advertising agencies, fine-arts certificate in purse. Must have filled out a million applications. Then, guess what? I became a receptionist at H. Charles Bronson! Yes, just like Doris out there." She gestured in the general direction of the lobby. "There wasn't another opening, they said, and women artists were buzzing the agencies like bees after honey. However, the employment chap told me that many receptionists moved into copy staff positions. This fellow, looked something like Dick Doyle, couldn't care less that I couldn't type my name. 'Just smile and look pretty,' he told me. There was a lot more to it than that, including being fast in the clinches, believe me. I was a receptionist for two weeks, and then they put me in one of those cubicles where the copy girls work outside Dick's office. They gave me a packet of pencils and told me to start drawing."

"I can see it," I said. "You in the lobby, with the agency sports jammed in like college boys in a phone booth. Did anyone ever get past you?"

Jo began to laugh, a merry constricted chuckle. "That's what Dick Doyle asked me. What a shame, he said, keeping all *that* hidden. Do you know, I spent a year in that honeycomb before I got up enough nerve to quit? Fortunately I was doing some volunteer work at the Foundation's aid-to-education campaign, and I knew George Rankin. When George's assistant, fellow named Frank Penwood, quit to join Leo Burnett's in Chicago, George asked me how I would like to be assistant to the director of information. *Would I?*

George and I had a few dates. That helped, I suppose. Anyway, I got the job, worked with George for two years, and then he quit to join Cotter's team, and I got George's job."

"It's a real success story," I commented.

Jo grinned. "Sure. Trouble is I'm only acting director of information. Any day they're going to hire somebody who knows something about public relations, and I'll be right back as assistant if they keep me. Unless--"

"Unless?"

She paused, as if considering whether she should tell me her thought. Her glance shifted to me and away. "I have a feeling I can trust you, Art. Not even Gideon knows this. I should tell him. But he wouldn't understand." She tapped out the cigarette. "I told Mr. Fletcher about the thesis that Professor Stoddard found."

I had no preconceived opinion as to whether the Foundation president ought to know about the thesis. Indeed, since I had no particular reason to wish he should not be told about it, I was surprised at Jo's agitation. While she was not apprehensive about telling me, she seemed concerned that I should know and not Gideon. I was beginning to understand something of Jo's position in relation to Gideon. He held some power over her, a power whose strength I did not yet know but which I was determined to oppose, if only because it was Gideon and not someone else.

More than that, however, I was aware, from my observation of Gideon's boss, Gibson Green, that Green had some plan of his own to keep Fletcher happy. The Foundation president was obviously eager to keep clear of Cotter if at all possible. On the surface it appeared that Fletcher did not even wish to be consulted on the case. On the surface, Fletcher was aloof, above it all. He did not want his name to be connected in any way with the ethical crime about to be committed, the crime of attack on Cotter's character. In taking the entire case to Fletcher directly, Jo was going over Green's head. What was more, she was going against Gideon, or why else had she not told him?

"What did Fletcher say?" I asked.

Jo stood up and went to the window. She gazed at the Empire State Building, from which the mist had risen. Now the tower shone in the sun. "Mr. Fletcher agreed with me that publication of Cotter's Moscow thesis in the Dispatch would be a more serious step than perhaps Mr. Green realized."

I came up beside her. "I've already written the story, Jo."

Her eyes opened wide. "But you could withdraw it?" she asked with alarm.

"I suppose."

"Not that I am asking you to," Jo went on quickly. "I know you are prepared to accept responsibility for--whatever happens." She rested her cheek in her hand. "If we only had more time. Gideon, he shows more foolhardy courage than good sense sometimes."

For the first time Jo had revealed to me her view of Gideon. To her he was a man of courage. Perhaps Gideon's roughshod recklessness was one of courage's many disguises. I was not prepared to admit, however, that I begrudged Gideon this advantage over myself. "We're fighting Cotter's deadline," I said.

Jo shook her head. "Gideon doesn't know Cotter very well," she said. "Not that I know him either. Call it a woman's intuition. Maybe I'm just plain scared. Anyway, how do we know that your story will turn people against Cotter? Maybe it will win him friends. Have we thought of that?"

I took her hand, more out of a sympathetic reaction to her overwrought condition than to make a pass at her, or so I thought. "It looks like you've thought of it, Jo. Who knows how the public will react? There isn't time for an opinion poll. Cotter's rally must be called off, or we have lost."

Jo clasped my hand. She looked up at me, her eyes shining with incipient tears. "Why, Art? Why are we so afraid of Cotter's rally? The schools will still be intact after the rally. Teachers will still be teaching. Their pupils will come and go as before. Teachers have survived extremist attacks in the past. They will survive Cotter's."

"But think of the harm he can do to your cause."

"I don't believe Cotter can hurt the Foundation, Art." She tightened her grip on my arm. "People are beginning to understand the basic issue, which is the freedom of teachers to teach. All we need is more time. A little more time." She took her hand away and wiped her eyes. "If we panic now,

Art," she said, her voice choking, "we may stop Cotter's rally, but we will still lose more to him in the end."

"Is that what you told Fletcher?"

"That's what I told him."

"What did he say?"

"He said he had already decided. You were to run your story."

I stepped away from her. "How nice of him! Does he believe he can tell the Dispatch what to print and what not to print?"

Jo resumed observing her view of the skyscrapers that cluttered Manhattan, where, here and there, new webs of steel were rising. "Did you ever have the feeling, Art, that you were just a minor piece on the chess board, a pawn, being pushed around by somebody? That's what's happening to us, Art. And you know--" She pointed to the Empire State. "That somebody is not Mr. Fletcher, it's really Cotter over there."

"But surely Cotter can't control Fletcher!"

"Can't he? How do we know? What can the Foundation do unless it has the financial backing of business? Mr. Fletcher thinks he has to go easy on Cotter, otherwise he'll get the Foundation embroiled in politics." Her face flamed. Skin tightened around her pursed lips. "The hell with the Foundation! The Foundation has no right to exist unless it's for the sake of the teachers. Isn't that the way things always end up? The cause we're supposed to be supporting becomes the one we're against?"

"Cotter has a good chance of turning public opinion against public education," I protested.

"What good will be accomplished?" Jo rushed on, her voice strident, "if teaching, the most important lay profession, is tarnished? We must avoid that at all costs. If we don't, then all our effort will be for nothing. That's why, if we do this to Cotter, there will be such a blight all over the country there will be teacher strikes and violence. And the teachers will lose. They will!"

"No, no," I said. "We will win, you will see."

Jo turned away, head buried in her hands. Her shoulders shook with her sobbing. "Oh, Art," she moaned. "I've worked hard, so hard."

I caught her shoulders, enfolding her in my embrace. Her eyes were veiled with tears. "Jo! I didn't realize this meant so much to you. I won't run the story, not if you don't want me to."

She tilted her head and looked up to me. Her tears ran unrestrained. "It's out of my hands now, Art." She pounded my chest with her clenched fists. "Oh, damn, damn, damn."

I laughed despite myself, holding her body still. "You should have been a teacher yourself, Jo. Repeat everything three times."

Her telephone rang. I let her go and Jo answered it. "Yes, sir. I understand. Right."

She hung up. "That was Mr. Fletcher. He said he could not condone giving the Moscow thesis to the Dispatch."

"What!"

"Wait, Art. That's Mr. Fletcher's official policy line. Mr. Fletcher talked with Mr. Green."

"Fletcher doesn't want to know what the thesis says?"

Jo nodded. "That's right. Perhaps you'd better make a last minute check with Gideon."

I dialed Gideon's number. Mary put me through to him. "Do we go ahead or don't we?" I asked Gideon.

Gideon's voice was husky, dry, like autumn leaves rustling at a curb. "Mr. Fletcher talked to Mr. Green, Art. Did Jo tell Mr. Fletcher? Well, it doesn't matter. Mr. Fletcher said he had heard the Dispatch had, somehow, obtained a copy of the Moscow thesis. He said he wanted Mr. Green to know that. Yes! And also he thought a Dispatch story on the thesis wouldn't do Cotter any harm. That's all he said. Nothing has changed, Art. Mr. Fletcher will maintain that he never heard of the thesis until he read about it in the Dispatch. Art?"

"Yes, Gideon?" I felt a chill, as if I had missed a deadline.

"I'm sorry, Art. There's no possibility of getting Foundation support, either now or later."

"There will be no follow-up statement tomorrow?"

Gideon was silent for a moment. "Not a chance," he said. "You're on your own, Art."

I said goodbye and hung up. I told Jo what Gideon had said.

"That's not fair!" she cried.

The shadow of the Empire State fell in a long narrow shaft over East Thirty-Fourth Street. My own dark image in the window glass stared back at me, mocking. How clever I had been! Secure in my feeling of superiority over Cotter, I had advanced against the enemy. Alone, as I had feared. My story could open a Pandora's box of recrimination, and the Foundation would feel nothing of Cotter's power. I wondered whether I ought to retrieve my story from Al's desk. There was still time.

I looked over at Jo. I was not alone, I told myself. I had found someone who believed as fiercely in freedom as myself. I put my arms around her again. "Jo, the hell with Fletcher. Let's give Cotter something to remember us by. Anyway, what are we afraid of? What can he do to us?"

She dabbed her eyes. "Sure," she said. "What can anyone do to us? Just give me time to fix my face."

While she was gone I stood looking out at the Empire State, which soared in lone majesty over Manhattan. There was the zenith, looking down on Zeus. This was the symbol of the shining city, the blunt column soaring, pure and noble in its naked power.

Only a few weeks before, during my first week in the city, I had gone up to the Empire's parapet, looked down on the pulsing streets, felt the gray mystery their allure. Then, looking up, I saw the thorny mast, protruding from the potent tower, and felt the desecration of the monument, the prostitution of the life of creation to the death of television. I had asked a guard, "Is it true that the zeppelin was to have anchored here?" The guard turned away. In anger? Or was he thinking of the flames at Lakehurst that flaked the skin from the cigar-shaped craft?

I wondered why Jo had come into my arms like that. When I held her, I was excited beyond anything I had ever felt before. Here was a woman more beautiful than any I had ever known. In my arms, her head on my chest, being comforted. How pale was Mary compared to Jo! Perhaps it was the mystery of Jo that excited me. But then again perhaps it was only the earthly longing. That it had happened was both natural and surprising. Natural, because she seemed much more human to me than any woman I had ever known. Surprising, because she was the creature of another world, the world of Madison Avenue. And yet it had happened. Jo was not the cold, hard sophisticated person I had envisioned. She was warm and tender, a child really, caught up in this cruel inhuman world where voices from above dictated policies that were no policies and left you in a vacuum of indecision. In comparison, how personal was the world in which I worked. It was I and Al and Fred and Mr. Marx and the Dispatch against the world, the brotherhood of journalism, unmatched for fellowship, unskilled in the subtler art of public relations, but honest for all that. Jo wasn't so far above me, after all. She was attainable. I wondered if I had the nerve to take her away from Gideon. Just the thought of doing that was a challenge. Wouldn't that be something? Jo and I. But what was I thinking? Had I fallen in love with Jo? Well, she was my own age. We had this feeling for humanity in common. Our fight against Cotter was not the play for power that it was with Gideon. It wasn't the chess-board gambit that it was to Silenus. Jo was tender. She hurt easily. And so did I. Well, I would have to take it easy. Jo was not the kind of woman you played around with without getting involved. I wasn't sure I wanted to get involved, not yet, not while I had the Cotter case in my hands. I still had to make a name for myself in New York. I couldn't, I wouldn't, ever use Jo to gain my own ends. And yet, I knew, I wanted her. I wanted her more than any woman I had ever known. More than Jenny Glen in Chesterton, more than Mary.

Jo's voice penetrated my foggy thoughts. Deep-throated, it purred across the room. "There's nothing either good or bad, but thinking makes it so," she sang with vigor.

"Who wrote that?" I asked.

I turned. Her lips were bright with new red, and her eyelids were shaped with shadow "Jo, if you only knew--"

"What makes you think I don't?" she asked.

I helped her into her white leather coat. I held her shoulders. "You're beautiful, Jo," I whispered in her ear. I felt her shiver.

"Don't Art. Not now. Not here. Later, perhaps." I felt her white-gloved hand. She squeezed mine, ever so lightly.

At the Press Gallery we paused outside the door until a waiter with a white napkin on his arm came up. He made a V-sign. "Two?" I nodded. As we passed between two tables, Jo in front of me, the men seated there made no effort to give Jo more room to pass. They turned around to watch her. One of the men said, "Hi, Jo." It was Dick Doyle. Jo introduced me and we shook hands. A sleek tanned man with long wavy hair, Doyle fitted in well with the Madison Avenue crowd. He reminded Jo of the scheduled copy conference at the Bronson agency after lunch. Jo said she would be there.

As I followed Jo up the stairs to the second floor, where I had eaten that first day in New York when Gideon and Mary were with us. I wondered why suddenly Dick Doyle constituted a threat to me. It must have been the way Doyle looked at Jo, the slight disappointment when he saw that Jo was not alone.

In the upstairs room, over coffee, Jo told me she was the daughter of a broken marriage. Nelson Davis, a Manhattan Bank vice-president, had been married to Marion Davis for twenty-one years when they decided to call it quits.

"Another woman?" I asked Jo.

She smiled, a crooked, rather sad, smile. "Yes. Me. Anyway, Mother said it was my fault. I was the cause of their arguments. Why couldn't I make up my mind what I wanted to do, she'd say. By that she meant be an artist. Father said 'Get out of the Village, they're all a bunch of bums.'" Jo sighed. "Anyway, we get along perfectly now. Father was marvelous. He gave Mother the Bronxville house, that's where she lives now. I see her once in a while, but Father I see a lot at his place on Morningside Heights. He's not stubborn or anything but we do have our arguments, over politics mostly." She looked around. "This is a nice place, isn't it?"

"Not bad," I said. I would have preferred the intimate Fanfanny's or the Madison Club, where the booths are semi-circular and the darkness is relaxing. Here the dark was not the romantic dimness of the true bar, but the fake gloom of a cavern styled for swift business luncheons. Besides, the wallpaper was a wretched maroon.

Jo picked up her coffee. "You're awfully quiet, Art. I know, the Foundation's let you down." She placed a hand on mine. "I've let you down. Don't worry. The Dispatch will stand by you."

"I'm not sure the Dispatch will print it. Mr. Marx may veto it."

"Who's he?"

"The managing editor. In serious stories like this one, he has the final say. If he vetoes it, where will I be?"

Jo leaned forward. She eyed me suspiciously. "Your greatest chance, Art? Because if you are using me and Gideon and Silenus and Mr. Green to set yourself up--"

"No, no," I protested. "Jo, I wouldn't. You don't know me. Let me tell you something that happened a long time ago." I told her about the Communist cell case at Richland University, how I had been double-crossed by Gideon and Senator Bentley. It took me fifteen or twenty minutes, longer than I should have taken, but I wanted her to know I had a stake in this venture.

"I find it hard to believe that about Gideon," Jo said.

"That's how Gideon got his start."

She bit her lower lip. "Gideon never told me."

"I know what Gideon means to you."

Her eyes flashed. "We're only friends, Gideon and I."

"I had it figured he was in love with you."

"Well, I like Gideon, even if he is--"

"Is what, Jo?"

"Gideon lives in two worlds, you know what I mean?"

"Sure. I know his wife and kids. Amy's a fine woman. I like her."

"Exactly," Jo said. "He comes to New York in the morning, and that's the Gideon I know. The Manhattan Gideon. Run for a taxi. Run for the subway. Run for the elevator. A scrambler, a positive thinker. Also a wolf, but a gentle one. Doesn't mean a tenth of what he says. Like he's always saying, 'Jo, let's fly away together to some sunny island.' Nonsense like that. Then I wonder what he's like in that other world he lives in, his married world. I know it must be a very good world, and yet Gideon gives the impression he'd give it up for me if only I gave him half a hope."

"I don't blame him for being crazy about you."

Jo bent her head to me. "Thank you, Art. I'd dismiss Gideon's possible infatuation, and I don't admit that he is at all serious, if it weren't for the fact that he doesn't pay the slightest attention to any other woman, not that I know of. Except Amy, of course."

"The faithful type," I ventured.

She knitted her brows. "No, not really. He is determined, up to a point, because he is proud, has real pride in doing a good job. But he doesn't believe, not in his heart, in what he is doing. He's only accidentally anti-Cotter."

"What do you mean, accidentally?"

"You told me part of the reason, the Richland University business. But there is something else, something that happened to him while he was in the Army in Korea. Did he ever tell you about it? No? Well, perhaps some day he will. Whatever it was it has something to do with the way, well, the way he is."

In the taxi on the way to the Bronson agency I asked Jo if Fletcher would be at the copy conference. She replied that it was possible. I was curious to know what the "great pooh-bah" of the Foundation, as Gideon titled him, was like. I told Jo about my meeting with Cotter, mentioning Miss Lawrence, Cotter's private secretary.

Jo clapped her hands. "Whee! Sexy," she cried. "Did you investigate the bedroom?"

I admitted I hadn't had the chance. She laughed about that all the way up Madison Avenue.

Oddly, the Bronson conference room smelled of pines. I padded across the spongy yellow floor to the chair moved out for me by Dick Doyle. I sank into it, rubbing sleek upholstery. Unlike the offices of the account executives, the conference was outfitted with polished walnut and leather, which Jo said was standard for Madison Avenue. We had gone first into Doyle's office, which was furnished like the breakfast nook of some English baronial castle: splintered cross-legged table for a desk, a leaded glass breakfront for a bookcase, a scored captain's chair. File cabinets were apparently not allowed. Doyle's office was unique, but so were the other offices, which were furnished with antiques. On the way to the conference room we had passed by executives lounging in Spanish splendor, French frills, Italian imitations, Portuguese pomposity, and, everywhere, Boston brass and trays.

Fletcher, stiffly erect, massive white-haired head held high in command, marched in. With him was Bronson, tanned and black-mustached, slightly stooped. After nodding to Jo and me they took their seats on opposite sides of the long table. Jo coughed. Fletcher and Bronson looked up. Jo introduced me to them. Each said, "Happy to know you." Looking around, I noted the wall on the other side of the room was half covered by a vertical paper poster. It was a Foundation advertisement I had seen on subway platforms. Designed by a Bronson artist, it displayed a teacher at a school black-board. Looking earnestly at the teacher were two young pupils, a white girl and a white boy. The slogan read: *Their future is in your hands. Support their teachers.* At the poster's foot, in much smaller type, was the name of the ad's sponsor: *Educational Foundation of America.* The copy committee's task was to put its stamp of approval on new theme art and slogan.

I nudged Jo's arm. "What are we waiting for?" I whispered. She replied that the meeting couldn't start without Gideon. When Gideon finally arrived, bowing apologetically, Jo smiled weakly at him. Gideon waved to me.

Doyle plumped a thin blue folder on the table, sat down and turned his attention to his papers. Gideon, however, was rounding the table shaking first Fletcher's hand, saying a few words in a whisper, and then giving the same double-handed grip to Bronson. If Gideon bore any ill-will toward either man he certainly didn't show it.

Now Doyle, looking quite pleased with himself by lounging, parlor-style, one arm flung over the back of his chair, opened the meeting by saying he was very pleased that both Mr. Bronson and Mr. Fletcher were in attendance. He distributed copies of the Bronson agency's proposal for the Foundation's basic theme advertisement to be used in the next year's campaign. In wide Latin font, the theme was: *Education Is the Strength of the Nation*. The painting showed a black-garbed professor lecturing a college class. Only two students were clearly pictured: a girl and a boy, both white.

"Let's play around with this for a while," Doyle said. Committee members were silent for a few minutes while they studied the proposed art.

Gideon was the first to speak. "Defense," he said loudly. "Today we have our backs to the wall. Education, particularly higher education, must be defended. May I suggest simply *Defend Education* with an exclamation point."

Doyle dismissed the suggestion with a wave of his hand and a toss of his head. He looked coldly at Gideon. "Our procedure," he lectured, "is to kick the ball around a bit before we try for exact wording."

Gideon reddened all the way to his receding hairline. "Sorry," he said. He sat down.

Fletcher clasped his hands over the table.

"Yes, Mr. Fletcher?" Doyle asked eagerly.

"I'd like to say," Fletcher began, clearing his throat, "that the Foundation has had a good response to the current theme. It rings the bell."

Bronson gave a puckish grin. "Might as well continue a good thing when we have it."

I caught Gideon's evil sidelong look, which lanced Doyle.

Doyle's greasy smile was like a gargoyle's: frozen. "With a slight twist," he said, addressing Mr. Fletcher, "just for something new. A theme soon gets stale. People say: What? The same old thing again?"

Jo held up her hand. "Gideon's idea makes sense," she said. "Higher education, especially, has been under attack for years. And it was Gideon who came up with the current slogan."

"Theme," said Doyle, correcting her.

Bronson licked his thin lips. "Gideon's theme is catchy and memorable. That's just the point. We've got to think ahead. What may be memorable today may be cliché tomorrow. I'm in favor of something new. We've saturated the country with the current theme. People get tired of seeing and hearing the same old words."

As Gideon slunk low in his chair, Mr. Fletcher pushed back from the table as if he had just finished a steak. "A year from now who knows what the world situation will be?" he asked nobody in particular. "We've got to think of the Russians."

Gideon's smirk was definite now.

Doyle reshuffled his papers. "That's it. Very good, Mr. Fletcher. The Russians are getting ahead in education. They have some themes that are pretty close to ours." He looked around as if to credit himself with knowing what those themes were. "What's the one thing the Russians are best at?" He pounded the table. "Advertising! It's become the backbone of their economy."

Fletcher said they were getting off the subject. Bronson disagreed. "Dick made a good point," the agency president said as Doyle beamed. "Think of the saving bonds appeal: Defend America."

Gideon raised his hand, much in the way I used to do in his class when I wanted to ask a question. "May I suggest," he said, "Education: Our Only Sure Defense."

"Please, Gideon," Doyle hissed, looking as if he had an ulcer paining him.

"Sorry," Gideon said again.

Doyle spoke to Branson. "If we can agree that we should work on the theme of defense, I am sure our copy people can come up with some suggestions."

Bronson nodded and stood up. "Shall we meet again? Say a week from today? Dick?"

"Fine with me, sir."

Fletcher went out with Bronson. Doyle shook hands with Gideon, Jo and I. "Thanks so much for coming," he said. He turned quickly and left us alone.

"That's all there is to it?" I asked.

"That's it," Gideon replied. He seemed oddly incognito, as if he hardly knew us. His mouth was stern. He shot sidelong glances at us, Jo and I, almost as if we were of the enemy camp.

I made a face like Doyle's, eyes ceiling-ward, brows angled. "Let's run this up the flagpole and see which way it waves," I said.

"Stow it," Gideon said morosely.

Jo went around the table. She touched Gideon's arm. It was a soft touch, a caress of Gideon's sleeve. "Doyle is an idiot," she said.

Gideon collapsed in the chair. "It's not Doyle," he said. His voice dropped to a mutter. "It's Fletcher. Well, his time will come. Some day he will see I'm right. One day he will come to me and I will--"

Gideon pursued the absent Fletcher for another minute or two. This was a Gideon I had never seen before: slouched, withdrawn, brooding. He directed his animosity toward Fletcher with wide barbs darted at Doyle. It was obvious to me that what griped Gideon was being forced to keep silent in Fletcher's presence. Gideon described Fletcher as he saw the pooh-bah: lordly brow, condescending glance, a smoothly polished white-haired Baal.

I pointed out that Fletcher had paid no more attention to Jo and me than he did to him, but Gideon was inconsolable. "Poor Jo!" he cried. "She's worked, God how she's worked for Fletcher. And does he thank her? He does not! The master-mind of the plot, the puppeteer pulling the strings." He slammed the table. The whack resounded through the room. "Idiot!"

Jo picked up her handbag. "I haven't told you this before, Gideon, but I'll be glad if the Dispatch runs Art's story."

If she had slapped his face, Gideon could not have been more chagrined. "Maybe you think that is the right thing to do, Jo, but you will change your mind later. Just wait until Cotter reads it."

Jo turned swiftly around to face Gideon. Her eyes burned across the table at him. "Do you know what you and Silenus are doing to Art? Don't you realize what Cotter can do to him? Without the backing of the Foundation, you see, Art is out there on a limb. And Cotter is the kind of brute who would chop the limb off behind him." She started toward the door, but turned around halfway there. She pointed at Gideon, index finger accusing him. "If I get through with this, Gideon, just remember, when Cotter gets his knife into Art, that you were the cause of it." With that she raced from the room.

Gideon looked at me, eyebrows up. "What was that about?"

I shrugged. "I'll let you in on a little secret, Gideon." I ambled over and slapped him on the shoulder. "Women always hurt the one they love the most."

Gideon frowned. A slow dumb smile crept over his broad face. "Jo!" he shouted. "You don't mean Jo?"

"Let's go, Gideon," I said, "before you faint trying to understand what life is all about."

Chapter Fourteen

"You both know the score," Mr. Marx said. "Cotter fumbled and we've picked up the ball. Now we're running with it. Let's make the touchdown."

My managing editor hunched his powerful shoulders and looked for all the world as if he was about to begin a sixty-yard dash, which, as a matter of fact, he had done more than once as a fullback for Michigan State.

Al closed the door of Marx's metal-and-glass office in the far corner of the Dispatch newsroom. "You think we can do it?" he asked Marx.

"I got coached by the publisher," Marx replied. He began pacing the office. I settled back in the beat-up brown leather sofa. "She says go," he continued, "so we go. The entire shop, nobody on the benches."

Al whistled. "Go for broke, Mr. Marx?"

"Every man up and at 'em." He stabbed a finger at me. "Art, you're the captain of this team." He was great on euphemisms. "It's your play, Art. Finding that thesis, that was great, really great! We've got to have a plan." He strode around his cigarette-burned desk, hands behind his back, head lowered, as if preparing to tackle.

"This is the play," Marx went on. "Art stays in the newsroom, takes stuff on the phone, does the recaps, the rewrites. Al, you assign as many reporters as you need to cover all sides of the Cotter story. This is the big one. The Rose Bowl!"

"Right!" Al cried.

Marx stalked the room. "Art, your first story will be on the street in an hour. Al, assign someone to get to Cotter with a copy, try for a comment. Have someone else cover the Garden, find out if Cotter's contracted for a rally. Hey! Al, someone in Sports maybe has a contact at the Garden. Next, get the Board of Education, the state Secretary of Education, everybody in that line. I want solid quotes, doesn't matter whose side they take. Keep 'em hollerin' between quarters. And don't forget the clergy. Monsignor what's-his-name will have something to say. Also, call the rabbis and the Protestant Clergy Council. Then the Teachers Union, Al, you know the others. Put a strong man in every position on this team. Let the cubs cover the regular beats, they're itching for the chance. I will watch the competition. Now, I'm going to blow the whistle every night on this. A conference tomorrow, same time, right?"

"Right," Al said.

"Right!" I echoed.

"The whole team," Marx said. "I want everyone out there running. Nobody on the bench."

Back at my desk I phoned Gideon at home. It was past six o'clock. I told him the signal was "Go!" Gideon's hurray was loud and clear. "We're in, buddy boy."

"What do you mean, we?"

"Whose idea was it to dig into Cotter's past?"

"As Mr. Marx would say, you refused to carry the ball."

"Art! I was willing. It was the Foundation that let us down."

"But you won't, will you, Gideon?"

"Buddy boy! You've got me all wrong. I wouldn't run out on you. You're not alone in this."

"But I am alone, Gideon. Only my name will be on that story. Not yours, not the Foundation's."

"Cotter won't dare to hold a rally now, Art. Your story will stop him cold."

"I'm only incidentally interested in Cotter's rally. This is a matter of the truth now."

"Let's not be extreme, Art."

"Tell Silenus."

"I will, Art."

An hour later the paper came up. The block Page One headline could be read across the newsroom: **SHOCKING!**

Underneath, the subhead read: **Cotter a Pink in the Twenties?**

Below was my byline, big and bold: *By Art James*

I dialed the Powers Hotel and asked for Cotter. Miss Lawrence came on the line. "Oh, is that you Mr. James?"

I replied that it was indeed *me.*

"When y'all coming to see us again?"

"Is Mr. Cotter in, Miss Lawrence?"

He wasn't in. I asked her to have him call me as soon as he returned.

Fred Roberts had the headphone on at the desk next to mine and was rattling off a statement someone was dictating. It was a clergyman. Fred kept saying "Yes, Reverend. Got it, Reverend. Go on, Reverend."

Beyond Fred three or four other reporters were busy on their phones. Dave Norman was reading my story to someone. Fred hung up. He tore the statement from his typewriter. "Protestant Clergy Council," he said. I spiked it. A copy boy handed me another one from Dave. I spiked that too. Later I would do a roundup of the reactions.

Al hailed me. At his desk he handed me a note from the Sports desk: *Hear Garden has a tentative reservation from Cotter November 21.* That gave Cotter only four weeks. Enough time to gear up a television campaign. He would have to pull out all the publicity stops if he wanted to fill the garden.

Al told me to borrow Max's radio and to listen for a news flash from Cotter's headquarters. "I wouldn't put it past Cotter," said Al, "to go on TV to reply to our story."

"*My* story," I said.

Al grinned. He pointed to the byline. "Look good to you?" he asked.

"I feel famous," I replied.

In Max's office I asked the drama editor, who as usual was listening to his radio, if he had heard any bulletins about the Moscow thesis. Max, bent over his typewriter with a pencil in his teeth, shook his head. I was disappointed. By this time the broadcasting stations would have had my story via Associated Press. I was eager to hear an announcer say *According to an exclusive story by Dispatch Reporter Art James tonight--*

Max permitted me to borrow his radio. I was going out the door with it when he called me back. He handed me a proof sheet. It was an advertisement for *Out of Eden.* My name was wide and deep under the quote: *Slice of life, succeeds magnificently, a powerful achievement: Art James, Dispatch.* Quotes from our competition followed.

"That's not what I wrote," I protested.

"Oh, but you did." Max said. He handed me a clipping of my review of Georgia Wilson's play. He read these words: "*Out of Eden* is a distorted slice of life. He has succeeded magnificently. He has also made a purposeful achievement."

"The ad takes those words out of context!" I cried.

"Every ad does. That's the way they get such good quotes. You knew how to do it, by instinct."

"I said the play was rotten. I wasn't trying for an advertising quote."

Max smiled. His yellow cracked teeth protruded. "Weren't you, Art?"

"No!" I shouted. Max kept smiling.

The pace of the past twenty-four hours was catching up on me. It seemed more like twenty-four years since I had discovered that Cotter had written the Moscow thesis, and longer since I had taken Mary to see *Out of Eden*. The advertisement's distortion of my review was more agonizing to me at that moment than Cotter's pending reaction. I asked myself if I had deliberately inserted those praising words in my review. And then I knew that Max was right. I had secretly hoped for a quotation in an advertisement. My name in an ad for a play set me up as an important critic. I couldn't blame Max for being sore. A pinch hitter, I had grabbed the spotlight from him. Was Max afraid that some Broadway tongue would wag: "Looks as if Max Jordan is over the hill. Newcomer, name of Art James, reviewed *Out of Eden!*" We are all afraid of something, I suppose.

In the newsroom I plugged in the radio and set it on my desk, twirled the dial to the Mutual station. I burrowed in on the reaction statements for a few minutes, and then the ten o'clock news came on. I turned up the volume so Fred could hear.

An item about the Moscow thesis came first. The announcer credited the Dispatch with the story. My heart thumped as I waited for a mention of my name, but there was none. I muttered a silent "Damn!" and flipped to CBA. The announcer was on the international news: a new crisis in Vietnam, and then a commercial, something about a mattress, seemed to last an eternity. At length the announcer came back on. He gave the Cotter story a more detailed treatment. He mentioned my name first. Fred raised his hand in salute. I turned the dial as fast as I could to NBC and ABC stations, but both had reached the weather report.

Al called me to his desk. "We're doubling the print order for the morning final, Art. "The *Times* and *Trib* will have to move over."

He told me that Circulation was yelling for more papers. The Times Square stands had sold out in ten minutes.

"And that's just the beginning, Art." Al rubbed his lean hard hands together. "You know, it's just possible you may be the man who saved the Dispatch."

I held up my hand, open palm toward him, in a gesture of modest dismissal.

"I mean it," Al said. "This is the kind of running story that can save our jobs." He ordered me to rush the reaction story for the next edition. The Dispatch was staking everything on a shaky premise.

I was no sooner back at my desk than the phone rang. It was Miss Lawrence. She put Cotter on.

"Hello, Mr. James, how are you?"

His voice was mellow. I had expected a deafening blast. "Fine, sir."

"My secretary tells me you called."

"Yes, I did call." I hardly knew what to say next.

"What can I do for you?"

Surely he had heard about my story by now. "It's about a story of mine in the Dispatch tonight, Mr. Cotter."

"Which one?"

He was playing a cat-and-mouse game. "The one about, ah, Moscow." I tapped a pencil as I waited for him to answer.

Cotter laughed. He must have moved the phone away from his mouth, or covered the phone with his hand. His laugh was hollow. "Shocking! Ha, ha! Yes, good headline. Shocking. I must say you boys sure know how to think up good one-line heads. Wish the other papers were more enterprising."

My stomach felt bound by chains. "I don't understand--"

"You don't understand what?"

"Nothing, Mr. Cotter. I, that is, we would like a statement from you, since you've seen the paper."

"Heard it on the radio just now. I would have called you before, but wanted to see if you were getting this thing around."

"You know how it is. The stations, they pick it up from us."

"I understand. You're doing a good job, Art. That kind of story, it's good for circulation." I swallowed hard. "Tell me, Art, how did you find my thesis? I thought I had burned every one in existence."

"Confidential source, Mr. Cotter." I looked up. Fred was leaning over my shoulder, and so was Al. I lifted the earpiece an inch away so they could hear.

"Very interesting, Art. You will go far in journalism, I'm sure. But I mustn't keep you from your very important work. Give me a few minutes, will you? I'll call you back."

"Thank you very much, Mr. Cotter," I said. I hung up slowly.

"I'll be damned," Al said as he shuffled away.

I picked up the sheaf of statements, but my mind was still on Cotter. He had let me off lightly. Perhaps he was only baiting a trap. Suddenly I wished that Gideon was with me. I needed his optimistic assurance that this was not the calm before the storm. The reaction statements were no more or less than I expected. The rabbi said he was shocked, but he was sure Cotter had merely committed a youthful indiscretion. The monsignor would have no comment until he consulted with the Cardinal in the morning. The Protestant Council spokesman said it only went to show that the pot was calling the kettle black. The Board of Education chairman was "upset," but he was certain there were extenuating circumstances, even though he disagreed with Cotter's methods. The Mayor was out of town, but a paragraph from the Manhattan Borough president said the thesis was a clear indication that Cotter was through.

There were more: the Teachers Union exulted that Cotter was a Russian bear in wolf's clothing. The AFL-CIO said everyone knew the Cotterites were anti-labor and claimed the Cotterite movement was a screen for smashing the union shop. The Chamber of Commerce claimed it was a frame-up. The Parent-Teachers conference said officers would have to see the entire thesis before commenting.

On and on the statements went. I sorted them into pro and con, just for the fun of it. The ringing of the phone interrupted me. It was Cotter with his statement.

"First I want to ask you about the rally in the Garden," I said.

"It's in my statement, Art."

I put on the earphones, flipped the switch that cut the sound into them and adjusted the mouthpiece. "Go ahead. Mr. Cotter."

He began dictating. His voice was precise, authoritative. Once or twice I wondered what sort of mind Cotter had that could twist so serious a charge to his own design.

When he finished dictating, he said. "Any questions, Art?"

I was exhausted. I said, "None, Mr. Cotter." I thanked him and hung up.

I took the statement to Al, who read it quickly, running his pencil over it, not touching the paper, as was his habit. "If that's the way he wants it," Al said, hissing the words, "that's the way he's going to get it. You can write another story on the thesis now."

At my desk I laid the statement flat and read it over. Fred was still busy knocking out reactions. He winked at me. "Give the bastard hell, Art."

As I read his statement I realized that Cotter had done none of the things I expected. He did not deny the existence of the thesis. He did not excuse himself for writing it. He didn't even belittle its implications for his position. No, Harry Cotter showed he was astute in his relations with the press. Cotter, it was evident, was the great realist. He knew that without the press he was nothing. I began to edit the document which has since become famous, hailed by extremists as a courageous confession of conviction, derided by the left as confused demagogic nonsense. As I read, the question teased me: how was Cotter able to come up with such a statement in the several minutes available to him? Who had tipped off Cotter about my story? I was convinced that the statement had been prepared well in advance. Here it is:

> *I am grateful to the Dispatch for bringing to the attention*
> *of its thousands of loyal readers the fact that I had a full*
> *year's experience in Russia during the early twenties. That*
> *one year gave me full opportunity to learn first-hand the*
> *evil notions which fomented the Bolshevist Revolution.*
> *I know what the Communists are up to. I am calling upon*
> *every citizen in New York with an ounce of conscience to*
> *come to Madison Square Garden at 8 p.m. Friday, the 21st*
> *of November. At that time I will issue a Manifesto which*
> *will demand that the President declare a national State of*

Emergency over the Communist menace. We must be on our guard against the Communist enemy. Appeasers and traitors must be eliminated. The truth about Communism must be taught in schools, colleges and universities, and in the Armed Forces. The time has come for ACTION!

How expertly Cotter had turned the disclosure of the Moscow thesis to his own account. He used it as a springboard from which to launch his rally. He knew he could count on the Dispatch's objectivity, knew that our next day's headline would have to be: *Cotter Sets/Garden Rally.*

Somehow I had been trapped into providing Cotter the attention he needed. Before that night I wouldn't have bet a dime that Cotter had a chance to fill the Garden. He and his movement weren't that well known. Now the public would be curious, eager to see what Cotter was like. I had played into Cotter's hands. Cotter would make the most of it. Now he would pull out all the publicity stunts. Posters advertising the rally would go up in the subways, buses and railway stations. Spot announcements would pepper TV and radio. The city would awake to find Cotter's gauntlet on its doorstep. In effect, he was sounding a national call to arms. He was announcing in advance that he planned to enlarge the scale of his attack by taking on not only public education but also the armed forces. By involving the President he was taking on the entire government. Cotter had chosen the date of his encounter and the battleground. His enemies were scattered and unorganized. Cotter counted on that. There would be little time for his enemies to arrange a defense, let alone a counterattack. Cotterite forces were mobilized to strike.

Al called me over. He had a new assignment for me: cover the fight that Doctor Canning, president of Richland University, was having with his Board of Trustees. "Got a tip from our Richland stringer," Al told me. "Canning has made a decision."

"Was his resignation accepted?"

"He withdrew it, Art. Find out why."

I protested that surely Al needed me to write follow-up stories on Cotter, including the reaction stuff. Al was firm. He had already assigned Fred Roberts to fill in for me.

"Who's the source of our information on Canning?" I asked.

"Managing editor of the Richland Monitor, guy named Harper."

"Surprise, surprise."

I took a cab home, which at that time was a one-room apartment on West 110th Street. I labored up two flights, fumbled for the right key. The hall was dark. I cursed the janitor for not replacing a burned-out bulb.

My room sprang into light as I flicked the switch. I tossed the Dispatch on my rumpled bed. The headline mocked me. *SHOCKING*. My byline stared back at me: *By Art James*. My reward for this scoop was to be sent back to the hinterland from which I had come.

I slipped into pajamas and turned down the bed cover. I glanced around the room, which still felt strange despite my two-month occupancy. My cufflinks, tie clip, comb and pen were in their places on the walnut bureau. The center drawer of my desk was slightly open, revealing the clutter of rubber bands, paper clips, pencils. My few books ranged the back of the desk against the olive wallpaper.

I sighed, reached overhead and pulled the chain on the lamp. From the window a soft glow from Riverside Drive spread over the room. I closed my eyes. I dreamed of Jo coming to see me, arms outstretched.

Chapter Fifteen

President Charles Foster Canning showed me the view from his office window overlooking the campus of Richland University. His stubby arm cut an arc, circumscribing the quadrangle, where students idled in the slanting sun. His voice was hoarse, dry as the leaves that peppered the dun autumn grass.

"Cotter is the most ignorant man in America," he said. His loose drooping jowls quivered. "Ignorance disguised as wisdom is the greatest evil. Men loved darkness rather than light, Scripture says. Cotter draws down darkness wherever he goes."

Imperceptibly the darkness thickened over the quadrangle. A shadow, pale as evening mist, crept across the plump olive carpet and nestled in the corners of the big square room. I jotted down what he had said, turned my head slightly to catch his next low-voiced condemnation of Cotter and his cause.

"Cotter snuffs out the flame of the lamp of learning," he went on as he leaned on one corner of the wall by the broad bay window. "With a snap of a finger he turns free men into quivering lumps. Like that." The echo of his snapping fingers died in the far reaches of the room. "This is the issue in America today. Shall we, who are born free, be slaves to demagogues who, because they are afraid, fear the freedom others demonstrate? Yes, I said demonstrate, because freedom is not only what you believe, it's what you live!"

I nodded my agreement as my pencil recorded his words in my own particular style of shorthand.

Canning pressed back his mass of white hair with both hands, as if he would exorcise the demon Cotter from his brain. He peered at me from ragged gray brows. "You alumni," he said, "you think the university will always be free. Sure, football games on a Saturday afternoon. Tenth anniversary reunions where you see one another growing old. You were free once, when you were students, free to probe and to pry, to question your teachers. You took that for granted. Not anymore. Today, for a professor to speak straight out on issues, concerns, is to beg for a Cotterite letter from the dean. Well, I defend my team. What's wrong with that? Ask your readers that, Mr. James. Shall I abdicate my responsibility on this campus. My God, no!"

All at once, as the sun went down behind the Arts and Science Building, the room was plunged into darkness. I looked around, intent on seeking the switch, but Canning hurried on.

"I do not intend to preside over this campus while it turns into a Cotterite fort." He swung toward me, bending his leonine head toward mine. His eyes glinted in the shadow. "I'm going to fight, Mr. James. Tell your readers that. I will never permit the return of Senator Bentley to the faculty of Richland University."

I was several words behind him in taking notes. I crushed the impulse to stop writing at the mention of Bentley's name. I could feel a cold sweat bursting. I shook off my desire to laugh, scream, cry aloud, anything to express my surprise that it was Bentley whom the university trustees were trying to foist upon Canning as their man to hatchet campus left-wingers. I was also delighted that I had the lead for my story.

"Let me get the facts straight, Doctor Canning," I said. "You are talking about the action of the Board of Trustees?"

He explained that the trustees had set up a committee with Senator Bentley as a member to investigate rumors, and outright charges contained in letters to the Richland Monitor, that fully a quarter of the faculty were left-wingers, as indicated by either their membership in organizations condemned by the Richland Cotterite Society, or by their advocacy of government programs and policies condemned by the Cotterites as socialistic.

"The committee recommended," Canning continued, "that I be authorized to dismiss faculty members whose names the committee presented to me. There was an alternative, permitted to preserve my public image, my public relations man tells me. The alternative is to hire Senator Bentley as vice-president for university affairs and give *him* the job of weeding out Cotter's victims from the faculty."

"Why Senator Bentley?" I asked.

"Experience plus availability," Canning answered. "Because Bentley has had experience as a member of the Senate Committee on Un-American Activities, and because he is not running for re-election. Canning crossed the room to the door and switched on the lights. He sat down behind his heavy dark desk. "Also because of his experience in getting rid of a leftwing cell several years go." He smiled at me. "Which you, Mr. James, no doubt recall."

"I remember it," I said. I sat down on a chair beside his desk. "But you have decided against employing Senator Bentley."

He swayed backward in his thick leather chair. He pressed the sides of his head again. "Headache," he said. "I'm going to take the assignment myself."

"What exactly will you do?"

Swinging himself back and forth in his chair, he pondered my question. "I will ask for a full report from the committee. I will insist that action is an administrative responsibility. I will consult with the faculty deans. We will come to a conclusion."

"Can you tell me what that conclusion will be?"

"We will conclude," he replied, leaning forward, "that the politics of a faculty member are his personal private business."

"And if the trustees don't buy that?"

"I will have no alternative but to resign."

"Then what you are thinking of doing is a stalling tactic?"

"Time heals many wounds, Mr. James. Cotter is at the height of his power. Your finding the Moscow thesis, that shows Cotter is on the way out." Canning stood up and came around the desk. "I think you may be known hereafter, Mr. James, as the Horatio who held the bridge."

"Thanks," I said, getting up, "but he's one hell of a big Etruscan."

"But dumb," Canning said, shaking my hand. "Big but dumb."

At the door he said "Keep in touch, Mr. James. And, by the way, Senator Bentley is in town, if you want to see him. I believe Mr. Harper of the Monitor knows where he is staying. His fellow trustees are interviewing him for the vice-presidential job."

"Why Mr. Harper?"

"Didn't you know? Mr. Harper is chairman of the trustees committee."

"Have you been in touch with Gideon Pratt in New York?" I asked. "He does public relations for the Educational Foundation."

"Gideon Pratt?"

"Used to teach English literature here."

"I don't recall him."

I boarded a bus a bus for the half-hour trip to West Lincoln, where Dad greeted me in the waiting room. His decade-old Pontiac awaited us. On Main Street we passed by his legal office, where Dad was the sole proprietor. He had a secretary and usually a part-time law student from Richland University. He asked me how my meeting with Canning went. I told him what I could and also about Cotter. I gave him a copy of the Dispatch with my byline on Page One. He congratulated me and said he would read it when he got home.

My mother swept me into her arms, which was a task because she was only five-six. Supper was on the table and my room was ready. "Oh, it's so good to have you home," she said. "When are you going to get married?" I was used to it. She never failed to ask me. She laughed when I said I had been too busy.

After supper I went to the parlor and was about to ignite a stack of paper and logs in the brick fireplace when Dad came in. I was struck by how thin he looked. He had always been slim. Lean, rather. His chest was heaving. He was out of breath. Narrow lines skipped around his thin mouth. "Good thinking," he said, as flames rose above the logs. "I was feeling a bit chilly. Let's enjoy it." We pulled up two leather armchairs. He spent a few minutes reading my Dispatch story. "That Cotter guy's a jerk," he said. "I'm more interested in how you like living in the Big Apple." He laughed. "I hope you've found a girl. Time's marching on, son. Your mother's always talking about it. She wants to be a grandmother."

I told him about Jo Davis. "I have hope," I said.

"And your job?"

"Exciting. Manhattan's got everything."

"And the people? They treating you right?"

I leaned toward him. "Dad, I think I'm really hitting my stride. I'm finding a cause that's worth fighting for. Exposing Cotter is right in line with what I've always wanted to do. Something meaningful. Something helpful. And I'm good at it. I really am."

"I never had any doubt about that, son, but be careful. There are plenty of people out there in the big cities that can do you harm." He picked up the Dispatch. "That Cotter guy, for instance. Don't trust him. Snake oil type."

"How's it going with you, Dad?"

He took a shallow breath. "Not so good at the office. Just lost the Tiber Trucks account. Son, don't take this as the gospel truth, but I think your stories about Cotter had something to do with it."

I felt a sudden chill, despite the warming fire. "How can that be?"

"You know the publisher of the Star?"

"Ewart France? I met him once. Why?"

Dad held his open hands toward the fire. "He's a consultant to Tiber Trucks. I got the word today from Tiber's attorney, fellow named MacDonald. He told me Tiber Trucks would not be renewing our contract when it expires at the end of this year. Financial reasons, I was told, although Mr. France's profits are higher than ever."

For what seemed an eternity I stared at him. Did Dad believe there was a connection between my story about Cotter and this loss of an important account? If that was true the Cotterites had struck with whiplash viciousness, as Al had warned me they might.

"Is Ewart France a Cotterite?" I asked.

"I don't know."

"He can't do this to you! Because of me? It's obvious. Cotter must have ordered France to find a way to punish me! Dad, I'm sorry. I'll find out."

"No, son. You will only cause more trouble." He held my hand. "You did what you had to do. You told the truth." His face brightened. He chuckled. "Anyway, I'm glad I found out about Mr. Barclay. Knowing what I suspect about him now I would have cancelled the contract myself."

Dad made a brave showing. I knew he was worried. He might lose other accounts in the same way and for the same reason: Me!

"I will quit the Dispatch," I said. "I will come back to Richland. When they can do this to you, the fight isn't worth it."

As I might have expected, Dad laughed again. "Now don't build this up into a national disaster, son. You've got to do your job the way you think it ought to be done. Nobody can ask more of you than that. Now sit still and tell me all about this guy Cotter."

For an hour I related all that had happened in New York. I told him how I was involved with my former teachers, Gideon and Silenus.

"Look out for that Gideon fellow," Dad said. "He doesn't sound to me like a man you can trust."

"Gideon's alright," I said. "After all, he's on my side." But I wasn't sure of that, even then.

My mother cheered us up by bringing us cake and ice cream to enjoy as we sat before the dying embers of the fire. We kept the bad news from her. When I was ready to retire she came into my room and sat down on the bed, as she used to when I was a boy, for a goodnight chat. It was amazing to me that she appeared to have aged years in the few months I had been away. Her hair was streaked with gray, although it was as carefully waved as ever. Perhaps it was the absence of her daytime makeup that gave her face a gray, drawn-out look. Her eyes, usually merry, were dull and withdrawn. I wondered whether Dad had told her after all. She bent to me and kissed my forehead. She smelled strangely of pine incense. I mentioned that. "It's the pine soap," she told me. At the door she blew me a kiss. "Goodnight, son. See you in the morning." She always said that. She closed the door silently.

I dedicated myself to staring at the gentle slope of the ceiling, which once was a comfort, but which was now restricting, overwhelming. In the morning I telephoned Gideon. He told me he had heard announcements on radio and television about the Cotterite rally. Also, Jo had heard a rumor, obtained from Dick Doyle, that Cotter planned to attack the Educational Foundation's program of scholarship aid to teachers. Gideon said he had traced this to Sammy Spurgeon's column in the News. "Just Sammy's usual speculation," Gideon said.

I told Gideon the whole story about Canning and the move to get Senator Bentley on Canning's staff.

"Burt would be a fool to take the job," Gideon said, "and you can tell him I said so."

"I will," I replied. "I know he always takes your advice."

"That's true," Gideon said.

He told me he had read Dispatch follow-up stories on the Moscow thesis with a roundup on reactions to Cotter's statement of rebuttal, and the next day with further quotes from Silenus' notes. An editorial condemned Cotter only weakly by accusing him of being insincere. I wondered what happened to slow down Mr. Marx's power play. I could not see myself meeting face to face with Harper, the Monitor's managing editor, so I telephoned Richland's downtown hotels and soon found the one where Bentley was staying, the Prospect. Bentley could not see me until that evening, so I dusted off my old portable typewriter, which I had left in the closet of my bedroom, and wrote a story based on my interview with Canning. As I was writing, the curious question nibbled at my mind as to why Al had assigned me to cover this particular story at this particular time. When he took me off the Moscow thesis story I felt I had a right to be annoyed. Now, apart from the obvious reason that I was the right man to cover the Richland University affair, I began to suspect Al's real reason: he wanted me out of New York to save me from Cotter's reprisals. But then, what could Cotter have done to me in New York that he couldn't do in Richland? I was no safer here than in New York, perhaps less so, since he had already gotten even through Dad. But I did appreciate Al's intention.

As I wrote I longed for freedom to express my growing personal animosity against Cotter. But my objectivity, that first rule of journalism, bound me to state the facts only. Nevertheless, I arranged my story to show the quiet subversion of faculty morale, the tearing down of traditional academic freedom, the slow erosion of free speech and unfettered inquiry. When I read over my story I realized that far from being objective I was now a dedicated enemy of Cotterites. From now on, I told myself, I would waste no time in second thoughts about the pure ethics of journalism. I was out to get Cotter and I would get him.

Senator Bentley met me in the Prospect Hotel lobby. His silken hair had grayed around the temples. He looked more than ever the slick operator of a small-town bookstore.

"Let's go, Art," he said, hooking his arm in mine. He pushed across the lobby to the revolving door, which I had just come through.

"Where?" I asked. "What?"

"Cotterite meeting," he said.

He lunged after me into a cab and gave the driver an address in Melrose Park, a Richland suburb.

"What's this all about, Senator?"

"Just got the invitation." He waved to a pretty girl on the sidewalk. The cab pulled away from the curb and immediately came to a halt in the stream of Main Street traffic. "Good experience for you," Bentley continued. "Background stuff. Ever been to one?"

I admitted I had not. I apologized for that. Bentley was the kind of man who made you feel ashamed of your shortcomings. He put on his pince-nez, squeezing it to make it stay put. His face had broadened considerably, which made his mouth appear like an undersized stitch. He seldom kept the stitch zipped up.

"Interesting phenomenon," he said. "Strange people. Get together for the social benefit, as much as anything. Thing to do. Especially in suburbs. Driver, can't you get going? Good folks. Middle higher income. Rising executives. Kids. Where you from, Art?"

I told him, "West Lincoln." I told it with pride. "Our house was an older modest type. My parents bought it before the ticky-tacky developments went up."

"Fine community," the Senator rattled on. "Backbone of America. Father's a lawyer, isn't he?" He shot me a swift sidelong glance. I nodded. I wondered how he knew Dad was a lawyer. "Fine reputation. One of best corporation men. May have something for him soon."

He was baiting me. He wanted me to ask him about Richland University. I said nothing. The cab began to move. Soon we were past Monarch Street and on the freeway.

"Saw Harper today," he said. "Remembers you. Mentioned your Dispatch story about Cotter."

"Why didn't the Monitor pick it up?"

Bentley smiled, a small twisted turning upwards of his lips. "You know why, Art."

"Alright, I know. What about the Star?"

"With Mr. France in the saddle? You will never work for the Richland newspapers again, Art."

He said it sympathetically, and, I thought, with a touch of admiration. At least I hoped so. "When I get back to New York, Senator, I'm going to give Cotter the full treatment."

The Senator tightened his gray silk tie. He took a small brochure from his pocket. "Background reading," he said as he handed it to me. It was entitled *Memo to High School Students*. "Cotterite literature," Bentley said.

"Not directly. From a group called Frontier Fathers. Cotterites picked it up. Here, want to read it?"

I flipped through the brochure. The tract warned high school students to be on the lookout for Communist teachers, or teachers who had Communist sympathies. I handed it back to the senator. "Keep it," he said. I slipped it into my jacket pocket.

"Fear literature," Bentley said. "Products of fear-twisted minds. Country is being overrun with them. Fear-mongers, peddlers of hate. Should be a law. Obscene junk. If I wasn't retiring I'd sure enough try to put a stop to it. Time and again I've told Harry Cotter to clean up the filth that's circulating. Doesn't do the Cotterites any good. May get them into trouble, disgrace. The *Black Book* is bad enough. But this stuff! Poison. Poison for young minds."

As the cab turned off the freeway into Melrose Park he asked: "How is my old friend Gideon Pratt?"

Bentley apparently knew about my relationship with Gideon. If he knew that, then he also knew what Gideon and I were plotting. I began to suspect that I was dancing to Gideon's tune. No wonder there had been no need to run very fast to catch up to Bentley.

The cab pulled into a side street lined with handsome homes fronted by fifty-foot lawns. We stopped before a particularly neat ranch with a white trellis. Bentley raced ahead up the walk. He pressed the bell. We were ushered in by a slight man who could have been no more than five feet tall. Bentley introduced me to Desmond Roach, the president of the Melrose Park Chapter of the Harry M. Cotter Society.

The colonial-style parlor was occupied by several men and women. All stood up for Roach's introduction of Bentley and me. There was considerable heel-clicking as Bentley passed around the circle to shake each hand and speak a word to each person.

Roach nudged me. I bent my head down a foot. "What's your name again?" he whispered. I told him. "The Star reporter?" I explained that I was no longer with the Star but had moved to New York. This displeased him, for he gave me a look of disbelief, shaking his small head in a kind of unbalanced awe. He went over to Bentley. A few words passed between them. Bentley took me aside. He told me that Roach was concerned about having a reporter in the house. With that Bentley silenced his audience with a cough.

"Ladies and gentlemen," he began, "Mr. James is a friend of long standing, whom I am happy to introduce to you as one of my most valued counselors. You remember his courageous reporting for the Star, with which he is no longer associated."

I acknowledged their surly nods and sat down in a chair opposite the sofa on which the three women plumped themselves. Bentley was given the honored position at the head of the semicircle. Roach presided. The first thing they did was stand again. Hands over hearts, we pledged allegiance to the flag, which stood in a corner. We sat down. Roach read the minutes of the last meeting, which detailed a lengthy discussion on membership dues versus the efficacy of voluntary contributions. Dues appeared to have won out.

Next was a report on a brief exchange over the application of a prominent Negro attorney. It was vetoed. J. Edgar Hoover's latest F.B.I. book was highly recommended. One man declared that it should be required reading, but this was voted down as being unnecessary. Roach put the motion for acceptance of the minutes as read. There was a vociferous "Yea!"

"And now," Roach said, beaming at Bentley, "I know you have all been waiting to hear from our distinguished Senator." He smiled broadly. "We are greatly honored, sir, by your surprise visit. I am sure that if we had time to announce your coming we would have had a far larger attendance. So many events vie for the time of--"

Bentley dismissed this apology with a wave of his hand. "Think no more of it," he said. "I know how busy you good people are, and I am delighted to see so many of you here tonight. It is I who am honored, deeply honored, by your presence. And may I say how proud I am of your distinguished president, Des Roach." He nodded to Roach, who smiled modestly all around. "I want to tell your friends, Des, that your assistance has been most effective in the Senate in helping to squeeze off and make non-effective our hypocritical relations with slave states, where our embassies and consulates have so easily been infiltrated by enemies who seek the downfall of our beloved republic. Des, my hat is off to you, and I am always ready to do what I can, little as it may be, to help you in your great patriotic effort."

Roach's smile broadened under this assault. His cheeks reddened with pure pleasure. "Thank you, Senator. Compared to your great influence throughout the country, my own is insignificant."

"We all have something to contribute," Bentley said.

Roach cleared his throat. "Ladies and gentlemen, with your permission I shall set aside tonight's agenda so we may hear from Senator Bentley. Sir."

"I don't have much time," Bentley said. It was interesting how the flavor of his way of speaking changed from the staccato conversational style to the more formal style of address, and back again. "Have to catch a train at ten. Always on the run, you know." He laughed a little. "I thought you might have some questions, which I will be glad to answer if I can. Is that okay with you, Des?"

Roach said that was fine with him. He asked for questions. The man with a toothbrush mustache beside me raised his hand. "Yes, Bud?"

Bud asked Bentley why Cotter was planning a rally in Madison Square Garden. Bud obviously took it for granted that Bentley had some working knowledge of the inside operations of the Cotterite movement, which came as a shock to me. Bentley's criticism of Cotter, made in the cab, left me with the impression that Bentley had suddenly become anti-Cotter. I had a lot to learn about senatorial politics.

"Good question," Bentley said. "Such a rally would never be held in Richland. Not necessary here. Not with so many fine folk as you keeping an eye on things. New York is a special case. It is so big, and there are so many foreign elements there, that even if there were a thousand Cotter societies it would not be enough to watch out for all the ways in which the Communists are subverting our most cherished institutions. The time is ripe to dramatize to the public that there are strong methods available to cope with the Communists. You see, the public is largely uneducated about the insidious ways in which the Communists get in. They are too prone to rely upon the police organizations, such as the FBI, to do the job that only alert citizens can do. Something is needed to shock them out of their apathy and also to give them courage to act. When you think you're alone in the fight against Commies you may lack the will to fight. But, united and disciplined, we can do something about the Communist menace. That's why groups like yours are so important."

If Bentley wasn't a Cotterite, he certainly knew the Cotterite lingo. I began to speculate that perhaps Cotter had sent Bentley on this mission to Richland to raise support for a new general tactic of public rallies. I could not believe Bentley's disclaimer that Richland had such well-organized societies that a public rally was not needed.

I anticipated the question of another man, a crew-cut rising young executive type. "I am not so sure that Richland doesn't need a similar rally," he said. "We're having a tough time right now in getting the school board to start a Junior Cotterite society in the high schools." This was the first time I had heard of a movement to organize youth at the high school level. I made a mental note to mention this in a Dispatch story.

Bentley clasped his hands tightly. No doubt he wasn't accustomed to having his authority disputed. "I'm not a prophet, as you know," he said. That little laugh again. "I don't like to predict the future. Circumstances do change. But as I see it now, we've got Richland pretty well sewed up. What I mean is, I wouldn't like to hear of any talk about a rally being held here."

His point apparently got across, for Bud said he understood. The third man's hand was going up, but Bentley turned to Roach. "Des, it's been great being with you, and I want you to know how much I appreciate the opportunity of being with you very very much." He stood up and went around the circle shaking every hand. "Let's go, Art."

I followed Bentley into the hall. Roach scurried after us, begging Bentley to come again. The taxi was there, which surprised me since I couldn't remember hearing Bentley ask the driver to wait.

"What was that all about?" I asked him as soon as I got in the cab, this time behind him.

Bentley seemed to shrivel into the corner. "All that nonsense about a rally in Richland. Who do they think I am, Cotter's press agent?"

I swallowed hard and asked my question. "Are you?"

Bentley squeezed the bridge of his nose and rubbed his eyes. "When you've been around as long as I have, Art, you'll realize it takes a lot of running to pay off old I.O.U.s. Especially when you don't have much time left."

"Then this was an assignment from Cotter?"

"Let's say that Cotter never forgets his friends." He opened his eyes and looked at me with pleading written all over his face. "Art, I did you a favor taking you to that meeting. You got some inside knowledge of the workings of a local society, didn't you?"

I agreed that the experience was valuable.

"Then you will consider my visit, any mention of it, even to your closest friend, as strictly off the record?"

"Sure," I said. "But tell me, Senator, are you or are you not a Cotterite?"

"No," he replied. He closed his eyes again.

On Main Street the traffic was unusually thick for a weekday evening. As we neared the Prospect Hotel I saw the reason. A crowd of perhaps a hundred was gathered on the sidewalk. One matronly woman with a mink stole carried a sign reading *Run Again, Senator Bentley.*

I seized the opportunity to question Bentley about his future. "I understand you are available for an important appointment," I said.

"I have several interesting propositions. But I haven't made up my mind."

"Perhaps you will return to the university."

Bentley laughed. "I can guess who told you that. No, I can't go back to the university, and I wouldn't even if I could. President Canning is too nice a guy to have me happen to him." The cab edged to the curb. Bentley welcomed his admirers, stopping here and there to sign an autograph. He kissed the woman in a mink stole, said a few words. She went with him into the hotel.

Chapter Sixteen

Jo's ebony velvet housecoat swished on the deep purple plush of the carpet. She seemed to glide, like a frocked Bolshoi dancer, to her parlor. "You're just in time," she said over her shoulder. She went before me down the two steps that led into a pit in which a coal fire blazed in a cup-like brazier. Blue smoke curled into the inverted funnel above the flames.

"Nice apartment," I said.

She glanced around with unabashed pride. "It is cosy, isn't it?" She looked up to where I was standing on the top step. Her red hair blazed in the firelight. I held her gaze a moment, all the while feeling a hot sweat breaking out on my forehead. Jo fingered the top button of her housecoat. It was a large button, a full inch wide, covered with the same black velvet as the coat. I stepped toward her. I almost fell into the pit.

Jo laughed as she steadied me. "Whoops!"

"I must like you an awful lot," I said, "to fall for you like that."

She touched my forehead. Her fingers were like cooling icicles. I pressed her hand. "That feels good, Jo. Do it again."

"A cold, miserable night like this," she replied, "and you're hot."

"Must be the rain," I said.

Jo told me to make myself comfortable in the parlor while she whipped up dinner. I offered to help, but she said no, she could manage by herself. The way she had set the stage for our first date made me feel both flattered and puzzled. The table-for-two was laden with two candles in tall silver holders, pewter plates, and immaculate linen. The only light in the parlor came from the fire and the candles. And there was something else: the faint pleasant aroma of Jo herself.

When we were seated at the table I touched the back of her smooth hand. The flame flickered in her eyes. I didn't say anything, but I hoped that my eyes conveyed my message: she was beautiful and I felt very much at home with her. We talked about Cotter for a while. I told her about my visit to Richland and my encounter with Bentley. She said that Green had been putting pressure on Gideon to come up with something that would stop Cotter's rally. Despite the gaiety of her voice, and the way she spoke brightly of the prospect that Cotter would be forced to cancel the rally on account of the continuing pressure of my articles in the Dispatch, I had the feeling that she was deeply depressed by the Cotter affair. However, I had other thoughts on my mind, so I did not ask her what else had happened while I was away.

She served chicken salad, warm rolls with coffee, then a sherbet dessert and more coffee. All through the meal, even while we talked about other things, I coddled the hope that I was not merely Jo's current partner in this rendezvous. It was atrocious, but I couldn't help it. I kept asking myself whether Gideon had often shared such an evening with Jo. Probably there had been others, maybe Dick Doyle or George Rankin. If these others had sat where I now sat Jo certainly gave no indication that she ever had eyes for anyone but myself. She began questioning me, in the most flattering way, about my years in the newspaper business, exclaiming frequently about my successes and comforting me over my failures. And all the while my thought was that Jo might be attainable after all. I suppose I was afraid of her. She belonged to that group of sophisticates who inhabited the Madison Avenue advertising and public relations world from which I felt far removed both by the Fifth Estate as my occupation and by my midwest background. I was not so naïve as to disbelieve the stories I had heard of the married Madison Avenue professionals, such as Gideon, making time with the unmarried glamour-gals such as Jo. They lived in a make-believe world where they were flung together in their work, and perhaps clung to one another for comfort and survival, as do survivors of a storm at sea clinging to a wave-tossed raft.

There was another aspect of my relationship to Jo. I had the vague, undefined feeling that this setting in which I sat with her was unreal. It was as if I was on a stage, where Jo was my leading lady, and I the hero attempting to win her hand. Was she merely playing a role, in which she was well rehearsed, the purpose of which was to cultivate the press? And, worse thought, was I still playing Gideon's puppet by participating in this all-too-obvious attempt of Jo's to retain my professional support by enticing me into her parlor? But this was cheap of me, I told myself, and unworthy of Jo. Why could I not take this meeting for what she said it was: a business conference, no more?

After we had finished eating, Jo showed me the products of her hobby: five wide brass plates, each embellished by a classic scene. Jo pointed to the plates on the wall opposite the fire pit. One plate pictured Diana, protector of the hunter, a long bow in her hand, the flowing gown draped over her left shoulder, her hair in Greek mode, long and ribbon-tied, breasts bare.

In her bedroom Jo led me to an archaic carved wooden chest. From a drawer she removed her metal-craft tools. She held up a hammer. "This is for chasing." Another odd-looking hammer was, she said, for planishing. Then a mallet, files, an awl, dividers, a hammer with a round ball on the end, and a punch with a long sharp point. A steel stake was shaped like a light bulb. Jo placed a square copper sheet on the stake. She hammered the sheet around the edges, and soon the metal took the form of a plate. The hammer blows cracked through the room.

"Don't the neighbors complain?" I asked.

I helped her put the tools away. "It's an interesting hobby," she said. "Helps pass the long evenings."

"I never thought of you being alone," I told her. I was being honest. It had simply never occurred to me that Jo, the cosmopolite, could be lonely.

She placed the final tool, a mallet, in the drawer. She laughed and looked up at me, a question on her face. "Do you think I entertain every night?" She sat down on the floor and gathered the housecoat under her legs. "I suppose, working nights, you don't know what it's like to be alone?"

I knelt beside her, balancing with one hand on the edge of the queen-sized bed. Her warm arms reached around my shoulders, pulling me to her.

When I engaged her warm body close to mine, she clung to me. I felt her back through the velvet and traced the arch under her raised arm. She pushed me back and turned her face away from me. "No, Art, no." I tried to hold her, but she broke from my grasp. She sprang to her feet and smoothed the housecoat over her thighs. "Let's go to the parlor," she said. "It's safer there."

We sat together on the love seat before the fire. Jo shrank into a corner. "I think the woman has to be the strong one, don't you?" she asked, not looking at me but at the leaping flames.

After a long silence, the flames died on the black coals and the pit was dark. I reached for her and she came into my arms. The smoke rose like incense from the fire. Then, far away, her telephone rang. Jo sprang up to answer it. She returned less than a minute later.

"Silenus," Jo said. "Pythia students are protesting in Washington Square."

Chapter Seventeen

He was hardly more than nineteen. With one commanding gesture: arm stiff, outthrust, he quieted the crowd. His voice boomed over a loudspeaker.

"Shush now. Be quiet now."

Everywhere, under the enormous Washington arch and the brightly lit park around it, in the brilliance of television camera lights and out of it, the Pythia University students hushed and were quiet.

"That's better," the boy said. He was standing at the top of the stairs leading to the main university entrance. "Let's have it quiet. Are you with me?"

The students, hundreds of them, roared "We're with you!"

A blond girl, standing next to the boy with the microphone, tossed a Dispatch into the air. A boy with an embryo beard clapped his hands over his head. The students screamed as if in pain. "Cotter no! Pythia, yes!"

The boy with the microphone called for quiet again. He looked around the gesturing crowd. His unruly hair tossed wildly in the slight breeze. "Did you hear? Did you hear? Harry Cotter is coming to town!" Yells of protest rippled all the way to the other side of the square. "You know old Harry? Of course you do. He's coming here, he is here, to tell you what to study and who you can have as a teacher. He's coming to tell you what books you can't read." An upturned palm, raised slowly over the boy's head, elicited a brazen shout.

I was standing next to Jo and Silenus inside the university's main hall, behind the closed glass doors. We were only a few feet behind the boy outside who was holding the crowd's attention. "One of your students?" I asked Silenus. He nodded.

"Cotter has come," the speaker went on, shouting now, "to tell us that we ought to drop the bomb first, and get it over with, and where do you think old Harry will be when the first bomb falls. In New York? No!

He will be safe in the hills! His mountain retreat, that's where he will be, where he has dug a safe shelter for himself. How many of you will he take with him? That's right. Not one. Because the Cotterites will be there, all his pals, all his top command. Does he care about you? Does he really care about you?"

Again the students roared at the boy's command, their angry stubborn voices joined and contorted in a chorus of *"No! No!"*

Jo touched my arm. "Gideon," she said, pointing. He was there, under the arch, talking to a Dispatch photographer.

"Who's afraid of Old Harry?" the boy cried out. He waited for effect, his hands on his hips, his black leather jacket open to the cold night wind. "Not one of us!" he cried. "We'll read the books we want to read, and if they fire one of our teachers because of him--what?" He cocked an ear to catch a muffled shout from someone in the crowd. "We won't let them!"

Again and again the students cheered their leader. The boy needed no encouragement. Now he really poured it on, punctuating his exclamations with fist-clenching and wild mid air punches. "Who is Cotter to push us around? Who appointed him? I'll tell you. He appointed himself, or should we say anointed? By what right? I'll tell you. No right at all, because Cotter is a Communist himself!"

Holding aloft a copy of the Dispatch bearing the headline SHOCKING! which surmounted my story on the Moscow thesis, the boy surveyed his audience with cold calculation. "Yes! Old Harry went to a university in Moscow. Old Harry wrote about the Communists. He praised them! It's all here, in the paper. And Old Harry wants to hold a rally in the Garden. I'll tell him now. We will be there!"

A burst of cheers. The students surged forward. "We will be there!"

The student ranks broke. Quickly, as if guided by some unseen commanding power, they lined up, two abreast. From out of nowhere placards were raised high. The students began to march, their thousand feet stamping in rhythm, their serpentine mass pressing forward around the arch and back again. Their placards proclaimed their protest:

Cotter Is a Communist.
Kick Cotter Off the Campus
See You in the Garden
Freedom Yes, Cotter No

Several photographers circled the marchers. The flash of their bulbs lit the inscriptions on the Arch honoring the *Father of Our Country*.

Out of the Arch's shadow Gideon came up the Pythia staircase. Silenus opened a door to let him in. While he was wearing a heavy black trench coat, his head had been bared to the chill high wind. "Let's go," Gideon said. "Let's join them." We exited to the stairway and marched down the steps. At the bottom, Jo linked arms between Gideon and Silenus. I walked behind them chanting my own private hymn of hate against Gideon's insulting intrusion of himself between me and Jo. I could forgive Silenus, for he was as joyful as I had ever seen him, patting Jo's hand and chatting amiably with her. Once, as we pushed our way through the line of marchers, he turned and called, "Coming, Art?' I waved my assurance that I would follow wherever he led. I was really following Jo, for I had come close, very close, and nothing would separate her from me.

In the Midas Tavern, a long narrow slot with booths along one wall, a bar on the other, we huddled together, Silenus and I on one side of the table, Gideon beside Jo on the other. After we ordered drinks Silenus asked me what I thought of the boy leader of the demonstration. His name was David Morgan.

"A born leader of men," I responded.

"I know the type," Gideon said. "The Army is full of them."

Silenus reared back. His beard waggled. "Whoa now! Just a minute."

"I knew a boy like him once," Gideon went on, ignoring Silenus. "It was in Korea. All tongue."

"David Morgan, he can think too," Silenus said. "Oh, I admit he's glib. But he knows what he's up to. You notice how he controlled every movement of the crowd?"

A waitress in a black outfit placed our drinks on the table. Gideon laid a ten-dollar bill beside his glass. His half-lidded glare punctured the distance between him and Silenus.

"What the hell's the big idea, Silenus?" Gideon muttered.

The professor was quaffing his vodka with distinct relish. He wiped his mustache. "That should be obvious to a professional like you, Gideon."

"What did you expect to accomplish?"

Silenus was silent. He put down his drink. He reached across the table with deliberate slowness and patted Jo's hand. "Tell you what, my dear, what say you and I lose your friend here and you come to my pad?" His eyes crinkled wickedly.

I laughed to myself over Gideon's discomfiture. His face was white. His lips moved silently over who knows what epithets.

Jo gently but firmly removed Silenus' hand. "I'd love to see your pad, Silenus." She blinked coquettishly at him. "You know I'm madly in love with you."

Silenus grinned. "I know, dear, but why did you have to tell your friend?"

"Just remember who's paying you, Silenus," said Gideon. He looked as if he was being strangled. He said little after that, although Silenus, Jo and I continued to discuss the character of David Morgan.

The leader of the demonstration, Silenus told us, was chairman of a student civil liberties group. He had long been a prime mover in peace petitions, and had often organized student rallies in support of favored professors who were in danger of being fired.

"Tonight's demonstration," I suggested, "was no doubt the star in his crown."

"Biggest thing he's ever done," Silenus agreed. However, he went on, the main purpose of the demonstration was to attract publicity for the anti-Cotter cause. He admitted that, as the power behind the scenes, he had informed the newspapers and television stations well in advance.

Gideon glowered into his drink. "Silenus is the model mercenary," he said. "Available for the fray if the price is right."

"Oh, lay off," Silenus growled.

"He doesn't care a fig for honor and glory," Gideon fumed remorselessly. "Just for cold cash. A man of pure and independent morals, that's our professor, the fearless foe of both Communism and Cotter." He slapped the table. The glasses jingled. "And who wouldn't for fifty an hour?"

Silenus coolly lifted his glass. "I'll tell you one thing, Gideon. If I stop working for you now, this minute, you won't get a single Pythia student attending Cotter's rally."

"Who needs them?" Gideon asked.

"You will, my friend. As many students as you can get."

"Who asked you to interfere?"

Jo, who through all this had been wringing her gloves, gazed levelly at me for support as she said, "If we're going to fight among ourselves we're never going to stop Cotter." She clasped and unclasped her hands. "Silenus, you ought to know better."

Silenus grinned triumphantly. "I *am* sorry, my dear. You understand, I have nothing against Gideon personally."

"Like hell you don't," Gideon muttered.

"I do want you all to meet David Morgan," Silenus went on as if Gideon had said nothing. "He should be in my pad by now. I asked him to come see me as soon as he could." He spoke to all of us, but he looked only at Gideon. "I'm inviting everyone. We'll have some coffee and--"

Gideon hollered for the waitress. It wasn't like him to be rude in a restaurant or bar. When the girl came over he handed her a tip and went with her to the bar to pay the bill.

Silenus leaned across the table. "What's got into Gideon?" he asked Jo.

"Orders from on high," she replied. "Meaning Mr. Fletcher. The order is that Cotter must be stopped. But how? Gideon doesn't have the faintest idea what to do next. And Mr. Green, he's been putting on the pressure too."

Gideon was putting on his overcoat. He brought over Jo's, the white leather one that I liked best. He helped her into it. Not another word was said as we left the Midas and went to Silenus' apartment. The first thing I noticed was that the Duchess painting was missing. David Morgan jumped off the sofa to greet Silenus. "Were you all at the rally?" he asked eagerly. We assured him that all of us had been there. Congratulations were in order, and David received these with what almost amounted to heel-clicking. He was shorter than he had appeared under the arch's shadow, and older too. His face, which had been as youthful-looking in the glare of the TV lights, was etched with small hard lines. And yet, gone from his voice was that commanding depth which had swayed the crowd to his will.

"It went alright?" he asked Silenus, his eyes dark and intent with excitement.

"It went fine, David."

"Perfect performance," said Gideon, smirking.

David kept his gaze on Silenus, his eyes begging further appreciation. "Was that you wanted, Professor?"

Silenus patted David's shoulder. "It was exactly what I wanted, David." Silenus excused himself and went off to the kitchen.

David laughed, a giggle. His black leather jacket crackled as he folded his arms.

"Professor Stoddard, he's alright, isn't he?" the student asked.

"Great guy," Gideon said sourly.

"You can say anything you want in his class," David went on. "You can talk about anything. Nuclear war, race, politics. Anything."

"I'll bet you say anything, too, David," said Gideon.

"Take the peace issue." David's voice became feverish. "We're all for the nuclear ban treaty, and its extension to all nations, because nuclear war would be mass suicide. That's what Professor Stoddard says." He looked up at the ceiling. "War as an instrument of national policy is anachronistic. That's exactly what he says. And he's right. And take the issue of military power--"

"You said it!" Gideon cried. He looked at David with new admiration. "Soon the military will be running the country."

"Where does the dictator begin?" David asked, looking at all of us as if he thought he knew the answer to that one. "By controlling the schools," he answered with a glint of triumph.

"Of course," Gideon aid. He sat down on the sofa. "The military dictates government policy. Civilians are yes-men. One mention of Russia and we run for cover. If it weren't for the common sense of the average American, well, Cotter would long since have taken over."

"Taken over what?" I ventured. I wondered what Cotter had to do with militarism, and also what caused Gideon to be so wound up about the threat of too much power in the hands of the military.

Jo sat down beside David. She patted his hand. "Doesn't it scare you, David," she asked, "to be able to manipulate a crowd the way you did?"

David shook his head, as much as to get his long hair out of his eyes as to indicate he wasn't scared a bit. "I just tell them the truth," he said. "Every group has to be led. Someone has to point them in the right direction."

"And a little child shall lead them," said Gideon.

"How many students do you expect to have at the Garden?" I asked David.

"At least a hundred, Mr. James."

There was a whistle from the kitchen. Silenus came in with a tray of cups and saucers. David stood up and clicked his heels. He begged to be excused. He had an eight o'clock class in the morning. As David was leaving, closing the door behind him, Gideon said "Our hero."

I telephoned Al at the City Desk. He said he didn't need a story on the Pythia demonstration. The photographer had obtained the necessary details. The Dispatch would run a photo with caption. "See you tomorrow," Al said.

Silenus phoned for a taxi to take Jo to her apartment. As soon as she left, Silenus went into his bedroom and returned with the Duchess. Gideon and I helped him return her to her place of honor.

Chapter Eighteen

Gideon, Silenus and I sat glumly on the sofa staring at the Duchess' enigmatic smile. It had not been my intention to stay, and I had in fact offered to take Jo home, but Silenus insisted that we three men had a lot to talk about. "There isn't much time left," he had said. "Not if we're going to stop Cotter's rally." Now, in response to his command, we were trying to think up some sort of strategy. Gideon called it *brainstorming.* Whatever it was, it wasn't successful.

Gideon yawned hugely. Silenus closed his eyes and rested his forehead in his hand. Because the apartment was stifling hot I removed my jacket. A piece of paper fell from a pocket. It was the Frontier Fathers brochure that Bentley had given me in Richland. Gideon picked it up and read the title: *Memo to High School Students.*

"Ever read it?" I asked Gideon.

He shook his head, then read the first paragraph. Silenus grabbed the brochure from Gideon's hand. "Let me see that!" He glanced through a few pages. "It's the same thing!" he shouted, his voice a curious blend of horror and triumph. He raced to his bedroom. I heard drawers being slid open and banged shut. Gideon kept on examining the Duchess. I poured myself a cup of coffee.

Silenus roared back into the parlor, his wild hair tossing. He waved a dark blurred book.

"What's that?" I asked.

Silenus lowered the book slowly and stared at it as if he had discovered a new scripture, like Joseph Smith and the Golden Tablets. "This is it!" he exclaimed.

He tossed the book toward Gideon, who fumbled the catch, then retrieved the book from the floor. He turned the book around, ran his fingers over the leather cover.

"Another of your treasured Cotter antiques?" Gideon asked.

"This is one you can't resist, Gideon." Silenus picked up the Memo brochure from his chair. "This Frontier Fathers tract, I knew I had read it before. I couldn't remember exactly where. Then I placed it. Turn to Page Seventy in the book, Gideon."

"First tell me what it is."

"Pythia's R.O.T.C. manual, used by our student Army unit."

Gideon fingered the black cover. He seemed transfixed.

"Hello, Gideon," Silenus said quietly.

Gideon looked up, eyes misted. "Sorry, I was thinking of David Morgan. You know, he reminded me of a boy I once knew in Richland. What was his name? He sighed, looked up at the ceiling. "Orson Barney. Improbable fellow. Orson was always looking at me as David looked at you, Silenus. From my class to my office, from my office across the quadrangle, to the library, Orson dawdled at my heels."

"What did he want?" I asked.

"To learn more than I was willing to teach," Gideon replied. The sweat suddenly stood out on his forehead. "You should have seen me. Like I was being shadowed by a private detective. I'd try to lose him in the corridors, dodging into the men's room, but Orson was always waiting for me when I came out."

"I know the type," said Silenus.

"I didn't dislike him," Gideon went on. "But he had an oppressive mask of a face. Know what I mean? Well, I played campus tag with him for weeks."

"If he only needed help--" I began.

"Help? He needed a psychiatrist! Trouble with Orson was he was a greedy burglar. Always wanting to pick my brains. Silenus, what does that kind want?"

"Knowledge free of charge," Silenus answered.

"I failed him repeatedly," Gideon said. "He was a masochist. Never gave up. Always came back for more punishment. Always asked me, why, why, why." Gideon gazed at the Duchess.

Silenus reached over and took the Army manual from Gideon's lap. He handed the book to me. "Gideon seems a mite foggy," he said. "Will you please do the chore of turning to Page Seventy."

I opened the manual to the page. Immediately I recognized what was there. "It's a reprint of the Frontier Fathers brochure!"

"Word for word," Silenus said. "Read us a few paragraphs. I have an idea. But first we ought to get the full flavor."

I began to read, starting at the top of the page:

While public education is dedicated to freedom,
equality and self-government, and to preservation of
our free-enterprise way of life, occasionally there are
Communists in the schools.

I looked up to spot the effect upon Gideon. While he appeared to have heard, he was looking through me rather than at me. "Something David said," Gideon muttered. "They have to have a leader. You know, I believe that. Did I ever tell you? Once, in Korea, there was this kid, name of Lenny. I forget his last name. I was a private then. Corporal Javits was leading our patrol. I remember we were in the woods. The firing stopped, I elbowed into the scrub, right onto Javits. He was bleeding from the head. No, I thought, he can't be dead, because Javits is the leader. I turned him over and I saw he was dead. He was dead, Silenus, Art. I lay there, I don't know, a long time. Then Lenny came up. When he saw that Javits was dead, he vomited. I said, 'Let's get the hell out of here,' and I led the way, you know, telling the others to follow me. We got into this ravine. The firing started again. I looked up, the others were crawling away. Lenny was leading them. I said, 'Follow me,' but they followed Lenny, only--" Gideon's voice drifted away. He closed his eyes.

Silenus and I exchanged puzzled glances. Silenus' turned-down mouth told me he was thinking what I was: that Gideon was attempting to delay the reading of the tract, like a fearful son delays reading his dead father's will. Nevertheless, I read on:

You may have been exposed to the subversive
influence of one of those Communists in your
years in elementary or high school. He or she
may have been one of your teachers, or your
librarian, even your principal.

Gideon worked his mouth. "Not the Army!" he cried. "Not the Army!"

Silenus, his forehead furrowed, obviously worried now over Gideon's agony, leaned forward, clasping his hands before him. "Why not the Army, Gideon? Why not the Army?"

Gideon opened his eyes halfway. "Remember the indoctrination lectures, Silenus? Who spoke out against the Communists the most? The chaplains!"

"They were professionally interested in God, Gideon," Silenus said.

I shrugged. I attributed Gideon's increasing distraction to the lateness of the hour, nearly midnight, and to the strain he had been under for the past few hours. I read aloud another paragraph:

Of course you may have no way of knowing which
of your teachers or school administrators was a
Communist---they are too clever for that. However,
in insidious ways, you may have been indoctrinated
in Communist ideology (another word for ideas).

"The Catholic chaplain," Gideon said, his voice low, guttural, "compared Communism to the anti-Christ. The Protestant chaplain, he thought the godlessness and atheism of Communism were almost as bad as sports on Sunday." Gideon laughed a half-giggle. "Those chaplains, they argued with each other for an hour. They cancelled each other out. We were then supposed to know enough about Communism to die bravely for America."

I slapped the book on my knee. "Gideon," I shouted, "shut up a minute so I can read this nonsense."

Gideon looked off toward the Duchess. "At Richland University," he said, "they had these courses on the meaning of freedom and democracy--"

Ignoring him, I read on:

Think! Were you told that the Communist takeover
was 'an agrarian reform movement'? Did a teacher
say that 'peaceful co-existence' was compatible with
Americanism? Did another advocate a socialistic
economic system for the United States?

"I used to get a regular stream of notes from the dean," Gideon went on, "suggesting that I emphasize the longing for freedom apparent in Russian literature. You know what my students emphasized in their papers? The Russian's love for his land!"

I continued reading:

Many of the history books, some of the social
studies books, were written, or at least inspired,
by Communists or former Communists. You
were not told this, were you? No one was.
No one is told.

"I told my students," Gideon said, "that as far as Russian literature was concerned, it was difficult to guarantee that the authors, such as Pasternak, were dyed-in-the-wool Communists. Those Russians, they're sneaky about it!"

I read more:

What can you do about it? Report these teachers
and these books to your parents. Ask them to
complain to the responsible, loyal leaders in your
community. Any officer of your local Harry M.
Cotter Society will be glad to help you.

Gideon clapped his hands. "Hey, Silenus, we didn't need Cotter around at Richland University to tell us what to do, did we? Seven Communists with one blow!"

Silenus snickered. "Things aren't much different today, are they, Gideon? Only the method has changed. Now we don't denounce the Commies to the university president. We turn the case over to Harry Cotter."

I closed the book. Whether Gideon had heard another word of what I read I cannot say. Now, like a drunk, he tried to restrain a laugh. "I hear that Cotter thinks *Swan Lake* is subversive. Did you hear what he said about the Bolshoi? Most of them are spies. Well, maybe he's right. Who can tell?"

"Gideon's sick," I said to Silenus.

"Just tired," Gideon countered.

"Let's hit the hay," I said.

Silenus laughed. He ruffled his unruly hair. "We have to decide what to do with Page Seventy."

"Do with it?" I asked. "Who wants to do anything with it? Cotterite material in an Army manual, what's so unusual about that?"

Again Silenus hollered. "Art's the one who's tired, Gideon. Weren't you listening, Art, when you read that stuff?"

"Gideon was making too much noise."

"Tell him, Silenus," said Gideon with a yawn.

"Tell him yourself, Gideon. I'll turn off the time-clock. Save you money."

Gideon seized the R.O.T.C manual from my hand. "Art, I'll tell you what I'd like to do with this damn book. I'd like to burn it. Damn you, Silenus! Why did you have to bring it out?"

"That's the way the ball bounces, Gideon."

"Thanks a lot." Gideon turned to me. His face was sallow, lined with fatigue. "What we have to do, Art, what I have to do, is to take this manual to Mr. Green. He will say take it to Jo. I will make copies of Page Seventy and give one to Jo. She will pass it along to Fletcher. The great pooh-bah will send it back, saying we can't use it. I'll take it back to Green. The chief will say we've got to use it, because Fletcher already called him and said that Cotter's rally has to be turned into an anti-climax. So Mr. Green, he tells me to do something. I do it."

He was leaving me way out in the dark. His passion displayed no common sense. "I'm stupid," I said. "Do what?"

Gideon stood up and pounded Silenus' shoulder. "Do what?" he cried. He paced over to the Duchess, looked fondly at her. "We protest! We holler like hell! What's the Army doing, telling our boys that the public schools are being run by Communists! It's an insult, that's what it is! They can't get away with it. We'll make them apologize!"

"Them?" I asked. "Who?"

Gideon swiveled about. He withered me with a condescending glance. "The Army, of course!" he fairly screamed.

"What are you looking at me for?" I asked.

"We need you, buddy boy. We need you."

Silenus was on his feet. "That's the spirit! We decide here and now to take on Uncle Sam's Army!"

I waved my hands about. "You can't do *that*. What can you do? The Army's the Army."

Silenus tugged his ear, mocking me. "A noble statement! Not helpful. It should be clear to you by now, Art. We go to Washington, demand that the Army apologize to the teachers of America, our most noble breed. We spread the word around the Washington press, call a press conference, give the reporters copies of our letter to the Secretary of the Army. He'll have to say *something*."

I was pulling off my shoes as he spoke. I massaged my burning feet. "So says something. Maybe. What good will that do? How does that stop Cotter?"

Gideon pounced and brooded over me. "You're the one who's tired, buddy boy. Get this. The Army has been using Cotter's propaganda. This piece was written for high school kids. Now it gets into an official Army manual for university units. God knows how many other such manuals it's in. Where does the Army get off maligning a quarter million American teachers. The teachers will be mad as hell. You just don't say that kind of thing about the schools, the country's pride. Better to blaspheme, to insult mother. Shades of the Adamses, both John and Quincy! Do you know how many loyal Americans went through public schools? Almost everybody! They've been insulted too. Will anybody admit they're Communists, that they've been indoctrinated in Communism? In the first place, to admit that would be to admit they were stupid, that their mothers were stupid, and their fathers were stupid, because morality is taught in the home, isn't it? Worse, nobody, but nobody, is ever going to admit they have ever been, not for a minute, slightly pink."

Silenus applauded Gideon's performance. "Great, Gideon. Great! Cotter will surrender now. Page Seventy will be his undoing."

I began to get the point. Page Seventy, seen in the light that Gideon saw it, was an Army mistake. It was also a mistake upon the part of the Frontier Fathers, the extremist Cotterite group that found a way to get the tract into the Pythia R.O.T.C. manual. Gideon's protest could catapult him into the national limelight. I yawned and couldn't stop yawning. I was too tired to pursue the matter.

I told Gideon and Silenus I would go along with the protest after clearing it with my Dispatch editor. We adjourned the session. Silenus raised his hand. "Partners in revolt," he said, "I salute you." He retired to his bedroom.

In the darkness, stretched out on the sofa, I listened to Gideon's deep breathing as he twisted and turned on the Murphy bed. I kept thinking what Gideon proposed was that we lance a mighty big windmill. I wondered about his strange behavior as I was reading Page Seventy. Gideon's dislike of the Army was almost an obsession. A car passed in the street. The Midas' blue light blinked on the window pane. Suddenly I was reminded about Jo.

"Gideon?"

"Yes, Art?"

"Wood Jo come with us to Washington?"

"Sure."

Why sure? Was Gideon even then thinking of her, as I was, and of the opportunity Washington would present? Just the thought of being near Jo filled me with fear. Yes, fear. Because she was Gideon's girl. Or was she?

"I had lunch with Jo the other day," I said, baiting him.

His voice was hushed, betraying his jealousy. "Is that so?"

"Yes, and I'm going to be seeing a lot more of her." I waited, breath abated, for his response.

"You wouldn't be thinking of taking her away from me?"

"From a married man?"

"There's a lot about me you don't know."

"What are you afraid of, Gideon?"

I heard only his full-bodied breathing. After a long while he said, "Don't push me too far, Art."

"I'm sorry," I said. "I'm sorry for you if you're in love with Jo."

"Are *you*?"

I pondered that for a moment. Love was one thing, lust another. How often this past week, since that day I had lunch with her, did I have a vision of her, coming to me, approaching me. How often I had imagined her beside me. Was I in love with her? I suppose I was. What claim could Gideon legitimately have upon her? None whatever.

"I am in love with her," I said.

"Then I am sorry for you, because Jo and I, we may have plans."

"What plans?"

His bed creaked. His voice came across the room in a bitter blast. "Don't touch her, Art. Don't touch her!"

I lay silent for a long while. Gideon's breathing was easier. I swore silently at him. If Gideon thought I was afraid of him! And then it began to get to me that he had taken for granted that I would go to Washington. Gideon always took me for granted. Well, the hell with him. I wasn't his patsy. Not like Lenny, the poor kid in Korea.

"Gideon, what happened to Lenny?"

"Who?"

"Lenny, the boy in the Army in Korea."

"He died."

"How?"

I really didn't expect an answer, but another surprising thing about Gideon was you never could tell.

"It was the Army's fault," he began, his voice clear, confident. "We were in this bunker, which our outfit had just captured. Did you ever smell burnt flesh? Well, that's what it smelt like. Lenny was lying down next to me. There was a shell hole in front of us and we were firing through it. Lenny's hands were shaking as he switched magazines, so I asked him, he was such a kid, if he was scared."

Gideon was silent for a moment. His breathing came in hard lumps. "That's when it happened. Lenny threw his carbine down, I mean threw it. You could see the yellow on his face. I told him to get the hell back in position, but he wouldn't move, didn't say anything, just lay there like he was made of stone. Then a machinegun opened up on us and I backed off from the hole and waited for it to stop. When it did, when the bullets stopped banging off the concrete, I lay down and began firing through the hole. I yelled for Lenny to hand me another magazine, and then I got this gas in my eyes and stopped firing and wiped my eyes. Lenny said to me, 'What are you crying for?' I didn't look at him, just as I heard a mortar coming. I yelled at Lenny. I flipped back, away from the hole, and then the place seemed to heave up."

Gideon labored for breath. I glanced over at him. It took me a while to sit up on the sofa and place my feet on the floor. Gideon lay rigid in the blue Midas light, his hands under his head, looking straight up.

"It happened so fast," he said. "I don't know how long it was, must have been only a minute or so, when I looked over, and Lenny was there under a part of the roof. He was buried in it. I found him at last, there under the rubble. Poor kid. He didn't have a chance."

"He was dead?"

"I started firing again. The gun got hot in my hands. I ran out of ammo."

"Lenny didn't get out of the way?" I asked. "Or he wasn't able?"

Gideon yawned. "It was the Army's fault, putting in a boy to do a man's job."

The Midas lamp went out. I lay back on the sofa. As I was falling asleep I was still wondering why Lenny refused to shoot.

Chapter Nineteen

Hatless, arms akimbo, Gideon stood on the rear deck of the ferry. His long straight graying black hair blew over his forehead. His unbuttoned dark blue raincoat flapped in the brisk Hudson River breeze. He gazed at the retreating Manhattan skyline. "I never get tired looking at it," he said.

We were on our way to Gideon's house in Rosewood, New jersey. It was two days after our midnight conference with Silenus. Everything was prepared for our flight to Washington that evening. Silenus and Jo were going with us, and Mary Wright, Gideon's girl-Friday, too.

"Don't you think it looks like a dragon?" Gideon asked, pointing across the river to Manhattan. I squinted. Manhattan did indeed take on the shape of a dragon: the raised wicked head of the Wall Street district, the dragon's tongue of Battery Park licking the bay, the bony torso north of Washington Square, the spiked tail of the uptown skyscrapers.

Near the Jersey Central piers in Hobocken a sign flashed in high white letters: *Cotter...Cotter...Cotter.* "Even on my way home," Gideon said, "there's no escape from him." Now another line of lights spelled out, below Cotter's name: *The Nation's Choice.*

"Very apropos," I said, "even if it does advertise grapefruit."

The ferry tilted, weaved, like a drunk on a train. Horn shrieking, the ferry turned north to circle a tall rusty freighter sloughing slowly to the sea. A brassy sun burnished the bay, struck gold on seagull wings. The Statue of Liberty, green with time, lifted her dark silent torch and the torch passed high like a fairy's wand over the piers where black webbed cranes bent like storks over cross-barred ships.

Our boat's broken boards clattered. The ferry barged against high wharf trunks, straightened out. The engines roared in reverse. The ferry moved slowly against the greasy concave buttress. A swarthy sweating man spun the ferry's spoked wheel. Corroded chains coruscated. The gangplank banged. The accordion gate parted and condensed. We crossed under the verdigris-coated arch.

On the local one-twenty train to Rosewood, Gideon flicked lint from the worn green mohair of the coach's seat. He sat down, lowered the shade, closed his eyes. I lifted my bag onto the overhead rack. Far-off windows of Bayonne flashed in the sun. The train clacked over the bay bridge, rattled into Elizabethport, stealthily crept across the tracks of the north-south line. Gideon seemed asleep.

We had risen early at Silenus' apartment, borrowed his electric razor, and went our separate ways. While I was at the Dispatch, Gideon phoned me to report that everything went as he anticipated. Green was delighted with Gideon's idea of demanding an Army apology for the Cotterite tract in the Pythia R.O.T.C. Manual. Green informed Fletcher, who approved the plan on condition the name of the Foundation would in no way be associated with the protest.

Green was in a dilemma. A protest by Private Citizen Gideon Pratt would open no doors to the Pentagon. A compromise was reached. Gideon drafted a letter to Louis E. Peters, Secretary of the Army, which Green signed. The letter was dispatched via airmail, special delivery, to Washington.

Still not enough. Some wire-pulling was needed. Gideon called Senator Bentley, who arranged an appointment with Secretary Peters. Jo and Mary began phoning the newspapers, the Associated Press, United Press, and television and radio stations to alert them to a press conference at the Woodrow Wilson Hotel. Mary mimeographed typewritten copies of Page Seventy, also Green's letter and a press release Gideon had written. These would be mailed to the news media.

Gideon had devoted himself without stint to these duties, even to the extent of staying overnight in Manhattan the past two nights. He did not say where. The thought flicked through my mind: had he stayed with Jo?

Cranford, Garwood, Westfield. The suburban New Jersey towns flashed by. Gideon was silent. He rested his chin in his hand, gazed out the window. Suddenly he said, "You know what I'm going to do if I pull off this Washington job?" The train crawled into Plainfield. "I'm going to ask Green to make me vice-president."

"And what if he doesn't?"

"He will."

Gideon's assurance struck me as being born more out of desperation than hope. Actually, he appeared to me to be indifferent to his fate. Perhaps fatalistic is a better word. He was never apathetic. When Silenus gave him the R.O.T.C. manual and the opportunity this presented to strike Cotter another blow, Gideon accepted the opportunity as a man with a clean conscience accepts death. He seemed unwilling, or unable, to do otherwise than to seize the opportunity that the manual made possible. I at least questioned whether action was necessary or advisable. He assumed that a protest had to be made, and since he was the only one in a position to make it, he would do it. He acted sometimes as if under the influence of some unseen diabolical power. This is not to say that he lacked self-control, for, in a way, he was one of the most controlled men I ever knew. I believe Gideon had a profound sense of mission in life.

Is mission too strong a word? I don't think so, not now, not in the light of what happened to him. He was a religious man, I gathered that much. He and Amy went to the Rosewood Episcopal Church every Sunday. Their children, Debra and Todd, attended Sunday school.

The conductor slammed open the end door. "Rosewood! Rosewood!"

From the Rosewood Station platform, set high on an embankment, I could see most of what there was to see of the town's business section. Across the narrow square was an A&P, Shaw's Hardware, Rosewood Radio, Newberry's Variety. Above Newberry's a fantastic name spelled out in foot-high gold letters: *St. John Robinson Bartholomew, Legal Service.* Next door were the seven windows of the Rosewood Medical Center. On the corner the tall twin columns of the Rosewood National Bank and Trust Company threw oblique shadows on the vaulted door. Beyond were spires of four churches, Gideon pointed out the Episcopal spire. Ivy-covered, it was the most gracious of all. We descended the dungeon-like steps to the dark concrete tunnel beneath the railway tracks, climbed the stairs to the waiting room, went by the wickets, turned right to the parking lot. Gideon raced ahead. He might have been blindfolded. I realized, with something of a shock, that Gideon had come this way twice each working day for nearly five years. It didn't fit into the picture I had of him as an unrestrained Madison Avenue type.

In his gray Ford we drove through the underpass, headed north on a street lined with beech trees, whose leaves were as dark as old varnish, and turned into a narrow winding drive. A milepost-type obelisk spelled out, vertically, *Park Terrace*. Gideon turned the Ford sharply onto the brick-topped drive of a white shingled split-level house.

When we got out, Gideon fingered the Ford's rain-spotted hood. "I'll wash it Saturday," he said apologetically. He took me around the side of the house to show me his Everlasting flowers, which looked like wax in the sun. Scuffing the curled crisp leaves on the grass, he said to me, as if I ought to do something about it, "I wish Todd would rake the lawn."

We entered the parlor from the front door, reached by a gray flagstone walk and a concrete stoop. The parlor was dead with silence. Gideon crossed the room to a lowboy stereophonic console, threw seven switches and turned five knobs. While he went into the kitchen to make coffee I surveyed the library. Books were shelved from the floor to the ceiling on either side of a red brick fireplace with a brass screen and a mantle decorated with photographs of Amy, Debra and Todd. Mostly the books ran to philosophy, religion, education, and psychology. They looked familiar. Then it came to me: these same books had lined Gideon's office at Richland University. I took down a book entitled *Familiar Operas*. Music suddenly blasted through the room. It was Bizet's symphony. The record must have been in the player, ready to roll.

I picked out a pint-size maroon-bound book labeled, in Old English type, *Prayer*. It was the *Episcopal Book of Common Prayer*. The book opened at a page marked by a purple ribbon. It was the catechism. Underlined were the words: *To keep my body in temperance, soberness and chastity.*

"We're getting Debra ready for confirmation." Gideon's voice startled me. I had not heard him approach. "Turn to Page five-seventy-six," he said.

I followed the words of the prayer as he recited them, speaking rapidly, running words together in a high thin tone: *O God, who knowest the weakness and corruptness of our nature, and the manifold temptations which we daily meet with; We humbly beseech thee to have compassion on our infirmities, and to give us the constant assistance of the Holy Spirit; that we may be effectually restrained from sin--*" Gideon hesitated. I read the final words*: and incited to our duty.*

"Oh, of course," Gideon said. "It's true, isn't it. That what you learn earliest stays with you the longest?"

I told him I had learned the answers to many of the questions in the Presbyterian shorter catechism when I was confirmed. "I can't remember a single one."

Gideon recited: "Imprint upon our hearts such a dread of Thy Judgments, and such a grateful sense of Thy goodness to us, as may make us both afraid and ashamed to offend Thee."

I complimented him upon his performance. Then a girl's voice called: "Daddy!" Debra came over. Gideon hugged her. "Hello, honey." Gideon introduced me to her. I told her I knew her seven or eight years ago. She tossed her armload of schoolbooks on the sofa. "What are you doing home today, Daddy? I thought you were a burglar." She gave me a bold accusing stare. Her pug nose tipped up with alarming impudence.

Gideon helped her out of her gray coat. "I was tired, Debra. Up late last night." His daughter pushed blond hair from her eyes. She hitched up the straps of her skirt. "Hey, Daddy! I learned a new dance. Watch." She began to clap and stomp.

Although her dancing did not fit with Bizet, Gideon clapped with her. "How about a twist?" he asked. Debra twisted vigorously, her nine-year-old body lithe and subtle. "I need the music," she said.

"Please, not now, Debra. Daddy has a headache." Debra reached up and touched his forehead. "If you're sick you should go to bed. That's what Mommy says."

He picked her up and swung her about. "I'm not *that* sick!" Debra clasped him tightly around his neck. "Daddy! Stop!" He lowered her to the floor. "Where's Todd? I want him to meet Mr. James."

She turned away pouting. "He had to stay after school." Then: "He was bad again," she said in a sing-song voice.

"What did he do?"

"I dunno. Do you want a glass of milk?" Gideon nodded. She went off to the kitchen.

"Where do they get the energy?" Gideon asked me. When Debra came back with two glasses of milk, one in each hand, and a white circle of milk around her pert lips, she handed a glass to her father. "Todd was late for school today," she said

Gideon frowned. "Is that why he had to stay after school?"

Debra raised her glass. Her brown eyes crossed as she watched the milk drain from the glass. "I dunno."

"Todd didn't go to school with you?"

Debra set down her empty glass on the coffee table. "Todd wouldn't get up, so I poured water on him. It was cold water."

Gideon patted her on the head. "You rascal!" Debra skipped from the room. Gideon took me to the basement to show me his workshop. He put on a paint-splattered apron, imprinted *Genius at Work*, and applied an electric sander to the latticed back of a dining room chair. Meanwhile he kept up a running commentary on the history of his acquisition of the saw, planer, drill and other power tools neatly arranged on board shelves above his workbench.

Suddenly they heard Debra screaming. Gideon switched off the sander. At the foot of the stairs he called up to the kitchen. "Debra! Todd! Stop that fighting. Todd, come down here."

Debra appeared at the top of the stairs. Her skirt was soaked. "Daddy, Todd splashed me!"

"Oh, that won't hurt you," Gideon said. "Tell Todd to come down."

Todd descended. "She deserved it," he said. Gideon put his arm around Todd's shoulders. "I will never ride the bus with her again," Todd said. "I'll walk."

"Then you will have to get up even earlier," Gideon said. "Sorry, Art. This is my favorite son. Todd, this my friend, Mr. James." I told Todd I had met him years before. The boy was silent. He shook my hand.

A car engine roared on the driveway. "Must be Amy," Gideon said. We quickly mounted the stairs to greet her.

"How nice to meet you again, Art." she said. "Gideon has been telling me about the exciting things you two are doing." Gideon helped her deposit a load of groceries on the kitchen table. She was still as pretty as I had seen her so many years before. Of course she was in her thirties now but she had aged gracefully. She hadn't neglected her appearance. Her long bleached-blond hair, parted in the middle, draped to her shoulders. "Well," she said with a sigh. "We might as well eat."

No sooner had I retired by myself to the parlor than I heard Amy exclaim "Oh no, no." I assumed that Gideon had told her we were leaving that evening to go to Washington. I crossed to the mantle to examine a studio portrait of Amy. It must have been taken recently. The photo showed a woman with a button-tipped nose, square jaw shallowly cleft, mouth generously wide, upper lip deeply fluted, cheeks highly arched. Altogether it was a sweet face, placid and undemanding. Apart from deepened lines at the corners of her eyes, she had changed little. She was small, not more than five feet. Her figure was doll-like, softly-rounded but with perceptible strength. She was not, knowing Gideon, what one would have expected his wife to look like. I had imagined that Amy would have matured, knowing Gideon's nature, into a woman damaged by his truculence and compliance to Madison Avenue's demand for both sophisticated manners and dominating audacity. I began to see Gideon in yet another light. He was the loving husband and father, the typical commuting suburbanite. At least this was the New Jersey Gideon. The speedy Madison Avenue manipulator and flirt was the Manhattan Gideon. I wondered whether Amy had the slightest knowledge of Gideon's other personality.

We gathered in the parlor for coffee. Even Debra and Todd knelt at the coffee table to prepare their own mixture, half coffee and half milk. There were cookies and small cakes on the table. I was about to help myself to one when Debra took my hand. Gideon's head was already bowed. Amy took my other hand, then Todd's. Gideon said the Grace Before Meat as I held Amy's and Todd's hands to complete the prayer circle: "Bless, O Father, Thy gifts to our use and us to Thy service, for Christ's sake, Amen." He spoke the words with intense deliberation, in the impressive deep clear voice that I had heard years before, when he lectured from the university stage. Amy squeezed my hand. That completed the ritual.

Debra picked up two cookies, one in each hand. Amy reprimanded her. Debra scowled and replaced one of her cookies on the plate. "You do your best," Amy said. Todd took his cup and cake toward the television, turned it on and sat down on the floor to watch. Amy touched Gideon's arm. "I still don't understand why you have to go to Washington," she said.

Gideon summarized our plot against the Pentagon.

"You will miss the Parent-Teachers meeting," she said.

Gideon winked at me. He held Amy's hand. "Dear, believe me, this is one of the most important thing I've ever done."

Amy leaned against the arm of the sofa. "Well, of course, I never did understand politics."

"It's not political, dear." Gideon patted her hand.

"Then what is it?"

I said "To me, Amy, Cotterism is a social symptom. It's a symptom of disease, a cancer eating at the character of American life. A manifestation of a vague sense of dissatisfaction with the way things are."

Amy knitted her brows. "Just because people feel insecure," she said, "I don't see why they have to blame Communism for everything."

"They need a scapegoat," I said. "They want to intimidate people."

I could see Gideon getting red. "That's a lot of nonsense," he said sharply. "I'm not excusing Cotter, but I think he's right on the basic issue, the issue of Communists infiltrating government, education, business, labor, all the rest. Maybe his methods are wrong, maybe he does think his end justifies the means, but I've never denied that Cotter was right in what he says about the seriousness of the Communist menace. After all, we have to be realistic."

"We still have to spike Cotter's guns," I replied.

"You don't have to tell *me* that," Gideon said.

Amy frowned. "Gideon, if you don't really believe--"

"I've got a job to do." Gideon sipped his coffee, not looking at me.

Amy smiled. "I haven't noticed any Communists around Rosewood," she said.

"Oh, haven't you?" Gideon asked harshly. "What about Sanderson? What about Walling?"

"He's talking about our school superintendent," Amy explained. "And the principal of the school Debra and Todd attend."

"Haven't they been telling us what the kids should study?" Gideon asked.

He ordered Debra to fetch her history book. She skipped up the stairs toward the second floor. "It's not just the books," Gideon continued. "It's the school board telling me what, as a parent, I should teach my own kids."

"They can't tell me what to do," Amy said, her voice suddenly hard-edged. "They can't run my house."

I looked at my watch. "Gideon, I think we'd better go."

Gideon finished his coffee. "Yes, I suppose. Are you ready, Amy?"

"Perhaps you'd better drive yourself, Gideon. Take the Ford. I'll need the Volkswagen."

Gideon went upstairs. He tousled Todd's hair as he went by. When he came down with his bag, Amy said "I don't mean to sound like a fretful wife, dear, but are you sure you're doing the right thing? I mean, is there no other way?"

He laughed, standing there beside her while the television blared. "Where there is no risk nothing much is gained," he said.

She grasped his arm. "But to put yourself in such a position! Cotter is no fool. What if he finds out it was you who gave Art the Moscow thesis?"

I was about to assert that I had found out about the Moscow thesis on my own, but I thought better of it.

Gideon kissed Amy on the cheek. "I have to do what I have to do, Amy. After all, Mr. Green asked me to do it, and Fletcher knows about the assignment."

Amy looked up at him, eyes pleading. "Oh, Gideon, you don't have to go through with it, not if you don't want to. I mean, this doesn't mean that much to you, does it?"

"It means my job, Amy! This is very important to Mr. Green, to the agency, to the Foundation. Mr. Green expects me to do this. And if I don't--"

Amy's eyes narrowed to cup the ready flow of tears. "I want to be brave, Gideon. I'm not just thinking of ourselves. Of the children, too."

Gideon put his arm around her. Her shoulders throbbed.

I said "I'll put your bag in the car, Gideon." I picked it up and quietly went outside. Debra followed me. I dropped the bag on the stoop. Debra picked it up and insisted on taking the bag to the Ford herself. I opened the car door and heaved it into the back seat.

"You're very strong," I said.

"You're going in an airplane, aren't you?" Debra asked. "Daddy's been on an airplane lots of times."

"Your Daddy is a very important man," I said sincerely.

"You're going to Washington, aren't you?"

I nodded. "I'll tell the President about you."

Her eyes widened. Then she frowned. "He never heard of me."

"He will when I tell him."

She threw her arms around my waist and hugged me. "I *like* you."

Todd came out with Gideon. The children kissed him goodbye. Amy waved through the screen door. As we were driving off, Debra called "Daddy, I couldn't find the book!"

Chapter Twenty

"How are ya, buddy boy?" Gideon wheeled the Ford out of Melrose Park.

I winced. "I wish you wouldn't call me that," I said.

"What's eating you?"

Crossing into North Avenue, he pulled sharply in front of a truck.

"You say Silenus is coming?" I asked.

"Said he'll meet us at the airport."

"We'll need him."

Gideon zoomed past a car. We were doing forty in a twenty-five zone.

Rosewood's business center was on our left, the Jersey Central station on our right. "Need Silenus?" Gideon asked. "Well, I think we can handle things."

"The professor's a good man to check things with."

Gideon snickered. "He thinks he knows what he's doing. But I wouldn't trust Silenus by himself in this assignment."

"How come you went on the fee bit?"

"Green hit the ceiling. But when I told him about Page Seventy he said Silenus was worth a thousand."

"Don't you think I ought to be given some of the credit?"

"Of course. Green had some suggestions for our press conference. But I think I've had enough experience along that line. We fly the kite in Washington and see which way the wind blows."

"I thought you ran the flag up a flagpole."

Gideon laughed. He beat an amber light at Walnut Street in Cranford and turned right. "Or pull the monkey's winding tail," he said.

"I wish I had your confidence, Gideon."

"Maybe you'll get into public relations yourself some day."

"I like writing."

"You can still write. After all, that's basic in public relations. You just give it a little twist."

"The monkey's tail?"

"First thing, you write to please the boss."

"What if he disagrees with you?"

"You change it to conform."

"Just like that?"

"Just like that," Gideon said. "It doesn't mean anything. You think of it like, well, baking a cake. The boss doesn't like the taste. You change the ingredients. Nothing personal in it. You're out to influence public opinion." Gideon slammed to a halt for the red light at Highway One. "As far as the writing is concerned, that's hack work. But it pays."

He hit seventy on the highway, passing everything in sight, although we had plenty of time. He overtook a trailer truck on the cloverleaf, swung in front of it as the truck's air brakes hissed, and turned into the Newark Airport drive. We left the car in a parking lot and walked to the terminal, where we bought our reserved tickets and checked our bags. As Gideon had arranged, we waited for Silenus, Jo and Mary by the shiny red Dodge revolving on a platform. At the other end of the vast concourse several panels of an illuminated poster rotated on their axels to reveal an advertisement for Pepsodent.

Silenus was the first to arrive, pushing his way through the crowd. He dropped a folded blue bag to the floor. "Damn near didn't make it," he panted. "Had to talk our young friend David Morgan out of holding another demonstration." Silenus' bag was well over the weight limit. Gideon insisted upon paying for the excess. "Sure you have enough cash?" Silenus asked.

"Except for liquor," Gideon replied.

"I only drink on the job."

"You'll be on the job in Washington."

"You call that work?" Silenus' beard waggled. "Shacking up with two beautiful broads?"

"That's not the way it's planned." Gideon handed some cash to the airline attendant behind the wide counter,

"The best laid plans, Gideon. Unless you're making prior claim."

"I'm all staked out, remember?"

"Whatever happened," the professor asked, looking around, "to good old American do-it-yourselfism, climbing to the top, making your own way, getting it while you can, otherwise known as free enterprise?"

"Silenus," I said, "are you really a socialist?"

"What political bed I sleep in is my own business," he replied darkly. "Hey, here come the girls."

Jo, her red hair upswept, her tall slim body hidden by a floppy white wool coat, broke through the surrounding crowd. Mary was behind her, a younger, smaller figure, neat, trim in her blue box coat, her blond hair fluffed in the current style. If I had to choose between the two women at that moment, I certainly would have chosen Jo. However, Gideon made the choice for me. He took Jo's bag to the weigh-in, which left me to do the same for Mary.

Our flight was announced. We walked gaily together down the long corridor to the exit. On the plane, Gideon ushered Jo ahead of him into a pair of seats, consigning Mary and I to the pair of seats across the aisle. Silenus was glad to have the next pair behind us to himself. Mary told me this was her first flight. The plane full, the engines revved up, taxied to the take-off strip, the wings shining in the setting sun. The plane slammed forward. Mary, sitting next to the window, gripped the chair's arm. I felt her hand. It was rigid, unmovable. The black-striped concrete tarmac fell away. The wheels clunked into the fuselage. Mary, jaw tense, opened her eyes. The plane slid over the square towers of Elizabeth's City Hall. The New Jersey Turnpike snaked south. Gray tassels streamed from the wings. The engines purred, propellers whirling.

"Now, that wasn't so bad, was it?" I asked Mary. She closed her eyes and sighed with relief.

Gideon was deep in conversation with Jo. He was leaning toward her, his voice low. I caught Jo's gaze. She smiled and blinked at me. I wished I was sitting beside her instead of Mary, who was fast asleep. I left her and moved away to sit with Silenus. We discussed the press conference, which Gideon had scheduled for the next morning. Silenus said he hoped for a good turnout from the Washington press corps. "We would be better off if we could use the name of the Foundation," he said. "It's ridiculous. But that's Gideon for you." He sighed. "In the good old days, if you wanted to say something, you stood on your box, gathered a crowd, and said it. Now you need a public relations man to speak for you. But when the p-r man is a scaredy-cat! I don't know. I guess I'm too old-fashioned."

I asked Silenus what he thought the chances were of getting Green's letter into the papers. "That depends upon the reaction of the Secretary of the Army," he said. "We'll need Senator Bentley's help, but I'm not sure Gideon really wants anyone's help."

"Then why did he ask you to go with him?"

Silenus stroked his beard. "I've been trying to figure that out myself. Moral support, I suppose. To tell you the truth, I'm glad he asked me. Between you and me, Art, I don't trust Gideon."

"Why, for heaven's sake?"

Silenus lowered his voice and shuffled closer to my ear. "You know the story of Gideon in the Bible? Well, he was chosen to lead his clan against the raiding Midianites. The poor soul, he didn't have a clue. He was the original Doubting Thomas. He required signs that God had really spoken to him. Before he'd do what God told him to do, he wanted God to prove His presence. He threw a fleece on the floor. God let the dew fall on the fleece but not on the ground. Still, Gideon wasn't satisfied. He asked God to do it again, this time in reverse. The dew fell on the ground and not on the fleece. Gideon had blown his trumpet to call thirty-two thousand of his men together to fight the Midianites. God thought that was a few too many and ordered Gideon to whittle the army down to three hundred. God wanted to prove what He and man can do together to save the world."

Silenus straightened up to see what Gideon was doing. Gideon was still intent in explaining something to Jo. Mary, now awake, was deep in a magazine. "Well, no wonder Gideon wavered between faith and doubt," Silenus continued. "But God had it all figured out. He told Gideon to order his three hundred men to arm themselves with jars and trumpets. Then Gideon was really scared. The Midianites filled the valley like a plague of grasshoppers. But Gideon did what he was told. He had each man put a lighted torch in his jar. Gideon's men surrounded the Midianites during the night. Blew their trumpets, smashed the jars and waved their torches like crazy. Well, between the blowing and yelling 'The sword of the Lord and of Gideon,' the poor Midianites didn't know what was going on. They started fighting among themselves. Then they all ran away. Gideon had saved his country."

"Which was a pretty good thing."

"Sure, but that's not the end of the story. Gideon ordered his son to kill two Midianite kings he had captured. His son refused because he didn't have the heart, so Gideon killed them himself. The people wanted to make Gideon king, but he refused the offer. It didn't do any good because after Gideon died, after forty years of peace, the Iraelites returned to their pagan god. But the old boy did leave seventy sons!"

"He was a brave man," I said.

Silenus gave me a half-smile. "Was he? What is bravery? Merely doing as he was told? No, Gideon of the Bible acted out of fear, fear of God, not in the sense of respect and awe of God, but out of downright fear of what God would do to *him* if he didn't obey. He was a scared little man."

"Still, God used him for His own purpose," I protested.

"True. But that didn't change Gideon's character. He blew the trumpet loudly, loud enough to create confusion in the enemy camp, loud enough to start his enemies fighting among themselves. It's a well-known principle of public relations. Gideon is following the classic procedure, but he doesn't know why."

"You mean the Israelites gave Gideon all the credit, not God."

"Human nature, isn't it? Our Gideon has to get all the credit. He needs a crowd around him as he charges off to Washington to attack the Pentagon. He has this fixation about the Army, because of what happened to a boy he knew in Korea."

"He told you about Lenny?" I asked.

"I'm surprised he also told you, Art. Well, no, I'm not surprised. You see, Gideon always has to be proving something about himself. He needs to prove that he's tough."

"When he isn't?"

"I didn't say that, Art. Gideon is tough, plenty tough. His battle experience was real. He earned his bronze star. No, what I mean is, he has to prove that he is astute, clever. He will never admit defeat. You and I might, but Gideon can't even admit it to himself. He has to win every battle. Not to say he's never been defeated. He has. But Gideon can see a victory even in defeat. And that's because Gideon personalizes, internalizes, everything. What's important in every situation is how it affects himself."

I told Silenus that it had often bothered me that Gideon looked upon Cotter as a personal enemy.

"That's because, for Gideon, Cotter symbolizes power," Silenus said. "And power is what Gideon wants but can't get. He'd like to have the power that Cotter has so he can crush Cotter."

"That won't change the basic threat," I said.

"Exactly. Supposing Cotter was thrown out as president of the Cotter societies. The Cotterites would still be with us. They might change their name, but never their stupidity. They're not so much anti-Communist as anti-democratic, with a small *d*. They've lost faith in the democratic process, if they ever had it. No, what I'm going to Washington for is not to attack Cotter but to prove that Cotterite stupidity led to Page Seventy, led to suspicion of one's friend, intimidation of one's neighbor, one's teacher. That's the crime the Cotterites have committed."

"Then Jo is right, in her way."

"Jo is very right," Silenus said. "And so is the Foundation. By restricting itself to shedding light on the issue of whether teachers shall be free or not, it has handicapped itself in its fight against Cotter. But, by refusing a direct engagement with Cotter, it is saving itself for the decisive battle, which will not be against Cotter but against the abysmal ignorance of the American people about what the teacher *is*."

"Still, the Foundation didn't back Green's protest to the Army."

"The Foundation has withheld its blessing, that's true. I think it should. The protest has to be made if only to flush out the enemy, to make it identifiable. But the enemy is not Cotter. The enemy is apathy and indifference toward education."

A flight attendant told us to fasten our seatbelts. I left Silenus behind and sat down beside Mary in the seat ahead. I felt my stomach sinking. The plane dropped through a cloud and there was Washington: the gray block of the Capitol, the greensward leading to the General's obelisk, with Lincoln's Memorial beyond. Then the sweep over the Potomac and the marsh grass under the wings. And then, gratefully, the runway closing in and the thump of wheels.

"Wasn't that exciting?" Mary said. "And so fast!"

"I hope we have a chance to see the city," I said. "Will you come with me?"

Her eyes sparkled. "I'd love to. Did you see the White House? I did. It was so clear!"

"Was President Johnson walking in the garden?"

"I couldn't make anybody out," she said seriously.

The plane approached the terminal. A man in a white coverall beckoned the plane to come closer and the plane obeyed. A final flurry of the propellers. We were there.

In the terminal, as we waited for our luggage, Jo came over to me. "I'm sorry we didn't have a chance to talk," she said.

"I'm sorry too, Jo."

"Your stories have been great, just great, Art."

She was very close, shedding her incense over me. The trip seemed to have tarnished her none at all. Her carmine lips opened in a bright smile. As she talked she never stopped looking at me. She was the kind of woman who seemed to beg to be taken in one's arms.

"I hope we'll get together here in Washington," I said. Already I had forgotten Mary.

"Let's do that," Jo said. She returned to Gideon's side.

In the taxi Mary and I sat on the bucket seats opposite Gideon and Silenus, with Jo between them. Gideon and his mighty band, I thought. All he needed was a trumpet.

Chapter Twenty-One

The taxi passed by the Potomac River Bridge, turned past the Jefferson Memorial and entered the congestion of Fourteenth Street by the Bureau of Engraving. "That's where the money comes from," I told Mary. The taxi turned up The Mall, giving us an unobstructed view of the Capitol. We rounded Union Square and crossed Constitution Avenue, and north of Capitol Plaza entered one of the narrow streets with a letter for a name. The taxi pulled up in front of the Woodrow Wilson Hotel.

In his suite, which consisted of a central parlor, a kitchenette and a bedroom, Gideon gathered his clan. He asked if we were settled in our rooms. We said we were. He asked room service to send up coffee and sandwiches.

He assigned Jo and Mary the task of telephoning the newspapers and television and radio stations to find out who was coming to the press conference the next morning. He ordered Silenus to check Bentley's office to find out when the Senator would be available in the morning, and also to find out from the Department of Defense press office whether Secretary Peters was in town.

Mary went to her room, which she was to share with Jo, to make her phone calls from there. Jo got busy on the phone in Gideon's parlor, while Gideon and I huddled on the sofa to compose questions I was to ask at the conference.

Silenus returned from the room he would share with me. He had used the telephone there. He reported that both Bentley and Army Secretary Peters would be in their offices in the morning.

Mary returned to report she had assurances from five newspapers, including two from Washington. Jo hung up the parlor phone and gave a list to Gideon. Not one of the television or radio stations was interested.

However, they wanted copies of Green's statement. Gideon asked Silenus to make the deliveries.

After Silenus left, Gideon read off the list of other newspapers that would be represented by their Washington correspondents: Chicago, St. Louis, Baltimore and Philadelphia. And, of course, the New York Dispatch. The wire services said they would rely on local reporters.

I phoned Bentley at his home to tell him about Page Seventy. "You should know, Senator," I said, "that the Educational Foundation is protesting, but not directly. Through its public relations agency, Gibson Green. No, he's not here. Gideon Pratt is. I'll put him on the line."

Gideon winked at me and grabbed the phone. "Hello, Burt. Yes, it's been a long time. No, Mr. Green sent a letter to Army Secretary Peters, asked for an apology. To the American people! That's right. And immediate withdrawal of the material. From every Army publication. All of them. I know. It is a pretty tall order. Yes. That's why we're holding a press conference. Tomorrow. Nine o'clock. Woodrow Wilson. Yes, Silenus is here. Oh, I see. A hearing. Well, if you can make it Burt, I'd appreciate it. Suite six-oh-six. Thanks, Burt. I'll call you tomorrow."

Gideon hung up. For a long while he didn't look at me. "Burt Bentley," he said. "I wonder if he's changed much. Of course we've been in touch, but I haven't actually seen him since Richland."

Somehow, sometime, there had been a falling out among Gideon, Silenus and Bentley. After leap-frogging into the Senate over Gideon's and Silenus' shoulders, Bentley had never looked back. Gideon and Silenus made it in New York on their own.

Early the next morning, except for Silenus, we gathered in the hotel dining room for breakfast under a portrait of Woodrow Wilson, the perfect picture of erudition. Overhead, cut-glass icicles dripped over flame-shaped bulbs. Mary asked where Silenus was. "Trying to get us some TV coverage," I told her. She had changed to an organdy blue cocktail dress. She giggled. Little lines dimpled her cheeks. "Professor Stoddard, he's kind of cute," she said.

Jo laughed. She touched Mary's arm. "Watch out for him, dear. He's a wolf in equine clothing." She twisted twin looping strands of pearls which emphasized the long smooth arch of her neck. Her sleeveless purple dress seemed tucked and cut purposely to keep my eyes pasted to the contours of her marvelously molded figure.

I don't know whether Gideon caught me in this staring act or not, but he slapped down the menu with such force that his fork went skittering and clanging to the floor. "Jo, you had better keep out of sight at the press conference," he said.

She looked up at him in surprise, and some shock too, for her lower lip trembled as she replied "Why, Gideon, in the name of common sense, shouldn't I be there?"

Gideon stooped and picked up the fork. "Far be it from me to deprive the press of an opportunity to drool over you, Jo. When I introduce you I couldn't tell the reporters you are on the Foundation staff. Now, could I?"

They shared dagger-stares for a moment. Then a waiter in a black jacket came over to take our orders. He was writing them down when Silenus came in and sat between Mary and Jo.

"I'll be darned, Jo, if you aren't a sight for sore eyes!"

"Guess what, Silenus, Gideon doesn't want me to be at the conference."

Gideon struck the table again. "I didn't say that," he protested.

"What's a press conference without a beautiful hostess?" Silenus asked, laughing. He glanced at Mary. "Two beautiful hostesses."

Jo patted Silenus' arm. "Thank you, sir. But let's remember that Gideon is in charge." She gave Gideon a curt smile. "Whatever you say, Gideon."

"I was only thinking," Gideon said, "of the need to keep the Foundation's name out of the papers."

"I'm hungry," Silenus said. He patted his stomach. "Besides Mary and Jo we will have something else to warm the cockles of a newspaperman's cold heart."

"Several blondes, Silenus," I suggested.

"I was referring," he replied with parliamentary dignity, "to liquid refreshment. What's a press conference without it?"

"A temperance conference," I suggested.

Gideon frowned. His face assumed its mask of stern command. "I didn't order liquor, Silenus."

The professor looked askance at him. "Still a teetotaler, Gideon?"

"I won an essay contest once," Gideon said. "On temperance. Gave me inhibitions. I'd suggest, Silenus, lay off the stuff today."

"You know I always drink on the job, Gideon."

"You keep telling me that."

"Alright, if you insist. You're the boss."

Jo touched Silenus' hand. This seemed to be a reflex motion with Jo whenever she wanted to gain someone's attention. "Yes, Silenus, it wouldn't do for you to fall flat on your--"

"Pratt?" Silenus said, raising an eyebrow.

Gideon gave his full attention to the waiter arriving with our breakfast. While we ate, Silenus told us he had succeeded in coaxing one television station to send a camera crew and reporter. One radio station had promised to use Green's statement and to pick up additional facts from the wire services. When Silenus suggested that Senator Bentley's presence at the conference would add importance to the occasion, Gideon objected.

"I hope he doesn't come," Gideon said.

"You told me it was a good idea," I put in.

"Well, I've changed my mind. His presence would only confuse the issue."

"We need all the help we can get," Silenus said. "The first question the reporters will ask is 'Who are you?'"

"Isn't it enough that I represent the Foundation?"

"That's just the point," Silenus said. "You don't."

Gideon could not be engaged in any extensive conversation after all. He ate moodily, picking at his food. I was still hungry for more toast when he pushed back his chair. "Let's go. We've got work to do."

Silenus said, in the same terse tone of command. "Yes, upstairs everybody. Every man to his station, every woman to her--"

"Camp," I suggested.

I marched behind Jo as we paraded Indian file among the tables toward the lobby. Men turned to gaze in amazement at Jo. I couldn't blame them. Her undulating walk, the fire of her brilliant red hair, the perfect curving lines of her dress, the slim taper of her legs, all attracted admiration.

In Gideon's parlor we hastened to our various tasks. Silenus lined up a couple of bottles of scotch and vodka on a table near the window. "It's tax-deductible," he told Gideon. I set up a semicircle of chairs, supplied by the hotel. Mary put out a stack of copies of Page Seventy and Green's letter.

We finished just in time. The bell rang. Jo opened the door. A lanky man with a small mustache raised his eyebrows. "Is this--?"

"Mr. Pratt's suite, yes."

Silenus stifled a giggle. He went over to shake the man's hand. "I'm Silenus Stoddard. Glad you could come."

"Rutherford. The Post," the man said.

Silenus took Rutherford's coat. He introduced us all.

"St. Louis?" Gideon asked.

"Washington," Rutherford replied dryly. He took a pack of cigarettes from his pocket.

"Hope I'm not too late for--" He spied the liquor and sprang across the room to the table.

When the bell rang again Jo admitted a huge balding man with a pipe in his grinning mouth. "Sun-Times," he said. "Claypoole."

"Baltimore?" Gideon asked.

"No way. Chicago of course," said Claypoole. He shook hands with each of us, taking too much time with Jo, then ambled to the table. Rutherford poured him a drink.

Next was Philadelphia: Dubrinski of the Inquirer, young, brittle. I almost heard his heels click as Silenus introduced him to Jo.

St. Louis came in, Gottlieb of the Post, a small man with long black hair and a slight paunch.

Finally, Baltimore: Vaccinni of the Sun, tall and dark and gray at the temples.

Gottlieb joined the party at the table. Vaccinni called Dubrinski into a corner.

Gideon went over to Silenus. "Shall we start?"

"Television, remember?"

"We can't wait too long."

"I'll keep the liquor flowing."

The professor went over to the table, where he joined Jo and the other reporters in a circle. Jo lightly touched Rutherford's arm as she laughed at something he said. Vaccinni and Dubrinski surrounded her.

After a while Silenus came through the reporters and sat down between Gideon and me. "They're in good hands," Silenus said. "What's the matter, Gideon? You look a little green."

The bell rang again. There were two of them: Oleson, stooped over a large black case marked WBQB-TV, and Aroulian, a cigarette drooling from his lips. They began setting up the camera and microphone, which they clamped to a lectern, also supplied by the hotel. Aroulian unveiled a portable mike.

After the two newcomers were introduced, the bell rang again. It was Kamkada, United Press. All bases were covered.

Gideon took his place behind the lectern. "Gentlemen, if you will please be seated." Rutherford led the way, sat down in an end chair, and the others followed. Oleson switched on the elevated television camera, located behind the reporters. A tiny red light below the camera lens blinked on. Oleson signaled "Go!" to Gideon.

"Gentlemen, before I take your questions, let me say first that we do appreciate your attendance very, very much. You will want to know why we are here, and I will come to that in a moment, but let me say for the second time my name is Gideon Pratt. I need not spell it for you as you will find it on the Gibson Green statement that has been given you." A reporter raised his hand. "Don't have one? Mary, would you be good enough?" Mary distributed the statement and at the same time made sure they also had Page Seventy.

"Where was I?" Gideon continued. "Oh, yes. I am associated with Gibson Green, a public relations agency in New York. That is, we have our national headquarters there."

Claypoole yawned.

"One of our accounts is a very, a very well known, extremely well known, educational organization."

Claypoole held up his hand. "What's the name?"

Startled, Gideon shook his head. "I'm really not at liberty to say."

Silenus coughed. "It's the Educational Foundation of America, fellows."

Gideon jerked his head. "Silenus," he hissed, loud enough, I was sure, for the reporters to hear. Silenus looked straight ahead.

Dubrinski lowered his drink. "You mean the E-F-A?"

Gideon nodded. "Off the record please."

Veccinni glowered at him. "Why?"

"Well, uh, you see--"

Silenus reached up and grasped Gideon's arm. "Our letter," Silenus said, "is from Mr. Green, not from the Foundation. The Foundation does not wish to be associated with this protest at the present time." He let go of Gideon's arm. "Men, I presume you received both documents in the mail and have perused them. You understand that they speak for themselves. Passages in an Army manual were copied from a Cotterite brochure. We are giving you copies so you can see for yourself. This is not a case of plagiarism. We are protesting that the Army's manual is undermining our educational system. You are free to inform the public of the existence of the Army manual and the Cotter brochure. Any questions?"

Kamkada smiled. "Any answer from Peters yet, Professor?"

"Peters hasn't received the letter yet, Steve. Won't until he opens his morning mail."

Clapoole's pipe admitted a cloud of smoke. "Have you read the letter to Peters, Silenus?"

"No."

I raised my hand. I asked the question Gideon had written for me: "Do you expect Secretary Peters to apologize?"

Gideon looked at me gratefully. "As Mr. Green's letter states," he said, "we expect Secretary Peters to apologize."

"To whom?" This from Dubrinski.

Gideon slammed his fist into the palm of his hand. "To the American people! To all the teachers in the United States!"

"And to withdraw Page Seventy?" I asked as fast as I could. It was another question Gideon wanted me to ask.

"Not only Page Seventy but also similar Cotterite material from any Army publications in which it appears, yes."

The reporters scribbled furiously.

"Can we quote the EFA?" asked Gottlieb.

"No, you can't," Gideon hollered.

Silenus clutched Gideon's arm again. "What we mean," the professor said, "is that what you write is, of course, up to you. The opinions expressed in the letter represent only those of Mr. Green."

Aroilian folded his arms and crossed his legs. "Who are you kidding, Silenus?"

"You know I wouldn't kid you, Arch. Any of you. We couldn't move the EFA. You know how they are."

"Sure," Aroulian said. He looked along the line of reporters. "Say, fellows, you heard about the award they're giving out this year? It's called the American Success Story award. A-S-S for short."

Claypoole's pipe shook. Ashes flew to the carpet. Laughter rippled around the circle. Rutherford and Caccinni went to the liquor table. "Hey, Silenus," Rutherford called. "We're running out."

Silenus phoned room service. He ordered another two bottles. He joined Jo and the other men at the table, leaving Gideon and me alone on the sofa. Jo detached herself from her circle of admirers. She came over and sat beside Gideon. "Too darn hot in here," she said. Gideon stared into space.

Veccinni stood over Jo, then sat beside her and put an arm around her shoulder. Gideon got up and went over to Oleson, who was still fiddling with the camera. "Do you want to start shooting now?" Gideon shouted over the general hubbub. Oleson shrugged and pointed to Aroulian. Gideon continued to argue with him.

Then, as a flame attracts moths, Jo attracted the entire crowd.

Suddenly Gideon was standing over us. "Mary, why don't you mix with the reporters?" he asked her, glaring.

She sprang up. "I will, Mr. Pratt. I didn't know--" She went over to Jo, who began introducing her.

"You don't have to get mad at Mary," I told Gideon.

Gideon frowned. "I asked her to come along because I thought she'd be useful. Instead of that she sits in a corner bawling."

"She's shy. She's not used to this sort of thing."

Silenus tottered over to us. "Wash the matter?"

"Go to hell," Gideon said.

"As ya whish." Silenus weaved away.

I picked up the notes Mary had made. "She was working on these," I said to Gideon, waving them under his nose. He grabbed the notes from me. He tore them up and threw the pieces on the floor.

"Come on, Gideon," I said, making one more attempt to bring him out of the funk he was in. "Let's join the party." I took his arm, intent on dragging him across the room if I had to, but he threw me off and sat down at the desk. He folded his hands, wrung them, stared at them. His face flamed. "That damned Silenus," I heard him mutter.

But I was off with the others. Jo and Mary were circled by the reporters. Jo was dazzling: they were delighted. Jo was enigmatic: they were enchanted. Jo, full-blossomed, hardly attempting, attracted. Mary, leaning against the windowsill, was a weak competitor. However, young Veccinni, his attention to Jo too widely shared, turned to Mary. She gave him her undivided attention.

Rutherford was saying, "You heard about the new Department of Public Education, members of which are otherwise known as DOPEs?" A roar of laughter all around.

Then it was Dubrinski's turn. "I hear the Senate has a Committee to Revise Administration Policy, otherwise known as CRAP."

Thus it went, each one attempting to outdo the other. I stole Gideon's joke and told the one about the National Union of Teachers, otherwise known as NUTs.

Still, Jo remained the center of attention. She laughed, head tilted, again and again, her fine white teeth gleaming.

"Hey, Jo, that was a good one, wasn't it?"

"Let me fill your glass again, Jo."

"Jo, have a sandwich, if you can call these little things sandwiches."

She seemed not at all aware of Gideon's silent scorn. Now Jo moved away from us, Veccinni clutching her elbow. Smiling Kamkada took over with Mary. Veccinni held Jo's hand. She seemed convulsed by a joke. Jo was saying something which caused Veccinni to hug her.

Gideon was looking at them too. Gideon covered his eyes. I went over to him again. "Come on, Gideon." He appeared not to have heard me. He swayed slightly, rocking back and forth. "Are you alright, Gideon?"

Looking up, eyes unnaturally bright, he said "Some day I will lead them. Some day I will lead them all."

I went over to Silenus. I nodded toward Gideon. "He's sick," I said.

Silenus got the reporters to leave. Oleson, grumbling, dismantled his camera and lugged it away. "What a waste of time," he muttered.

"Let's go to lunch," Jo said happily. Silenus, Mary and I joined her at the door. "Coming, Gideon?"

"You go ahead," Gideon said with a wave of his hand. "I have to stay. Senator Bentley may call." He mumbled something about everybody deserting him. We left Gideon to his solitude.

Chapter Twenty-Two

In the lobby Jo had her hand on Silenus' arm as if to steady him. "All the reporters gone?" I asked.

"To their terrible typewriters," Silenus replied. He appeared suddenly sober.

In the hotel's coffee shop we all ordered coffee of course.

"We left Gideon alone," I said, somewhat glumly and somewhat with a feeling of guilt.

Mary was the one looking truly guilty. "Maybe I'd better go back," she said quietly.

"He's best left alone to cool off," said Silenus.

Jo began taking off her pearl earrings. "Gideon was doing alright, Silenus, until you butted in."

Silenus calmly stirred his coffee. "The principle of taking the press into your confidence."

"Gideon should have known that," I said.

"It couldn't be helped," Silenus added. "Gideon was making a mess of it. You shouldn't try to kid the papers, should you, Art?"

"Never," I agreed. "The ultimate sin."

Mary laughed.

"What's so funny?" I asked her.

"Nothing. I didn't have a thing to do."

Silenus scratched his beard. "What did we need notes for anyway? Gideon was just trying to be officious."

"And you were offensive," Jo said sharply. She toyed with her earrings on the table. "Really, Silenus, I think you owe Gideon an apology."

"Oh, I'll apologize. But what will that teach Gideon? Only that he was right and I was wrong."

"You shouldn't treat people that way," Jo said.

"Don't generalize. Anyway, I had to step in before Gideon wrecked the entire plan."

"Silenus is right," I said. "You just can't treat reporters as if they were messenger boys."

"I can see that," Jo said. "What I can't see, Silenus, is the way you took over from Gideon. It was his show."

The professor compressed his lips. "There's more involved than the way Gideon feels. He's feeling a mite peevish now, but he'll get over it. Why don't you go and cheer him up, Jo? Tell him for me that I'm sorry."

"I will," Jo said. She stood up. "Coming Mary?"

Mary said, "If you don't mind. Miss Davis, I think I'll go to our room. I have a few more notes to write for Mr. Pratt."

"Thanks. For everything, Mary," Silenus said. "See you later."

Jo and Mary went off together, Jo directly into Gideon's bedroom. Silenus and I sat together on the sofa for fifteen minutes or so as we discussed what happened at the press conference, all the while hearing the murmuring voices of Jo and Gideon emanating from Gideon's room.

"Hope they are behaving themselves," Silenus muttered.

"At least you can't make out what they are saying," I said.

Silenus was in a mellow mood. Perhaps it was the vodka. We were conversing about our forthcoming conference that morning with Senator Bentley. Silenus was the complete pragmatist. Now that Gideon had lost his self-control, Silenus considered himself in complete charge of Operation Pentagon, as he called it. Aparently he never questioned his right to assume command. He lived by his own rules, and one of those rules seemed to be *Trust yourself only.*

He considered Bentley to be a fair man, his own man, one who took the side he thought was right regardless of whether it was left or right, regardless of political party. "Bentley would spit on me if I told him he was fair," Silenus said. "He'd as soon scorch me as Cotter would, depending upon the action. That's because he's concerned about what happens to the truth in a fight."

"Both sides can't be right!" I protested.

Silenus refilled his cup from the coffee flask. "Can't they? It depends upon which side you're on. When you're out to get a guy, you don't quibble about the method. We have our job to do and we do it with whatever weapons are handy, without regret. But Bentley, he looks at our weapons. And Cotter's. His concern is that, in our wild swinging at one another, we may be damaging some pretty important liberties."

"Just the same," I said, "I don't see how Bentley can condone Cotter's tactics."

"He doesn't," Silenus replied. "Of course he's against the Communists as much as Cotter. All I'm saying is, Bentley and Cotter, they differ in their choice of weapons."

This was a subtle distinction, one I was not prepared to make. I am by nature, I think, an uncomplicated guy with the usual prejudices and appetites. Silenus' ability to qualify everything, to see both sides, to choose one form of action over another hardly different, was foreign, both to my experience and my inclination. Either I liked someone or I didn't. That's the way it used to be. Now I was being forced to associate, even follow, people whom I did not wholly respect and yet sometimes were worthy of my grudging admiration. Perhaps I was beginning to see Silenus' faults. In any case, the brilliant strategist paled, and in its place I saw before me the sideline critic, the above-it-all cynic, one who had complete confidence in his ability to rise above every situation, especially when it meant superseding those placed in authority over him. I do not accuse Silenus of being disloyal to Gideon. Perhaps he did what he did out of a sense of greater loyalty, to save Gideon's cause in spite of Gideon's inadequacy. Still, Silenus' star had now ascended as Gideon's had dipped. There was a relationship between these events. I was not sure just how much one was the cause of the other.

Silenus said he wanted to visit an old Washington friend. I had little doubt his friend was female, so I let him go.

I was about to enter Gideon's room, in fact had my hand on the knob, when the door swung forcefully open. Jo, face contorted, lips parted, held the other knob in both hands. She was bent forward, heels dug into the carpet. Gideon had his hands around her waist. He pulled her back a foot even as Jo strained to get away from him.

It was a moment before either of them saw me. They remained frozen in their tug-of-war position, as if in a tableau, with neither making progress to win the struggle. Finally, Jo must have noticed my feet protruding inside the opening door. She looked up slowly. She grinned. "Hello, Art."

Gideon, who was in his dressing gown, held his head low. He seemed to be resting up for another tug at the immovable object. When Jo let go of the doorknob Gideon fell backward with a thump on the floor. Spread-eagled, he gazed up at me with such a look of amazement and incredulity that I felt more sorry for him than amused.

"Excuse me," Jo said. She tugged at her dress as she looked furtively into the parlor, zipped past me and Silenus, opened the door to the corridor and disappeared.

"You take care of Gideon," Silenus said. "I'm out of here." He put on his raincoat and fled.

I tiptoed over to Gideon's room and opened the door. He was lying on the floor. I helped him to his feet, guided him to the parlor and plunked him on the sofa. He reached for a half-full glass on an end table and downed the contents with a single swallow. Then he slumped, chin on his chest. His rumpled hair fell over his eyes.

I peered into his flaming face. "Gideon, are you with us?"

He raised his head, looked at me blankly, without recognition. "What?"

I took the glass from his hand. "I think we ought to get you to bed, buddy boy."

"Bed," he muttered.

"Sleep, remember."

His head lowered again.

"How about a cup of coffee?" I asked.

"Coffee?"

I took his reply as consent. Leaving him toppled over on the sofa, I went to the kitchen, filled a small kettle and put it on the stove. I switched on the electric coil. I found a jar of instant coffee in a cupboard. I put a spoonful in a cup and returned to Gideon.

"Whatsa matta, buddy boy?" I asked.

He wobbled his head. "Sick."

"Oh, you're not sick. Just a teensy-weensy bit drunk."

"Sick," he said again. He tried to get up, fell back, tried again. This time I helped him. He was half-way to the kitchen when I realized he was looking for the bathroom. I steered him around a full turn, headed him in the right direction. Gideon fell on his knees in front of the toilet.

I returned to the kitchen to fill the cup with hot water. I could hear Gideon retching horribly. I decided that what Gideon needed now was milk. I found some in the tiny refrigerator. I heated a cupful.

Gideon stumbled to the parlor and lay down on the sofa. I placed a pillow under his head and pressed the cup to his lips. "Down the hatch," I said. The milk dribbled down his chin. "You need a bib," I said. He eyed me with a baleful stare. His face was like chalk. He held his stomach and groaned. "You bastard," he said thickly.

"You don't like me anymore?" I asked.

"I like you," he replied.

"You're not mad at me?"

"Silenus."

"He did it for the best."

I placed the cup to his lips again. "Here's to success," I said.

"Go to hell."

He drank the milk without further complaint. "Feel better?" I asked.

I pulled him up by his arms and propelled him into the bedroom. Gideon flopped on the bed. I tucked him in. Gideon closed his yes. "You're my friend, Art," he said.

I went to Jo's room. I knocked, a gentle tap. There was a stirring inside, then a soft voice. "Who is it?" I told her. The door chain jingled. Jo opened the door a crack. "Mary's taking a nap," she said. "Meet me in the lobby."

A few couples occupied other tables in the coffee shop. I told Jo that Silenus had gone off to parts unknown. We clinked coffee cups. "To Gideon, poor soul," Jo said.

"I suppose you would say my entrance couldn't have been better timed," I said. "Art James to the rescue of fair maiden."

Jo laughed heartedly. "Did you put him to bed?"

I nodded. "Like a baby. Gave him some warm milk first."

She looked at me seriously. "I want you to know, Art, that I had been sitting a long way from him while I tried to calm him down. He was lying on his bed the entire time." She fingered her cup. "We had quite an argument. Mostly about the way I behaved. He was simply livid about Silenus."

"And wild about you?"

She only smiled. "Don't you feel proud, having rescued me?"

"From a fate worse than death? Anytime, miss."

She traced a pattern on the table. "I'm worried about Gideon, Art."

"He brought it on himself."

"Did he? Aren't we all responsible. In a way? Silenus simply overshadowed him. And I didn't help, drawing attention away from him. Gideon was right. I shouldn't have been there."

"Well, his big show is still to come."

"I hope Gideon will be alright. We can't let him bungle everything."

"Then you do have doubts about Gideon's ability?"

She looked away. "Especially after this morning's episode," she said. She looked at me, her eyes dark and serious. "Art, do you think there's something wrong with Gideon? I mean, is he emotionally unstable or something like that?"

Her questions were leading me to a conclusion I had postponed. Gideon acted erratically. Knowing his history, his peculiar combination of overbearing obstinacy and his compulsive obedience, his capacity for tenderness coupled with his hardly-concealed hostility, I was perhaps in a better position than Jo to judge him. Still, I hesitated. A psychiatrist might first find Gideon a simple case to diagnose. Because I had only a layman's superficial understanding of these things, I was reluctant to state an opinion which could be far off the mark and do Gideon an injustice.

"I know he's in love with you," I said.

"Apart from that," Jo said flatly, as if I had merely stated the obvious. "Isn't there something about Gideon that leads you not to trust him?"

She was putting me on the spot. I tried to ease off it by saying that Gideon was not an easy type to categorize. Besides, I wanted to talk about ourselves. I was getting a little tired of Gideon being the topic of our conversations. "He isn't your type?" I asked, indicating my interest in her by daring to stroke her smooth hand.

Without withdrawing her hand she gave me a coquettish look, batting eyes and a coy lip-rounded "Oh?"

"What type am I, Art?"

"The Manhattan type. You know. Sophisticated."

"Woman of the world?"

"Something like that," I said.

"You surprise me, Art. You really do. If I didn't know you I'd suspect you were on the make."

"You don't know me that well."

"Don't I?" she asked, arching an eyebrow. "Don't forget I'm a woman of vast experience, a passionate past."

"You're kidding me now."

Her other eyebrow rose. "Am I?"

Completely unnerved, yet rising to the challenge, I moved closer to her. I put my arm around her shoulders. I caressed her hand.

"You have such nice hands," I said.

"Have I?"

"Yes." I gave her hand a gentle squeeze. I leaned toward her, intending to kiss her.

"No," she exclaimed, withdrawing her hand. "Not here. Not now."

I leaned back and sighed.

"What's that for," she asked.

"You are a puzzle."

"Oh, I don't think so. Just an average woman with average instincts."

Every word she said seemed tinged with invitation. My face was burning. "I mean, I wish I knew you better," I said. "You must be fun to work with."

"We're working together now, aren't we?"

"I mean, like Gideon. You see each other often, don't you?"

"Three or four times a week, sometimes."

"I met his wife for the second time yesterday. The first time was seven years ago, in Richland."

"I like Amy."

"They have two great kids, a boy and a girl."

"I know," Jo said.

"I wish I could work with you."

"Maybe you will some day, who knows?" She smiled sweetly. "By the way, you did a marvelous job today, simply marvelous."

"I didn't do anything."

"Oh, but you did! You got United Press there. And you got Senator Bentley interested."

"It was Silenus' show."

"Isn't he amazing? Really, is there anyone he doesn't know? I wasn't too impressed with him at first. But now I think he's absolutely indispensable, even if he was overbearing with Gideon."

"Gideon doesn't have Silenus' experience."

"We must be patient with Gideon, Art. He's trying to do his best."

"He won't get the Army to apologize."

"Gideon thinks he will," Jo said.

"We'll find out today," I replied hopefully.

Jo smiled. "Good luck," she said.

Chapter Twenty-Three

We crossed Capitol Plaza under a turquoise sky. Gideon set the pace for Silenus and I as we loped over Delaware Avenue against a red light, then across First Street to the new Senate Office building. We went through several marble corridors and at last found Senator Bentley's office. We were ushered through a foyer by his secretary, a spectacled, bony woman with glistening blue-gray hair. On the other side of the vast office, Senator Bentley rose from behind a wide polished desk. We shook hands all round and then formed a conference circle on a red leather sofa and matching chairs.

"Good of all of you to come," Bentley began, adjusting his pince-nez. "Think of it! We're all from Richland! It's like a reunion, isn't it? Art, looks like your trip to Richland was worthwhile. To think that a little brochure you picked up there would lead to this. Silenus, you old rascal you. Leading a student protest! What's the world coming to? And Gideon, you've hit the big time. Say your prayers. You'll need all the help you can get."

"Thank you, Burt. Remember that Communist cell?"

Bentley brushed him off. "Silenus, Secretary Peters specifically asked that you be there. Is that okay?"

"Okay. It will be good to see him again," Silenus said. Gideon and I joined in expressing our surprise. It was news to us that Silenus was acquainted with the Secretary of the Army.

Gideon raised his hand to gain Bentley's attention. "I mailed Secretary Peters a copy of Mr. Green's statement, also Page Seventy," he announced. "He should have them by now."

Silenus laughed. "Not a chance, Gideon. Mail takes longer than that. I took them to him this morning. Also copies I made of my notes on Cotter's Moscow thesis. He was attending a meeting of the Joint Chiefs of Staff, but an aide told me that the Secretary would take a good look at everything so he would be prepared for our meeting."

"Good work, Silenus," Bentley said. "Meanwhile, the Senate Committee on Anti-American Activities will be meeting soon and I've asked the Chairman for the privilege of being called as a witness. Also, there's a chance of the committee also calling Peters to testify." He glanced severely around at the three of us. "I want your word that none of this will reach the media until the committee meets. Okay?"

The three of us voiced our pledge that it would be so. "Whatever the Senator wishes," Gideon said.

"This goes for you too, Art. This is strictly off the record. It would do our cause great harm if it ever got out that an employed newspaperman was working with us."

"I understand, Senator Bentley. I am only here as a reporter. As far as I'm concerned this is solely an interview for background, off the record."

"Good, Art. Gideon, how did your press conference go?"

"Get the early Post tonight, Burt," Silenus said.

"Incidentally, Gideon, I told Secretary Peters who was behind Green's, that is, Gideon's statement. I told him it was the Education Foundation."

"You did!" Gideon exclaimed. "Mr. Fletcher specifically asked that the Foundation not be mentioned."

"That bone-head," Bentley said. "Everyone knows Gibson Green has the Foundation account. You can't keep *that* a secret. In any case, I called Fletcher and told him so. I asked him straight out if he was going to join the protest against Cotter, or wasn't he? Well, we'll see."

"I told the press this morning," Gideon said, "that any mention of the Foundation or Mr. Fletcher was off the record."

Silenus smirked. "Useless, Gideon. Any reporter could find that out."

"But I promised Mr. Fletcher!" Gideon protested.

"Listen to me, Gideon," Bentley said. "You would never get to see Secretary Peters if he thought you only represented Gibson Green."

Looking as if he were the victim of some monstrous force frustrating his plans, Gideon gaped. "Page Seventy is a slap in the face for every teacher in the country!" he cried.

"That reminds me," Bentley said, "there's a woman staff member of the Foundation in your party?"

"Miss Davis," Silenus replied.

"Take her along," Bentley said.

"I don't know about that," Gideon said weakly.

"It's essential," Bentley said firmly. "You will see she's there, Silenus?"

Silenus nodded. "Do you have an approach to recommend, Burt?"

Gideon leaped up. "There's only one approach that Peters understands," he shouted. He strode behind Bentley's chair. "Demand an apology." He slammed a fist into the palm of his hand.

"Take my advice," Bentley said quietly. "Take it easy on Peters. He's only human. And don't use the word apologize."

"The hell I won't," Gideon said. He went off to the broad window. He stood there, hands in his pockets, back arched, looking down into the street.

Bentley took Gideon's place between Silenus and I. "You will have to keep a firm rein on Gideon, Silenus." He spoke softly so that Gideon would not hear. "This Miss Davis, she's a good looker?"

"She's a doll," I told him.

Silenus smiled at me, perhaps knowingly.

"Let her do some of the talking," Bentley said. He winked at me. "You can always depend upon Peters to pay attention to a pretty girl. Surprised you didn't bring her to see me."

"It was Gideon's idea," I told him. "He likes to keep her hidden." I said that loudly enough so that Gideon would hear me. He turned around and glared daggers at me.

"Well," Bentley fairly whispered to Silenus and I, "maybe some other time I will have the pleasure. Meanwhile, I have something more to say about this apology business." He lowered his voice even further, because Gideon had turned to give us a look full of injured dismay. "On the whole," Bentley said, "Gideon did a good job on the letter to Peters. However, it would have been enough to ask for withdrawal of the Cotterite tract from the Army's manual. Peters can feel sorry that the material got into the manual. But to ask him to apologize to the American people for an oversight, that's too much."

Bentley stood up. "Sit down, Gideon," he commanded. He pointed to the chair. Gideon obeyed. "Listen to me," Bentley said, addressing Gideon directly. "If Peters had to apologize for every piece of propaganda that finds its way into Army publications, of which there must be millions, judging from the appropriations for paper, well, it's impossible. After all, Peters doesn't edit every page of every manual."

Gideon's mouth worked. "It's an official publication of the United States government," he said. "Page Seventy could be taken to represent the view of the United States. Think of our overseas relations!"

"Knock it off, Gideon," Silenus said.

"Think of what you're up against," Bentley went on, still attempting to mollify Gideon. "Even a U.S. senator couldn't get the Secretary of the Army to apologize. Would be next to censure. Besides, who's asking for the apology? Gibson Green. Now, if the Foundation, Fletcher himself, were to ask for it. We know that's not going to happen. And I for one am glad Fletcher was smart enough to keep himself and the Foundation out of the issue." Bentley replaced his pince-nez. "You've gone as far as you can go, Silenus. We can get withdrawal of the material, and a statement saying Page Seventy was a mistake, praising the teachers as loyal and all that." He looked pointedly at Gideon. "But not an apology. Never an apology."

"He'll apologize," Gideon said stubbornly. His face was masked in misery, mouth turned down, eyes narrowed, forehead furrowed.

"The demand for an apology was a strategic error," Bentley insisted. "I'm surprised that Fletcher approved it."

"He didn't exactly approve it," Silenus admitted.

Bentley adopted that sonorous tone for which he was famous. "You know as well as I do, Silenus, that I won't stand for anything that hurts the Senate's relationship with the Army. Remember McCarthy and what the Senate did to *him*!"

"Well, *he* had a point," Gideon said.

"His tactics stank," Bentley replied. He looked at his watch. "Unfortunately there's a pack of my loyal constituents outside."

"I have the feeling, Burt," Gideon said, his voice threatening, "That you think the Army is justified."

Bentley peered at Gideon over his pince-nez. "By printing Page Seventy, Gideon? No, that wasn't justified. I'm not defending the Army. Makes the same kinds of mistakes civilian organizations make. After all, this Cotter tripe is flooding the country. We ought to sympathize with the Army when some of that tripe turns up in an Army publication."

Gideon shrugged. He stood up. "I suppose," he said, "that all we can do is advise people to read the books of J. Edgar Hoover and to say our prayers." He went to the door and opened it. I was on my feet now. I could see a crowd of faces through the open door. "Burt," Gideon went on, "you're as naïve as a Sunday school teacher. You think that only God can preserve the country from being taken over by the Communists. You think we shouldn't be too hard on the Communists for fear of offending Russia." He swung the door wide open. "Thanks for your help, Burt. Thanks for nothing." He disappeared among Bentley's ardent supporters.

"Go after him, Silenus," Bentley ordered. "You can handle Gideon."

Silenus crashed his way into the gesturing crowd and Bentley followed. "Hello, folks," Bentley said brightly. He made his way among them as an aide closed the door behind him. I could hear him vaguely as he addressed his fans with kind, soothing words.

I paced the room, looked down into the quiet street below. In the distance the Washington Monument loomed high into the brilliant October sky. Thinking about Gideon, I had a feeling of impending doom. He was a loose cannon. Even Silenus was finding it difficult to control him. Something in Gideon had snapped. Perhaps something in his past. He was a man of ambition stuck in a subservient position, subject to the inordinately undefined whims of men in high positions, themselves unsure of where they were going, subject to the prevailing winds of wild public opinion, bewildered by forces beyond their control. Still, Gideon strived for control, which he lacked, and he knew it. His frustration was driving him away from his compatriots into a valley of deceit and envy, forces that were fighting for control, when all the while the Cotterites and their ilk laughed heartily over their confusion.

I went to Bentley's desk and read the statement he had prepared:

The entire nation is disturbed today to learn that a dastardly attack has been made upon the distinguished name of our public school teachers. This attack has been published, inadvertently, I am convinced, by the U.S. Army. That this could happen in a society that prides itself upon its sense of fair play is to be deplored. The attack itself is reprehensible, and I do not condone the officers whose oversight caused this attack to be printed in an official publication. The attack has been published, although it is supported by no evidence whatever that what it purports to say is true. Toying with the truth is the danger; our freedom from fear of this kind of group suspicion has been dearly paid for. I am aware that military officers cannot be held responsible for every foolish and despicable charge that finds its way into publications. Nevertheless, I am asking the chairman of the U.S. Senate Armed Services Committee to schedule a hearing on this matter at the earliest possible date. At that time it is my hope that both the complainants and those responsible for Page Seventy will be heard and a judgment rendered that will forestall recurrence of this unfortunate slur upon a fine group of American citizens.

When Bentley came back, I sat down to question him. He reached for a cigar and lit it. "Fire away," he said.

"Since your statement indicates sympathy for the Foundation," I said, "does that mean you're against Cotter?"

He examined the hot end of his cigar. He leaned back in his chair and swiveled toward the window. "Well, Cotter has a role to play in a complex society such as ours. Powers must be balanced. By powers I mean groups that have solid support among significant segments of the population. Cotter has a right to his opinions. So have other people. My constituents out there are as frightened as Cotter about the Communists, but they don't yap about subversion and infiltration. They don't think the Communists are about to take over the country. They have more common sense. Trouble is Cotter has appointed himself guardian of the common man's loyalty. And that's where he's wrong. We don't need a loyalty czar in America. You see, Cotter doesn't qualify or document his charges. He lumps whole groups, like the teachers. That undermines everybody's faith in teachers in general. You've heard about Cotter's idea of having teachers pass loyalty tests imposed by boards of review?" I said I had. "Because such a board would be required to test an intangible, the teacher's spirit. Not character, mind you. Spirit. The Cotterites think they can judge a person's loyalty. I don't think they can."

I asked Bentley about the announcement in his statement that he planned to ask the Senate Armed Services Committee to hold a hearing.

"I think I have enough support to cause that to happen," he answered. "Off the record of course. I want to head off another investigation."

"By whom?"

"By the distinguished senior senator from Colorado, McLeod. Know what he wants to do? An immediate session of Un-American Activities to investigate the Dispatch."

"I'm not surprised," I said. "As long it's not me."

"Don't worry about it," Bentley said. "Mcleod's mostly sound and fury. I don't think he will go as far as calling a meeting of his committee. What he might do is mention it in his newspaper column. They've stirred up a hornet's nest, Art."

"Appears that way," I replied.

On my way back to the hotel I realized I still had no answer to my question whether Bentley was a Cotterite. He was against Cotter's methods, but I wasn't sure how far he would go in trying to rid the country of Cotter himself. If Cotter was only a symptom, as Silenus believed, then there was no urgency to dethrone Cotter from his place of power. The root of the problem was fear, the fear expressed by many Americans that ballooned the real Communist menace into a super-bogeyman. Such scared people were at the mercy of demagogues like Cotter. He played upon their fears, built fires of hatred, fanned their hate into a conflagration, heaped faggots of fear into the flames of their hatred. Thus he was able to turn neighbor against neighbor, turn a teacher into an informer on fellow teachers. But condemnation by rumor and suspicion wasn't the American way. It was also not our way to rely upon amateur sleuths, as Cotter did, to root out communists. That was applying the ax to the root of democracy. This was the real evil of which Cotter was the symptom: vigilante intimidation masquerading in the Stars and Stripes.

Late that evening I telephoned Al. He told me the Dispatch's first edition was out. He read me the headline: *Cotter blasted. Army manual reveals indoctrination.* He had received my wired report on my interview with Bentley, plus Bentley's statement. He said he would save it for the next day. I mentioned that an interview with Secretary Peters would follow.

I descended to the hotel lobby and picked up the Post. A report on our press conference was confined to half a column on an inside page. Both Green's statement and Page Seventy were briefly summarized. Back in Gideon's suite I showed it to Silenus.

"It's a fizzle," he said.

Chapter Twenty-Four

Jo was all excitement. She waved a piece of paper at me. It was a list of people who had telephoned. All of them wanted to see Gideon. I glanced down the list. There was Reverend Jones of the All-American Group, Inc.; Judge Dement of World Justice, Inc.; Leverett Walker of The Pilgrim Pointers; Doctor (Mrs.) Foxe of the Revere Rovers; Francis Wakefield of The Peace Parade; and Starbuck Smith of The Frontier Fathers.

"We sure don't want to see those nuts," I told Silenus. "They are all extremists." I followed Jo into the kitchen. I kicked the door closed behind me. She was standing on tip-toe looking for something on the top cupboard shelf. Bouquets of lavender flowers danced on her dotted Swiss dress. I put my arm around her and turned her about. She put an arm around me. She laughed at me. "Now, really, Art. What if Gideon should see us?"

"The heck with Gideon." The doorbell rang. Jo pushed me away. "We have work to do, mister hotshot reporter."

We were returning to the parlor when Silenus opened the door. A tall man topped by a white Texan hat stepped inside without invitation. "I," he announced loudly, "am General Quince!" He wore a dark blue business suit and a floppy black bow tie that wobbled with his Adam's apple as he spoke.

Silenus exclaimed "General!" and boldly shook the man's hand. They hugged each another. Silenus held the man at arm's length. "You son-of-a-gun! Let me look at you. Say, you haven't changed a bit. How long's it been?"

The General scratched the long black hair over his left ear. "I dunno. Must be nigh on ten year. What 'n tarnation yuh doin' here?"

"Business," Silenus said. "I might ask you the same."

General Quince took a newspaper clipping from his pocket. "This!"

"Oh, that. Now, General, it isn't anything to get excited about. Nothing against the Army personally."

The General put the clipping back in his pocket. "Better not be." He looked around the room, as if aware of Jo and me for the first time. "Who might they be?"

Silenus introduced us. The General tipped his hat to Jo. "Please t' meetcha." He turned to Silenus. "Can I talk the truth to yuh, private, Silenus?"

"We can talk here, General. I can vouch for each of them."

"Yur sure?"

"Sure, sure. How about a drink? Jo?"

"All gone, Silenus."

"What do you mean, all gone?"

"It's a long story," Jo said.

General Quince tipped his hat. "Nevva mind, y'all. It's too earla in the mawnin' anyway."

Silenus bid the General to sit down, but the General preferred to stand, tall and free. "What ah have t' say can be said standin' up."

"Oh, talk English, General," Silenus said curtly.

"Suh? Oh, alright, Silenus. Glare and Glory protests your, uh, protest."

"What in the world is Glare and Glory?"

"You never heard of us?"

"Never."

"You've heard of Old Glory?"

"Yes."

"You heard of the rockets' glare?"

"*Red* glare."

"Suh! That word!"

"It's in the anthem," Silenus said. His hand on the General's arm, Silenus explained that no insult was intended, and certainly he had no desire to restrain the Army from getting rid of Communists.

Mollified, the General expressed his pleasure at "Meetin' y'all" and invited us to visit him at his Texas ranch "Anytime ya'll can come." With that the General about-faced and marched from the room.

Jo laughed loudly. "What was that about?" she asked.

Silenus explained that General Quince was an old Army buddy and that, while he was quite over the hill, he was still a good sort and meant well.

Glare and Glory was, apparently, the latest of the extremist groups the General had either organized or loaned his name. As for the invitation to the General's ranch, that was genuine, because Silenus had been there and remembered getting lost on it--while he was driving. He had no idea what the General was doing in Washington.

Gideon and Mary came in from the bedroom. Gideon said he had been busy on the phone. Mary waved pages of paper. She explained that she had been taking dictation from Gideon, who then ordered us to sit down. Once we were arranged on the sofa to his satisfaction he stood before us to outline his battle plan. He began to pace back and forth.

"The way I see it," he began, "the appearance of General Quince is our first sample of group reaction." Silenus winked at me. I figured that Gideon must have overheard the confrontation with the General. Now Gideon was giving it all he had to gain control of what he called "Operation Pentagon." He held up Jo's list of people he had phoned.

"We may expect visits from many of these people," he told us in a stern, no-nonsense, voice. "I want everyone to greet these visitors cordially. And leave off the levity, Silenus. Some of these people may be sympathetic to our cause." He caught Silenus and I expressing our doubt by shaking our heads. "Well, they might! The more groups we can line up on our side the better. Let no one misunderstand," he cried, "we are in this fight to the finish. This is our command post. Yes, that's it! Let them come here! We will enroll all volunteers right here. We can't use General Quince, because he's on the opposition side. I don't know whether these groups are on the right or on the left."

"They're right-wing," I told him.

Gideon pointed to Mary. "Some research on these groups, please." He handed the list to her.

"Yes, Mr. Pratt."

"Find out all you can about these organizations."

"Where, Mr. Pratt?"

Gideon scowled at her. "I don't care where."

Silenus raised his hand. "May I suggest the Library of Congress?"

"Of course," said Gideon, looking evilly at Silenus under thundercloud brows. Art, you have your own stories to write, I realize that. Perhaps you wouldn't mind putting together some pieces on these groups so we can release them to the wire services tonight. Silenus, you and I could visit some of the Washington headquarters of the national organizations, try to win their support."

"Such as?" Silenus asked.

"The AFL-CIO, the National Council of Churches, the General Federation of Women's Clubs, the National Catholic Women's Conference." Gideon rattled off the names rapidly, proudly.

"That will take time, Silenus, especially since some organizations are headquartered in Manhattan, not in Washington."

"Then I suggest we get right to it, Silenus. I've been phoning some of these people. We can knock off a few today, can't we?" He clapped his hands. "I guess that about does it. Any questions?"

There were no questions. Gideon told Mary to take a taxi to the Library of Congress. Silenus retired gracefully to our room. Jo took the first of another round of calls on the parlor phone.

Gideon drew me to one side. "I want you to know, Art, that I appreciate all you have done. Really, I don't know what I would have done without you."

This was so unlike Gideon that I didn't know what to reply. His sincerity was transparent. Or was it? Was he attempting to provoke me? I held up my hand in a gesture of dismissal. He invited me into his bedroom. I followed him. He began making coffee. "Of course Silenus tries to be helpful," he said. "Actually, I don't know why I asked him to come along. Doesn't he think I know what to do? Well, of course, I realize he arranged our conference with Senator Bentley, but he's pretty expensive just to get a few phone calls taken care of."

Taking mugs from the cupboard, spooning instant coffee, poring the water, lacing the coffee with sugar and cream, Gideon puttered about. His pace decelerated. As he kept talking he seemed to turn into a man in slow motion. He never stopped talking.

"I could have handled Burt myself," he rattled on, his voice increasingly edged with a rasping quaver. "After all, I know Burt as well as Silenus does. And then that busy work of getting a television man to the press conference.

And letting the cat out of the bag by mentioning the Foundation! We'll be lucky if none of the papers use it. Silenus hasn't had the experience. Silenus forgets that I'm in charge here. If he tries once more to take over I'll fire him! Yes I will. In a minute. Just let him get out of line once more. Of course I wouldn't fire you, Art, not if you were on my staff. I need you. You're not like Silenus. If he wasn't getting paid fifty an hour he'd have left me long ago. Well, everyone can be bought. Since I'm paying him, the least Silenus can do is keep out of my hair. You don't think Silenus can do better than me, do you, Art? How do we know Silenus won't be drunk next time?" He paused and sipped his coffee. "You're my friend, Art. You wouldn't leave me, would you?" Again he halted, eying me suspiciously. "You bastard! You stood there and said that. It was you! You came in, when Jo was--"

I caught a glimpse of his balled fist slashing toward me.

Then: a sharp click inside my head.

I sensed, rather than knew for a surety, that I was lying on the sofa, with Jo's foggy figure bending over me. Yes, it was Jo herself, forehead creased, cheeks sunken. Her hand was cold upon my forehead. I reached up and pressed her hand. I tried to get up.

"No," she said. "Lie still."

I think I asked her where Gideon was, although I had no interest in him now. Jo said he had gone out, she didn't know where. My eyes, for some reason, kept closing. I heard the dull clicking of the telephone being dialed, the full cycle, once, and Jo's voice saying, over and over, "Doctor! Doctor!" I tried to form the words "No need," and I thought I was deaf because I could not hear my own voice. The mist drifted down again.

I awoke to the sharp shame of ammonia forking my nostrils. I sprang up, alert to the doctor's presence. A depressant struck down my tongue. I gagged. I blinked fiercely as a brilliant peering eye pierced my own. "He will live," I heard a male voice say. "I'm glad to know that," Jo said with a laugh. I was not sure myself, for the pain stabbed my brain and stitched my neck. I felt my calf twitch as the mallet stung my knee. I sprang up again. "Okay," I cried. "That's enough." My head awhirl, the room spiraling, I heaved toward the window. In the panes I witnessed my ghostly image, then Jo's appeared behind me, then the vaster figure of the doctor. I reached for the window's handle, tugged it. "I'll help," Jo said.

Her hand on mine, she depressed the latch and shoved the window out. The cold air smote me. I inhaled deeply, coughed as the cold cut my lungs. Breathing softly, slowly, I sensed the sweet smell of fallen leaves, saw their oxide umber.

I hardly heard the opening of a door. "Where the hell is Gideon?" Silenus asked. He strode past me, ignoring us, and entered Gideon's room. Not finding him there, Silenus returned to confront Jo and I. "I've set up an appointment with the I-B-C," he said. Then he noticed that Jo was holding my arm, guiding me back to the sofa. "What's going on? What's the matter with you, Art?"

"Gideon hit him," Jo told him. She took Silenus aside, out of earshot. I wondered what Jo was telling him.

"It wasn't anything," I said, not knowing whether they could hear me or not.

"Maybe not," Silenus said, looking down at me. He shook his head. "Damn fool. Well, we'll take care of Gideon later. Right now we've got to see Brownell."

"Who's Brownell?" I asked. "I'm a little foggy. What's the I-B-C?"

"International Brotherhood of Caretakers. Brownell's the business manager." Silenus raced out.

Jo had no idea where Gideon had gone. "I never saw him in such a rage," Jo told me.

She had no sooner gone to her room--"To rearrange my face."-- than the doorbell rang. I thought it might be Gideon. But Gideon had a key. I struggled up from the sofa, crossed the room and opened the door.

"How do you do?" the man said. "I am Reverend Jones."

He was wearing a sports jacket crossed with pink lines and a tie with pink polka dots on it. His trousers were as white as an altar cloth. He handed me a business card. I read the words: *All-American Group Inc.* "You were looking for me?" he asked. I ushered him to the sofa. He smiled at me through his balloon features, his jowls fighting one another.

I sat down on a chair opposite him. "That's better," he said with a deep voice. "Now we can talk."

I excused myself, went over to the telephone and dialed Jo's room. "Come rescue me," I whispered. "I have a guest here. *Reverend* Jones."

I returned to the chair. "What shall we talk about, reverend?" I asked.

"About Mr. Cotter, of course," the minister said. "You are crucifying him!"

"If I had only known he was Jesus Christ," I said.

"Sir, you blaspheme! May God forgive you, son. I can see you don't see the error of your ways. You are blind to the evil of Communism. You don't realize the Communists are Satan's instruments."

"Like hell, you say."

His jowls jounced. "You hate sin, son?"

"Like the devil."

"Then help us wipe out the Communists! Your talent is needed. God gave you the ability to write. Think of the power of your pen!"

"I use a typewriter."

"I was speaking figuratively. Your skill is God-given. God wants you on His side!"

"God hates the Communists?" I asked.

"Loathes them."

"I thought all men were his children. He loves us all."

"Ah, but the Communists are not men. They are beasts."

"They look like men," I said.

"Ravening wolves!"

"How about bullying bears?"

"You mock me, sir!"

"Forgive me."

"I do, and God bless you. Now, as I was saying, you hate sin and you hate Satan. You must hate the Communist beast too. You've read Revelation?"

"Well, yes," I replied. I was getting tired of this nonsense.

The Reverend Jones took a New Testament from his pocket, turned the pages from the back. "God tells us to destroy the beast. For we read: 'And I saw the beast, and the kings of the earth, and their armies, gathered together to make war against him that sat on the horse, and against his army. And the beast was taken, and with him that false prophet that wrought miracles before him, with which he deceived them that had received the mark of the beast, and them that worshipped his image. These both were cast alive into a lake of fire burning with brimstone.'" He paused for the full impact of the verses to make their expected effect upon me.

217

"Shades of Jonathan Edwards," I said.

"You see!" the minister said. "The Lord is telling us what is going to happen. The beast is Communism. The false prophet is, you know who. All those whom Communism deceives bear the mark of the beast, the hammer and the sickle. They worship his image. You know how they put his picture up everywhere. The Bible tells us of the coming conflagration, when the beast will be destroyed, and his false prophet."

"And be thrown into hell?"

"Exactly. Prepare for the glorious day, son. Join our cause! We are on the march!"

"For all America?"

"For the sake of our dear land, for which our fathers so gloriously fought and died, yes. But for God's sake! There are many more among us who bear the mark of the beast. They have been deceived by the false prophet. We must seek them out."

"And cast them alive into a lake of fire burning with brimstone?"

"God is merciful. The Lord is just. They must repent of their sin."

"And if they don't?"

"Ah, then, they must suffer the consequences of their sin."

"Your's is indeed a noble and righteous cause," I said. "I wish you luck."

The Reverend James blinked appreciatively. "Then you are with us?"

"Actually," I whispered, bending forward, looking furtively around the room as if for spies, "I'm an undercover agent for the FBI. There are so many Communists in my line of work."

The minister pulled a wallet from an inside jacket pocket and took out a small card. He wrote *Gideon Pratt* on the back of the card. I decided not to enlighten him. "This card," he said, "identifies you as an official member of the All-American Group. Use the card carefully. It means you are a dedicated, fighting defender of Christianity against Communism." The minister paused a minute, looked at me dubiously. "On second thought, since you are already a Hoover man, you had better not carry the card with you. If you were captured, they would search you. That would give your game away."

I took the card from him and looked at it. There was a Sign of the Cross in the upper left corner. "How much?" I asked.

"Oh, don't worry about that," the minister said. "We will send you a bill."

"How much?"

"Sixty dollars. Of course, that is our suggested annual gift to the double-A-Ginc. Actually we depend upon love offerings, freely given."

"You have my love."

"Sir?"

"Love is stronger than death."

The door opened and Jo entered. She was wearing a black sleeveless dress and black net gloves which came to her elbows. "Oh, excuse me," Jo said. "I didn't know you had a guest."

I stood up. "Please come in, Miss Davis. May I introduce you to Reverend Jones?"

The minister rolled off the sofa and put out his hand. "How do you do?"

I took the minister's arm and guided him to the door. "Unfortunately Reverend Jones has to hurry away, Miss Davis."

"No, really, I--"

"Goodbye, Reverend. Good to see you." I shoved him out the door, closed it, leaned back upon it. "Thank you, Jo."

"One of the saner types, I presume," Jo said.

I showed her the card. "Gideon's now a Double-A-Ginc."

We stood next to one another at the window looking down at the sunlit terrace. Leaves, lemon and rust, rustled in the gutters. "I love this time of year," Jo said.

"Most people don't like November."

Jo breathed deeply. "It's such a peaceful time."

I took her in my arms. "Jo, I think I'm in love with you,"

Her eyes resumed their amused crinkle. "Aren't you sure?"

"I'm sure," I said.

Jo hugged me with sufficient assurance.

Gideon Pratt was eclipsed.

Chapter Twenty-Five

Silenus introduced me to Worth Brownell, whose frayed tweed and scuffed shoes hardly fitted with the palatial marble splendor of the I-B-C headquarters, shook my hand vigorously. He scanned me from head to toe. "How do you like this joint?" he asked.

For Brownell's benefit I looked around the temple-like lobby. The International Brotherhood of Caretakers had spared no expense in building its headquarters. Tablets on the walls bore deeply etched testimonials to labor's unity. One text proclaimed *Justice for All*, while another, just below the union's name, announced *We Take Care of You*.

We paused for a moment on the building's porch to admire the view of the Capitol's soaring magnificence. Brownell escorted us around the corner of Pennsylvania Avenue to a seedy lunch counter. We sat on stools, Brownell between Silenus and I. We ordered corned beef on rye. Brownell told us he was in a rush because he had to catch a plane to New York. "Got orders," he said, "to get our locals in all five boroughs to attend Cotter's rally."

It was the first tip I had that organized labor was planning a counterattack upon Cotter. I took out my pad and began taking notes.

Silenus snorted. "No offense, Worth, but how come you, as business manager, got this assignment?"

"Best man for the job," Brownell replied. "Used to do it full-time when I was director of political relations. Which in some quarters is known as political agitation."

"The politburo?" I asked.

"We're as much against Communism as anybody. You can print that."

"Watch out, Worth," Art may do that. "Did I tell you, Art, that Worth taught economics at Richland University? That was before your time. He taught the theory that the laborer is worthy of his hire." Laughing,

220

Silenus slapped Worth's back. "You would go back to teaching in a minute, wouldn't you, Worth, if you weren't taking so much graft?"

"Hah! Look who's talking. Who's bankroll are *you* on today, Silenus?"

"Help me earn it, will you, Worth? We need a union statement supporting Gideon's protest to the Army."

Brownell yelped. He almost fell off his stool. "Are you crazy, Silenus? You think the IBC is going to take on the Army? Things are tough enough as it is. Anyway, we've got our own little bandwagon rolling against Cotter. And you started it, Art." He pounded me on the back. I started to choke. "Yes, sir, your torpedo about Cotter in Moscow is going to blow a hole in him a mile wide. Listen! We're going to squeeze Cotter's grapefruit until he drowns in his own juice. The Caretakers are ready to go. Strike every Cotter Grapefruit plant in the country. Besides, the IBC is lining up some other pretty big unions."

I told Brownell that this sounded to me like economic blackmail to gain a political goal. "Listen!" he said sternly. "Would you rather we struck the schools? What would happen if school building staffs walked out? It would be worse than teacher strikes. No heat. Heck, there would be such a holler as you never heard. Teach Johnny what you like but keep him warm! Of course we're *not* going to strike the schools. We've got a sense of civic responsibility."

"Sure you have," I said.

"Disregarding your emotional outburst," Silenus said, "you mean you seriously intend to try to bankrupt Cotter?"

"What keeps Cotter in the anti-Commie racket? Grapefruit. Squeeze that dry and we put the skids on his far-right crusade. We strike for sixty days, starting Christmas Day, height of the season. Yes, sir. We're going to take care of Cotter."

Brownell picked up his bill. Silenus snatched it from him. "I'm paying, Worth."

"No you're not," Worth said as he took his bill back. "You want those Senate guys to nail you for un-American activity?" He hopped off his stool, paid his bill and took off. "See you in the Garden," he called over his shoulder.

"Whatever happened," Silenus asked, "to the downtrodden masses?"

Silenus and I sat in silence as our taxi passed over the Potomac River bridge into Virginia, then over the Jefferson Davis highway to the ponderous mass of the Pentagon.

Jo was waiting for us. She walked between us as we marched in time through monotonous corridors. Before the door with the words *Secretary of the Army*, printed in gold, we paused a moment, took stock of one another. Jo was trim, alert, in her black dress. Silenus stroked his whiskers.

Inside, Gideon was sitting, head down, hands clasped between his knees. A girl in a stiff white blouse was typing at a desk. I went over to Gideon, stood in front of him, hovering.

He looked up sheepishly. "Hello, Art." His eyes were red, misty. I was sure he had removed his contact lenses. "I'm sorry, Art. Are you okay?"

"Sure," I said, "What about you?"

He stood up, staggering. "Jo. Silenus." He nodded to them. "We will be called in soon," he said. He had such a hangdog look I felt sorry for him.

The girl at the desk flipped a switch. "Mr. Pratt," the girl said, "you and your party may go in now."

The Honorable Louis E. Peters looked innocent enough, I thought. His face was firm, rose-flecked, and not at all flaccid, as coarse-screen newspaper pictures led me to expect. He peered at us from behind a desk nearly the size of a billiard table. His bright eyes were like blue buttons about to pop. He gestured to us to sit opposite him. Silenus, Jo and I sat on the sofa. Gideon took the chair to my left.

Peters' thin voice belied the strength of his position. He leaned forward over the desk. "Silenus, what the hell is this all about?"

The professor tickled his beard. "Now don't get excited, Lou. I'm only the temporary counsel to Gibson Green. Mr. Pratt is the head of this delegation."

"Well, what do you want, Mr. Pratt?"

Gideon seemed to be tracing the lacy edge of the desk. "About the letter from Mr. Green, Mr. Secretary--"

"Yes?" Long and drawn out.

"We have issued copies to the press and--"

"I've read the papers."

"I think the public expects a reply." Gideon looked off across the room. He gazed at a gilt-framed portrait hung deep in the shadow above Peters.

"How do you know?" Peters asked.

"Know what, sir?"

"You have asked the public?"

"Well, no. But the newspapers are waiting."

Peters leaned back. I could see only an arc of his thin white hair. "I know that, Mr. Pratt. The reporters are in the press room now, waiting to hear me apologize. Isn't that right, Mr. James?"

"Well, I wouldn't go that far, Mr. Secretary."

"But Mr. Pratt would."

Sun glinted from Gideon's temple. He gripped the arm of his chair. "Then we may expect a statement from you, sir?" he asked.

"I due time, Mr. Pratt. In due time."

"Tonight, then?"

Peters' slim mustache curled. "Very kind of you to give me so much time, Mr. Pratt."

Silenus coughed. He leaned forward. "Then we may tell the press, Lou, that you decline to comment?"

"But I haven't declined, Silenus."

Gideon looked away, inspecting, it appeared, the sunlight on the maroon carpet.

Since the letter was from Green, said Peters, he would reply to Green. And then, seeming to take notice of Jo for the first time, he asked her what her connection was with the Educational Foundation. Gideon was blatantly indicating his contempt for Peters by swiveling about and looking around the edges of the room, where shadows hid the corner furniture from my peripheral vision.

Jo's voice was husky, entreating. She asked Peters to clarify what the role of the Army would be in withdrawing the offending Cotterite tract from the R.O.T.C. manual. Peters' reply was long and rambling, full of assurances that the Army appreciated the feelings of teachers and recognized their undisputed loyalty, and desired to do nothing to harm their good name. Meanwhile Gideon had turned his attention to Peters. He examined the Secretary's face as if counting the capillaries on his red-hued nose. Peters gave his full attention to Jo. I was reminded of what Bentley had said about Peters weakness for pretty women, and that caused me to smile.

"Do you wish me to clarify the procedure?" Peters was asking. "If I may identify myself with the service for a moment, rather than the executive branch, I would say that in an organization of such vast complexity as the Army, this sort of thing is bound to happen. I am by no means excusing it, even as I am not apologizing for it."

I glanced anxiously at Gideon. He was rocking his head back and forth, as I sometimes would do to ease headache tension. Peters cast a furtive glance in Gideon's direction. "I agree with Senator Bentley's statement about the request for an apology," Peters said meaningfully, all the while looking at Gideon. However, the import of this statement was surely lost upon Gideon, but not upon me. It was clear that Bentley had checked his own statement with Peters. A small smile on his mouth, Peters addressed Silenus: "I think proper adjustments in procedure may be made through channels, and I can assure you that everything will be done so that material of this nature will be carefully screened. That is, checked for accuracy and propriety."

Gideon muttered something. His eyes were closed. His face was placid, revealing nothing of his thoughts. I wondered if he was, in his mind, stripping the flesh off Peters.

"We appreciate your action," Silenus said. "We expected you would act with dispatch in this matter, knowing that our only means of rebuttal was through the civilian authority."

"Well, you know these generals, Silenus, They don't like to be pushed around."

Silenus' returned laugh was gay with confidence. "You should know, Lou. Now, about Mr. Green's letter. Mr. Green asked me to explain about the request for an apology."

This caused Gideon to half open his eyes, for he cast upon Silenus a full contemptuous smile. I thought that perhaps Silenus deserved it, for Silenus had not told me he had been in touch with Green about the letter. I presumed he was referring to a phone call that very morning, before we left the hotel.

"What does Mr. Green want me to do, Silenus? Retract the paragraph? Apologize?"

I was close enough to Gideon, closer than the others, to recognize that his mouth formed the word *Apologize.*

"Depends upon how you define the word," Silenus said.

Again Gideon hurled the silent word at Peters.

"I think it is clear enough," Peters replied. "I have already said I am sorry."

"Well, the letter having gone to the press, Lou--"

"That's not my concern, Silenus. I didn't release the letter to the press. Mr. Pratt here did that." He looked over at Gideon, but Gideon now had turned his back on Peters. I wasn't sure if he was trying to stand up until that is actually what he did. Silenus went over to Gideon and grasped his arm to steady him.

"Thanks for everything, Lou," Silenus said.

I expressed my own thanks, and Jo did the same. We turned and raced after Silenus, who was guiding Gideon toward the door. Gideon thrust off Silenus' grasp. Gideon's mouth was contorted. Tendons on his neck tensed.

"Apologize!" Gideon cried out, pointing a finger at Peters.

It all took only a second. I sprang to the aid of Silenus, pushing Gideon around and out the door that Jo was holding open. Some demon had Gideon in its grasp. Gideon broke from us, ran like a deer to the outer door and burst into the corridor. Although we chased him a distance we lost him in the labyrinth.

Puffing, Silenus was the first to give up the chase, in which a pretty WAVE was knocked to the wall, a Marine tried to block us with his bulk, and a soldier began chasing us. I suggested to Silenus and Jo that they accompany me to the press room as I had to knock out a story for the Dispatch. We received directions but I can't say how we got there. All I know is that we turned at least a dozen corners.

I was in the midst of typing my story, lost in the composition of phrases which I knew Al dearly loved, when Gideon burst in. His hair was wild, his eyes wilder. He strode over to Veccinni's desk, picked up a paper weight and banged it down.

"Gentlemen! Gentlemen!"

There were perhaps twenty reporters in the room. Silenus and Jo huddled on a bench near the door.

"My name is Gideon Pratt! I've just seen Secretary Peters!"

Conversation died. All heads turned toward Gideon. Jo visibly gasped. She clapped her hands over her mouth. Silenus was on his feet. He made a move toward Gideon.

A jostling of reporters, a coming together, a pulling apart. They waded among the desks, I with them. We came to the open space in front of Gideon and formed a circle around him.

Gideon took a piece of paper from his pocket. He held it up. I recognized the copy of Page Seventy. A flashbulb popped.

"Now get this!" Gideon cried, his voice raw. "Peters refuses to apologize to the American people!"

Veccinni waved at him and turned away.

"The teachers have been insulted!"

I stepped toward him. "Gideon!"

"Our boys are being indoctrinated!"

"Gideon," I yelled at him.

"This extremist propaganda--"

Someone in the back shouted. "Come off it, Pratt. We already have Peters' statement."

"Propaganda against liberty, freedom!"

The reporters began drifting away.

"Wait! Wait!"

A voice, trailing over a retreating shoulder: "Who the hell are you?"

Hands and arms flailing, Gideon floundered, begging, around the circle of backs. "Art, tell them!"

Entreating, cajoling, Gideon pursued the reporters. I followed after him, touching his arm, calling his name, doing what I could to calm him. "Listen, Gideon." I grabbed his arm and held on. His eyes skidded, as if he had just come out of a tailspin. "Listen, Gideon! Page Seventy has been withdrawn!"

Eyes glazed, he folded on a chair like a dropped napkin. I thrust Peters' statement at him. He took it, turned it upside down. I righted it for him. Still, I could tell, he didn't know what he was looking at.

I read the statement to him, although I was convinced he couldn't understand a word:

My attention has been called to the fact that certain
material which does not represent the official view of
the U.S. Army with regard to the nature of Communism,
has been included in an Army training manual, whose
distribution was confined to a limited geographical area

of the continental USA. I have ordered this material to be
withdrawn immediately, and I have asked that careful scrutiny
be given to the sources of such material in the future.

If Gideon had struck me again I would have understood him better, but he slowly lowered his head into his hands. His entire body was rigid, as if burdened by some unseen load.

"You've won, Gideon," I said slowly. "You've won. You got what you wanted."

Gideon stood stiffly, as if he was made of marble. At last his fingers fluttered. His mumble was hardly audible. "No, no, that's not what I wanted. Not what I wanted," he proclaimed in a tremulous voice. "The Army has made a mistake." His voice rose slowly to a wail. He certainly wasn't aware that, all over the room, reporters stopped typing, ceased talking, were listening. Jo, white-faced, approached furtively.

"He has to apologize," Gideon continued. He grabbed me by my coat's lapels. "Why didn't he apologize?" he pleaded. "They've got to say they're wrong." He began to shake his head. "Can't they see that? Don't they know that? They've done wrong. They've got to be sorry for that. They've got to tell the people they're sorry for what they've done."

Silenus was by us now. His face was stern, commanding. His eyes were hard, his mouth a firm line.

"Shut up, Gideon," Silenus commanded. "Stop making a scene. Control yourself."

"Leave him alone," I told Silenus.

"The coward," Silenus said.

At once Gideon spun around. His arm came back, weakly, I thought, and his blow, although aimed at Silenus' lowered, threatening face, did not reach its target. Silenus, with a motion so swift I did not see its beginning, grasped Gideon's arm, twisted it behind Gideon's back, turning Gideon about. With a fury born of utter frustration Gideon broke loose and bolted to the door. He wrestled it open, thrashed through a corridor crowd, and was gone.

Chapter Twenty-Six

Outside the Pentagon we boarded a taxi, a Checker with jump seats. "Where do you want to go," I asked Silenus, who, I assumed, now that Gideon had left us, was in charge.

"Who cares?" he replied as if he really didn't care if we stayed or went back to New York.

"If we've got the time," said Jo, "and since we're already on the Virginia side, I'd like to see Arlington National Cemetery."

We arrived at the Tomb of the Unknown Soldier as the guard was changing. Stiff-postured, the guards marched, stripped of pretense.

Together we went over to the Amphitheater, entered one of the boxes between the mighty columns which overlooked the circling marble benches. Except for the vaulting sky a Roman senate might have sat there, dealing justice to the state. Here heroes were immortalized, heroic deeds recalled. This was a memorial, not only to an unknown man, but also to men known. War destroyed the other; man created the art. A wind blew under the benches, turning the yellow leaves of fall. The shadowed benches blended, moved. The branches were undisturbed. How could the winds of controversy destroy this? Gathered here, Cotterites on one side and liberals on the other, would be indistinguishable, each hushed by history. Quiet the query: here questions were irreverent. Now the benches curved away, iridescent, golden haze and rose, ripples on an oval pool. Argument was quelled, peace restored. The agony of our quest seemed irrelevant.

Then the Lincoln Memorial, the matchless phrases read and re-read. Jefferson's *We hold these truths.* Hence to the Washington Monument and up the elevator to the pinnacle, the view down The Mall and the glorious Capitol beyond. Past the museums to the Capitol itself. The great heroes, large as life, encircling, ennobling. On to the Smithsonian and across to the National Museum, a dash through each. Then old Ford's Theater and the dreadful derringer: *Sic semper tyrannis!* Across the street, the shadowed room where Lincoln lay dying. Somehow it was fitting, after such magnificence, that our tour should end in a red brick house. How fraught with fate.

Exhausted, we entered a corner restaurant on F Street, were shown to a quiet booth padded like a nineteenth century Pullman, thick brown mohair and gleaming walnut veneer on the walls. We ate in black silence, unable and unwilling to discuss Gideon. I got up once to call the Wilson Hotel, discovered that Gideon had checked out. Mary, forgotten, was there, in tears I suspected. I told her to pack her things and Jo's too, as we had decided to take the evening train back to Manhattan.

"Poor Mary," said Jo when I returned to our booth. "Did she see Gideon?"

"I didn't ask."

Silenus was picking his teeth. "It appears our friend Gideon has run out on us. Well, I'm to blame, I suppose. If I hadn't kept interfering with him this wouldn't have happened."

"That's true," Jo said, causing Silenus to adopt such a mournful *et tu Brute* expression, all drooping beard and downcast mustache, that I almost burst out laughing.

"I didn't expect you to agree with me, Jo," Silenus said.

"I know you didn't," Jo replied. She moved closer to me. Our thighs touched, sending me a message I hardly dared believe. "That's you all over, Silenus. You say things you don't mean. We never know when you're sincere. If you and Gideon had an understanding, if you had coached him gently beforehand, he would have behaved differently."

Silenus put one hand to his whiskered chin, like a scolded child. "I didn't come on this junket to be Gideon's baby-sitter. Anyway, did Gideon ever once ask me what to say, what to do? He did not! All I did was pick up the ball when he fumbled. What else was I to do? Sit there and let him throw the game? I understood that's what I was being paid for. Anyway, I've plenty of tricks left up my sleeve. Such as asking Art to publish the entire notes on the Moscow thesis and the full text of Page Seventy. Did Gideon bother asking for that? No. All he was interested in was getting Peters to apologize. Because he hates the Army. Well, I'm sure a lot of vets may feel the same way, only they don't get psycho about it."

229

"You're full of hot ideas, Silenus," I said. "Who asked you to be the leader?"

Silenus pointed his fork at me. "Someone must lead. Might as well be me."

"Just because you were a major in the war, I suppose," I said.

"Suit yourself, Art."

I got up without excusing myself and went over to the pay phone. I called Al collect to tell him I'd be back at the Dispatch in the morning.

"Art, I've been trying to get you all afternoon."

I explained I had been tied up at the Pentagon and that my story was on the wire.

"Well, this is important." Al spaced his words. "Cotter was calling you. From Washington."

"You mean he's here?"

"Apparently. Want the number?" I jotted it down. It was the number of our hotel.

I said goodbye and hung up. I dialed the hotel and asked for Cotter. The room clerk gave me Cotter's message.

Returning to Silenus and Jo, I must have been wearing a smile of mystery, for Silenus asked "Did you catch that look from Moner Liser?"

"Fasten your seat belts," I said, sitting down as close to Jo as I could. "Guess who's in town? Cotter! Yes! Here! He left a message, wants to see me, couldn't wait, is taking the train to New York tonight."

Stunned is a cliché word, but that's the way they looked. Jo's mouth popped open. "My God!" she said. Then: "That's why Peters put us off. Oh, I should have known. I should have thought of this."

"What, for heaven's sake?" I asked.

"Mr. Fletcher, he used to be a director of the Louis E. Peters Company, industrial chemicals." She looked at us as if we were dunces for not getting the point. "Don't you see? George Rankin, my former boss. He went to work for Cotter. And Dick Doyle, he's in it too."

I still didn't get it. "What's he in?"

"A Cotterite cell! In the Bronson agency, of course. I bet Bronson himself is a Cotterite. Oh, it's clear now. A phone call to Mr. Fletcher, from Bronson, I mean, who phones Peters--"

"My dear," Silenus said, "you're a genius. But Cotter wouldn't have to act through Bronson. That's why Cotter's here in Washington. Cotter visited Peters *before* we did!"

"And Bentley too," I said.

"Let's get out of here," Silenus shouted.

Washington was quiet again, the city of dreams. We walked east on F Street to the Woodrow Wilson, Jo between me and Silenus.

"The Woodrow Wilson!" Silenus cried as we neared the hotel. "How appropriate! Princeton's pride, education's gift, democracy's savior."

Why had our hopes been vitiated? We had come to Washington proud of education's vitality, prepared to sacrifice ourselves to its cause. Was this merely a rationalization? Perhaps I, at least, had come only to fulfill a selfish lust for fame. Well, at least we had come, whatever our separate reasons. We had come, we had seen and Cotter had conquered. Or had he? I wasn't finished with Cotter yet. I could still write stories about him that would fire public indignation to a fever pitch. Perhaps this would win me promotion to feature writer, King Arthur and the Round Table, working knights! Out Excalibur! Good will triumph yet!

"Why would Cotter come to Washington if we didn't have him on the run?" Silenus asked cheerfully, waving his arms, as in celebration.

Jo wasn't so sure. She leaned to the theory that Cotter was capitalizing on the publicity my stories had generated. I agreed with her.

In Gideon's suite at the hotel, Mary told us an excruciating tale of being utterly lost in the Library of Congress. It was a while before I succeeded in calming her. She didn't want to give me her notes, saying they were for Gideon. She had no idea what had happened to him. He had returned to the hotel before she returned from the library. There were some signs of his hasty departure: his toothbrush still on the rack in the bathroom, a sock curled in a corner of a bureau drawer. I told Mary I was sure Gideon wanted me to have the notes for use in the Dispatch. At last she agreed to give them to me. I sat down at the parlor desk to go over them. Mary and Jo went to their room.

Mary's notes disclosed a pattern in the groups she had investigated. Each group had a single titular leader with a background of failure in a profession. The Reverend Jones was pastor of a fundamentalist church for only two years, after which he had circulated around the backwoods of

Kentucky and Tennessee as an itinerant evangelist with no visible means of support beyond love offerings. He was the founder and the sole executive of All-America Group, Inc, the Double-A-Ginc as he called it. I had no doubt that the Reverend Jones was getting fat on extremism.

As for General Quince, he had indeed won his laurels legitimately under fire during World War Two, but he had been retired under covered-up circumstances having to do with indoctrination procedures. He had known Silenus during the fighting in Europe. Silenus was in psychological warfare for a time until he transferred to quarter-mastering, where his commander had been none other than Louis E. Peters, Secretary of the Army. There was a footnote on Peters here: he was actually Louis E. Peters *Junior*. The vast chemical empire he ruled was founded by his father. Defense contracts provided a large part of the Peters Company business. Louis Peters took care of the conflict-of-interest issue by transferring his stock in the company to a family-operated foundation

Memberships in the extremist groups seemed to divide along geographical, wealth and social lines, sometimes all three. Both the All-America Group and Quince's Glare and Glory were comprised of southern conservatives. Both were Christ-centered. They differed in that Jones had his tens of thousands from among small-town shopkeepers and farmers' widows, while Quince's few were a roll-call of the rich ex-military elite. Judge Dement's World Justice was confined to a small New York element of anti-intellectuals whose principal perspective was assistance to escapees from behind the Iron Curtain. Leverett Walker's Pilgrim Pointers appeared on the surface to be more interested in museums and the preservation of historical sites connected to the Civil War than in fighting Communism. Walker was a Boston bluenose who had once been a distinguished member of the bar. Francis Wakefield's Peace Parade had nothing whatever to do with parades, and even less to do with peace: Paraders, who were mainly located in Washington, demanded the closing of all embassies in Communist countries and the severing of diplomatic relations with all nations doing business with Communist countries, including England. Wakefield had once been a lower-echelon secretary in the State Department. Doctor (Mrs.) Foxe, leader of the Revere Rovers, was a Johns Hopkins graduate with years of private practice in the Massachusetts hills. Now she was arming the hill country women with hatchets. They would be ready for the Communist rape, when it came. Starbuck Smith's Frontier Fathers were strongest in the Allegheny mountains, and Daniel Boone was their hero. They sought to influence public relations through propaganda circulated to Parent-Teacher presidents.

Whether these people were Cotterites or not was a moot point. The danger of Cotter's movement was that it attracted every breed of would-be demagogue. These small groups, many of them splinters of more powerful dissident and patriotic elements, discovered in Cotter a focal point around which they coalesced. While they represented varied, often opposing, goals, they knew the power of united action. They had chosen Cotter as their leader, and Cotter was making the most of it. His coming rally in Madison Square Garden would center attention upon the growing strength of the extremist amalgamation and would attempt to make it appear that they represented a powerful segment of the American population. Cotter himself was not the crowd-whipper that Hitler was: He was more of an organization man, an expert at propaganda and the wielder of influence in high places. The time was ripe, I thought, as a chill crept up my spine, for an orator to emerge, one with the aggressive animal instinct to dominate the herd, to merge and lash the myriad little tongues of extremism into a single resounding voice of intimidation and execration.

As I thought about it, the horror of what might happen filled me with fear. Cotter's money and idealism had purchased for him a significant following among liberals and conservatives alike: the frustrated, insecure, fearful, maladjusted, angry. These were Cotter's followers. Little people with big egos, neurotics with externalized phobias, constant complainers, the lonely, the unloved. Whoever harnessed their fears, focused their insecure outlooks on life, would be their leader. And that emerging leader had to be one who was driven by the fear of both heaven and hell.

Silenus was in a riotous mood as we left the hotel. "Exit laughing," he said, as we merged into the street.

"What's so funny?" I asked him. I was still depressed over the implications of Mary's report.

Jo was beside me, choosing me, and leaving Silenus to accompany Mary. Jo started laughing, an extraordinary giggle thrown in. "Something Mary said, Art."

Mary heard her. She hastened to catch up with us, eager to explain. "Mr. James! All I said was, was that Mr. Cotter was a very nice man."

That made me quite hysterical.

"Well, he is!" Mary insisted. She told us of a meeting at George Rankin's apartment that Cotter had attended. Apparently the others were friends of Rankin, who at the time was Jo's boss. Only later did Rankin go to work for Cotter. The group was obviously the Cotterite cell whose existence Jo had suspected.

Jo turned around. She gripped Mary's arm. We were waiting for the light at Capitol Street. Union Station rose high and shadowed beyond the Plaza, beyond the Supreme Court. "Tell me, Mary," Jo said. "Did Mr. Pratt attend Mr. Rankin's meeting?"

Mary shook her head. "No, Mr. Doyle took me."

"I know that," Jo said. "But was Mr. Pratt there too."

Mary shook her head. "No, I didn't see him there, Miss Davis. Of course Mr. Rankin worked at the Foundation then."

Nothing more was said as we crossed to the railway station. Looking up, I read the inscription on the fantastic facade:

Sweetener of hut and of hall
Bringer of life out of naught
Freedom O fairest of all
The daughters of time and thought.

We passed through the station's central triumphant arch into the vast waiting room. "Ah," Silenus cried, "classic Burnham!" he craned his neck to look into the vault. "The noblest Roman of them all. Next chariot stops at Nova Yorka."

Silenus set the pace across the concourse, with Mary tagging after him. Jo kept by my side. I followed Mary up the cross-hatched steps to the Pullman. "We're in here, Art." Jo and Mary had adjoining rooms.

On the pretext that I wanted to buy the evening papers, I left Silenus and went back to the station's concourse. It was a hunch, but I had to find out. I asked the Pullman attendant for Harry Cotter's room number, as if I had no doubt he was on the train.

I was right.

Chapter Twenty-Seven

On the train I knocked on Cotter's door. The master plotter appeared. He was holding his cane. The white pearly knob glistened. His right hand grasped the gleaming black stalk. Easily he shifted the cane to his left hand, put out his right.

"How are you, Art?" he asked cheerfully as he shook my hand.

Here was no menacing monster. Merely a man clad in a gray business suit. His white hair was sleek on his slanting skull, his eyes dark, his thin lips arched in a biting smile, his nose sharp and pinched. His clasp was warm and enfolding.

"Please come in," he said.

I sat down beside him on a long brown couch. "This is a pleasant surprise, Art. I tried to reach you at the hotel."

A train on the next track was filling. A blond girl stared back at me. The train lurched. We began to move. The girl vanished in a kaleidoscope of blurred faces.

"So you found me," I said.

"It wasn't difficult." Cotter polished the knob of his cane. "We have a mutual friend, General Quince."

"He's not a friend of mine."

"Silenus then. We've crossed swords often, Silenus and I. It was valuable for you to have had the benefit of his advice and counsel."

"Gideon Pratt didn't think so."

Cotter lit a cigar. The flame died in his narrow eyes. The suburbs of Washington flashed by the window. "He makes a magnificent enemy," he said. "He hates so utterly."

"What about me?" I asked.

"Your youthful idealism shows through. You trust too much."

I laughed. "Funny, I always thought of myself as a hard-boiled, don't-care newspaperman. A cynic."

"You credit yourself with too little goodness, Art. Hate is an art only the holy can handle. Others give up too soon."

"I haven't the slightest idea what you're talking about."

"You take Gideon," he went on, concentrating on polishing the cane between puffs on his cigar. "He led you so far and then he left you. Those left behind, those stones on which he stepped, suspect his defeat, but they are wrong. He is not defeated, for he had no cause except his own, and his own is always served."

I shook my head. I was puzzled. I didn't have a clue as to what he was talking about, not then. I thought I knew Gideon better than anyone. Cotter was good at talking in riddles. I changed the subject.

"You saw Senator Bentley this morning," I said.

Cotter nodded.

"And Secretary Peters?"

He nodded again.

"You think you're unbeatable, don't you?"

Cotter puffed hungrily on his cigar. The image of its fire glowed in his eyes. "When you love enough," he said, "you hate enough to defend what you love."

"And you think you're going to win the country?"

"It's only a matter of time."

"It's as simple as that, is it?"

Cotter rubbed the knob of his cane again. "It's not simple, Art. The country is in the possession of the apathetic. They are angry only with the past. They blame a previous generation, a prior government administration. They learn nothing from history, which is to say they haven't learned that evil exists in present time alone and must be dealt with daily. The evil is within us."

I watched the flow of the flame in his eyes. "I'm not sure I understand you."

"Look at it this way. Certainly there are root causes for present evil, but these causes we can leave to philosophers like Silenus. Theologians tell us that man is by nature sinful. So be it. I have no argument with that.

Sin is admitted. It is present. It must be rooted out. That is because sin is contagious. It afflicts the undisciplined, the immature in mind and spirit."

"But how can the weak be strong?"

"Our strength lies in our right-thinking, tough-minded leaders, who are not swayed by sentimental pleas about individual liberties." Cotter paused to observe the descending darkness outside the single pane that separated us from the night sky. He held the cane up high. It wobbled in his tremulous grasp. "The safety of our country is at stake, Art. We must rid the country of those who would corrupt the nation's soul. It is the Devil's trick to say that good and evil can exist side by side."

I stood up. I needed to stretch, to give myself a moment to distance myself from his enticing words. Cotter rolled the cane on his knees. "You better watch out, Mr. Cotter," I said, "because it's going to be either you or me."

Cotter laughed, a rasping chuckle. "Why, I could thrash you anytime." He brandished the cane.

"Your power doesn't frighten me."

"They all say that."

"I'm not afraid, Mr. Cotter. What have I got to lose?" I laughed in his face. "You're getting old, Mr. Cotter."

He leaned back, looked out the window, where night had fallen. "There are others to come after us."

"Such as?"

He continued to gaze out the window. "Oh, Bentley, for one. Although I don't completely trust him."

"Then he is a Cotterite?"

"Most effective. But Peters is an embarrassment."

"You mean because of Page Seventy? That was merely embarrassing?"

"Embarrassing to our entire program for the armed services," he replied. "It was Wakefield's fault. Stupid thing to do. Brings open the issue of the use of public funds to promote the views of the private group."

"Then why don't you give me a statement, denying responsibility for Page Seventy?"

Cotter sighed, as if I was a dunce to whom his logic was quite beyond my ability to comprehend. "Because that tract is within the spirit of the Cotter societies. Besides, the Frontier Fathers is one of our best contributors."

"You don't care who your bedfellows are?"

"As long as they're fighting Communism."

I touched the cane, which Cotter had laid on the seat beside him. "That's a fancy cane," I said. I picked it up. It's weight surprised me. "Quite a weapon."

"It could be," Cotter replied. "Picked it up in a Moscow antique shop. The dealer said it belonged to the Czar. Not, of course, that I put any stock in that."

"You didn't mention the cane in your Moscow thesis."

"I've explained that!" he cried testily. "I was glad to see the overthrow of tyranny."

"And the beginning of a new one?"

"It was only later that the aims of the revolution were betrayed!"

"It took you a while to find that out."

Cotter glared at me. "I wasn't alone in my admiration of the Communist experiment." He picked up the cane and tapped its knob on the couch. "Later it became an international conspiracy. My experience in Moscow gives me a certain authority."

"You didn't exactly make it public."

"Except for suppressing my thesis, I never tried to keep my experience in Moscow a secret. Lots of other Americans were in Moscow at the time. And they are still loyal Americans."

"I may quote you on that?" I asked, smiling.

"Not yet. I will explain everything in the Garden," he said.

I thanked him for the interview and went back to my compartment, Silenus wasn't there. I suspected he was in the bar. I swayed through the corridor, leaped the crevasse to the next car, stopped to watch the moon-swept Maryland meadows march swiftly past. Now, I thought, I could apply my talent to bring down this demagogue who tampered with my life. For, I realized, while I had been crusading against him, Cotter had been above the proscenium arch, wielding his awesome power, working his violent will. In a way, I had been no more than a puppet dancing to his manipulations. Cotter had tested my mettle. He would soon see I was equal to his testing.

Above meadows the moon rose high and slim under thin narrow clouds. Down the track a red light swung and clang went a crossing bell and clang again. Low on a road a car honked its moaning horn. Tall poles, laced by threading wires, clicked past. Stooks of standing corn stood silently sentinel in cut stubble fields. Lonely houses shut against the cold edged sharply up not far from the tracks. Stark rusty single lightbulbs probed station platforms and merging rails, tightly bonded, forever wedded.

Beyond the bar, where a mustached man gestured wildly to a girl in a tight silvery dress, Jo sat in one of the parlor chairs, Silenus next to her. I stepped over his out-thrust legs and sat down by Jo. Silenus raised his glass. "Here's to the nation's unsung heroes," he said. "Those untiring battlers against Communism."

Jo clinked her glass against that of Silenus. "You're a joy and a pleasure to be with, Silenus," she said brightly.

"Thank you, my dear," Silenus replied jovially. He downed half the glass.

"What are you celebrating?" I asked. "We didn't win anything."

"Our reward is in playing the game," Silenus said. "No matter who wins, as long as it isn't Cotter."

"He's won this time, Silenus. You will want to tie one on, so you might as well start now. Drink up!"

Silenus did as I suggested. I told them about my interview with Cotter. Jo paled. Silenus sank low in his chair, drinking steadily. When I finished, he sat glowering for a while.

"Gideon rejected all of us," he said. "He didn't understand what was happening. He thought he could conquer by his own resources. He's never learned it's not that kind of world, not anymore."

"Jo leaned toward him." She was wearing a scarlet tight-fitting robe. "What kind of world is it, Silenus?"

Silenus put down his glass. He leaned toward us. A serious cloud of concern veiled his face. "Listen," he said. "This is a world in which the wise are aware that power sits only in the seats of the mighty. A world in which that power is preserved by gentlemen's agreement: You keep your hands off my field of control and I will keep my hands off yours."

"You make it sound quite hopeless," I said.

Silenus waved his hand groggily. "I'm just a simple-minded professor, Art. I couldn't live in that kind of world myself, although I understand it. Gideon tried to live in it, but he failed, for whatever reasons I don't know."

"I think I know," Jo said. "I think it was my fault."

"Your's!" both Silenus and I cried in unison.

"Well," she said, rocking back and forth, digging her heels into the carpet. "Perhaps we are all guilty. We drove Gideon pretty hard, you know."

On the other side of Jo two women in jackets with ermine collars talked together in whispers. Next to me a man with white hair was deep in the Washington Post. I looked back at Jo. Her eyes were clouded with tears. "I don't understand," she said. "I will never understand. Gideon was always so sure of himself."

"Like a fox," Silenus muttered.

"No," Jo said softly. "Not cunning. Ambition, perhaps. But not mean."

"One thing's certain," Silenus said. "He bit off more than he could chew."

I disagreed with Silenus about that. "Cotter was too smart for us," I said. "Too powerful."

"Gideon used to say," Silenus went on, "never wait for opportunity to come knocking on your door. Something his father told him, no doubt."

I took Jo's hand. It throbbed in mine. "Come with me, Jo." I helped her up. Silenus was deep in his drink. I don't think he saw us leave.

When I closed the door to my compartment, Jo turned from me and sat down on the couch and looked out at the passing dark night. I took down a blanket from the overhead rack and tucked it around her. She dropped her black spike-heeled shoes to the floor. Still she continued to look sadly out the window. I sat down beside her. "Jo, are you in love with Gideon?" I asked.

"No," she replied, not looking my way. "To be honest, Art, I don't know. He has been attracted to me, I know that. But then, he's married. I kept reminding him, and myself, of that. He didn't like it. It was silly, the way he flirted with me. Because I know Amy, and I like her. I thought I had a lot in common with Gideon. We talked together by the hour, had lunch together quite often. I'm sure he didn't tell Amy about that. I thought I could count on Gideon. Now he has run away, deserted us, just when we needed him most."

I reached for her hand, but she pulled away. "Gideon said a strange thing last night," she went on, her voice edged with some uncontrollable grief. "Was it only last night? Gideon said, 'They all work together. They work with one another so we can't do anything.' I asked him who he was talking about, and what was it we can't do anything about. 'Everyone,' he said. 'Don't you see? What's the use of all our plans? They've made up their minds to be against us. You have to work with them.' Now, wasn't that strange? I told him he was talking nonsense, but he raved on like that. I told him the world isn't like that at all. You have to know where you stand, and stand there, on your side, despite everything."

"You don't have to tell me more, Jo," I said. I took her soft hand in mine. "Jo, I want to tell you. I love you, Jo."

She entwined her fingers in mine. "That's what Gideon said. I asked him what hope was there for us."

The tears came, long streams of tears on her pallid cheeks, staining the pale flesh and falling from her face to her upraised hands. She covered her face. I bent to her and put my arms around her and drew her to me. I unfolded the dress from her soft white shoulders. The swaying of the train on the driven rails swept our pain away. The comfort of swishing wheels sang of our joy.

Chapter Twenty-Eight

Two weeks later I was in Green's office to be considered for Gideon's job. Gideon had been fired. The order had come from Fletcher. Our mission to Washington had been a failure. Green got an ultimatum: either fire Gideon or lose the Educational Foundation account. Green complied, gave Gideon three months' separation pay and let him go immediately. All this I got from Jo, who had been frantically trying to reach Gideon but without success. He had dropped out of sight. His home phone had been disconnected.

Green rose from behind his desk. The room looked even more Spartan than before, all steel and linoleum. "Art!" he exclaimed. "Great to see you!"

"I'm sorry about Gideon," I said, sitting down.

Green scratched his stubble beard. "I am too, in a way."

"Do you know what he's doing?"

"He made us look like damn fools, that's what," Green said. "Getting his picture in the papers like that. Well, I suppose he was only trying to do his job. It was my fault. I shouldn't have asked him to go after Cotter by himself. He didn't have what it takes." He looked at me through half-slitted eyes. "You think you have?"

"I know I have."

"I'd hire Silenus if he was available. Best damn public relations man I ever saw, when you gave him his lead. But he turned down the job." He looked at my brief resume, which I had sent over the day before. "You've had a lot of newspaper experience, Art. And you already know the Cotter case. What do you think it would take to hire you?"

"Whatever Gideon was getting would be fine," I said coolly.

He threw back his head, laughing. His wild white hair tossed. "Sorry, Art. Out of the question. We'd have to start you out lower, much lower."

"Whatever you say."

"You don't sound much like you want the job."

"If I can have a free hand with Cotter."

"Well, as I said, it was too much of a free hand that got Gideon into trouble."

"I'm not so sure of that."

"Supposing I let you know."

"When?"

"After the rally in the Garden."

I agreed. I said I would be thinking about it, too. I went into Gideon's office. I sat down at his desk. The overhead vent gave off a murmur. Here in this office, I thought, I could be close to Jo. I could have lunch with her two or three times a week. I could work with the advertising men of Madison Avenue. I could work against Cotter. I telephoned Jo.

"Guess where I am," I said.

She couldn't guess, of course. I told her. There was a dead silence on the phone. Then: "Art, you can't."

"I'm considering it." I thought she should be pleased.

"Let's talk about it," she said

I stood up and looked around the windowless room. Gideon's failure, I told myself, resulted from the fact that he had become too emotionally involved in the Cotterite case. Was I not the cool, calculating newsman, with the newsman's detachment? Surely I could fit in well with Gibson Green's organization. I would be working days, have my evenings free for Jo. I would make more money. I could afford an apartment, be able to move from my small room. Then, maybe, a car. Finally, I would marry Jo. Yes, all these things would be made possible. All I had to do was to say yes to Green. I shivered. Gideon's ghost seemed to haunt the room. I went out to visit Mary.

She seemed oddly detached, as if she had not known me. Or as if, I guessed, she knew something she didn't want to tell me. She adjusted her brown framed eye glasses. I could not recall having seen her wearing them before. They added years to her appearance. She crooked a finger, beckoning me to come closer. "Mr. Doyle wants me to work for him," she whispered.

"No! Really?"

"I have to look more mature," Mary said, flashing me one of her shy smiles. "Actually, the lenses aren't lenses at all. Plain glass." She tapped them, as if that would prove they were false.

"Good luck," I said. I noticed the absence of carnations on her desk. "If you hear from Mr. Pratt," I said, "tell him I was asking about him, will you?"

She nodded, then answered her ringing phone.

If there had ever been anything between us, I thought on my way down on the elevator, it was certainly over. While Mary had come from my part of the world, something had happened to me in New York that had severed any feeling I had for the midwest simplicities. I knew the main cause of this was Jo. She was a Manhattanite through and through. I wanted to be part of her world. Suddenly I realized I was taking the same emotional journey that Gideon must have taken. The difference between us was that I was free to love, to marry, and Gideon was not.

As the time approached for Cotter's rally in the Garden, and for Green's decision, the hours, the minutes, dragged. At my Dispatch desk I wrote furiously, like one possessed. I had stories every day on the Cotterites. I rehashed the Washington episode. I was given greater freedom to editorialize, since every story was under my byline. I began getting fan mail, and much criticism too, even threats. I started toying with the idea of starting a column, and I even wrote one on speculation for Al's comment in which I answered all my critics. I never got up enough courage to show it to Al. I locked it in my desk drawer. It would be something new to take to Al if and when I needed it.

Cotter's publicity boy, George Rankin, kept feeding me stuff about the rally. Senator McLeod would introduce Cotter. There would be delegations from almost every New England state. Worth Brownell told me he was raising the anti-Cotter temperature among the New York local unions of the Caretakers. One item I gave special treatment: Silenus was elected president of the Platonic Society. The Dispatch even ran his picture.

As for Jo, we saw one another often, sometimes at the Press Gallery, sometimes in her apartment. But she kept putting me off, and not once would she say she loved me.

244

Chapter Twenty-Nine

Outside Madison Square Garden, David Morgan and his lieutenants marshaled the Pythia University students. Paired off, led by a bugler playing *Semper Fidelis*, they marched into the Garden. I went in behind Jo and Silenus, who leaped the stairs. The students filled the top rows of our section. When we were settled, the bugler sounded *Taps*. Banner-bearers pounded poles. Echoes of the bugling rang off the steel arches and died. A policeman pounced toward the bugler. Waving his arms, the cop argued. Their words were lost in an avalanche of student protest.

The banked seats opposite us filled. The crowds darkened with battalions of students from New York and Columbia universities, then other regiments from Rutgers, Long Island and Brooklyn. There was a sound of faraway feet ascending aisles. A demonic murmur rose and ebbed as if the protest, already begun, fought containment.

In the arena the chairs filled with the mink and velvet-collar crowd: the Cotterites, the thousands of them, silent and disciplined. Soon the lower boxed-in seats were filled by ticketed well-dressed guests, obviously the right-wing crowd.

From the rear entrance to the arena now emerged the Manhattan High School cadet corps. Paced by a brass band playing *Stars and Stripes*, the boys marched around in circles, splendid in their scarlet tunics.

High above, on the topmost rows of seats, David Morgan stood up. He raised his arm. His bugle blared. The arena's overhead lights dimmed. The arena's stage burst into focus with the stabbing beam of a spotlight, which searched the platform like the giant beam of a Cyclop's eye. Onto the stage marched a row of tiny figures, like ants on parade. Althea Ringwood, the full-bosomed opera star, trailing a dazzling white gown, began singing the National Anthem: *Oh say, can you see---*.

Senator McLeod introduced himself. "You all know me---" The Senate, he said, was very much interested in what was going on in the schools. Un-American activities, he promised, might conceivably begin hearings on what very much looked like a successful Communist takeover of the classroom.

Strangely, the stands were silent. Around the arena, all was darkly quiet. Then, as if abashed by their sparse numbers, the Cotterites applauded politely. They appeared fearful, oppressed by the enormous weight of the opposition, the gulf that separated them from the people in the vast balconies above them. I glanced down the row to David Morgan. He was hunched forward, chin resting on his clenched fist.

Senator McLeod, face pale in the lancing light, introduced several "prominent educators" whose high positions in public education, the senator said, qualified them to state the validity of Cotter's claim that the Communists were scuttling the schools. Each educator paid tribute to the Senator as a fierce fighter for freedom, and to Cotter as a plain-spoken businessman whose great loyalty and deep convictions, to say nothing of his courage, made him the arch enemy of the Communists.

Another selection by the cadet bands: *My Country 'Tis of Thee*. A solo by the opera's pride: *America the Beautiful*.

Cotter came out of the darkness and crossed to the front of the stage. He leaned his cane against the lectern. He posed in the spotlight to acknowledge the burst of cheers from the arena's standing audience and boos from the upper galleries. He posed and waved, smiled and grinned.

Finally the outburst subsided. Slowly his vast audience assumed their seats and there was silence.

"Always remember this night," Cotter began in a dry monotone. His pudgy hands flailed the air. "What is happening here will go down in history as the turning point, the night the tide reversed. I promise you this: tomorrow the tide of Communism, which now threatens to engulf this nation, will be on the ebb." His voice was dry, almost hoarse. A smattering of handclapping seemed to please him. "Why do I say this? Because of the spirit of Americans, shown by you young people here tonight." He waved toward us. "Because of the unconquerable spirit that is stronger than Communism." He paused for the effect. The arena was slow in responding. There were a few cheers. "Day will dawn," Cotter continued, "on a new era in American life. We will awaken to the danger, the terrible threat, of Communism. Not Communism far away in another country, but Communism here in our midst, tearing away at the foundation of American freedom."

There was a restlessness in the stands, some stamping of feet. "But I will have more to say on this later, my friends. Meanwhile, I want to present to you a man, a young man, who represents the finest ideals of the republic, a man who has just joined my staff."

Cotter looked around, gripping the lectern. The spotlight struck a halo around his head. "Ladies and gentlemen, it is my great pleasure to present to you--my vice-president for public relations, Mr. Gideon Pratt!"

"Oh, my God," Jo gasped.

My breath bolted. "Gideon?" I asked Silenus.

Silenus looked as if he had been struck dumb. "The bastard," he hissed.

Gideon was shaking Cotter's hand. Now he was alone at the lectern. He posed, as Cotter had, in the spotlight. Cotter raised Gideon's arm, then turned quickly away and vanished into the darkness.

Gideon gripped the lectern and then, with one mighty upward and foreword gesture, raised his right arm, palm down, thumb tightly pressed against the remaining commanding fingers. Slowly he swept his arm over the arena. He began.

"Comrades!" He waited. His arm was still, stiff, in control. Was that a hush of horror in the arena? "Yes, it can happen here!" Gideon's voice rang like thunder from huge loudspeakers. "Some day soon, from this very platform, where I stand, a Communist could stand!"

He looked around to the heights of the Garden. "You young people up there, answer me! Is that what you want?"

Utter silence in the darkness.

"Do you want the Garden filled with Communists? Is that what you would rather have?" Gideon waited for a response. "Answer!" He shouted "Yes or no?" He leaned forward and spoke directly into the microphone. "David! David Morgan!" Gideon looked up and pointed, finger lancing, toward me. No, it was toward David.

David rose from his seat. Row on row, the Pythia students turned to look at him. "David," Gideon called again. "You're there, I can see you. Answer me, David. Yes or no?"

Hypnotically, David Morgan whispered.

"What's that, David?"

As in slow motion, David raised his hands and cupped them over his mouth. "No!" His word bore down on the Cotterites, tore across the arena and into the opposite stands. "No!" It came again, an echo of itself.

This time it was Gideon repeating the word. "No! That's right!" He cried triumphantly. "No one wants the Communists to rule America!"

Gideon turned his attention to the students far away. "You students, you don't want it. You Caretakers, yes, I know you are here, you don't want it. You businessmen, down there, you don't want it!"

From the arena there arose a thumping sound.

"This country," Gideon thundered, "is in mortal danger, not from the threat of the enemy without, but from the enemy within. Moral sickness, a weakness that is wrecking our strength."

Gideon paused again, bent slightly and picked up Cotter's cane. "This is what we need," he hissed, holding the cane on high. "The power that will drive out the Communists!" He brought the cane down with a crash on the top edge of the lectern. "Power!" He held the cane above his head. "That is what they understand!" His manner of addressing his audience echoed his performance in Bond Hall years before, when he enthralled Richland University students with his practiced way of lecturing.

Behind him, others on the platform leaned forward. Cotter remained hidden in the shadows.

"I tell you," Gideon cried, "their wickedness is beyond belief. They lie their way into the noblest professions, they hide their vile intentions behind a veil of loyalty, but are they dangerous? Yes! They plot our ruin, they steal the treasure your fathers died for, they hate you! Yes!" He drew a breath that could be heard throughout the garden. "Yes, they hate their country!"

Now there was a murmur, rising into audibility. It came from the arena. There was a muted echo, sharp and crisp.

Gideon turned toward the Pythians again. "David!"

David, still standing, said "Yes?" Certainly few could hear him.

"Do you hate the Communists, David?"

"Yes!" This time David shouted so loud that it was evident he could be heard in the arena, whose audience clapped loudly. I looked closely. David was speaking into a microphone!

"You will fight the Communists, David?"

Then, cane out-flung, a sword point: "You love your country, David?"

"Yes! Yes!"

I was on my feet, moving along the row, tripping. Silenus followed. We made our way, despite the difficulty, to David's side.

"David," Silenus commanded. "Follow me!" But now a large number of other students had risen. They were singing a chorus: "Yes! Yes!" Forced back, I fell on a bench.

Gideon, his hand on the cane's knob, passed it over the crowd like a magic wand. It's path cut a whistling swath.

"You hear?" His voice was cutting, shrill. "Pythia students hate the Communists. You, you other students over there. Do you hear?"

A gutteral roar from the opposite side.

"Two weeks ago, just two weeks ago, I was like you were. I scorned Harry Cotter. Yes! I scourged him, He was an enemy to be fought. I was out to win. But then, but then, Harry Cotter came to me. Yes! To me! You never heard of me before, but I was like you were. And you know what he said? He said: Son. Yes! He called me that! The one I had persecuted."

From the stands David cried "No!"

"Yes, David," he said softly, his mouth close to the microphone. He turned about and pointed the cane at Cotter. "This good man," he said, raising his voice, "who loves his country so much, who loves us so much. O! when I think of it. O! how could I have done it? I will tell you why." He raised the cane again. "It was because I couldn't see. I didn't know what I was doing. Then, when he came, I was blind with ignorance of the meaning of his coming. And I said, Why me? Why choose me? And, you know what he said? He said 'Gideon, why are you doing this to me?' And I had no answer, because I was like you were, before tonight. Oh, what have I done? I was as zealous as you were in persecuting him and his followers. No, more than that, I was one of his chief persecutors, I was paid to persecute him, it was my job! Then, he spoke to me. Yes! Harry Cotter showed me why I was like that, like you are. Oh, the great goodness of the man! Oh, Americans! Americans! You don't know what your name means! That we should turn on *him*! You see! You see! This is what the Communists have done. Yes! They have turned one American against another. They have planted evil ideas in our minds. They have made us question one another.

Why? Why? Because they are not Americans! No! They are loyal to another country, our country's enemy. Yes! Harry Cotter knows that enemy, knows him because he was there when the Communists made slaves of the people there. When all the world was saying how wonderful those devils were, he was warning us that they wanted to make slaves of us too. Yes! You newspaper and television people there."

He raised the cane from the lectern and pointed it at the reporters' tables beyond the arena. "He thinks you're there," Silenus said to me.

"You reporters," Gideon went on accusingly, "you are persecuting him too. Are you enemies of America? Of course not. You follow those who say that slavery is better than to die in the defense of your country. Americans!" He circled the Garden with his gaze. "Wake up before it is too late! The enemy is there before us, we surround him, he is in the midst of us. What are you waiting for? I will tell you, you don't know who he is. Yes! You are blind. You feel the enemy is here, but you cannot see him. And that is because he is so evil. He dresses like an American. He speaks like an American. He acts like an American. But you can tell. You can tell! Does he say we should give up our nuclear power? Does he say we should try to live like the Russians? That they have better education? You have heard these things, but you close your ears to them. You close your eyes to the books they place in the schools and universities. You know what I mean! Soft-headed, socialist, leftist books by writers who have been listed as subversive by the Department of Justice and the FBI! These writers are everywhere in America. They sneer at our flag and everything it stands for."

Gideon brought the cane down again. The cane hit the microphone. The thud whined against the Garden's roof. He looked straight ahead, beyond the thousand arena chairs, to the Caretakers banked above them. "Brownell!" he shouted. "Yes, Brownell. You're here, Brownell, making traitors out of honest working men, men whose fathers and fathers' fathers came to America to escape enslavement. Men! Do you want the slavery of Siberia?" A chorus of "No! No!" Gideon stormed on: "Then follow me! Follow Harry Cotter! Cut the chains that bind you to your hypocritical leaders who work in marble halls. You have Communists among your members. Where is your pride? Gone with your freedom?"

Now the Caretakers were on their feet, their applause clapped like thunder and arched across the vaulted hall.

From the students on the left a rising cheer, mounting wave on rising wave, merging with the beat of five thousand hands, the pounding of student feet, and the tremulous soaring of trumpets blowing from on high. Suddenly lights on the arena's ceilings flashed, on and of, on and off. Gideon turned and slashed the cane through the vibrating air. He crossed the wide space between the lectern and the waiting officers of Cotterite societies. He handed the cane to Cotter, who embraced him heartily.

It appeared to me, standing with Jo and Silenus, silent, drained of all feeling, that Gideon pulled on the cane and tugged Cotter to the lectern.

Cotter's speech was anti-climax. There were some boos at first, subdued and halted by hisses of annoyance. Cotter referred to a forthcoming manifesto that, he said, told the truth about the Moscow thesis and Page Seventy. He received a standing ovation, polite but not prolonged.

Cotter beckoned Gideon to the foreground. A roar of excited approval, applause and foot-stomping shook the Garden to the rafters.

Chapter Thirty

The wind had come up. Dark clouds raced to cover the last of the stars. We waited, not speaking, as the students emerged, clustered. There was little talking. David Morgan was not among them. We stood on the corner of Eighth Avenue, a tight little knot.

"Will Gideon be the leader now?" Jo asked.

Silenus, beside her, thrust his hands in his pockets. He hunched his shoulders. "The Good Lord save us," he said. "Gideon got what he wanted."

"Then there is no hope," Jo said, her face a forlorn mask.

"None at all," Silenus agreed. "Tomorrow it will be in all the papers. The Cotterites have a new leader. One of the takeover generation."

We began walking north. "But the story," I said, "is not in what happened in the Garden tonight. The story is in what happened in Washington."

"No," said Silenus. "It's not there, at least not all of it. It's in what Gideon has been all his life, how he got that way."

"What we know," said Jo, quickening her pace, "is very little. We know where he was born, who his parents were, what his father did. We know how he served so well in Korea. We know how and why he became a teacher and where he taught. We know about his career with Gibson Green. I wonder--" She looked curiously at Silenus. "I wonder if even Cotter knows him, if anyone really knows him."

"My dear," said Silenus, "I don't very much care."

I grabbed Silenus' arm, stopped him, there amidst the descending crowds.

"Well, I do!" I said. "I know him now. I know him beneath the surface details of his life." I smiled at Jo. "I know him because I know myself." I took Jo's hand.

We crossed Forty-Second Street, where the million lights glittered fitfully all the way to Times Square. We entered the gloom of the blocks beyond.

"I wonder what will happen to Gideon?" Jo asked.

There was no answer.

Silenus asked me "You will fight him?"

"I will fight him," I said.

"I hear," Silenus said, "they got you all sewed up."

"Not yet, Silenus. Tell Green I am not sorry. Thanks, but no thanks."

"You're young," Silenus said.

Jo looked up at the clouded sky, as if there were stars to be seen. "Yes, isn't it wonderful? To be young in New York, I mean, with all this to look forward to?" She gestured, indicating she meant the city.

We walked again in silence for a while. I halted. Jo and Silenus stopped with me.

"What are we stopping here for?" Silenus asked. "I thought maybe you would both like come down to my pad and--"

"The Dispatch," I said, looking up at the high noble façade. They looked at me: my friends. When they understood, Jo kissed me.

Silenus shook my hand. "Goodbye," he said. "Good luck."

"Not luck," I told him. "Courage, perhaps."

Jo took my hand. We marched into the dim, dingy lobby. It looked beautiful. I was home again. The elevator's clatter was like sweet music.

In the wonderful cluttered newsroom, my reporter friends stared at Jo. There were whistles and a few cheers. I drew up a chair for Jo and sat down beside her, facing my desk. I put a sheet of copy paper in my beat-up typewriter and typed my name in the upper left corner. My fingers flew on the keys of power.

Al came over from the city desk. He welcomed Jo with a warm welcoming glint in his eyes. "We heard about Gideon on the radio, Art. What's your angle?"

"The truth," I replied. "About Cotter. And about Gideon Pratt."

Al called loudly to Fred Roberts, who had been covering my beat while I was away. "Okay, Fred, knock it off. Art James is back!"

Later, on the street, I looked both ways on Eighth Avenue. Not a cab in sight. "What will it be, Jo? Wait for a taxi or take the subway?"

"Let's live it up, Art. Let's take the subway to my place."

The End

Printed in the United States
By Bookmasters

Journeys of Loss; Horizons of Hope

Meredith Shave

WESTBOW
PRESS®
A DIVISION OF THOMAS NELSON
& ZONDERVAN

Family photo by Jess Henderson.
Author photo by David Longobardo, DL Captures.

Unless otherwise indicated, all scripture taken from the New King James Version®. Copyright © 1982 by Thomas Nelson. Used by permission. All rights reserved.

Scripture quotations marked (NIV) are taken from the Holy Bible, New International Version®, NIV®. Copyright © 1973, 1978, 1984, 2011 by Biblica, Inc.™ Used by permission of Zondervan. All rights reserved worldwide. www.zondervan.com The "NIV" and "New International Version" are trademarks registered in the United States Patent and Trademark Office by Biblica, Inc.™

WestBow Press books may be ordered through booksellers or by contacting:

WestBow Press
A Division of Thomas Nelson & Zondervan
1663 Liberty Drive
Bloomington, IN 47403
www.westbowpress.com
1 (866) 928-1240

Because of the dynamic nature of the Internet, any web addresses or links contained in this book may have changed since publication and may no longer be valid. The views expressed in this work are solely those of the author and do not necessarily reflect the views of the publisher, and the publisher hereby disclaims any responsibility for them.

Any people depicted in stock imagery provided by Getty Images are models, and such images are being used for illustrative purposes only. Certain stock imagery © Getty Images.

ISBN: 978-1-9736-4232-9 (sc)
ISBN: 978-1-9736-4231-2 (hc)
ISBN: 978-1-9736-4233-6 (e)

Library of Congress Control Number: 2018912059

Print information available on the last page.

WestBow Press rev. date: 10/25/2018

To Jon ...

Kind-hearted and selfless, you have become my favorite person and very best friend. You, my darling, take "saving the best for last" to a whole new level. Encouraging me to share my past to give others hope is just one of the many reasons I love you.

Together forever,
Mer

Contents

The Empty Chair

The picture for the cover of this book revealed itself as I searched through hundreds of my sunrise photos. I kept going back to the ones of the aged Adirondack chair.

When I lived near the ocean, it sat in the sand at the end of the path that led to the beach. Before dawn, I walked by it every morning. I was drawn to its splintered wood and rugged beauty. I wondered who had left it there. Among the seagrass, it seemed strong yet weary and worn.

The wooden chair became a focal point of many of my photos; something beckoned me to focus on the light surrounding the old chair. The emptiness represents loss and grief. In my own journey, it portrays a divorce, the passing of my beautiful mother, and the sudden and tragic death of a husband.

But it also depicts any kind of loss—perhaps a loss of innocence, the death of a child, the end of a career, a decrease of physical mobility, or the devastation of a dream.

Look higher and turn your gaze beyond the chair. The sun, rising on the horizon, brightens the picture. The radiant light symbolizes hope— the kind of hope that always is there, just like the dawning of a new day.

Jesus is our hope. In fact, He is our only hope.

Jesus is the one who redeems pain, heals lives, and turns sorrow to joy.

1

Walk With Me

How many times have you heard me cry out "God please take this?"
How many times have you given me strength to just keep breathing?

—PLUMB, "NEED YOU NOW"

My mother named me well. Meredith is Welsh and means "guardian of the sea."

Before dawn, I stand on the sand where the water meets the shore and look out over the vast expanse, taking it all in. I adore the ocean breeze on my skin and the sound of the seagulls. The dancing waves are enchanting, and the sun cresting over the horizon never fails to bring a smile to my face.

Truthfully, the ocean ministers to me.

The Virginia horse country claims my roots, but the northeastern coast of Florida is my home. I have a deep love of horses in my bones, and I often run to the ocean to meet the sunrise. Maybe that's why I'm most content astride a horse or on the beach—or even better, galloping the length of the shoreline. The steady pounding of a horse's hooves and the rhythm of the waves are melodies to my ears.

God meets me at the beach. My soul feels absolutely at home walking the shore at sunrise. As the day breaks, hope wells up inside me. I enjoy watching the master artist paint the sky, and I soak in the warmth of the rising light.

My heart carries some hurtful memories; there have been seasons of storm-tossed seas in my life. But the salt air is a healing balm. I dig my heels into the sand, and step after step the world and its problems fade away. Over the pounding of the surf, I hear His whisper. I feel the Lord's presence and know He's walking beside me, even when joy and sorrow meet. Every smile and every tear are noticed by my loving Father.

> *My* heart carries some hurtful memories

The seagulls' morning singing brings a song to my lips. I'm thankful God gifted me with a voice to sing His praises, and that He breathed me into being within the love of a musical family. Melodies and lyrics fill me—songs and psalms, stories and prayers. I mostly listen to praise and worship music now, but my mind often drifts back to the beauty of the old hymns. Music moves me; it is my favorite form of worship, responding with humble thanksgiving to the faithfulness of my Savior, who has never forgotten nor forsaken me.

Along with a passion for music, I enjoy reading and writing. Words leap off pages, probably inherited from my mother, who was a high school English teacher. The songs she wrote for our family to perform are tucked inside my heart in a very special place. Three are included at the end of this chapter.

The book you hold in your hands is my song—a pouring out and back, of sorts, to the waves of grace that sustain me. It is a love story. It traces the route of my life's journey thus far. Like the sprinkling of wrinkles that prove I'm inching toward my fiftieth birthday, these pages reveal years that have been as unpredictable as the ocean, some calm and some stormy.

I'm a mother and a grandmother, yet my heart is as tender as when I was a child. I've weathered a few knee-buckling breakers, as well as some that have knocked me flat and left me gasping for air. First and foremost, I am God's daughter and a woman grateful for the saving grace of Jesus Christ. Every favor and every trial are His.

The sweet innocence of my childhood echoes the words I remember so well: "Jesus loves me this I know, for the Bible tells me so. Little ones to Him belong, they are weak but He is strong." Although I gleaned my faith from my parents, it began to grow as they taught me Scripture from the King James Bible and modeled God's nurturing love.

My memories of church are pleasant. I accepted Jesus as my Savior when I was seven, during an altar call, but it was more a physical action than a response from my heart. I learned more about living a life of faith as I attended Sunday school and youth group, as well as watching my parents live out their faith on a daily basis.

Religion became an intimate relationship for me at the age of twenty-four. The moment my faith became personal remains imprinted on my heart. It was a cool September evening on a church trip that I welcomed Christ's indwelling through the Holy Spirit. I felt an assurance, a blessing, like never before.

It is as true today as it was then: the Lord is my guide, my strength, my peace. Ever since that September night, I have pledged to myself and others, "God has a plan." The role He's writing for me, for my life, is part of His greater love story for the world. It's perfect and purposeful, even through betrayal, divorce, illness, addiction, and death. There are many things I'll never completely understand on this side of heaven. But I look forward to reuniting with my mother and other loved ones one day, and I'll see this truth face-to-face, when all things will be made known. I may not always understand or like God's plan, but I trust the Planner.

> *t*he Lord is my guide, my strength, my peace

Plumb starts her song affirming, "Well, everybody's got a story to tell, and everybody's got a wound to be healed." Like her, I believe there's beauty and meaning in pain. I know that in the hands of God, nothing is wasted.

The words on these pages are simply an act of obedience to the one who inspired me to write them down. The paragraphs are soaked with vulnerability, and this experience has been cathartic and liberating. I pray you will receive the genuine wonder and wonderfulness of God's redeeming love with open hands.

> We are hard pressed on every side, yet not crushed; we are perplexed, but not in despair, persecuted, but not forsaken; struck down, but not destroyed. (2 Corinthians 4:8–9)

Sweet Friend,

The Master Artist is writing your story too, painting a beautiful horizon of hope just for you—a sign of His redeeming grace. Be encouraged. Remember that God can use it all, and you will survive.

As my father used to tell me, "Baby, hindsight is twenty-twenty." Maybe, you've heard it as well. As a child, I didn't know what it meant, but if Daddy said it, it must be true. It's easier now to mentally revisit certain life circumstances and think, "Oh, maybe that's why I went through that," or say, "I'm glad God allowed that door to close!"

My prayer is that within these pages, you will find hope amid His plan and a loving purpose in the middle of your pain.

I hope you enjoy the words of three of my sweet momma's songs. From your mind to your heart, may the love of God our Father wash over you.

Walk with me …
Mer

—— "Changed Like a Butterfly" ——

Jimi Buck

One autumn day, I watched a caterpillar climb a tree.
He wrapped himself in silk and thread; safe from the world was he.
Then winter came with cold and rain, but he was safe inside.
Then with the spring, a miracle: God made a butterfly.

Amazing grace, how can it be? Oh, praise His holy name.
He's wrapped me in His threads of love; I'll never be the same.
One blessed day, I'll see His face. He'll split the eastern sky.
Then with His shout, I'll fly away, changed like a butterfly.

My life was ruined; I had no hope; a hell-bound road I trod.
But then I met the savior, the blessed Son of God.
He changed my life; I've been set free from this old world of sin.
In Him a new creation, I have been born again!

Amazing grace, how can it be? Oh, praise His holy name.
He's wrapped me in His threads of love; I'll never be the same.
One blessed day, I'll see His face. He'll split the eastern sky.
Then with His shout, I'll fly away, changed like a butterfly.

The Bible tells of mystery and how we'll all be changed.
Mortal to immortal, it cannot be explained.
But I will be like Jesus and reign with Him on high.
How can I doubt His promises? I've seen a butterfly.

—— "The Pearl of Great Price" ——

Jimi Buck

At the bottom of the ocean, a tiny oyster
lay wounded by a grain of sand.
It seemed it was all over, as its life just slipped away.
Then, a miracle began ...

Layer upon layer of its essence wrapped around
that tiny stone embedded in its side,
Transforming something hurtful into something rare:
A pearl, the pearl of great price.

Down from heaven's glory, the Savior came
to be, wounded by mortal man.
It seemed it was all over as they nailed Him to a tree.
Then a miracle began ...

Layer upon layer of His blood was wrapped around the very ones
who pierced Him in the side,
Transforming something sinful into something rare:
A pearl, the pearl of great price.

The pearl, the pearl of great price, purchased by our Lord Jesus Christ,
Wrapped up in His blood, transformed by His love.
The pearl, the pearl of great price.
One day in heaven's portal, a bride in spotless
white will stand before a gate of pearl.
There she will be united with the one who bled and died,
Ransomed for this sinful world.

Layer upon layer of His love will wrap around
whosoever on His name has cried,
Transforming something mortal into something rare:
A pearl, the pearl of great price.

—— "THE ALABASTER BOX" ——

Jimi Buck

A woman came to Jesus and knelt before Him there.
Her tears fell on His dusty feet; she wiped them with her hair.
Her repentant heart was aching for things that she had done.
She broke a box of ointment and anointed God's dear Son.

So, break the alabaster box and spill love's precious ointment.
Mingle it with tears to cleanse your troubled soul.
Just break the alabaster box and say, "My Lord, I love You."
He will give you joy, mend your heart, and make you whole.

In love and deep compassion, the Savior saw her sin.
He knew the life that she had led, her sorrow deep within.
But He said, "Because you love Me and prove it willingly,
Your sins, they're all forgiven; your faith has set you free."

The Savior's heart was broken, as He died for you and me.
His blood, like healing ointment, flowed down from Calvary.
And I know that God the Father shed great tears of sorrow when
His only Son beloved paid the price for all our sins.

So break the alabaster box and spill love's precious ointment.
Mingle it with tears to cleanse your troubled soul.
Just break the alabaster box and say, "My Lord, I love You."
He will give you joy, mend your heart, and make you whole.

2

Safe Harbor

I've anchored my soul in the Harbor of Hope,
where the peaceful waters of His love flow.
A place of rest and refuge from the howling winds that blow,
A haven from the hurricanes that rage against my soul.
Jesus is my Harbor of Hope.

—THE RUPPES, "HARBOR OF HOPE"

My story begins on August 4, 1969. It was one of the hottest days of the year in Manassas, Virginia. I am a middle child, and I like to think I was a pleasant surprise.

I was the fourth of six daughters born to Sidney and Jimi Buck. The first two, Phoebe and Ellen, were born sixteen months apart; Amanda came along four years later. I arrived two years after Amanda. I can imagine my parents' disappointment when I looked up at them with long lashes and the all-too-familiar girl parts. Momma and Daddy just knew in their hearts God would have blessed them with a boy; that was the plan, anyway. But as the old saying goes, "If you want to hear God laugh, tell Him your plans."

Six years later, Kimberly was born. The youngest, Patricia, joined our family four years later, on my tenth birthday. She's never lived down the total wreckage of my special day. For years we heard the tale of when Daddy found out she was yet another beautiful baby girl. When he walked into the delivery room and heard the news, he shook his head and, with tears in his eyes, turned and walked out. He wasn't insensitive, just disappointed.

Our father loved all six of his girls well. In fact, he taught us to ride horses, shoot guns, and kick butt if we ever had to. Momma prayed *a lot*. Most of my sisters loved the outdoors and getting dirty. I was a cross between tomboy and girly-girly with long blonde hair. I ran everywhere I went, and my feet always were bare and dusty.

I lived the first six years of my life on a thoroughbred farm, where our dad trained racehorses and our mom broke them for riding. She hardly weighed more than a hundred pounds, and she never thought twice about jumping on the back of one thousand pounds of horseflesh. Mom fondly referred to riding these amazing animals as "like riding a locomotive." She also would breeze them (exercise them on the racetrack) once they were ready.

Of course, I began riding my own horse at a very young age. It was my very first happy place. In fact, one day my Mema lost me. She searched the house and yard, and when she finally found me, I was on my pony, Tiny Tim. I was facing backward with my head on his rump, sound asleep.

Sometime after second grade, we moved to a little town in northeast Florida that was about thirty miles inland. Mom eventually became a high school English teacher, and Dad was a foreman at a dairy farm. Later, he became a deputy with the sheriff's office; he retired as a captain after serving the county for twenty years.

We lived in a small, three-bedroom, two-bathroom home. Six girls shared two bedrooms and one bathroom. We slept in bunk beds, sharing beds until the two oldest left home. Our bathroom was busy. No, it was grossly overcrowded *every* morning. Nevertheless, we were a tight-knit family and loved each other immensely (unless one of us used all the hot water). The Buck household rarely was quiet. We laughed a lot, fought some, and played outside every day.

Some years, we had a television. Birthdays were not expensive parties with friends but family dinners featuring the birthday girl's favorite meal (within reason) and a homemade cake. I never expected, or received, extravagant gifts for my birthday or at Christmas; it was disappointing at times to just get an orange, a candy cane, and a pair of socks in my stocking. But I always knew Momma and Daddy did the best they could. In high school, I had to do small jobs in the neighborhood to earn money in order to attend events.

My childhood was not filled with prestige and wealth, but it overflowed with love. Like the wood pilings under the docks at the marina, the foundation of my childhood was strong and sturdy.

> *L*ike the wood pilings under the docks at the marina, the foundation of my childhood was strong

Sidney and Jimi were well-known about town and very involved in the small Baptist church we attended. Daddy and Momma lived the same faith at home as in public. They led us in prayer before every meal, and we often had family Bible study at night. Many evenings we sang around the piano. We were a family who loved the Lord, and He was a very real presence in my life as far back as I can remember.

Mornings before sunup, I'd crawl out of my bed to go to the bathroom, and my dad would be sitting at the kitchen table reading his Bible. Mom was ready to answer any why questions I had, such as, "Why do I have to be nice to her, when she's always mean to me?" and she backed up everything she told me with Scripture. "Love your enemies, do good to those who hate you" (Luke 6:27). "If your enemy is hungry, feed him; if he is thirsty, give him a drink" (Romans 12:20).

Momma also was a singer and songwriter. The Singing Buck Family performed at churches all over the southeast. We originally sang southern gospel songs written by others; our first record was a compilation of those. Once my mom had written more than thirty songs of her own, we performed only her music and produced two more albums. All eight of us either sang or played an instrument. When I was young, I sang a solo once in a while and played my beloved maracas. As a teen and into adulthood, I sang alto and broke out the tambourine on the upbeat tunes.

On these occasions, I dressed girly. My older sisters wore matching dresses, and I was so excited when I was finally old enough to wear an identical dress instead of a little girl's dress. My favorite was a long dress with flowing sleeves and a belt with a butterfly buckle. I felt a lot like a butterfly when I wore it.

It also was special because Momma loved butterflies. The very first song she wrote was "Changed like a Butterfly." She told us she was sitting in Sunday school one morning, and "God just poured the words" into her heart, flowing so fast. She quickly jotted down the words on a napkin she pulled from her purse. Each of her songs was a beautiful picture of God's love for His children.

I loved listening to my parents share their testimony of God's mercy and grace during our performances. When Mom sang, I was mesmerized. She praised God with a passion I'd never seen before. Momma loved to worship the Savior. She lifted her voice to her Father in heaven with a smile, and often tears streamed down her face. She taught me to worship without ever knowing it, because she sang to an audience of One.

The Bucks slowly stopped performing as each of us girls grew up, got married, and followed different paths. Singing with my family is a time in my life I always will cherish. The hymns and songs are carved deep into my soul. At night, I still often fall asleep humming and wiggling my toes under the sheet to the sweet melody.

Wondering whether my parents were happy never entered my mind; I knew they were. They adored each other and always had each other's backs. They had endured some personal battles before they started having children, and their love had a strong foundation and very deep roots. Even though I saw them face trials together, they never

> *W*ondering whether my parents were happy never entered my mind; I knew they were.

yelled at each other (not in our presence, anyway). They hunkered down and prayed together through every challenge that arose.

Our parents were the picture of true love and determination. They taught their six girls to love God, be honorable, work hard, and fight for the things we knew to be right. Daddy and Momma were married for more than fifty years, until my mom died at the age of sixty-nine from breast cancer in 2010. Daddy had to lean into Jesus for comfort and hope after she died. Momma was finally in the arms of the Savior.

> Whoever dwells in the shelter of the Most High will rest in the shadow of the Almighty. I will say of the Lord, "He is my refuge and my fortress, my God, in whom I trust." (Psalm 91:1–2 NIV)

Sweet Friend,

Childhood memories can be priceless or painful. Perhaps you didn't grow up in a loving family like I did, and for that I am so sorry. Can you remember a person who nurtured and encouraged you, such as a teacher, a coach, or a neighbor? Someone who made you feel worthy and brought a smile to your face? If he or she is still alive, reach out and say thanks. God knew you needed that person; he or she was His gift to you.

But remember that people inherently disappoint. God created you with soul space designed only for Him to fill. He is waiting to be whatever you need Him to be for you, and it's never too late to ask. He wants to hear the prayers (even if they are merely groans or whispers) from your heart.

Find a safe harbor in Him.

Mer

Have you ever thought your life or current situation is too messed up for you to show your face in church? Do you think you need to get some things in your life right before you begin to pray?

God wants you just as you are. In the Bible, Jesus says, "Come to me, all you who are weary and burdened, and I will give you rest" (Matthew 11:28). He doesn't say *if* or *when* you have it all together. The churches I know are filled with nothing but broken, imperfect people—including those who are called to ministry. Everyone messes up; everyone is a sinner who will never reach complete holiness.

People who go to church, know a few Bible verses, and pray certainly haven't "arrived." Those who think they have arrived are mistaken.

Trust me, you can run straight into Jesus's arms, especially when you feel too angry, too sad, or too unworthy of His love. That's when He does His very best work. God entered this world in a dirty stable and slept in a feeding trough. The Light of the world came in the darkness for those who recognize they need a Savior.

Dressed not in royal robes but in simple cotton, Jesus said to a crowd, "It is not the healthy who need a doctor, but the sick. I have not come to call the righteous, but sinners" (Mark 2:17 NIV).

Everyone falls short of being holy; sin is part of living on this earth. There's the obvious stuff (abuse and murder) and also the not-so-obvious sins (bigotry, envy, gossip, pride).

God sees it all and wants it all. He wants you to trust Him with it. Here is the beautiful thing: the closer you get to Christ, the more like Him you become. If you think you're in bad of shape, the timing is perfect. Come to Jesus just as you are. Don't stress about not having your life cleaned up. He wants to heal you and mend your broken heart. He will pursue you, but He won't force you.

The door is always open. Seeking God is about a relationship—an intimate friendship that is full of forgiveness and grace, mercy, and peace.

—— Deep Breath ——

Throughout my school years, I would run to my mom if I was worried about something, or if I had a big homework project due. Sometimes she would ask, "Darling, how do you eat an elephant?" Then she'd always answer her own question: "One bite at a time."

Her nugget of wisdom is something I often recall when I face monumental tasks. I have to step back from my overachieving multitasking, take a deep breath, and focus on doing one thing at a time.

God instructs us similarly. "Be still, and know that I am God; I will be exalted among the nations, I will be exalted in the earth!" (Psalm 46:10) Are you like me? Do you sometimes get so busy trying to fix something or make everything fall into place that you completely leave God out of it or miss what He is trying to teach you? Especially when what's in front of you is daunting, a huge challenge, or an issue where you feel so very small? If you are like me, then you tend to panic and become fearful.

Here's the deal: I just want the elephant gone now—outta here! If I don't take the time to seek God in the situation, then I'm trying to do His job. I'm relying solely on myself. Do I not trust the Almighty? Is He not more capable and powerful than me? Read about timid Gideon in Judges 6 and then find out how God uses him to defeat the Midianite army in Judges 7. Consider David the shepherd boy against Goliath the giant (1 Samuel 17). And there's also Daniel in the lions' den (Daniel 6).

You will always have elephants in your life. Maybe it's a seemingly overwhelming project at work, a relationship that's creating anxiety in your life, a debt, an illness, or a wayward child. God knows every detail of your situation, and He wants you to lean into Him. God is faithful and trustworthy. Nothing is impossible in His kingdom.

Right now, stop, take a deep breath, square your shoulders, look the elephant in the eyes, and be still. God's got it.

—— Default Focus ——

My earliest childhood memories include riding a horse. The world around me fades away, and I become one with the horse. All the heartache and problems of the world are momentarily forgotten as I completely focus on the one thousand pounds of horseflesh beneath me.

Often I think of my daddy as I break into a nice, steady canter. I remember the many times he'd tell me, "Baby, when you're on or around your horse, always pay attention and stay focused. If you don't, you or someone else might get hurt." It's still wise advice. I strive to focus only on the present moment, and when I do, all seems right with the world. What do you focus on when you are alone with your thoughts? It's common to rehearse life's disappointments and problems. That's where Satan wants you to stay, going over the "If only …" and "What if …?" scenarios of the past and the unknowns of future.

But with God as your default focus in the present, you can breathe easier. He is the air that fills your lungs, your breath of life. The story of Job in the Bible is about the temptation to believe Satan's lies. Afflicted and under assault, Job claims in faith, "The Spirit of God has made me, and the breath of the Almighty gives me life" (Job 33:4). Turn your focus to gratitude. Train your mind to count blessings instead of disappointments. The Bible says you have access to divine power that can "take captive every thought" (2 Corinthians 10:5 NIV) in order to demolish anxiety and fear.

Reading Scripture is one way to develop contentment. Learn to focus on how much Jesus loves you and all He wants to offer you. Peace in the present is found there. "But blessed is the one who trusts in the Lord, whose confidence is in Him…. like a tree planted by the water that sends out its roots by the stream. It does not fear when heat comes; its leaves are always green. It has no worries" (Jeremiah 17:7–8 NIV). When difficult times are at hand, you won't be uprooted. I have experienced a lot of distress throughout my life. Only with Christ as my guide, my default focus, have I been able to be okay. He has a plan for you too. Believe it. When you are distracted by pain, turn your attention to Jesus. Stand firm in His love and let Him heal your heart.

3

Sandcastles

I have won and I have lost,
I got it right sometimes
But sometimes I did not.
Life's been a journey;
I've seen joy, I've seen regret.
Oh and You have been my God
Through all of it.
—COLTON DIXON, "THROUGH ALL OF IT"

Little girls often dream of fairytale marriages. Princesses are swept off their feet by handsome princes and ride off to kingdoms of happiness and prosperity. Their homes are fortresses with long, winding staircases that lead heavenward. Love is professed over and over again on moonlit balconies, and romantic nights produce perfect children who play on grassy lawns.

As I walk the beach, I reflect on my childhood fantasies of having a marriage just like my parents. (Well, minus a few children. No way was I going to try to raise six—too much work and noise!) I remember the white Cinderella-style fluffy wedding dress I wore thirty years ago. It makes me smile; I certainly felt like a princess.

I fell madly in love when I was sixteen. Flirtatious and funny boys caught my eye in high school, but I only agreed to date a couple of them. Robert, however, was musically gifted and intriguingly sarcastic—familiar territory for me with five sisters. We started dating when I was a senior. He was two years older than me and already out working. At the age of nineteen, on April 15, 1989, I said, "I do," with the full intention of being married for life. I wanted more than anything to be a wife, and to love and be loved.

> *I* wanted more than anything to be a wife, and to love and be loved.

I tried to love and nurture my new husband in a way that I felt he had missed. Sadly, his mother had died when he was twelve, and his father never remarried. Robert Sr., a wonderful person and high-ranking military man, did his best to love his son. I came into the marriage desiring to feel seen and valued, which was attention I always had craved from my dad. I thought we would complete each other, and in my naiveté, I believed I could teach him to love in the way my heart so desperately longed for.

Robert was a police officer, and I worked in banking. We lived in the same town as where we'd graduated high school and had a small, rented townhouse in Fernandina Beach. Finding a church that suited our style was easy, and we found a home and a shared passion in the music ministry. He played the drums and sang; I was a vocalist.

We attended church weekly, and I often felt the Spirit move. But something still was missing for me. As a child, I had gone through the motions of receiving salvation and living rightly under God. I was doing the work of the Lord, but I had not made Jesus the Lord of my life.

I received a precious gift one night in September 1994. We went with our church to Roanoke, Virginia, to be a part of the annual Blueridge Baptist Church Jubilee Revival. Our pastor delivered the sermon, and during that evening's invitation, he said, "God is speaking to someone here."

I heard the Lord whisper to me, "It's you." At that moment, I wholly received Christ as my personal Savior. God's timing was (and always is) perfect. His omniscient sovereignty and faithfulness washed over me, and I was awed. We sang "Amazing Grace" to close the evening service.

Although it seemed I had sung that song a million times since I was a little girl, it was new to my ears. The words "How precious did that grace appear, the hour I first believed" brought tears of both release and joy. I wept with gratitude and hope.

Our daughter, Jimi, was born early in the marriage in 1991, and Bobby followed eighteen months later. Not yet twenty-five, I was a wife, mom, employee, and part-time student. I was very tired. When Robert worked nights, I'd tuck the kids into bed and hit my pillow too. Often rest eluded me. I would listen to the police scanner on the bedside table and imagine all sorts of bad things. We tag-teamed a lot. There were many times we would meet in the late afternoon and pull over on the side of the road to exchange quick hellos and move the children from his police car to my car.

When Jimi and Bobby were in school, it was homework, cheerleading, volleyball, basketball, and baseball. I tried to be the best wife and mom I could be. Everything I did to win my husband's attention and approval seemed futile, and I was frustrated much of the time. Outsiders saw our marriage as picture-perfect. Disney vacations created happy memories. But in the marriage, I felt unseen, unworthy. I later learned that it was unfair of me to put my self-worth and joy on his (or anyone's) shoulders and expect to be made whole.

The mortgage business, however, was booming in the early 2000s, and I enjoyed financial success and working with satisfied customers. Thankfully, my job provided for our home and lifestyle, and Jimi and Bobby were healthy and carefree. This was a source of happiness for me in my early thirties. Whether in the living room or the bedroom, there was plenty of activity. Yet, I felt alone.

For seventeen years, we tried to fill our own voids. My "happily ever after" ended, as did the marriage. I was just thirty-six. Yesterday's castle was now unrecognizable, much like when a child's sand fortress is washed away with the tide.

There was never going to be a good time to endure divorce, and for Jimi, fifteen, and Bobby, thirteen, it was brutal. Years of heartache and the betrayal I felt left me empty.

I felt guilty about what we had done to the children, and it nearly tore me apart. I felt like God no longer would use me—a woman with a big "D" stamped on her forehead. I was broken. I was a failure. No one would ever want me.

Walking through that season of bitterness was miserable. I was the living picture of the saying "Unforgiveness is like drinking poison and hoping the other person dies," and I was gulping down the poison.

After many years, the biggest takeaway for me was this: a God-honoring marriage is built on love, respect, and the firm foundation that only a relationship with Jesus offers. In addition, wound-healing and soul-filling love comes only from the Savior. And I had one final choice to make: I either could hold onto the hurt, or I could forgive and move forward.

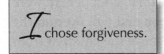

I chose forgiveness. "When everything in you wants to hold a grudge, point a finger and remember the pain, God wants you to lay it all aside," says R. T. Kendall in his book *Total Forgiveness*. It also taught me that the change of heart and resulting peace I wanted wasn't something I could make happen. It only would come from Him.

The waterfall of calm that washed my tears away began to flow when I placed all the pain at the feet of Jesus. I asked the Holy Spirit to empower me to forgive and extend grace over and over again, not only to those who had hurt me but also to myself.

> Therefore whoever hears these sayings of Mine, and does them, I will liken him to a wise man who built his house on the rock: And the rain descended, the floods came, and the winds blew and beat on that house; and it did not fall, for it was founded on the rock. But everyone who hears these sayings of Mine, and does not do them, will be like a foolish man who built his house on the sand: And the rain descended, the floods came, and the winds blew and beat on that house; and it fell. And great was its fall. (Matthew 7:24–27)

Sweet Friend,

Trust and be obedient—not always easy, and certainly letting go of the past is a process. I had to learn the hard way that continually looking back into the past made me stumble. Glancing back is necessary for remembrance and learning, yet forward focus is required for growth. Proverbs 16:9 says, "A man's heart plans his way, but the Lord directs his steps."

It's a cliché, but it's true: The windshield is bigger than the rearview mirror for a reason. Ask God to help you forgive those who have hurt you. Or do you need to forgive yourself? He will help. Surrender to His healing. Leaning into Jesus brings a more intimate relationship and steadies your faith walk.

Go ahead. He is waiting, and He has unimaginable peace waiting for you.

Build your castle in His kingdom.
Mer

The Beatles song "All You Need Is Love" is a catchy tune and a universal truth. As children, when my sisters and I would fight, Momma would make us hug and tell one another, "I love you." I'm sure she knew that in that moment, we did not feel very loving, yet she wanted us to remember that even in the midst of the battle, we were still family, and we loved each other no matter what.

Even though we are called to love one another, often we're more so concerned with judging the people around us. God *is* love, so it's no wonder the word appears hundreds of times in the Bible (more than three hundred times in the King James Bible, nearly three hundred-fifty times in the New American Standard Bible, and five hundred-fifty times in the New International Version). It's of utmost important in God's kingdom: "And now these three remain: faith, hope and love. But the greatest of these is love" (1 Corinthians 13:13 NIV). Then there's this passionate proclamation: "Above all, love each other deeply, because love covers over a multitude of sins" (1 Peter 4:8 NIV).

Certainly it's easy for me to love kind, "normal" people, and it's much more difficult to dredge up love for those I think are weird or mean— those who make me uncomfortable. However, I'm commanded to love not just inside my safety zone but also outside my box of comfort. Jesus says, "But I tell you, love your enemies and pray for those who persecute you, that you may be children of your Father in heaven. He causes his sun to rise on the evil and the good, and sends rain on the righteous and the unrighteous" (Matthew 5:44–45 NIV).

In many instances, this is extremely difficult. Abusers and murderers too? Yes. With all the atrocities in the world, it's easy for our human minds to justify hatred, but Almighty God calls us to love, forgive, and even minister to cruel, hurtful people. He doesn't say it's easy, but it's necessary. Justice belongs to Him.

Love must be a choice. As we follow the example of Christ, we will grow to be more like Him—more faithful, more hopeful and more loving. He loves us when we are unlovable, He died for us while we were still sinners, and He has gone to prepare a place for us so that we can live eternally with Him.

Thank John Lennon and Paul McCartney for the catchy tune, turn up the volume, and sing along with the love song of the Savior. In fact, put it on repeat.

—— Nothing Less Than Love ——

Many years ago, I met an older gentleman, and he challenged my mind. Although I don't remember his name, I remember the wisdom he shared with me: "Anything less than a loving thought is toxic."

Radical, huh? But the more I think about it, the more it makes sense. It's even in the Bible.

Sin begins in our thought life. Satan is sly and loves to fill our brains with garbage. Negative thoughts create doubt, hateful thoughts create division, anxious thoughts create disbelief, and self-critical thoughts create isolation. But God's Word is the soap for "stinkin' thinkin'." Scripture teaches the remedy for a toxic mind: in the words of the Apostle Paul, "bringing every thought into captivity to the obedience of Christ" (2 Corinthians 10:5). Paul also says,

> Whatever is true, whatever is noble, whatever is right, whatever is pure, whatever is lovely, whatever is admirable—if anything is excellent or praiseworthy— think about such things. Whatever you have learned or received or heard from me, or seen in me—put it into practice. And the God of peace will be with you. (Philippians 4:8 NIV)

Wouldn't it be nice to think beautiful thoughts and speak lovely words most of the time? I can, and you can too. It takes a mind shift. Move your thoughts from this world to God, from scarcity to abundance, from darkness to light.

Try it and see what happens. Think love, be love, and give love.

4

Sea Glass

This is my temporary home, it's not where I belong.
Windows and rooms that I'm passing through,
This was just a stop on the way to where I'm going.
I'm not afraid because I know,
This was my temporary home.

—CARRIE UNDERWOOD, "TEMPORARY HOME"

I remember a beautiful spring day in 2006, when my mom called me twice in a row on a workday (which was unlike her). I stepped out of a meeting to call her back.

"Sweetheart, Daddy and I just left the doctor's office. I have stage four breast cancer."

She continued to talk, but I desperately tried to process those six words. When I zoned back in to the conversation, she was saying something about needing a lumpectomy right away and beginning chemotherapy and radiation. Then, in true Jimi Buck fashion, I heard her say with a smile in her voice, "Don't worry,

> "*Don't worry, darling. God will work out all the details.*

darling. God will work out all the details. I'm not worried, and so you shouldn't be."

The thing is, she meant it. My mom trusted that the same God who had been her lifelong provider and protector would also be her healer.

For four years, I watched my mom walk the arduous road of late-stage cancer and the "treatment" that was the protocol to extend her life. Through it all, my sweet, optimistic mother never lost her humor, and not once did her faith or trust in the Savior waver. The cancer journey was very difficult for my introverted dad, and my mom wanted to make it easier on him. My older sister, Phoebe, shaved mom's head when her hair began to fall out. Mom told my dad that this was his chance. "Daddy, pick any color you want," she said in her witty way.

Standing in the wig store, my dad said to Momma, "I think I want a blonde, a brunette, and a redhead." Like they always had, they made the best of a hard situation.

One afternoon, I went to see my parents, and as soon as I walked in the door, my dad said, "Me and Momma have a new song." He already had it cued up to play, and moments later the twangy voice of Randy Travis singing, "I'm Gonna Love You Forever" floated through the air.

I smiled and said, "That's sweet, Daddy."

"No, listen to this verse," he said. My quiet dad wanted my mom to know he loved her no matter what. And as Randy crooned, the strong and tough-as-nails Sidney Buck pointed at the radio and said through his tears, "This part right here."

"They say time take its toll on a body, makes a young girl's brown hair turn gray. Well, honey, I don't care, I ain't in love with your hair and if it all fell out, well, I'd love you anyway."

I had credited my mom with most of my life lessons up to this point. My dad was the disciplinarian, whereas mom always was sharing an antidote or one of her sayings in order to create a teachable moment. However, in this moment, my stoic, earthly father was shining the light of the heavenly Father and making an eternal impact.

So began another layer of love between my mom and dad. When I thought they could not comfort, support, and encourage each other more, I watched them do it. My parents leaned into each other and together pressed into Jesus, the

> *My* parents leaned into each other and together pressed into Jesus

author and finisher of their faith. "A cord of three strands is not quickly broken" (Ecclesiastes 4:12 NIV).

Momma was my best friend and a role model like no other. Once again, she didn't disappoint. She battled cancer with the sword of faith. During the last few months of her life, I spent Wednesdays with her. I asked her questions because I wanted to be prepared. Nobody else was asking her what the doctor was saying, in terms of her life expectancy. Daddy knew, but he had a difficult time talking with us about her death. He couldn't fathom life without her.

One day I asked point-blank, "Mom, when do you think you will die?"

With a twinkle in her eye, she answered, "Sweet darling, I may have cancer, but you could be hit by a truck today. When we are going die is known only by God."

Another time I asked, "Mom, are you afraid of dying?"

She smiled as tears streamed down her face. "No, sweetheart, I'm not afraid to die. Heaven is going to be marvelous! I just worry about your daddy. I hate to leave him here, but I am ready to see my Savior."

On May 14, 2010, I sat at the foot of my mother's bed as she breathed her last breath and was received into the arms of the heavenly Father in her eternal home. I had prayed for four years asking God to heal my mom from the cancer in her body, and for four years, I felt like God wasn't answering my prayer.

As I lay at my precious mom's feet, having felt defeated in my prayers for healing, I cried. I wept for the loss of my mother—caregiver, companion, the only one who had ever loved me unconditionally, and my best friend. I questioned God. This woman had loved Jesus more than anyone I had ever known, and He had just allowed her to die.

As I cried, the Holy Spirit whispered to me, "She is healed."

Immediately, pieces of scripture came to mind. Later that day, I opened my Bible and found the comfort I sought. When Mom had talked about death, she quoted, "We are confident, yes, well pleased rather to be absent from the body and to be present with the Lord" (2 Corinthians 5:8). I also remember many times when she talked about heaven, and she reminded people, "And God will wipe away every tear from their eyes; there shall be no more death, nor sorrow, nor crying. There shall be no more pain, for the former things have passed away" (Revelation 21:4).

Today, as I think about my mom's life testimony, I know she is completely healed. In fact, she received her heavenly reward! She didn't want to leave my dad in this old world because she knew how wonderful heaven would be. Mom longed for her eternal home, where there would be no more pain, tears, or sorrow, but only living in the presence of Christ.

God answered my prayers after all. Maybe not how I would have done it, as selfishly I wanted her healed here on earth. He did, however, answer my pleas perfectly. Do I miss my mom? Yes, every day. Yet I smile knowing she is worshipping at the feet of Jesus, completely whole, completely healed.

For me, the grief of missing my mom felt like a sailing vessel with a broken mast. My sails were lifeless; I felt dead in the water. My mom was my go-to, my phone-a-friend lifeline. She always was my compassionate comforter, trustworthy confidant, and wise counsel. To me, the most beautiful human on this earth was gone, and I was never to hear her call me darling again.

> To me, the most beautiful human on this earth was gone, and I was never to hear her call me darling again.

Even years after her death, I would pick up the phone to call her just as I always had on my way to work in the morning. There remain days I wish I could call her and share all that is on my heart. When I am sad or disappointed, I imagine her saying, "My darling, this too shall pass," or, "All will be well."

Just a few months ago, I attended an award meeting. On the way back to my car afterward, someone stopped me and asked, "This may sound crazy, but is Jimi Buck your mother?"

I said, "Yes, she is."

"I knew it! You have her smile," she responded. The woman had been one of my mom's students and had moved out of town. She hadn't known of mom's death. I cried all the way back to work, missing her. Yet, my heart was filled with joy because she was not forgotten.

I carry her smile with me.

> And we know that all things work together for good
> to those who love God, to those who are the called
> according to *His* purpose. (Romans 8:28)

Sweet Friend,

Have you ever lost someone who was precious to you? Maybe a parent, spouse, or child? There is no other pain quite so excruciating. It may not feel like it at the time of your grievous loss, but God sees your pain and feels it with you, and He has never left your side. David reminds us, "Yea, though I walk through the valley of the shadow of death, I will fear no evil; for You are with me" (Psalm 23:4). He is holding your hand and sometimes even carrying you through the valley. So, just be held.

I am excited to share with you devotions about some of the things my mother taught me. Those who knew my mom know that she was always on the lookout for a teachable moment. She was a wise woman and was quick to speak truth in love.

Lean into the lessons.
Mer

When we were children, Momma sometimes would tell my sisters and me, "Children should be seen and not heard." She didn't want mute children. She simply wanted us to be respectful and less rowdy when she had company or needed some peace and quiet. As a child who craved attention, I didn't like her words; I liked to be heard.

Similarly, as a child of God, there have been times in my walk when I knew He was there. I knew in my heart He could see me. But I questioned whether He could hear me, because God did not answer my requests within my timeframe. (I chuckle as I write this. Here I am, the creation, wanting the Creator to be at my beck and call.) I recall Daddy telling me that God answers us three ways: yes, no, and wait a while. It was during the waiting that I sometimes felt like God wasn't hearing me.

Quite the opposite was true. The loving Father heard me and was allowing me to learn to trust His timing. God was building my character and enlarging my faith. "My brethren, count it all joy when you fall into various trials, knowing that the testing of your faith produces patience" (James 1:2).

When you feel like God has gone radio silent, know that He hasn't. He most assuredly sees you and hears you. Scripture declares, "Your Father knows what you need before you ask Him" (Matthew 6:8 NIV). Isn't that reassuring? As a matter of fact, it should take the pressure off. God's got whatever is troubling you.

Take a deep breath and know God's timing is always perfect. He is never late. Keep trusting, believing, and praying. He's all ears.

—— GREENER GRASS ——

I did not grow up in a wealthy home. My parents were loving yet strict. To say I never got away with anything is an understatement. There were times I wasn't allowed to buy something or go somewhere my classmates were able to go. When I expressed my opinion that I wish we were rich or that they weren't so strict, my mom always told me we were rich in love.

"My darling, the grass may look greener in the neighbor's yard, but if you look closely, it is usually directly over the septic tank," she said.

It didn't sit well with me when I was a teenager, but as I have experienced life more, I see what Momma meant. It's easy to gaze at someone else's life, especially through the lens of social media, and think a situation is better than yours, maybe even perfect. Upon closer inspection, you realize someone's stuff may not be as flawless as you envisioned. Scripture warns, "A sound heart is life to the body, but envy is rottenness to the bones" (Proverbs 14:30).

Looking back, I realize I had so very much for which to be thankful. My less-than-emerald yard wasn't so bad after all. What about you?

Comparison isn't realistic or beneficial. When you obsess over what you don't have (or think you don't have), you forget to thank the heavenly Father for all of the blessings He is providing. Don't let envy grow weeds in your heart.

GLASS HOUSES

I was fourteen the first time my mother scolded me with the proverbial, "Sweetheart, those who live in glass houses should not throw stones." I had just told her about someone at school who did something I thought was wrong. Instead of the hoped-for response from my mom, proclaiming me the perfect child and telling me what a good person I was for not doing those things, she busted my self-righteous bubble with truth.

Her words hit their intended mark and got me thinking about my own sins (gossip, lying to my sisters, etc.). I realized it's easy to pick apart another person, because looking inward is quite difficult.

> Why do you look at the speck of sawdust in your brother's eye and pay no attention to the plank in your own eye? How can you say to your brother, "Let me take the speck out of your eye," when all the time there is a plank in your own eye? You hypocrite, first take the plank out of your own eye, and then you will see clearly to remove the speck from your brother's eye. (Matthew 7:3–5 NIV)

Jesus also taught this when a crowd was accusing a woman who had been caught in the act of adultery. The religious leaders told Jesus the law demanded she be stoned for her sin. Instead of condemning her to death, while the crowd awaited His thoughts, Jesus bent down to write in the sand. Then, He said, "He who is without sin among you, let him throw a stone at her first" (John 8:7). He bent down again to write in the sand, and this time when He looked up, every persecutor had dropped his stones and left.

> Jesus straightened up and asked her, "Woman, where are they? Has no one condemned you?" "No one, sir," she said. "Then neither do I condemn you," Jesus declared. "Go now and leave your life of sin." (John 8:10–11 NIV)

Our God is just, but here Jesus chose to be merciful to this woman. I think about the many things I have done wrong and displeased the Father. He commands me to love others as He mercifully loves me. Let's drop the rocks. Rather than being ready to accuse and condemn, live with hands free to reach out in Christlike love.

5

Jumping Waves

Tell your heart to beat again,
Close your eyes and breathe it in.
Let the shadows fall away,
Step into the light of grace.
Yesterday's a closing door,
You don't live there anymore.
Say goodbye to where you've been,
And tell your heart to beat again.

—DANNY GOKEY, "TELL YOUR HEART TO BEAT AGAIN"

I remember going to the beach with my family as a little girl. My sister Amanda would run into the rushing breakers without fear and begin jumping the waves. But I was timid and small for my age. I was intimidated and afraid I would drown.

Daddy would often hold my hand at first if I asked him, and so we walked deeper into the water together. His strong grip helped calm my nerves. Ankles wet, then knee deep. Soon, I was confident enough to jump and play in the surf with my sister. It was so freeing.

After the divorce, I felt much like that scared little girl. I wanted to jump the waves again, to go out and laugh with friends, to be carefree and have fun. But I needed the guidance and strength of the Father to lead the way.

Even though I was the one ready for the marriage to be over and had been planning to leave for some time, the divorce was difficult. It was a scary time for Jimi, Bobby, and me. I rented a condo near the beach, which was my first taste of coastal living. Little did I know then how much living near the water was just what my soul needed during that season spent deep in the throes of healing.

I wanted to hide and lick my wounds, but a disappearing act isn't easy in a small town. I mustered up a bit of courage every morning and held my head high as I went to work, and as I took Jimi to volleyball and Bobby to basketball and baseball. Sometimes it seemed like the other moms were gossiping and whispering behind their hands, or all eyes were on me because I was the hot topic of conversation. I tried to not let it bother me because I knew the truth. I limped as best I could through those early months of singleness.

During this time, I claimed these words: "If I ascend into heaven, You are there; if I make my bed in hell, behold, You are there. If I take the wings of the morning, and dwell in the uttermost parts of the sea, even there Your hand shall lead me, and Your right hand shall hold me" (Psalm 139:8–10). This Scripture reassured me that no matter the season of my life, God always is and will be with me.

Most people thought I had a lot of friends, but I have just a few intimate girlfriends with whom I share my life. Lots of people in town didn't even know Robert and I had been having problems; I'd tried to protect my family in the hopes that one day, everything would work out.

In His infinite faithfulness, God kept the most amazing friends close to me during my transition. They didn't judge, they listened, and they prayed for all of us. The "couple friends" Robert and I shared were great too, praying for us and not picking sides. They loved us well and respected our privacy.

When the kids were with their dad, I tended to isolate myself, walking the beach to think and pray. I had so many emotions to sort through, fears to talk with Jesus about, and unknowns to face, and so I walked and walked, until the ocean became my dearest friend. The sunrises called to me with God's promises of protection and provision, and each sunset brought the calm of His peace.

The church we had attended together remained important to me. I decided to step away with the hope the kids' dad would continue going. He did for a while, and I was thankful. Our pastor, Jeff, and his wife, Cheri, were good friends, and I knew they always would love and pray for Robert, the children, and me. I began spending Sunday mornings with my parents at the small Baptist church in Callahan that they attended. When Jimi and Bobby were with me, they came too. After church, we went back to my mom and dad's house to eat lunch and hang out. Those Sundays together were a precious time.

Riding the roller coaster of good weeks and not-so-good weeks the first few months eventually slid into a new, steady routine. I did things a little differently as a single mom. I still was fairly strict, and the family values did not change, but I tried to create a less stressful, laid-back environment. For example, Jimi wanted a white Christmas tree the first time it was just the three of us, and so we looked everywhere until we finally found one. I let Jimi and Bobby pick out the ornaments, and they chose bright colors ... and nothing matched. It was wonderfully different!

We ordered Chinese food at least once a week and ate in the living room—a huge hit. After living in the beach condo for six months, we moved to a cute cottage in the center of town. My goal first and foremost was to give Jimi and Bobby love and stability. And I needed it as much as they did.

The one-year anniversary of my divorce came around without fanfare. Although I had thoughts of someday finding someone to spend the rest of my life with, my heart wasn't all that hopeful. I wasn't excited about joining the dating pool. Besides the children, my companions were work, the barn (and riding my horse, Patches), and the TV remote (oh, how I loved having the control!).

But there was one guy in whom I gradually became a bit interested. Lee Lewis and I worked together, and when I realized I had grown attracted to his exuberant demeanor and somewhat zany ways, I was surprised.

I'd met Lee about eighteen months earlier, while I was still married. One afternoon at the office, he walked in with a big smile on his face. He had on nice slacks and a dress shirt with the sleeves rolled up. He was cocky and sure of himself; I was not impressed. *Who is he?* I thought after he walked right up to my desk and extended his hand in greeting.

"Are you the famous Meredith?" he asked.

Not certain how to respond, I replied, "And you are ...?"

Like I should have known, he beamed and said, "Lee Lewis!"

Many women probably would have blushed under the attention of such a good-looking man with olive skin and dark hair, but I was married. That day, I honestly didn't notice his looks, only that he was very sure of himself. It was a busy day, and I didn't have time for his spiel, but I tried not to be rude. I let him stand there next to my desk and heard him out.

Lee also was in the mortgage industry and was opening a new office in town. Although he tried hard to convince me I needed to change offices and work for him, I politely turned him down. The bank I was working for at the time had recently sold, and I already had verbally committed to another bank. I explained this, but that didn't seem to deter Lee.

"Timing is everything," he said. Persistence is one thing he had going for him. Eventually I caved in and joined his team. Lee was kind to everyone in the office and was always quick with a smile and a compliment. He loved to make people feel good about themselves.

Extremely friendly and passionate, Lee made everyone feel like they were his best friend in a very genuine way. He used to quote Teddy Roosevelt: "People don't care how much you know, until they know how much you care."

Lee asked me out on a date a year after my divorce. We had become friends, and I was comfortable around him, so I agreed. We went to a movie with another friend; I enjoyed myself and the easy laughter. Although we worked together, Lee rarely was in the office. When he did come in, generally we were too busy to chat. A short time later, he joined another bank as a commercial lender.

We continued to date, and as time moved forward, I learned more about Lee. Even though he had shared with me early on that he was an alcoholic in recovery, as we became better acquainted, I realized what a daily struggle it was for him. Lee regularly attended Alcoholics Anonymous meetings and was devoted to helping others become and stay sober. He was a fitness enthusiast and was in phenomenal physical shape. Lee told me his addictive personality required he focus on healthy ways of living.

He threw himself into whatever ignited his passion: his faith, his daughters, and his friends. Lee loved Jesus. Because of Christ's saving grace extended to him, Lee wanted everyone he met to experience that same grace, and he was not ashamed to share his story with anyone who would listen. He didn't judge others; often he would say, "But God ..." and it reminded me of the Scripture in Ephesians. "But God, who is rich in mercy, because of His great love with which He loved us, even when we were dead in trespasses, made us alive together with Christ (by grace you have been saved)" (Ephesians 2:4–5).

Lee loved his two little girls fiercely and wanted more than anything to be a good daddy to Sarah Katherine, five, and Caroline, three. He did all he could to protect them and lead them to a life of faith. He told me once, "I may not be able to give them all the things money can buy, but I can show them the way to a relationship with Jesus."

Lee and I came from different denominational backgrounds. Lee's Granny Lewis took him to a Billy Graham crusade, and at the age of twelve, Lee dedicated his life to Christ. While growing up, he often attended a Presbyterian church with his parents, however as a young man he strayed from the path of faith. When Lee began his journey to sobriety, he knew that he would need the help of the heavenly Father and leaned into Him. Thankfully, we found an amazing non-denominational, Bible-teaching church together, and I watched Lee's spiritual walk blossom.

We dated for about seven months and then got married in December 2006. As a fifteen-year-old, Jimi struggled with having to share me. She'd had visions of us being like the Gilmore Girls. Bobby, on the other hand, was thirteen and seemed like he could have cared less.

I moved into Lee's house, and we settled in as a blended family with Jimi, Bobby, Sarah Katherine, and Caroline with us when they weren't with their other parents. Lee's girls lived with their mom about an hour and a half away, and they hung out with us every other weekend. I had my two teens half the time; they rotated a week with their dad and a week with me. Needless to say, some weeks for Lee and me were quiet, and some were filled with beautiful chaos.

"Okay, here is my second chance," I thought, planning to be the best wife, mom, and stepmom I possibly could be. "Everything is going to work out." My heart beamed. Although it wasn't easy, we did our best and made some amazing memories.

Like most marriages, we had our struggles. But we were committed to putting God first, faithfully staying married, and growing old together. Lee and I each had brought some emotional baggage into the marriage. Lee was fighting his own inner demons, and I still was trying to claim self-worth. We worked hard to help each other be the best version of ourselves, and we woke up early in the morning to read the Bible together over coffee. Sometimes we walked the beach at sunrise and would stop to read God's Word and pray.

As he got down on his knees before the sun, the beginning of Lee's prayer was always, "Good morning, God. This is Lee checking in. I am an alcoholic and a dipaholic, so please help me to resist both today. Help me to be the best son, brother, dad, husband, and friend I can be today." Lee told many people he wanted his life to glorify the heavenly Father.

One day before heading out of town, he gave me a five-page letter. In it he wrote, "I wish—no, I pray—God will use me in a way that is justified and pleasing to Him." Lee may as well have written the words of Paul to the believers in Roman: "Therefore, I urge you, brothers and sisters, in view of God's mercy, to offer your bodies as a living sacrifice, holy and pleasing to God—this is your true and proper worship" (Romans 12:1 NIV).

We'd been married for just over seven years when Lee went on a short trip to visit his daughters and attend their softball banquet. Because the real estate market was in full swing that spring on Amelia Island, I stayed behind to work. We talked for a long time as he sat in his hotel room in Lake City that evening. His plan was to come home the next morning.

I awoke to a call from Lee at six o'clock, and he told me he was going to drive to Sarasota instead, to encourage a friend. I was surprised and not pleased. He told me it was his friend's birthday, and he was worried about him and wanted to go cheer him up. We traded texts throughout the day, and at six thirty that evening, he messaged me, "I love you. I miss you." I still wasn't happy he had detoured from our plan, and my response wasn't loving. We both knew the environment of the destination was not healthy for him in maintaining his sobriety.

Lee encouraged me not to worry. He said, "God's got me."

Later that night, I got news that rocked my world and changed the course of my life forever. Lee's friend called to tell me he was dead.

"No! It can't be. He just text me!" I screamed into my phone.

I collapsed to the floor and held my head in my hands, trying not to throw up. When I asked if Lee was in a car accident, I was shocked to hear the details.

"No, Meredith. We were eating dinner, and he choked to death."

When I finally got the whole story, I found out Lee was at his friend's mother's house, celebrating over a birthday dinner. There were twenty-five or so people at the party, and Lee had taken his first bite of beef tenderloin.

Lee loved to eat. Lee loved beef.

His first bite was a large medallion of meat. Apparently when he realized the meat was stuck and he couldn't swallow, he got up from the table and headed to the bathroom. (Caution: If you are choking, *never* leave a crowded room for an isolated one.)

An unsuspecting guest thought he was going to be sick and led him down the hall so he would not be embarrassed. When she realized he was choking, several people tried to do the Heimlich maneuver, but they weren't able to dislodge the meat. Someone called the ambulance, but Lee died in the arms of his friend's mother before the paramedics arrived.

His body was taken to the medical examiner's office because anytime there is an unexpected, in-home death, an autopsy is required. Several days later, the medical examiner called to tell me the piece of meat was lodged so tightly that even if the medics had been on the scene at the time of the incident, they would not have been able to reach or dislodge it. She also said she'd never had had a forty-three-year-old subject with a heart, lungs, and liver as healthy as Lee's. (Much later, this fact would be important for me to remember.)

> So teach us to number our days, that we may gain a heart
> of wisdom. (Psalm 90:12)

Sweet Friend,

Have you ever felt that you had a perfect plan, only to suddenly have it crumble into pieces at your feet? Me too. But, hear me on this: God can take the shattered pieces of our lives and mold those fragments into something precious. Like artists who collect broken shells or glass that wash ashore on the beach and craft the colorful bits into stunning sculptures, He takes what we think is destroyed and useless, and He creates beauty out of brokenness.

I pray everyone who is reading this will find encouragement. I pray they will, by the power of the Holy Spirit, hand over their worries to God, trust His plan and live a life, not paralyzed by fear but energized by faith, sustained by His promises.

Take the hand of your good Father.
Mer

── Why Worry ──

As I walk the beach some mornings, I marvel at how the skies could change so quickly. Some sunny mornings are bright and beautiful—the weather mild and the ocean calm. And then *bam!*—hours later, the wind is cool and crisp, the misty rain is falling, and the waves are dark and luminous.

What do we really have control over? I wonder. Certainly not the weather. I shout to the wind, "We don't have control over anything!"

Scripture points out this truth: "Can any one of you by worrying add a single hour to your life?" (Matthew 6:27 NIV) There's also the saying "Worry does not empty tomorrow of its sorrow, it empties today of its strength." My personal favorites are, "Don't miss the sun today, worrying about the rain coming tomorrow," and, "Worry doesn't take away tomorrow's troubles. It takes away today's peace."

I can assure you that the job or bank account you depend on, or even the person you think always will be there, is fleeting at best. Nothing is guaranteed or permanent in this life. After my losses, James 4:14 really hit home in my heart: "Whereas you do not know what will happen tomorrow. For what is your life? It is even a vapor that appears for a little time and then vanishes away."

I've seen disappointment, as well as how short life can be. The soul was created by God to be filled only by Him. He is a dependable, trustworthy Father. A relationship with Jesus is fulfilling, and when life gets tough, only His love comforts and sustains.

Now, I pray as the ocean pounds out its praises to the Creator, and I release everything! I give over my children, my granddaughter, my past, my present, and my future to God. I release all the things that Satan uses to try to cripple me with worry. I know every morning, He is the only one giving the grace of new mercies so that I can hold my head high.

But let me be real. I am not so spiritual that I never struggle and am never tempted to worry. At times I do drive home from the beach to get ready for work and begin my day in the world, and my heart starts pounding as thoughts of giving God total control of my life (like it's even mine to give) enter my mind. I have to unclench my grip on the steering wheel and pray, "Okay, Lord. I gave it all to You just a few minutes ago, and now I am having doubts? Please give me the strength to follow through."

His Word whispers back, "My grace is sufficient for you, for My strength is made perfect in weakness" (2 Corinthians 12:9). Often we must give our worries to Jesus ten, a hundred, and even a thousand times a day. Lean into His grace and trust Him.

—— THINGS UNSEEN ——

Life is disappointing. Plans are made, and expectations come into play.

When things don't turn out, spirits sink, and bitterness tries to creep in. There's no way that at sixteen, I'd ever have imagined being divorced at thirty-six after seventeen years of marriage. Or that I'd be remarried for seven years only to end up a widow at forty-three. To say life didn't go as I had planned is an understatement.

Here is the beauty: God was not surprised. In fact, Jesus clearly says, "These things I have spoken to you, that in Me you may have peace. In the world you will have tribulation; but be of good cheer, I have overcome the world" (John 16:33). He doesn't say *if* we encounter trouble. For every valley I walked through, as well as the disappointments and trials I will face in the future, He works for my good to glorify His name.

God is the great Redeemer. Yes, it's easier to focus on the pain rather than any good that comes from it. But consider this: doesn't sorrow often prompt a turning toward God? How often does a particular struggle teach a personal lesson? Don't new, different directions often result in even better outcomes than what was planned? What if a disappointment is protection from something that could have been devastating?

These are what can be seen and experienced. However, redemption often happens through other lives that are changed. A faithful and God-seeking response to a terrible situation often impacts people who are watching from the sidelines—people who see what a relationship with Jesus offers and want that for themselves.

God sees a future we cannot. He can turn disappointment into delight.

I've learned that if I truly believe my purpose on this side of heaven is to glorify God and build His kingdom, then it's not all about me and my little world. I have to consider the bigger picture, the one He sees.

Blame can hurt both sides. I've blamed someone for something and later realized the person didn't do what I had presumed. With misplaced anger and hurt, I've sat and felt horrible after having avoided someone and allowing the relationship to suffer.

Incorrect assumptions also can be unleashed on God. When something unpleasant or tragic happens, God often gets the blame—even if the unpleasant circumstances were a result of poor choices. The outcome? Isolating from family and friends, staying away from church, avoiding prayer, and withholding worship. The mind can conjure up how mean God is for having allowed bad things to happen, thinking that He's distant and doesn't care.

"Why? Why me? Why now?" is the string of questions uttered when darkness threatens, and the reason or answer is rarely clear. Yet God is never surprised by anything that happens. My dad always says, "When you feel like God has abandoned you, turn around. He is standing right where you left Him; He is the same yesterday, today, and forever. God didn't move—you did."

Isn't it easier to trust God when life is going smoothly? As soon as things start going sideways, His sovereignty comes into question. But whereas earthly eyes focus on earthly things, the Creator of the universe has the good of His entire creation in mind. "So we fix our eyes not on what is seen, but on what is unseen, since what is seen is temporary, but what is unseen is eternal" (2 Corinthians 4:18 NIV).

Faith is trusting the unseen. Choose to live a life of expectancy, trusting God has a plan that is good, even if it may not be free from heartache. I have heard it said, "The plan is only as good as the planner," and I know the heavenly Father is the ultimate Planner. He is love, and He is a good, good Father.

6

Riptide

I know someday,
I know somehow,
I'll be okay.
But not right now,
Not right now.

—JASON GRAY, "NOT RIGHT NOW"

Collapsing to the floor in shock. Feeling utterly alone and terrified. Swimming against the current, blinded by tears. I've lived it, and I know what it's like when nothing makes sense.

On the evening of Thursday, May 16, 2013 I was on the couch with a book waiting for a call from Lee because he was out of town. My cell rang at 9:28. His friend said, "Meredith ..." There was a long pause." "Lee is dead."

What? How? Where? Lee was very athletic and the picture of health. He was supposed to live to be an old man, not die at forty-three. My husband was dead. I didn't get to say, "I love you." I never said goodbye. Our last conversation was an argument.

In a matter of seconds, I went from wife to widow. The swirling waves of shock kept crashing over me, and I didn't know which direction to turn. I desperately wanted to grab my mom's hand and have her pull me in close to safety. I needed her to rub my back and assure me everything was going to be okay as I cried an

> *I*n a matter of seconds, I went from wife to widow.

ocean of tears. But Momma was dead, and Lee was dead. The dark sea was pulling me under.

Once I could breathe a bit, I called my longtime friend and my pastor's wife, Kara. She and her husband Darryl, jumped in the car and were by my side within twenty minutes. Kara had called Lee's mentor and friend, Billy, and his wife, Lindsay. My living room quickly became a circle of comfort for me and a lifeline of strength.

I knew Lee's girls and their mother, as well as his parents and siblings, had to be told. God provided the courage and strength to make those difficult calls and visits in the middle of the night. Sometime around three o'clock in the morning, I tried to close my eyes. There was no sleep, only the lonely nightmare of despair.

Lee's body was at the morgue four hours away, and so I wasn't able to see it immediately. Several days later, the funeral home in town called to say Lee was "home." No one else in the family wanted to go, but I had to. I needed to see and touch him one more time to really believe he was gone. I prayed for strength as I prepared my heart to see the lifeless body of my husband. I longed for my mother once again.

The heavenly Father heard my prayer, and the phone rang just as I was ready to leave. Of course it wasn't my mom, however, it was one of my dearest friends. In her loving fashion, Judith Boyle had called to see if there was anything she could do to help. When I told her I was headed to the funeral home, she told me to sit tight. She came over in a dash to pick me up.

God knew exactly whom and what I needed. With the love of a mother, she held my hand, prayed with me, and held me when I cried. She even went in to see Lee first to make sure I could handle what I was about to face. Judith eased my fears and assured me Lee looked like he was sleeping peacefully and was smiling.

Sure enough, Lee was smiling, and he looked as if he would wake up any second. Judith encouraged me to take my time, and I did. In my mind, I knew what I saw was simply Lee's shell, but my heart needed to talk, touch, and pray with him one last time. Judith stepped in and walked with me through one of the hardest experiences of my life. I was grateful beyond words.

After making the arrangements for the service, I left the funeral home knowing I had one additional task that needed to get done. I had to find an important document—one I knew was somewhere within an enormous stack of boxes in our storage unit. I had told only my best friend Angie about my dilemma, and she was flying in from Texas the next day with a promise to help look for the proverbial needle in a haystack. The dread of searching for what could have been hours nearly paralyzed me. As I pulled into my garage, I put my head down and pleaded with God for help. "Please don't let it be in box ninety-nine, Lord. I just don't think I have the energy," I prayed. What happened next was otherworldly.

When I got out of my car, I noticed a single white sheet of paper lying on top of Lee's flip-flops, which were by the door leading into the house. When I bent down to pick it up, my mind could barely comprehend what it was or why it was there. It was exactly the document I needed. This may be difficult for some people to believe; it was for me at the time. However, I felt God had heard my prayer and answered in a supernatural way.

The Bible says, "For He will command His angels concerning you to guard you in all your ways" (Psalm 91:11 NIV). Also, "Are not all angels ministering Spirits sent to serve those who will inherit salvation?" (Hebrews 1:14 NIV)

Even though I had been freed from that worry, continuing to prepare for Lee's service was still mind-numbingly difficult. Lee, being the man he was, had once shared with me his wishes. Yet going through pictures for the slideshow (thank goodness his sister Virginia was there to help) and listening to the songs he liked was beyond brutal. It took a few days, but I was determined to get everything just right. Jimi barely left my side, and my sister Amanda was a sentinel at the front door, greeting those who brought food and offered condolences and protecting me from being overwhelmed with callers. My friend Kara coordinated most of the actual service and reception with the help of family and friends, relieving me of that huge task.

Eight days after Lee died, we held his celebration of life. It was a beautiful day, but I didn't want to get out of bed. I wanted to crawl under the covers and never come out, feeling like I had aged twenty years in one week. Only for Lee and his daughters, Sarah Katherine and Caroline, did I put on my big-girl panties and face the day.

The church was standing room only, packed with more than seven hundred people in attendance. Worried about walking into the church with people crying and the huge picture of their dad on the screen up front, the girls held tightly to their mom and me and sat sandwiched between us. Both girls stood bravely during the service, and they each went up front and spoke about how their daddy loved God so much and taught them the importance of having a relationship with Jesus.

My counselor, Dr. Linda Miller, later shared with me how touched and impressed she had been regarding their courage. "Lee equipped his children to be able to walk through grief by pointing them so often to Christ," she said.

Everything about the service was nontraditional. I wore a vibrant royal blue dress instead of black. Our pastor and close friend Darryl preached a salvation message at the request of Lee himself. Our friend Chris sang "The Stand" by Hillsong United. People laughed, cried, and had the opportunity to give their lives to Christ. I thought afterward, *I can only hope my funeral will be as impactful.*

We gathered in the lobby following the service, where normally there would be a reception line. Instead, more people had the opportunity to tell "Lee stories." I felt like I hugged a million necks. I don't think I really saw everyone I spoke with, but friends later told me I'd done well. Obviously I was still in shock and doing what I had to do to get through the day, consoling others in their mourning.

> *I*n the days to follow, I fell into a vortex of grief.

In the days to follow, I fell into a vortex of grief. My daughter and a close family friend, David, stayed with me in the evenings. I couldn't sleep in the bed Lee and I had shared, so I camped out on the couch. Dreams of my second chance and growing old with Lee filled my head. To say my life plan had changed yet again was a gross understatement.

I couldn't get my bearings; some days I felt like I was swimming through pudding, and others felt like I was sinking in quicksand. At times, I didn't think I could take my next breath. The grief often was suffocating.

I questioned God's wisdom and His love for me. I pleaded for answers.

"How could You allow Lee to die, and how do You expect me to endure this?" I asked God to turn back time, to give me just one more chance to tell Lee I loved him, assuring him I wasn't angry. Our last words to each other had been strained.

Wrestling with this, I prayed for sleep so I could forget my reality. But then I'd wake up and remember the nightmare. I went over and over the what-ifs, and sometimes I wished I'd had a warning. I wanted to push rewind, but a blank road ahead was all I could see. Sometimes I barely whispered, "Help me, Father." I knew my faith was the only thing that would get me through. I clung to Christ and did my best to praise Him despite my fear and grief. But in the dead of night, sometimes I would wake up and wonder whether I would survive.

Scripture pointed me to truth. "'For My thoughts are not your thoughts, neither are your ways My ways,' declares the Lord. 'As the heavens are higher than the earth, so are My ways higher than your ways and My thoughts than your thoughts'" (Isaiah 55:8–9 NIV). But, oh, how I wanted God's way to be my way.

My next move was hasty and probably not the smartest, but I needed something to focus on besides my loss. Staying home and being in our space wasn't helpful. I returned to work the week after the service. My co-workers Ben and Bianca were amazing, letting me ease back in and do things that didn't require customer contact. They shielded me from the more stressful situations the mortgage business brings. Ben and Bianca had become like family over the years, and they reacted like the brother and sister they are to me. I will be forever grateful for their love and care; simply getting through the day was a major feat.

In my journal, on day fourteen after Lee's death, I wrote,

> It was a really hard day. I could hardly make it up the stairs after work before I started sobbing, so I just laid down right there. I called out to God for comfort. This Scripture from Psalm 56:8 came to mind. "You keep track of all my sorrows. You have collected all my tears in Your bottle. You have recorded each one in Your book." I told a friend yesterday that I see two choices: (1) curl up in a fetal position and wait to die, or (2) glorify the Savior, knowing His ways are higher than my ways. I know the loving Father cares enough for me to collect

all my tears, so I'm going to choose #2. As Lee Lewis used to say, "It's not easy, but it's the right thing to do."

Others around me got back to their normal routines. It was weird. My world had fallen apart, but the rest of the world was still functioning. The sun kept rising. The woodpecker outside my bedroom window continued drumming his morning tune. People were laughing. I thought many times, *Mer, you are never going to feel joy again. Life as you know it is over.* I was right about one thing: Life as I had planned it was over.

The firsts were the hardest—Father's Day, Lee's birthday, and our anniversary. These days screamed reminders of who was missing. Except for Thanksgiving and Christmas, most people weren't aware of how much I was struggling. Jimi, who had grown very fond of Lee, always remembered the hard days and reached out to me. In fact, there was a role reversal, and she became my pseudomom, hovering like a mother hen and telling me how much I needed her. Jimi insisted on moving in with me as a twenty-three-year-old woman, and we enjoyed an adult mother-daughter friendship. Bobby visited us when he could, and I always wished he could have expressed his sadness more, but like most men he kept it all inside.

On my most difficult days, I went to the beach to face the ocean and cry. The vast expanse of water easily could have been my tears as I attempted to cry myself empty of the grief.

Exactly one month after Lee's death was Father's Day. His daughters and their mom came to church with me. It was a difficult morning, especially for the girls, who saw other dads holding hands with their daughters. Yet I knew in my heart that Lee was looking down from heaven, thrilled that we were worshipping together. Our courage and strength that day came from God. We had chosen not to let the sea of grief pull us under.

> When you pass through the waters, I will be with you;
> and when you pass through the rivers, they will not
> sweep over you. (Isaiah 43:2 NIV)

Sweet Friend,

God is for you and will walk with you through your disappointment, heartache, loss, and grief. The verse above from Isaiah is a reminder that there is no escaping trouble in this earthly life. But God is with you every day and in every circumstance. He will even carry you, if necessary.

Have you ever felt like you were running out of strength, or that you couldn't keep your head above the waves any longer? Stop striving, stop struggling. The loving Father is there to catch you and hold you when you feel you can't go on. Surrender to His everlasting arms.

God hears your cries for help. Rest assured in His promise to never turn away from you or leave you—this is His comfort for your weary soul. I pray a few of the things I wrote in my journal that first year after Lee's death may help you during a time of needed encouragement.

Christ reaches to rescue in strong currents.
Mer

── A Safe Haven ──

July 2013. I headed to Starbucks after leaving the beach this morning. Just before I opened the door, I look down and saw a little bird on the pavement. She was very still and dangerously in the traffic pattern of customers. I bent to take a closer look, careful not to touch her. The little bird was very much alive; her heart was beating fast and hard. She didn't look hurt, just stunned. I thought she must have flown into the Starbucks window. The poor thing didn't know what hit her.

Afraid someone would walk by and accidentally step on her, I put my finger in front of her. The tiny bird stepped on. As I relocated her to a safe patch of grass, I whispered, "I know how you feel, sweet sparrow."

Continuing on my way, I was reminded of a cherished Scripture from my childhood. "Are not five sparrows sold for two copper coins? And not one of them is forgotten before God. But the very hairs of your head are all numbered. Do not fear therefore; you are of more value than many sparrows" (Luke 12:6–7). The little bird had needed a safe place to rest until she could take to the sky once again.

There are days that I too feel stunned and not quite sure what to do next. I long for a quiet place to heal. I am reminded that just as God had allowed me to help one of His little creatures, He lovingly takes care of me.

It's time for sleep. I pray my mind will give in to rest tonight. The Comforter is here—the one who gently whispers in my ear that He is very aware of my tears and my every need.

Jesus is my resting place.

——— Beauty in the Storm ———

August 2013. Lee loved a good storm. Me? Not so much. Lee always opened the windows and the sliding glass door so he could see the ocean and hear the wind and rain. He'd say, "Mer, this calls for a pot of coffee." He celebrated a storm. I would curl up next to him as the lightning flashed and the thunder boomed, and I felt safe.

The past months have been the hardest of my entire life. The pain of missing sometimes physically hurts, so much so that it leaves me crying out to God to wrap His arms around me and hold me during the storm. And the fear. Oh, the fear. It keeps stalking me.

My counselor, Linda, tells me to look at it like fear and I are playing a game of tag. She reminds me of when, as a child, I got all quivery while waiting to be tagged. But once I actually was tagged, the fear left, and I had a feeling of being in control again. I love this analogy and keep thinking about it. I have decided to be still and name my fear of being alone for the rest of my life. I'll let it touch me and feel it, and then it will no longer control me.

"I sought the Lord, and He heard me, and delivered me from all my fears" (Psalm 34:4). I am learning to focus on Jesus rather than my fear.

There is a storm rolling in tonight. I sit with the sliding door open, and I smile. The sound of the rain makes me feel closer to Lee. I keep finding the little notes Lee stashed for me all around the house. Little signs of his presence are popping up for me everywhere. Soon, there won't be any more left.

I'm also discovering daily encouragements from Jesus, the lover of my soul. The Scriptures I have read many times mean so much more to me now, and the peace that fills my heart when I pray is amazing.

Even this storm tonight is a reminder that God paints beauty out of tragedy. I am going to celebrate this life storm and give thanks for His deliverance.

—— Legacy ——

September 2013. *Death* was the word I whispered today as I passed the funeral home. The place was packed with cars, and even though I didn't know who had died, my heart squeezed with sorrow for the people left behind. Life doesn't go on forever. I once heard someone say, "Statistics prove that ten out of ten people will die this year."

Perhaps for some, it isn't as scary, especially if you know where you're going and that it's going to be a holy place without any sickness or tears. My mom wasn't afraid of dying, but she wasn't looking forward to leaving Daddy all alone. Lee and I talked about dying too. He used to say, "I'm not afraid to die. I am just afraid of the process." He was most concerned with being a sickly burden to his loved ones.

For Lee's sake, that never happened. But I was not prepared. I was left without a plan. I'm a major planner (always prepared and even overprepared), and so life has been pulled out from under me. There's no reaching into my magic Mary Poppins bag to get needle and thread to patch my broken heart, or a salve to soothe the burn of my anger over life's unfairness.

There's one thing I've learned I can be prepared for: to meet Jesus face-to-face. Lee had been ready. He had accepted Christ as Lord of his life and was all set to meet the Savior. When his daughters talked about him at the service, they didn't recall his accomplishments in business or all the cool stuff he'd bought for them over the years. Rather, they recounted how much their daddy loved everyone and told everyone about Jesus. They told the entire church about how his favorite saying was, "Girls, God's got it."

There is comfort in knowing where Lee is spending eternity. He was not perfect, but he left a legacy. Oh, that Nichole Nordeman song to Jesus: "I want to leave a legacy, how will they remember me? Did I choose to love? Did I point to You enough to make a mark on things? I want to leave an offering, a child of mercy and grace who blessed Your name unapologetically."

I don't think it's morbid for people to ponder what others will find when they sift through the ashes of a life, or even to consider what kind of eulogy will be spoken, and whether others will be comforted, knowing greetings of "well done good and faithful servant" (Matthew 25:23) were given in heaven.

God, help me be mindful of living and leaving a legacy of faith.

7

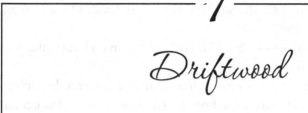

Spirit lead me where my trust is without borders,
Let me walk upon the waters
Wherever You would call me.
Take me deeper than my feet could ever wander
And my faith will be made stronger
In the presence of my Savior.

—HILLSONG UNITED, "OCEANS (WHERE FEET MAY FAIL)"

Spring is a particularly beautiful season on the Florida coast. There are days when I think there couldn't be a more perfect place to live.

For me, the month of May is bittersweet. May 8 is Momma's birthday, and sometimes it's also Mother's Day (six times since I was born, and twice since my mom died). May 14 is now Mom's heaven-versary. May 16 is the day Lee died, and May 1 is the day I got married again.

In 2013, just eight days before Lee died, he and I talked about my mom in Heaven. It went something like this.

"Happy birthday, Jimi Buck!" he shouted to the sky.

"Hey, do you think they have birthday celebrations in heaven?" I wondered aloud.

"Hmm, I don't know, sweetheart."

"Nah, I bet they have rebirth day celebrations," I said.

"Heaven is going to be so cool; I can't wait to go there. Hey, if anything ever happens to me, I want my funeral to be awesome," he said emphatically. "Ask Pastor D to preach salvation, because all my fraternity brothers will be there. He can do it in a way that it won't be like cramming it down their throats, but they will get it! Oh, and sing that song I love, 'I'll Stand,' okay?"

"Lee, you're as healthy as a horse! You're going to live a long time. But whatever you say," I agreed.

Remembering that conversation reminds me of the tree branches and limbs that have been washed ashore by tides or waves. This ocean debris often is transformed into appealing works of art. Dry, hardened driftwood provides perches and shelter for birds, and it can become the foundation for erosion-preventing sand dunes. Though once soggy pieces of wood floating aimlessly in the sea, driftwood is remarkable after the storm.

Similarly, as I began to dry out from my painful days and nights of crying, I reflected on all the eternally changed lives because of Jimi Buck and Lee Lewis. Their lives and deaths were not in vain.

I read once, "To have suffered much is like knowing many languages: It gives the sufferer access to many more people." I don't know who said it, but I certainly believe it's true. The loss of my loved ones put me through a level of suffering I never had experienced before. Affliction softens the heart, and mine had been torn and left incredibly tender. Yet in His perfect plan, the Master Potter gently restores the broken pieces.

My woundedness allowed empathy for others' challenges to grow deeper. I became less judgmental and more tolerant, maybe even curious. People's stories are the truth of who they are; appearances often mask the pain inside. God uses pain to bring people together. Scripture says,

> Blessed be the God and Father of our Lord Jesus Christ, the Father of mercies and God of all comfort, who comforts us in all our tribulation, that we may be able to comfort those who are in any trouble, with the comfort with which we ourselves are comforted by God. For as the sufferings of Christ abound in us, so our consolation also abounds through Christ. (2 Corinthians 1:3–5)

Although it might seem easier to suffer in silence, God anoints His people to be bravely vulnerable, walking alongside one another in compassion. Personally, I've found a kinship in shared pain, an unspoken understanding. Those who walk through deep water generally find God reveals His hope through them to others.

As Christians, we know evil abounds in this fallen world. But God is a purposeful and loving father who is involved in every detail of what happens on this earth. When bad things happen, His people are not forgotten and abandoned to fend for themselves. While grieving, I grew to know and love the heavenly Father in a more intimate way. He became my constant companion as I talked to Him about my sadness while walking the beach. I felt His Spirit of healing every time a beautiful sunrise lifted my heart.

> While grieving, I grew to know and love the heavenly Father in a more intimate way.

God also revealed Himself as the Sustainer, helping me stay afloat when the weight of the loneliness almost was too strong. And He also became the Protector, guiding me to safe people and places where I could be myself—not just a widow. The first time I was able to go out with a friend and laugh felt strange but also freeing.

Building a new routine was not easy. After years of being a wife and mother, little by little I began to rediscover Meredith the woman, including what I liked and disliked. I realized I was fairly boring (compared to most single women), and I was okay with that. Waking before the sun came up gave me time in God's Word with a comforting cup of coffee or hot tea. Then I'd go to the gym, catch a breath of the sunrise, and head to work. Later in the afternoon, I'd sometimes stop at Publix (buying food for one was a whole new experience). Evenings were too quiet, so it was not unusual for me to be in bed by eight thirty.

Weekends were filled with reflection and self-care. I spent a lot of time reading (more than one hundred books in the first year). I also wandered around some of the downtown shops and got a pedicure once in a while. I spent lots of time at the barn. Even though I had sold my horse years earlier, sweeping the floor and cleaning the stalls was therapeutic, and sometimes I rode a friend's horse. I eventually bought a new horse, and MoJo became the man in my life. He was spirited and loving—the perfect horse for me, except he never laughed at my jokes. I was mostly content, but a bit lonely for a friend who could share in this new normal with me. The majority of the amazing friends I had were married with families, and I didn't want to impose.

Then it happened. God showed up through a woman I'd met a year or so earlier in the grocery store. She was vaguely familiar, and I sort of remembered her from church.

"Meredith, I am so sorry to hear about your loss, and I'm sorry that I'm just reaching out to you," she said, walking right up to me one morning as I was leaving the gym. The woman explained she had been recovering after having a cancerous tumor removed and was just getting back into her exercise routine. "My name is Lynn, and I have been praying for you. In fact, can I pray with you right now?" And she did, right there in the middle of the gym.

We exchanged phone numbers and talked about getting together for coffee. A few weeks later, we enjoyed getting acquainted and had a long, lovely conversation about our lives, the ups and the downs of raising children, and being middle age. Lynn and I laughed some and cried some, and just like that, a beautiful friendship bloomed.

Lynn was in a season of singleness too, and we became inseparable, nearly glued at the hip. We worked out together, went to church together, and spent most of our free time together. When I met Lynn's son, Murphy, I immediately thought he and my daughter Jimi would hit it off. But my matchmaking fell flat when, after meeting him, my free-spirited, hippie Jimi assured me he was "too preppy."

As winter turned into spring, Lynn invited me to her youngest son's baseball games. As a fan of the game (and Lynn's energy and contagious laughter), I accepted and was eager to cheer on Carter and my high school alma mater. After the first game, I was hooked and bought a season ticket to support the team. I felt calm sitting in the bleachers, and it was great to decompress after work.

Meeting Lynn certainly was a divine appointment. God gave us each other to walk through a season of singleness. Her invitation to a baseball game changed the course of my life forever. The boy who wasn't at all the type for my daughter became my son-in-law, and I received the precious gift of a granddaughter. Jimi and Murphy are amazing together, shining the light of Jesus to their generation through serving in the youth ministry at their church. They are marvelous parents to sweet Willow. Lynn and I are connected forever—as friends, in-laws, and grandmothers.

I love the good gifts He sends me: new beginnings, new friends, and a newfound sense of purpose. He showers me with beautiful moments and even has a sense of humor. My sweet Willow and her playful giggles and precious kisses are like parachute drops from heaven. She makes me laugh and brings light to any cloudy day.

When I stop long enough and pay attention, God gives the best hugs.

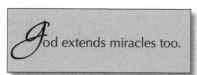

His arms reach through the people in my life. In the warmth of the sun around my shoulders, the feel of the sun on my face, and so many other ways, I feel His divine embrace. God extends miracles too. I have experienced them. He answers prayers (even though sometimes the answer is no) and loves with an everlasting love.

God is relentless in His pursuit. My proof is that I was able to settle into a newness of life and go days without crying. Wearing a genuine smile—not a forced, fake "I'm fine" one—felt so awesome.

The things that were once ordinary, everyday activities became the very things that filled my soul. Previously taken for granted, now time with my children brought such joy. Conversations with dear friends were deeper and more intimate. Nearly every flower caught my eye. Even the pieces of driftwood on the sand brought awe, not indifference.

And the birds. Since that encounter with the sparrow at Starbucks, it seems my ears grew more attuned to their lofty melodies.

> Look at the birds of the air, for they neither sow nor reap nor gather into barns; yet your heavenly Father feeds them. Are you not of more value than they? (Matthew 6:26)

Sweet Friend,

God is good, and His plan is amazing and perfect. Even though there are times in life when it seems like all has been lost and there's wreckage everywhere, He is still beside you. The Savior sees every tear and wastes nothing. He loves you very much, and He is trustworthy.

I pray the healing Holy Spirit pours comfort and hope into your heart. Allow Him to be your safe place to land.

Let the Good Father of the universe repurpose your broken places.
Mer

—— In His Arms ——

People often ask others who are walking through a trial, "How do you cope?" or "I'm amazed at your strength. What keeps you so calm?" They may even ask, "How can you praise God in this tragedy?" Anytime someone asks me this type of question, I think of the poem I read and loved as a child. The poem is called "Footprints in the Sand" by Mary Stevenson. It was about a man who had a dream he was walking on the beach with the Lord. As they walked, scenes from his life flashed before him. During the display, he noticed that sometimes there were two set of footprints in the sand, and at other times there was only one set. This really bothered the man because it seemed that during the most difficult times, he only saw one set of footprints. So, he questions the Lord.

> "Why, when I needed you most,
> you have not been there for me?"
> The Lord replied,
> "The times when you have
> seen only one set of footprints,
> is when I carried you."

I can imagine the light going off in the man's mind at the Lord's reply. I certainly recognize the many moments that I never could have gotten through without the strength of the Father. Jesus carries those He loves. "The Lord is close to the brokenhearted and saves those who are crushed in spirit" (Psalm 34:18 NIV).

Hear Him whisper to your soul, "Child, I feel the pain of your heart right now."

Years after Lee's death, I had a coffee date with a friend whose husband had died suddenly at forty-four. Just two months after the loss, Amy was trying to figure out the day-to-day effort of getting through. She expressed the plethora emotions, specifically anger at God.

As Christians, we think it's taboo to admit we are angry at Him for allowing bad things to happen. When blame needs a scapegoat, God often is the target. It's okay. He understands human anger and can handle it; He loves us anyway. God isn't disappointed when His beloved children are confused. He is a patient father. He sticks close, and when the light bulb eventually comes on for us, God is complete in His forgiveness (Psalm 86:15). He always is generous with His grace.

Others who have not walked the path of pain don't get that grief has no limits. It's so personal that it's difficult to explain, even to the ones closest to us. And sometimes the most well-meaning people try to offer comforting words that hurt more than help. As Amy and I sat together, my mind went back to the moment I broke the silence of my own anger with God. It was a Sunday morning after church. As I drove home, the heat inside me started to rise, and before I had gone more than a mile, my distress turned into a full-blown ugly, sobbing cry. Anguish built and was released in a wail of frustration. I eventually pulled over to continue my rant. I beat the steering wheel and screamed at God, "Why would you do this to me? I am so mad at You!" As soon as those words came out of my mouth, I winced, even though I felt like God could have healed my mom and saved Lee.

As cars sped past, I felt a whisper in my heart say, "It's okay, I get you … even in your anger." I looked across the table at Amy and smiled. She didn't know then that she eventually would be okay, but I did. I told her it was normal to be angry, hurt, and scared, because grief stinks. I knew one day she would laugh again and realize God had not done this *to* her, but that He had walked *with* her through it (Psalm 138:7). Amy simply needed someone to share her pain with—without expectations, without judgment, and without setting a timeline on her grief. She needed a friend to sit with her. These lyrics by Jason Gray express what my friend and many others try to say but don't know how: "While I wait for the smoke to clear, you don't even have to speak. Just sit with me in the ashes here, and together we can pray for peace to the One acquainted with our grief."

8

Morning Light

I will run and not grow weary,
I will walk, I will not faint.
I will soar on wings like eagles,
Find my rest in your everlasting name.
You are my revival,
Jesus on you I wait.
And I'll lean on your promise,
You will renew my strength.

—LAUREN DAIGLE, "MY REVIVAL"

> "*Never give up on your dreams.*"

"Expect the unexpected."
"Never give up on your dreams."
"Miracles happen to those who believe in them."

These words of wisdom are easy to dismiss with an offhanded, "Whatever." But ask people who have suffered a tragedy, and they'll tell you about God's almighty power to change lives.

My friendship with Lynn led me to a ballpark, and the course of my life changed beyond my wildest dreams. Some friends had started asking me when I would be ready to date again, but I politely told them I wasn't at all interested and might never be. I'd always felt I was meant to be a wife, but my third time in a season of singleness felt right. I was content.

One afternoon while I was standing by the bleachers, an acquaintance of mine approached. And just like my first encounter with Lynn, the moment was another restart that happened in God's timing.

Jon Shave and I had attended the same high school and had run into each other occasionally over the years, but we'd never really known each other well. Yet one of the pros (or cons, depending on the situation) of living in a small town is that many people keep up with who's who and the juicy tidbits of each other's lives after graduation.

He had left Fernandina after high school to play college baseball and then was recruited by a professional team. After fifteen years, he returned to Fernandina and married, although it ended in divorce. Jon was single with two children.

When he walked up to me, I thought two things. *He's a nice guy, and he probably wants to get to know Lynn.* My dark-haired friend always turned heads. After making small talk for a few minutes, Jon walked away, and Lynn leaned over to me.

"Mer, I think he likes you." Apparently, I had been oblivious to his flirting.

"Huh? Nah, he was just coming over here to look at you."

Lynn assured me this wasn't the case. Jon didn't really have a reason to be at the ballpark, because his son was not old enough to play high school baseball. But he lived nearby and loved the game. Of course, I now know it was another divine appointment set by the Author of my life.

Later that night, I thought more about Jon. I remembered him as being shy and quiet, like my dad, and less like the men to whom I previously had been attracted. We talked more as the season progressed and we saw one another at the ballpark. Jon was refreshingly humble and sincere.

I was very attracted to him, but I was in a much different place emotionally and spiritually then I ever had been. I was not looking for a romantic relationship.

When Jon finally got up the nerve to ask me out, I was honest with him about my reservations. If he was looking for a rebound, for sex or adventurous drama, I was not the girl. My boring interests? Sitting at home and watching a movie or walking the beach. I kept waiting for his eyes to glaze over and for him to say, "Never mind."

"Okay, let's be friends and see where it goes," Jon said instead. "And if we only end up as friends, then we're friends."

Jon became my very best friend. Most mornings, he would come and pick me up, and as I took pictures of the sunrise, he would fish. Our dates were simple and comfortable, talking for hours and never allowing pretense to invade. We were up front and real with each other about every area of our lives, the good, the bad, and the ugly. He made me laugh, and better yet, he laughed at my jokes.

Not long after we started dating, I knew I could spend the rest of my life with this extraordinary man. Jon had a way about him. When I was with him, I felt like I was home. As our relationship grew more serious, I broke some news to him, wondering how he would respond. Once I explained what was on my heart, I think Jon was relieved.

> *When I was with him, I felt like I was home.*

As we talked, I explained to Jon that although I realized I had been so busy trying to feel loved in my previous relationships, I had forgotten my true love. I had gone from living in my parents' home to being a wife and mother. I had always had others to nurture and rescue, but I'd never allowed someone to rescue me. Throughout my first and second marriage, God always had been there, waiting for me to turn to Him, but I kept pushing Him to second or third place.

The Scripture says, "Nevertheless I have this against you, that you have left your first love" (Revelation 2:4). Throughout my life, I had put unrealistic expectations on others' natural love, assuming earthly love could fill my love tank and make me feel worthy. Only supernatural love can do that. The extravagant love of Jesus is enough. It fills, assigns worth, calms, heals, and restores.

Jesus had become my all in all, and so I told Jon that he could not be my first love. When Jesus held my head above the waves and carried me out of the treacherous water to the safety of the shore, He became my everything. He became my refuge and strength (Psalm 46); my rock, my fortress, and my deliverer (Psalm 18); and the one in whom I put all my trust (Psalm 91). The intimacy Christ offers is incomparable. There is so much freedom—freedom from fear (1 John 4:18), freedom from abandonment (Deuteronomy 31:6), and freedom from feeling unworthy.

Jon asked me to marry him after we had been dating about a year.

He was coaching baseball at the time, and so we casually agreed to wait until the season was over, which was late April. My mom had died on May 14, and Lee had died on May 16. We chose to get married on May 1, creating a happy start to what otherwise was a difficult month for me.

We decided on Wednesday to get married that Friday. I hadn't even thought about a dress, but a quick trip to one of our downtown shops delivered. I told the clerk I need a wedding dress to wear the next day. Without hesitating, she said she had the perfect dress.

And it was. It wasn't too fussy, it was knee-length, cream-colored, and sleeveless with a shear overlay that gave it just the right elegance. The ceremony was a small, quiet one with only a few family members by our side at our favorite spot on the beach. At sunrise, Jon and I pledged our forever love to each another and began the rest of our lives together.

Jesus was in His rightful place as my first love, and my love gauge read full. I was complete already, which meant so much freedom for Jon. He didn't take on the pressure of fulfilling my soul's desires. Jon was free to be himself, as well as my partner and helpmate in our marriage.

With Jon, God certainly blessed me beyond my imagination. Our blended family now also includes his children, Cisco and Katy, as well as Jon's mom, dad, and brother. I love them all and am constantly amazed at how the heart expands to hold so much affection and happiness.

Cisco, who just started college, is a quiet and very kind young man. He doesn't let things bother him but goes with the flow. I asked him one time why he doesn't get stressed about much. He replied, "I don't worry about stuff I can't control." A lot of wisdom for an eighteen-year-old.

Katy, eleven, sees the positive in most everything. One morning as she walked out of the front door, she noticed the sky was cloudy and growing darker. Her excitement bubbled over with, "Oh! It's going to rain. I think there will be a rainbow!" She's definitely a glass-half-full girl.

Jon's dad, Tommy, affectionately known as Papa, is a good man who is loving and wise. He always has a smile and a kiss on the cheek for me, and he makes me feel special. God even provided a mother when I didn't even realize I needed one. Jon's mom, Joyce, aka Mimi, is feisty and opinionated. She's passionate in the love she has for her children, grandchildren, and now me. We talk every morning on my way to work, on my way home, and whenever I need a mother's love and advice (which is often). When God does His work, He leaves no detail undone.

My children, Jimi and Bobby, are healthy young adults, having survived some hard situations and making difficult decisions. Over the years, I explained to both of them many times about the choice of being a victim or a victor, of living a life of excuses or pushing forward despite the past.

At twenty-seven, Jimi is an independent and fiercely loyal woman. She's a non-judgmental, people-loving disciple of Jesus, and she's an amazing wife and mother. Jimi has become my closest friend. Bobby is twenty-five and has more talent in his little finger than ten people put together. He is more reserved now compared to the extremely funny child who always had a hilarious remark growing up, however I still can see glimpses of my witty little boy. Bobby has a compassionate heart, and I see God doing an incredible work in his life. God has big plans for my son; I love watching it unfold.

I never will understand every twist and turn of my life on this side of heaven, but I do know the loving Father is patient and kind. He is the God of second (and third) chances. The joy I am experiencing as I walk through the rest of my life with Jon takes my breath away. Being his best friend, wife, and forever love feels so right. In fact, it feels like it has always been meant to be.

I often tell Jon I wish we had noticed each other in high school, fallen in love, and married, and that there always had been an us. In his wisdom, Jon smiles each time and says, "Darlin', God knew what He was doing. We might have messed it up way back then. His timing is perfect."

Jon is my blessing from the greatest and most gracious gift giver of all.

> By night on my bed I sought the one I love;
> I sought him, but I did not find him.
> 'I will rise now,' I said,
> 'And go about the city;
> In the streets and in the squares
> I will seek the one I love.'
> I sought him, but I did not find him.
> The watchmen who go about the city found me;
> I said, 'Have you seen the one I love?'
> Scarcely had I passed by them,
> When I found the one I love.
> I held him and would not let him go. (Song of Solomon 3:1–4)

Sweet Friend,

Do you think you'll never feel joy again? Let me assure you that although the night seems long, God always makes the sun rise. Kristene DiMarco of Bethel Music sings, "Take courage my heart, stay steadfast my soul, He's in the waiting, He's in the waiting. Hold onto your hope as your triumph unfolds, He's never failing, He's never failing."

God knows your deepest aches and all your soul's desires, and He cares. He is the precious Savior who tends to the brokenhearted, and He works out His good plan. Be thankful because God is faithful in His promises, and He never forsakes those He loves.

Keep your eyes on the hope of His horizon.
Mer

—— Becoming a Butterfly ——

When I first accepted Christ into my heart as Lord and Savior, I surrendered my life to Him. As a new, on-fire Christian, there was an overwhelming sense of freedom. But as life moved forward, some days His freedom from temptation and sin felt less filling than my desire to please myself. It was hard to turn away from how I was used to living and turn toward what I knew to be right. Yet it is exactly what God called me to do.

Transitioning from one world into another is a difficult journey, much like becoming a disciple of Christ. The good news is that God does the changing. He leads; we follow.

As an example, Jon ate, worked, and slept baseball from childhood into adulthood. It was his entire life and was all he knew. When his career as a professional ballplayer ended, and he didn't wake up every day with that purpose, it was challenging for him physically, mentally, and socially. He felt out of place in so many ways. However, Jon kept looking forward and wanted to embrace the opportunities he hoped lay ahead.

This ability begins as soon as we look to the cross. In the Bible, Paul explains it this way: "Therefore, if anyone is in Christ, he is a new creation; old things have passed away; behold, all things have become new" (2 Corinthians 5:17).

In my mother's song, "Changed like a Butterfly," she compares the caterpillar's metamorphosis to a hell-bound life being born again as a new creation in Christ. The change is not without pain, however the result can only be described as amazing.

Living as a Christ follower is a transformation of heart and mind. "Do not conform to the pattern of this world, but be transformed by the renewing of your mind. Then you will be able to test and approve what God's will is—His good, pleasing and perfect will" (Romans 12:2 NIV).

Let's not be willing to settle for good, when God wants great for us. Although His perfect will doesn't always turn out how we expected, God longs to give us abundant life. Change is never easy, but it's always worth it. Just ask the caterpillar.

I often talk with Jon on the phone as he drives to work. One morning, I heard him exclaim, "Wait, little guy! Hey, Mer, I'll call you back." A few minutes later, Jon told me he'd seen a deer caught in a fence by the side of the road. He stopped to help, and the deer was able to free itself. The poor animal was totally panicked, but Jon shooed him away from the danger of traffic.

In my mind, I saw how it had played out: the fear of the deer and Jon's desire to rescue it. There have been times when, like the deer, I have been in total panic mode. I've gotten so focused on the crisis that I forget about the One who calms and saves. I often tell myself, "Hey, you're only human." But is that an excuse? Is it really the reason for the fear, or is it my unbelief?

I used to tell Jimi and Bobby when they were young, "Stop, look, and listen so that you don't have to stop, drop, and roll!" Similar advice for Christians is, "Be still, and know that I am God" (Psalm 46:10).

If the deer had only remained calm during its duress, it would have experienced the comfort of knowing someone bigger and stronger was there to help. It simply had to be still and trust. Jon's encounter with the deer reminded me how unpredictable life really is.

The choice is this: panic or trust? When I told a friend the story, she reminded me of the scripture that says, "The Lord will fight for you; you need only to be still" (Exodus 14:14 NIV).

Not long after we married, Jon took a new job that required him to travel. I freaked out during his first trip. I was so full of fear, worrying he might not come back alive (just like Lee), that I became physically ill. I tried to hide my panic from him when he called to check in, but Jon already knew me well enough to know I was struggling. He reassured me that God was in control and that everything was going to be fine. He called me often, and finally the three-day trip ended; he returned home.

Around his fifth trip, I began to relax and was able see what God was up to. The heavenly Father loves me so much that He was allowing me to heal from post-traumatic stress. Jon's traveling gave me the opportunity to work through fears I hadn't even realized I was harboring. I would like to say I never had another worry and was completely healed, however I'm still growing.

Life is the long process of becoming whole in Christ. Every time fear creeps in or total panic attempts to take over and paralyze, remember to take a deep breath and just be still.

Allow God to bring peace and direct those next steps. Take Him up on His promise to fight for good. He's trustworthy.

Nothing. Nada. Zip.

During the process of writing this book, I sat down a few different times at my keyboard, and no words came to mind. Not good. I had always enjoyed journaling, and writing during those times was like a God-fountain of words almost effortlessly flowing from my heart to my fingers. I clicked away until my fingers cramped.

These new blank-slate moments were frustrating. I chatted with God and reminded Him that I was doing this for Him. Still, zilch. I questioned whether I should be trying to write a book at all. *What if I fail? What if it's terrible, and no one wants to read it?* I quickly identified Satan as the author of these doubts.

Then, the soft whisper came. "I am your muse. Aren't you doing this with Me and for Me?"

The Spirit followed with this reminder, "Be strong and take heart and wait for the Lord" (Psalm 27:14 NIV).

I had tried to charge ahead, forgetting the only audience that mattered: my audience of One. God sees the motive of the heart, no matter how good the intention may be. The world of writer's block, the land of nothingness, is a scary place. But it got my attention and prompted me to look Godward instead of inward and how the world might judge me.

Desert places are times of waiting and feeling fruitless. The wilderness is where God does His most meaningful work. Faithfulness during days of drought gets rewarded. He pours His Spirit into thirsty souls, proving He is willing and able to do great things.

God is still good through writer's block. He is almighty when we are running through fields of flowers and when we feel stranded in the desert places of our lives. He teaches and has purpose in every season.

The focus and hope in all things is God, not self. He is the inspiration, the resolve, and the stamina.

> But those who wait on the Lord Shall renew their strength; They shall mount up with wings like eagles, They shall; run and not be weary, They shall walk and not faint. (Isaiah 40:31)

Tidal Waves, Tributaries, and Treasures

Sweet Friend,

When I get out of bed before dawn and go down to the beach with my camera in hand, I am hoping to catch a beautiful sunrise. On relatively calm mornings, I wade out as far as I deem safe, sometimes waste deep, and wait.

Hope. The dictionary defines it as "a feeling of expectation or desire for a certain thing to happen." (Of course, most mornings I hope there are no sharks scouting for their breakfast!) On a day-to-day basis, I think most people's earthly desire is to live a life of contentment with minimal stress and avoid pain. But when the ocean begins to get turbulent, often hope is lost.

Sometimes I have to remind myself that hope has nothing to do with the absence of trouble but everything to do with a relationship with Jesus, the Savior of our fallen world. He is the hope when storms come. Choosing to see the goodness of God, even in the most tragic situations, brings the remarkable realization that He is the lifeline to peace.

Perhaps you just have been hit by a tidal wave, that unexpected blow that knocks your feet out from under you, and now you're trying to catch your breath. Or you may be wading through a tributary in a season of waiting and searching. Maybe you are sifting through the memories of both, like sand falling through your fingers, and recalling the treasures provided along the way. No matter where you are on your life journey, God is with you and for you.

The Apostle Paul writes,

And we boast in the hope of the glory of God. Not only so, but we also glory in our sufferings, because we know that suffering produces perseverance; perseverance, character; and character, hope. And hope does not put us to shame, because God's love has been poured out into our hearts through the Holy Spirit, who has been given to us. (Romans 5:2–5 NIV)

Don't lose heart, friend. God has a good plan for your life that is full of hope. His name is Jesus. He is steadfast in every season, He wants to walk with you through each one, and His hope is on the horizon.

As I continue to praise God in every sunrise, I know there will be more trials and sadness in my life. God doesn't promise a pain-free journey to heaven, but He does promise His presence and His strength to get through anything. And through the death of His Son on the cross, He promises an eternal home in Heaven for those who accept that sacrificial gift. In the words of the late Billy Graham, "My home is in Heaven. I'm just traveling through this world."

Thank you for reading my story. I pray that in some way, it has offered encouragement to press on. The next portion of this book is a compilation of thoughts or devotions I have written throughout the years. Please read through them in any way your spirit is stirred.

Allow God's waves of grace to wash over you as He wraps you in His love.

Love,
Mer

——— God's Tapestry ———

Have you ever looked at the backside of a section of tapestry while the artist is still working? It looks like a mish-mash of colorful lines. Not until the last thread is woven in can the beauty of the completed work be appreciated, and generally from a bit of a distance.

A child feels despondent when the sandcastle, nearly complete at the edge of the water, gets flooded and parts are washed away with the tide. Dad can envision the finished product, but for the child, it's disappointing.

Life often feels this way. When struggle, heartache, and tragedy are woven into our lives, it's difficult not to focus on anything but the immediate mess. God's Word promises, "Being confident of this very thing, that He who has begun a good work in you will complete it until the day of Jesus Christ" (Philippians 1:6).

The Master Weaver, the Great Architect, wants His very best for us. In the middle of the chaos, we forget to look at the Creator.

Accepting that God is working all things for good is a matter of trust. The seemingly tangled threads of our lives at a certain time may be what turn into a pattern of purpose. As others look on at what we see as a flattened heap of nothing, God could be revealing His steadfast faithfulness. And though we may never know this side of Heaven those who've watched us prevail as overcomers, God uses our lives to bring precious souls to the saving knowledge of Jesus.

Turn your eyes from what is temporal to what is eternal, from what's only for a brief season in this earthly life to what will endure through the ages, and fulfill the Almighty's purpose.

Consider these words: "While we do not look at the things which are seen, but at the things which are not seen. For the things which are seen are temporary, but the things which are not seen are eternal" (2 Corinthians 4:18).

Take a deep breath. If you are sitting on the beach and reading this, maybe wiggle your toes deeper into the sand and whisper, "I trust you, Jesus." God may not answer every why, but maybe, just maybe, He will allow you to catch a glimpse of His beautiful design, His tapestry of love.

There's a silly folktale about a fear-filled fowl. While Chicken Little is taking her morning walk, an acorn falls on her head, and she immediately thinks worst-case scenario. She starts telling all of her friends, "The sky is falling!" In other words, the world as she knew it was coming to an end.

Her friends believe her. Chicken Little, Henny Penny, Ducky Lucky, Turkey Lurkey, and Goosey Loosey are in an all-out panic. Their anxiety is through the roof, and they are not thinking clearly, which makes them a perfect target to fall prey to the enemy. Sly ol' Foxy Loxy, acting concerned and seemingly having all of the answers, offers to point them in the right direction ... or so they think. "Run into my den," he says. "You will be safe there while I go tell the king." Then, Foxy Loxy eats them all!

I never liked that story. I mean, really? Overreacting because of an acorn? How dumb.

Oh, wait. I have been a catastrophic thinker from time to time, focusing on all the what-if, worst-case scenarios. I've used so much energy worrying about something that never came to be or was totally insignificant. I have allowed so much anxiety into my heart and mind that I momentarily forgot I have a mighty warrior, God, on my side. He is for me and with me.

Irrational catastrophic thinking is never good. Truth is best. "Fear not, for I am with you; be not dismayed, for I am your God. I will strengthen you, yes, I will help you, I will uphold you with My righteous right hand" (Isaiah 41:10).

Too bad no one shared Apostle Peter's warning with Chicken Little. "Be sober, be vigilant; because your adversary the devil walks about like a roaring lion, seeking whom he may devour" (1 Peter 5:8). Satan, the opportunist, is looking for any occasion to trip us up. Being sober (clearheaded) and vigilant (keeping careful watch for possible danger or difficulties) is our defense against his attack.

When panic begins to tighten in our chests, we must take a deep breath and remember the truth. "For God has not given us a spirit of fear, but of power and of love and of a sound mind" (2 Timothy 1:7).

The Savior is completely trustworthy. When it seems like the sky is falling, run to Jesus for the calm reassurance that everything will be all right.

Perseverance

One late afternoon, my daughter, Jimi, and I were strolling through Fernandina's historic downtown. We saw what I thought was an amazing sight. A beautiful purple flower was growing up through a crack in the base of a hundred-year-old brick building. I don't know the type of flower, but I named her Perseverance.

Precious little Perseverance had grown in the most unlikely of places. Against all odds, she had bloomed right where the Creator had put her.

At the very beginning of this book (chapter 1, "Walk with Me"), I include the lyrics of a song by Plumb: "How many times have you heard me cry out, 'God please take this?' How many times have you given me strength to just keep breathing?" Oh, how those words resonate! We beg God to relieve our pain, and instead He helps us survive the trial.

The Bible instructs us to "be joyful in hope, patient in affliction, faithful in prayer" (Romans 12:12 NIV). From my experiences, I believe God is more concerned with the development of our character than our comfort. Miss Perseverance surely didn't find it easy or comfortable flourishing between brick and concrete, but it was the only way she could live in total dependence on the Maker and grow to her full potential. I like to think God simply put her there just for me, as a reminder of His love.

The Apostle Paul, who wrote many of the New Testament letters from prison, testified, "I served the Lord with great humility and with tears and in the midst of severe testing" (Acts 20:19 NIV). We too are called to endure with patience and hope.

The next time you're in a tight spot or are weary from difficulty, remember the purple flower growing up through a crack, and keep pushing forward. Persevere and show others that they can too.

The Battle

The bad news: We're in the midst of a battle.

The good news: We have a warrior God.

Is the struggle an illness, a failing marriage, a wayward child? Maybe it's fighting against fear, grief, or depression. The Merriam-Webster dictionary defines a battle as "a combat between two persons, to fight or struggle tenaciously to achieve or resist something."

Scripture confirms, "For our struggle is not against flesh and blood, but against the rulers, against the authorities, against the powers of this dark world and against the spiritual forces of evil in the heavenly realms" (Ephesians 6:12 NIV). Spiritual warfare is real. Satan wants souls, and he uses feelings and emotions like shame, loneliness, and unworthiness. He's cunning. In fact, he "walks about like a roaring lion, seeking whom he may devour" (1 Peter 5:8).

But we have a God who is victorious. He is the light that shines in the darkness, and it cannot be overcome. Our God is personal. He fights for and with, us. "But the Lord is with me like a mighty warrior; so my persecutors will stumble and not prevail. They will fail and be thoroughly disgraced; their dishonor will never be forgotten" (Jeremiah 20:11 NIV).

One of my very favorite reminders of God's greatness is found in 2 Samuel, when David inquires of God regarding an upcoming battle. God tells him, "As soon as you hear the sound of marching in the tops of the poplar trees, move quickly, because that will mean the Lord has gone out in front of you to strike the Philistine army" (2 Samuel 5:24 NIV). David was obedient and waited for the signal, even though he was a man of action and war. I'm almost certain waiting was not his forte, but David had learned over time, from one battle to another, about God's faithfulness to His promises. Obedience equals victory.

God's victory is our victory! "If God is for us, who can be against us?" (Romans 8:31) God knows our struggles, and He cares. If we can be still and calm our breathing, tilting our ears toward the sound, we will hear the marching of the celestial army arriving to win the battle.

Believe. Trust. Be faithful and wait on the Lord.

Know God and embrace His victory.

—— THE KEY ——

Trying to unlock a door with the wrong key is frustrating. And it's futile, to say the least.

Often it is obvious because it won't even fit in the keyhole. But then there are the keys that fit well and simply will not unlock the door. No matter how much we jiggle it, it's the wrong key.

The door to life, with its many twists and turns, requires the correct key as well. I didn't write *keys* plural, but the singular *key*. There is only one key to get through this life and into the eternal kingdom. His name is Jesus. "Jesus said to him, 'I am the way, the truth, and the life. No one comes to the Father except through Me'" (John 14:6).

God knows we struggle with accepting that Jesus is the only answer to every question. He strategically reminds again and again that His ways are better than our ways. "Trust in the Lord with all your heart, and lean not on your own understanding; in all your ways acknowledge Him, and He shall direct your paths" (Proverbs 3:5–6). We do not have other choices. There are no alternatives, just Jesus. We make it hard, but really it is so simple.

Perhaps a bigger house or a vacation will fix the marriage. A night out with friends and a few drinks certainly will make the loneliness go away. I picture people walking around like the janitor with a hundred different keys, trying each one, when all that's needed is the one key. Such a collection of fake keys is heavy and weighs us down; they cause confusion.

It's time to lighten the load. Throw away all the other keys except for the master key. Don't call the local locksmith. Reach for the One who works perfectly every single time. Jesus is all we need.

I read some very sad words in Lisa Bevere's book, *Lioness Arising*. The author wrote, "Because of fear, I had forfeited strength, life and beauty. I had lost a sense of my true self and, with that loss, so much of what God wanted for me was yet unrealized."

Fear certainly has a way of keeping us from realizing all God has for us. As women, we sometimes want to put a finger to the chest of this world and scream, "I am woman. Hear me roar!" Yet we're scared inside. We wear our game faces and then wait for the world to tell us we are not worthy, not part of the in crowd, or not a good wife, mother, friend, or co-worker.

It's no wonder that *empowered* is a buzzword among women. The dictionary gives this definition: "give (someone) the authority or power to do something, make (someone) stronger and more confident, especially in controlling their life and claiming their rights." We desire to be liberated, not shackled by our fear of failure, rejection, and other's opinions. Yet we can't seem to break out of the bondage of self-depreciation.

Studying God's Word together as sisters in Christ is a tool to freedom. "And He said to me, 'My grace is sufficient for you, for My strength is made perfect in weakness'" (2 Corinthians 12:9). The Apostle John lovingly tells us, "You are of God, little children, and have overcome them, because He who is in you is greater than he who is in the world" (1 John 4:4).

We are cherished, loved, favored, treasured, and precious. We are worth dying for and staying for, beloved and empowered. It's not because of the balance in our bank accounts, the brands we wear, or the crowd we hang with. It's not because of who we are but because of *whose* we are and *whose* strength is in us.

Chin up, shoulders back! We must claim our rightful place. We are daughters of the King of kings!

—— Come Home ——

I remember my children singing songs about Jesus when they were young and coming home from Sunday school with Bible verses memorized. Innocence abounded. I never thought they one day would go down a wayward path ... but they did.

Thankfully, God pursued and drew them back to Him. The waiting was hard. As a mother, I did everything I could to make them see truth, but at the end of the day, they had to make their way back to the Father.

I love the parable Jesus tells about the prodigal son. The youngest boy wanted his inheritance early, and when he received it, he left home and spent all of it on "riotous living" (Luke 15:13). Leaving the protection of his father's house in order to follow his own desires, the son lived it up and did what he wanted to do. When he hit rock bottom, he returned home with intentions to humble himself and be a servant in his father's house.

Then comes my favorite part: "And he arose, and came to his father. But when he was yet a great way off, his father saw him, and had compassion, and ran, and fell on his neck, and kissed him" (Luke 15:20). I love the middle part the most. "But when he was yet a great way off, his father saw him." This tells me the father knew his child well and was watching with expectancy for his return.

Waiting. Watching. The father had gone about his daily routine, all the while watching for his precious child to come home. It didn't matter how many months or years the son was gone; the father never stopped looking down the road that led to home.

Like the prodigal son's father, we have the faithful, heavenly Father who loves us even in our wandering. My daddy would say, "When you feel like God has abandoned you, Meredith, turn around. He didn't move—you did. God is the same yesterday, today, and forever."

Poor choices, detours, and even pigpens don't mean the end. God's love is unconditional and everlasting. He is the compassionate Father and does not lay on guilt trips or say, "I told you so."

"Then I will give them a heart to know Me, that I am the Lord; and they shall be My people, and I will be their God, for they shall return to Me with their whole heart" (Jeremiah 24:7). The Father is watching with expectancy and waiting with open arms. Turn around and return home.

A Man of Sorrows

In a week's time, a friend of mine was diagnosed with cancer. Another had a miscarriage, losing the precious baby she and her husband had been waiting on for over two years. Yet another friend's husband went to heaven after a long battle with brain cancer. All these dear ones grieved, and most likely they grieved differently.

One of the many beautiful attributes of the good Father is the way He loves us right where we are. When we are crushed beneath the wave of sorrow, He loves us there. When we are screaming the anguish of "Why?" He loves us there. Even when we turn our back to His comfort, He loves us and is patiently waiting for us to turn again into His faithful arms.

I love the many reminders in scripture. "Even though I walk through the valley of the shadow of death, I will fear no evil: for thou art with me; thy rod and thy staff they comfort me" (Psalm 23:4). "And the Lord, He is the One who goes before you. He will be with you, He will not leave you nor forsake you; do not fear nor be dismayed" (Deuteronomy 31:8). These verses gently whisper to our hurting hearts that our loving God is with us through every tear, every anxiety attack, every fit of anger, every fragmented prayer, and every effort just to breathe. He holds us in His arms when we can't walk, and He stands beside us, holding our hand when we start taking those baby steps out of the valley of despair.

While going through a trial or tragedy, often well-meaning people offer, "I know how you feel." But everyone deals with grief differently; a more accurate sentiment may be, "I don't know exactly what you are going through, but my heart hurts for you and I am praying for you."

Jesus is the only one who can understand entirely what we are feeling and how we hurt. "He is despised and rejected by men, a Man of sorrows and acquainted with grief. And we hid, as it were, our faces from Him; He was despised, and we did not esteem Him. Surely He has borne our grief and carried our sorrows" (Isaiah 53:3–4). There is no suffering Jesus the man, or God the Father has not faced.

We must not be ashamed of how we are feeling while walking through a dark valley, because Abba Father already has been there ahead of us, and He doesn't leave us to face it alone. It may be hard to see in the midst of sadness, but there is a comforter and a light in the darkness.

There is an exquisite artist who creates "beauty from ashes." His name is Jesus.

—— Be the Door ——

You know by now that music inspires me. I like rhythm, but I'm a lyric listener. As a child, when a song came on the radio, I would say, "Momma, listen to these words."

Jason Gray's "With Every Act of Love" includes a line that says, "God put a million, million doors in the world for His love to walk through and one of those doors is you." Many songs are inspired by God's Word, and we who are created in His image are meant to worship Him and point others to Him.

"He who does not love does not know God, for God is love" (1 John 4:8). Do we ooze the love that resides in us? Are we a door, or even just a welcome mat, to His kingdom for everyone with whom we work and play?

Consider a room filled with vases of gardenias or roses—the pleasant aroma fills every corner. The same is true for us: whatever we fill ourselves with the most will pour out of our mouths and show in our actions (2 Corinthians 2:15).

Minds and hearts filled with Jesus radiate love. Spending time in the Bible and praying for God to use us helps us to be on the lookout for opportunities to be the hands and feet of Christ. We'll also see others through the eyes of Christ. We will love with no agenda, no self-driven motive and no expectation of a payback.

Holy obedience opens up opportunity for an abundant harvest of souls. We share God's love and He does the rest. Let's be gentle, kind, cheerful, and encouraging. Helpers and compassionate listeners. Let's be doors.

Oftentimes words and phrases nearly jump off pages and beg for my attention.

Recently, while reading the book of Ruth, I noticed something new. Naomi forgot who she was. After her husband and two sons die, she and her daughter-in-law Ruth returned to Naomi's hometown. When people recognized her as she entered the gate, she told them to no longer call her Naomi, but to refer to her as Mara, which means "bitter" (Ruth 1:20).

I sat in the sorrow she must have experienced. She told her friends, "I went out full, and the Lord has brought me home again empty." She was understandably focusing on her loss.

As I kept reading, I was intrigued. The author, most likely Samuel, never stopped referring to her as Naomi. The inspired Word of God continued to call her by her given name, not her self-proclaimed one! Renaming ourselves by our current state of mind does not accurately define who we are in Christ. He always sees us through the eyes of His unchanging love.

Life is unpredictable. Plans change and life can take unexpected twists and turns. It may even resemble Kingda Ka at Six Flags (the scariest roller coaster in the world), but we have a dependable God. When tempted to exist only as anger, bitterness, broken, hatefulness, failure, unworthy, or unwanted, we must stop and remember *whose* we are.

The loving Father wraps His arms around every broken heart, every broken life, and whispers, "You are My precious daughter, you are My greatly loved son; I see your situation and haven't forgotten you." Even when we try to change our names due to temporary memory lapse, rest assured that we are known by God.

Soak in the comforting words from the Redeemer: "Fear not, for I have redeemed you; I have called you by your name; you are Mine" (Isaiah 43:1).

—— Shark's Teeth ——

I remember a time when I was trying to figure out God's will for my life. It seemed as elusive as finding a shark's tooth on the beach. I searched and searched, and I even thought I found one. But it wasn't a shark's tooth at all; upon closer inspection, it was only a broken shell, a counterfeit. Sometimes we feel like we're looking in the right places and heading in the right direction, certain the path we're on is God's will. Then a look in the mirror reveals more self-serving intentions than selflessness. I have made decisions based on what I wanted and then tried to justify my actions by claiming God's will. But they were my own selfish desires— broken pieces trying to look like something genuine and valuable. Maybe we make it too hard. We want so badly for God's will to match our agenda that we pick up anything that's shiny, but all He really wants from us is our devotion. If our purpose as Christ followers is to worship Him and build His kingdom, then the particular path we walk is not as imperative as the way we walk it. Maybe it isn't in all the tiny details. The often quoted scripture "For I know the plans I have for you ... plans to prosper you and not to harm you, plans to give you hope and a future" (Jeremiah 29:11NIV) entices us to think God wants to pave the road we travel here on earth with gold. Jesus actually is talking about our salvation, our eternal life with Him.

Instead of desperately trying to discover what we believe is His will for us, why don't we desperately seek Him? We can worship and serve God in any city or job.

He vows, "You will seek Me and find Me, when you search for Me with all your heart" (Jeremiah 29:13). Eyes open to the possibilities will find the true treasure.

One morning at therapy—actually, I was getting a pedicure (which *is* therapy!)—my friend and pedicurist Rhonda and I were talking about life and dysfunction. For years over a spa tub and nail polish, she and I have dug deeper, well beyond the normal salon chitchat.

That morning we were talking about how we think God allows tribulations so that His children don't get too comfortable here on this earth. Many are merely existing, paralyzed by uncertainty, rather than living with expectancy of God's goodness and favor.

We talked about Lee, and Rhonda told me how she thought others viewed our marriage. After hearing that they thought we had the absolute perfect marriage, I felt I needed to clear up some things. Lee was not perfect (and certainly I'm not either!), and our relationship was not without fault. Two flawed people doing life together isn't always butterflies and rainbows.

We tried to make the best of what we had to work with, and the only way we were able to maintain a healthy marriage was with God at the center. Lee would say, "Mer, I'm glad we are in this foxhole together, but we're only going to make it with Jesus in here with us!"

Jesus taught, "But seek first the kingdom of God and His righteousness, and all these things shall be added to you" (Matthew 6:33). Making God's will a priority in marriage helps to ensure sustainability. Relationships are where Satan likes to meddle. Two people can resist an attack, but with God in the circle of intimacy, the devil can't distract and destroy (Ecclesiastes 4:12).

Be careful not to underappreciate your mate in the mundane of the everyday. Don't compare your relationship to others. That's in Satan's toolbox too. Be vigilant to tell the people you care about that you treasure them. Don't make them guess.

Keep God where He longs to be: at the core of marriage. That way, love flourishes.

—— DNA ——

Oh, the intrigue. A TV commercial offered to use my DNA to reveal my heritage, and the possibility of knowing from where my ancestors came, and the different nationalities that could be embedded into my genetic makeup! Every time the commercial ran, the more I really wanted to know the history of my maternal grandmother's Native American tribe. Imagine my delight when my mother-in-law gave me a DNA kit for my birthday.

It's amazing the things science can discover. All this information at my fingertips from just a small amount of saliva? I followed the directions with precision and mailed in my DNA with excitement. Waiting for the results certainly was a lesson in patience. When the data arrived, revealing I am less than 1 percent Native American, I was sorely disappointed. My entire life, I truly had believed I was part American Indian.

Instead, I found out that I am Irish, Scottish, Welsh, German, and Scandinavian; I even have some Russian thrown into the mix. If anyone asked, I told myself, it may be less confusing to say, "I'm a little bit country and a little bit rock 'n' roll" (people my age will get it).

My Godly lineage (and yours too!) isn't confusing at all. It is exact, and there is no guessing as to my heritage. The Word tells me, "But as many as received Him, to them He gave the right to become children of God, to those who believe in His name" (John 1:12). Once we accept Christ as the Savior, the buck stops here, so to speak. We don't really need further instruction, but the words "I am the Alpha and the Omega, the Beginning and the End, the First and the Last" (Revelation 22:13) seal the case.

We no longer need to search through the ashes of time for our origin and the origin of our forefathers because once we belong to the household of faith, the family line begins and ends with the blood of Jesus.

As a child of the living God, I know who I am and *whose* I am. There's nothing wrong with curiosity as to earthly ancestry, but with Jesus, there's powerful confidence in claiming birthrights to the Eternal King.

A local church youth leader and dear friend recently shared that she was in a slump and feeling "kind of blah" about everything. She was discouraged and wondered whether she was doing enough for the teens God had placed in her life to nurture and guide.

As Christians, we have a desire to help others find the path to everlasting life. When that doesn't happen in our timing, we can feel not enough, like we are not making a difference or living up to expectations (often our own).

When my children were teenagers, my mother's heart wanted them to be happy. At the same time, I wanted them to make wise decisions and stay out of trouble. I prayed, spoke God's truth to them, nagged, and worried. Yet at the end of the day, who they were going to become and what they were going to stand for was their decision. As much as I tried to be their junior Holy Spirit, I was simply their mom. I had to trust God to do His work in their hearts.

Don't go thinking I'm a spiritual supermom! I released my kids into the hands of Jesus kicking and screaming. In one breath, I said I trusted Him to protect them, and in the next breath I practically curled up in the fetal position with worry.

Many seasons of life can feel like the land of blah: mothering little ones, when never getting out of the house is a constant; working fifty-plus hours a week, month after month; and wandering around an empty nest, silently grieving a lost purpose. The mundane certainly can seem purposeless.

But in God there is significance in every season (Ecclesiastes 3:1–8). We simply need to stay close and seek Him. When discouragement comes, take time to still the questions. Sit quietly with Him and repent, refocus, and regroup.

First, I ask God to reveal anything in my life that I need to repent of or dispose of so that I can be useful for His kingdom. Maybe I'm not trusting Him or His plan? Second, I refocus my attention on Jesus, my savior, refuge, and warrior. Perhaps I'm too focused on myself? Then, I regroup and remind myself, "You are a child of God. You belong to Him, and your life is for Him." I spend time in prayer and then meditate on

Paul's words: "I press toward the goal for the prize of the upward call of God in Christ Jesus" (Philippians 3:14).

Shine His light in every season and every place. Trust and pray for loved ones and friends, encouraging and speaking truth with grace. Be available, be expectant, and be ready.

Stand back and watch as Jesus illuminates souls!

—— Bend Your Knees ——

Pulling a muscle often happens unexpectedly. Move the wrong way or don't lift properly—and ouch! A muscle strain is painful and often inconvenient. When I strain a muscle at the gym, it's usually because I haven't stretched enough or worked out consistently.

The same may happen to our spirits. If we aren't in the Word regularly and praying, we can easily get offended by others. Certainly there are times when someone says or does something intentionally, but many times it doesn't have anything to do with the offender. He or she may not even know feelings have been hurt.

When we're overly sensitive, likely there's something much deeper going on inside. Often the offense really isn't worth getting our feathers ruffled or allowing it to distract us from our walk with Christ. I once had a friend who would say, "I just let things go, like water off a duck's back." He didn't obsess over little annoyances and kept smiling.

But that isn't as easy as it sounds for some. Ultrasensitive people have tender spirits, and asking God for a confidence boost and to fortify the spirit is important. His strength is the answer.

Satan tries to steal our joy with offenses. Jesus warns, "The thief does not come except to steal, and to kill, and to destroy. I have come that they may have life, and that they may have it more abundantly" (John 10:10). When insults sting, look to Jesus.

The rule of thumb for heavy lifting is to "bend your knees and lift with your legs." The same goes for dealing with life's offences. If we bend our knees in prayer and give it to God, we can get up and walk confidently the path set before us.

Consider the lies and betrayals Jesus endured in order to give us the ultimate abundant life. He knew His truth and was sustained by His purpose to fulfill the Father's plan. We must do the same.

── GOD-SIZE DREAM ──

What were your childhood fantasies? Whom did you aspire to be when you grew up?

When I was thirteen, I was certain I would be a successful jockey, riding in the Kentucky Derby. In high school, I dreamed of traveling the world as a National Geographic photographer. Neither of those ever came to fruition, and at twenty-one, I was a wife, a mother, and a fulltime bank employee.

I'm not saying children's dreams are silly or their aspirations are never fulfilled—look at all the Olympic athletes—but often the ideas we have for our future are shortsighted. God's plans, on the other hand, are good and perfect. "In their hearts, humans plan their course, but the Lord establishes their steps" (Proverbs 16:9 NIV).

Although math has never been my thing, I am still in mortgage banking twenty-seven years later. As I reflect on my life, I know my job doesn't define me, and my work rarely is about numbers. The relationships far outweigh the worksheets and closing documents. God has put me in a place to help people and be His mouthpiece; He knew my sweet spot wasn't on the back of a horse or behind a camera in some faraway land, but rather face-to-face with those He wants to reach.

As a mother, I had dreams for my young children as they grew into teenagers. The potential I saw in certain areas of their life lured me to map out in my mind possible career paths for them. When Jimi was a freshman in high school, she could argue so well and convincingly that I was sure she would be a powerful lawyer one day. I had Bobby ready to be a Major League Baseball prospect when he was seven. But even the most elaborate dreams we parents have for our children cannot compare to the Father's dream for them. The world's view of our children's accomplishments is about how popular they are and how much money they will make someday. God sees how much like Himself they are becoming.

In ancient times, the shepherd boy David dreamed only of leading and protecting his sheep. However, God saw a king of nations and a "man after His own heart." Joseph dreamed that he would rule over his brothers one day. That paled in comparison to God's plan: ruling over all of Egypt, which included saving his family and an entire generation from starvation. Mary was looking forward to being a wife and someday a mother, but God asked her to give birth to and raise His Son.

The Sovereign One is a game-changing God. No matter what we dream up for ourselves, He has an even better plan. Let Him dream for you!

── One True Self ──

While I was growing up, especially during my teen years, my mother occasionally would quote Shakespeare: "To thine own self be true." The first time I heard it, I asked her what it meant. In *Hamlet*, Polonius, the advisor to the king and father to Laertes, gave his son this advice as he was leaving on a trip.

Mom explained it was a reminder to Laertes that even though he would be away from home, he should always remember who he was inside and should live a good and noble life. Then she told me that she and Dad had done their best to instill in their girls the truths of faith, but it was up to us to embrace those truths and decide whose we are. Needless to say, when I often faced temptation, I heard my mother's voice in my head saying, "Meredith, remember whose daughter you are, and to thine own self be true."

As the years passed, I appreciated my mother's wisdom. But as I became more acquainted with Scripture, I struggled with the philosophy of the old adage. In fact, the New Testament says, "I have been crucified with Christ and I no longer live, but Christ lives in me. The life I now live in the body, I live by faith in the Son of God, who loved me and gave Himself for me" (Galatians 2:20 NIV). Also, Jesus declares, "Then He said to them all, 'If anyone desires to come after Me, let him deny himself, and take up his cross daily, and follow Me'" (Luke 9:23).

We are to die to self. I wondered, *Could Mom have been wrong?* She was a godly and wise woman, and I was certain my mom would have thought this advice through and measured it against God's Word before imparting it to her children.

Deciding to try to think like Jimi Buck, I searched the Scripture some more. "For in Him we live and move and have our being" (Acts 17:28). Also, "But he who is joined to the Lord is one spirit with Him" (1 Corinthians 6:17).

Being true to ourselves is being true to Christ. We are made in the image of the one true, holy God, and the Spirit of truth lives in us to keep us from all temptation and evil.

I concluded my mom was giving us biblical wisdom. We are one with Christ and indwelled with the Holy Spirit so that we can confidently heed, "To thine own self be true."

Gnats

Those irritating little creatures! Biting gnats, or swarms of no-see-ums, as we call them in the South, are pesky and downright distracting. The teeny, tiny things buzz around ears and bite like crazy.

These pests certainly can be a distraction from doing the work of the Lord, particularly mission work outdoors. But what about the spiritual pests on our everyday faith walk? The annoying co-worker, the rude clerk, the inconvenient car breakdown, the bad hair day, the sarcastic friend. They're not major disturbances, to be sure, but people and situations can sting our spirits. Such annoyances can veer us off course, make us cranky, and cause us to miss opportunities to minister to others.

Jesus affirms living this earthly life isn't easy; it means "tribulation" (John 16:33). Satan loves to mess with our marriages, friend circles, and daily agendas. He probably mutters to himself, "I can't have her soul, but I can bug (no pun intended!) the living daylights out of her and make her feel like she isn't any good to God."

How do we stand firm against this evil? "For God has not given us a spirit of fear, but of power and of love and of a sound mind" (2 Timothy 1:7). The Holy Spirit is our inner safeguard.

Like bug spray, we're instructed in Ephesians how to repel Satan. "Finally, be strong in the Lord and in His mighty power. Put on the full armor of God, so that you can take your stand against the devil's schemes" (Ephesians 6:10–11 NIV). Additional verses describe that "mighty" as "the belt of truth," "the breastplate of righteousness," "the shield of faith," "the helmet of salvation" and "the sword of the Spirit."

When gnats try to swarm our faith, we must swat them away with the goodness, faithfulness, and power of God. Instead of becoming preoccupied with all the little frustrations in life, let's praise God for our blessings, allowing the annoyances to blow away on the breeze of His grace.

—— Come Alive ——

I woke up one morning with a song in my head. *(Thankfully, it wasn't* "We all live in a yellow submarine ...") The chorus of "Come Alive (Dry Bones)" by Lauren Daigle kept repeating in my mind and flowing from my lips as I went about my morning.

> As we call out to dry bones
> Come alive, come alive
> We call out to dead hearts
> Come alive, come alive
> Up out of the ashes
> Let us see an army rise
> We call out to dry bones, come alive

I was overwhelmed by the absolute power of God. I thought to myself, *Wow, there have been so many times the Holy Spirit has renewed me and brought me back to life. I am so thankful.* Then it occurred to me, this is about so much more than just my renewal. It's about the one and only miraculous power.

I was compelled to open my Bible and read about how God set Ezekiel in a valley with an army of dead people. They were not only vast, but the bones were "very dry," meaning the men had been dead a long time. God asked Ezekiel, "Son of man, can these bones live?" Ezekiel answered, "O Lord God, You know" (Ezekiel 37:3).

The Holy Spirit reminded me, just as He may have reminded Ezekiel, that with us things may seem impossible, but with God anything is possible. I wept with relief.

Ezekiel knew the God he served and obeyed was a God of hope in hopeless situations. He relayed the message from God to the piles of bones, telling them God would cause breath to enter them, and they would live; He would restore flesh over the bones, and they would know He was the Lord.

Today, as disciples of Christ, we are called to proclaim the message that God can save and has the power to breathe life into dead things. We are to be obedient and share the gospel ... and then stand by and watch as the Holy Spirit breathes everlasting life into hearts once dead.

As a former corpse myself, I can attest that nothing is too difficult for God.

──── Peeling Eggs ────

Most mornings, I boil eggs for my two co-workers and myself. Sometimes the eggs peel with ease, the shell and skin seeming to slip right off. But other times I'm tempted to throw the egg in the trash for all the frustration and trouble it causes.

Life is like that. Some days and weeks are easy, dreamlike almost, and we feel like we're walking on clouds. Then other times, everything is more complicated. Our families or our jobs are like the uncooperative eggshell that sticks to the tender egg white.

"For He makes His sun rise on the evil and on the good, and sends rain on the just and on the unjust" (Matthew 5:45). Being a Christ follower doesn't protect us from the yuck in life. It's what we do with the unpleasant or downright horrible days that make a difference.

We have a choice: scream, throw a fit, and toss the proverbial egg in the trash, or remember it's just life. "This is the day the Lord has made; we will rejoice and be glad in it" (Psalm 118:24). It's really a matter of perspective and purpose. There is good in the midst of bad, and difficult times often are when our character is developed and we grow. We must fill our minds and hearts with God's Word (His love letter to us) and lean into His will.

God doesn't leave us without a reprieve. Jesus invites, "Come to Me, all you who labor and are heavy laden, and I will give you rest" (Matthew 11:28).

My mother would say, "Darling, this too shall pass." No matter how messed up the day may seem, even if the egg white is demolished, remember that there's always the yoke, nourishment for survival.

God is the God of both great days and horrible eggshell days. Chin up! God has a plan.

Go Organic

It seems a lot of people are going organic these days—fertilizer, food, cleaners, and even cookware. With such a desire to live chemical-, hormone-, synthetic-, GMO-, and BPA-free lives, we should also be choosing organic joy.

Wait, what? Organic joy is the difference between being happy for a time and living a truly joyful life. Let me explain. Although many people strive to be happy, their happiness may be full of synthetics. Perhaps they're seeking fulfillment through a relationship, their job, their wealth, their children, or even their social circle. These may bring moments of temporary external happiness, but true and lasting joy isn't found in any person or thing other than Christ.

It's easy to get caught up in the hype of creating our own happiness. Sadly, that never lasts. Happiness is circumstantial. The joy Jesus gives is internal and everlasting; it remains even when tragedy strikes. Joy is knowing there's always hope, always a reason to praise God. Speaking from experience, any other substitute leaves us in want.

Jesus said, "I am the true vine and My Father is the vinedresser" (John 15:1). Jesus goes on to give us the recipe for joy. He says, "Abide in Me, and I in you. As the branch cannot bear fruit of itself, unless it abides in the vine, neither can you, unless you abide in Me" (John 15:4). Then He puts a bow on it with, "These things I have spoken to you, that My joy may remain in you, and that your joy may be full" (John 15:11).

The main ingredient for lasting and true joy is to abide (obey, hold on) in the vine. It's a fruit (like love, peace, and self-control) that grows out of a life with Jesus (Galatians 5:22). Then it's passed on. Once we have the joy that comes from Christ, we want to share it with others. Much like when we start eating healthier and see the benefits.

Bottom line: True and lasting joy, the peace that surpasses all understanding, is the result of an intimate relationship with Christ. Oh, and it's free! Jesus already paid the exorbitant price for us when He died on the cross for our sins.

This is the real deal. No gimmicks, no hidden ingredients, no sleight of hand … just Jesus. Pure "organic joy" can be found only in Christ. Don't wait. Go organic.

──── The Good Investment ────

I had a dream one night that I'd made a good investment and came into a lot of money. In the dream, a friend hugged me the next day and said, "You don't feel any richer."

"That's because I was rich already. The other is just money." I woke up, and even though I was a little disappointed a windfall wasn't sitting in my bank account, I knew the dream was God's truth.

I am rich. God has blessed me abundantly. I may not have a large bankroll, but I have things money can't buy, and I am extremely thankful. The priceless gift of salvation is enough, and yet He has given me so much more: health; an amazing family and group of friends who are Christ followers; a precious, healthy granddaughter; a safe home; and a fulfilling job. I even count the trials in my life as blessings because those times grew my faith and trust in Christ.

Jesus teaches, "But lay up for yourselves treasures in heaven" (Matthew 6:20). Investing in earthly possessions brings only temporary happiness. Using our time, talent, and resources with a cheerful, generous heart for God's kingdom is eternal. Sometimes I feel a bit sad when I think about the early years with my children. I worked hard to make a living and provide for what we needed. Long hours at the bank meant missing out on moments I can never get back. There were times I was physically present but not mentally; —my mind was working a mortgage deal or worrying about clients' needs.

As a citizen of Heaven, the urgency of my loved ones requires my wholehearted devotion. Even though I cannot retrace my steps, I have learned that the "stop and drop everything" response to my family's needs (while still being responsible at work) pleases God. Paul wrote to the Christians in Corinth, reminding them, "But this I say: He who sows sparingly will also reap sparingly, and he who sows bountifully will also reap bountifully" (2 Corinthians 9:6).

Jesus often went out of His way, or stopped what He was doing, to help those in need. Consider the time Jesus took the road through Samaria to meet the woman at the well, or how He passed through Jericho and made time to dine with the tax collector Zacchaeus. He also pardoned the woman caught in the act of adultery, healed the bleeding woman in the crowd, and restored the sight of blind Bartimaeus. What if He had said, "I'm too busy with my ministry to help these people"?

Sometimes we don't see what's right in front of us because we're too focused on the important work we're doing—and often it's church work! Let's make sure we let Jesus have control of our calendar and our time-management bank account. I want to invest in the immeasurable abundant riches of Heaven. Don't you?

We've all done something we are extremely ashamed of in our lifetime. Admit it. Maybe we never told another soul; in fact, we most likely desperately tried to forget. We cringe when a memory creeps back up, and we wish we could have a do-over. Unfortunately, we can't.

Guess what? That thing, that terrible sin, doesn't keep God from loving us! In fact, when Jesus was carrying His own cross to the place where He would die, He didn't rehearse our indiscretions and reconsider sacrificing Himself. No, it was the opposite. Jesus looked through the mist of time and saw me, and He saw you, knowing every bad choice we had made and would make in the future. Yet He was determined to pay the ultimate price to save His creation!

When we feel weighed down with the guilt and unforgiveness of the past, we have to open the Bible. There is no sin more powerful than the blood of Jesus Christ. When we feel unworthy of this loving sacrifice, we can read and be reminded that we did not make Him give up His life for us. Jesus willingly gave His life in exchange for ours.

"But God demonstrates His own love toward us, in that while we were still sinners, Christ died for us" (Romans 5:8). It's scandalous in its truth! Because of this great love gift, we are worthy to be called the children of God.

We can't go back and we don't need do-overs. Trying to hide from the hideous is needless. We live today in freedom from sin. "Looking unto Jesus, the author and finisher of our faith, who for the joy that was set before Him endured the cross, despising the shame, and has sat down at the right hand of the throne of God" (Hebrews 12:2).

We have a reason to rejoice today. God loves us and willingly died for us.

HURRICANES

Wind, rain, and storm-surging seas are a frequent occurrence on the Florida coast from May through November. We sit glued to our televisions, like the rest of the world, wondering, "What's going to happen?" For most residents, when the weather threatens disaster, the song "Should I Stay or Should I Go?" by The Clash plays in our heads.

When the wind kicks up in life, we're tempted to shake with fear too. We may panic and lose sight of the one who is ultimately in control. The twelve in the boat is a familiar Bible story. "The disciples went and woke Him, saying, 'Lord, save us! We're going to drown!' He replied, 'You of little faith, why are you so afraid?' Then He got up and rebuked the winds and the waves, and it was completely calm" (Matthew 8:25–26 NIV).

So often we ride the waves of anxiety when we worry about the trajectory of our future. I have experienced tragedy, and I know bad things happen. There's no trying to "figure it out." It's a matter of choice for me: I will trust the Sovereign Lord who loves me completely.

When my stomach starts to feel queasy and my nerves begin sizzling with fear, I lean into His Word. "The name of the LORD *is* a strong tower; The righteous run to it and are safe" (Proverbs 18:10). "But let all who take refuge in You be glad; let them ever sing for joy. Spread Your protection over them, that those who love Your name may rejoice in You" (Psalm 5:11 NIV).

Still, I sometimes waver, and I want to put my trust in my earthly capabilities and allow my finite mind to fret, "What is going to happen to me and the ones I love?" Even though the loving Savior has shown me time and again that His ways are perfect, I tend to want to believe my escape plan might be better.

With eyes glued on the storm, it's difficult to see anything else. We are creatures of survival; we fear disaster, and we want to live. Therefore we cry out, "Have mercy on me, my God, have mercy on me, for in You I take refuge. I will take refuge in the shadow of Your wings until the disaster has passed" (Psalm 57:1 NIV).

Turning our focus from the possibility of impending doom to Jesus, we'll likely discover that God has the best plan. He may not move the storm from our path, but only He can calm the "category five" in our hearts.

Backstory

We can learn a lot about people from their Facebook pages. Most of the time, it is simply the highlight reel, the parts of their lives they want to be seen. Sometimes, though, there is real insight if we stop to look closer.

I recently noticed a post from a mother who had lost her child to drowning several years ago. Her post pled, "If I have been unkind or short lately, please forgive me, I am just having a hard time dealing." This stayed with me throughout the day. I knew others who didn't know her or her situation may think she is quick-tempered. But by knowing people's stories, we are likely to be more understanding and extend more grace.

We come across people every day who may not be very pleasant or outgoing. They may need our smile, kindness, encouragement, and grace the most. We don't know what others are going through or what their backstories might be. When people are experiencing emotional or physical pain, it often affects the things they do and the way they act.

It's like the story of the woman at the well (John 4). With five previous husbands and a current live-in boyfriend, I'm certain she had a backstory. Did she have a father wound? Was she looking for love in all the wrong places? Jesus knew what she was struggling with and offered her everlasting love and "living water" (John 4:13–14).

Shouldn't we follow the example of Christ? Sometimes people might simply need to know someone cares, or they may need to hear the good news of the Living Water. We usually don't know people's backstory, but we know the one who can step into stories to mend broken hearts and heal wounds. Let's not keep Him to ourselves.

"Because of the Lord's great love, we are not consumed, for His compassions never fail" (Lamentations 3:22–23 NIV). God's mercy is new every morning, and He is faithful beyond our imaginations.

If we can recall the time Jesus walked into our stories and changed our lives forever, then we must pass it on.

Intentional Living

Not too long ago, I decided that I was going to get back to the gym. I already had a membership at a local fitness center, but a new spot opened that offered Pilates, yoga, and kickboxing. I joined that place too.

Three months later, I hadn't gone once. The problem? I was not being intentional about my health. A well-toned body wasn't going to magically happen. I had to start being deliberate about making wellness a priority.

We also must be intentional—do something on purpose—in our relationship with Christ. Activities important to our spiritual growth must be at the top of our list. Reading the Word, praying, telling the lost about Jesus, spending time with and encouraging other believers, and being the hands and feet of Christ enrich our relationship with the Savior.

Good intentions are great, but allowing other things to sneak up and take precedence is the downfall. There has to be action behind intent.

"Faith by itself, if it does not have works, is dead" (James 2:17). We must believe God and live a God-centered, Jesus-following life. When we see a person in need and have the ability to help, then we must take action.

> "For I was hungry and you gave Me food; I was thirsty and you gave Me drink; I was a stranger and you took me in; I was naked and you clothed Me, I was sick and you visited Me; I was in prison and you came to Me." Then the righteous will answer Him, saying "Lord, when did we see You hungry and feed You, or thirsty and give You drink? When did we see You a stranger and take You in, or naked and clothe You? Or when did we see You sick, or in prison and come to You?" And the King will answer and say to them, "Assuredly, I say to you, inasmuch as you did it to one of the least of these My brethren, you did it to Me." (Matthew 25:35–40)

When we see others through the eyes of Christ, we respond as He would.

Being a disciple of Jesus Christ is not always convenient, but it is always beneficial. If there is someone the Holy Spirit places on our hearts to reach out to, then we must give that person a call.

I tell myself, "Meredith, having a gym membership does not guarantee you a fit body. You must do something!" The same goes with being a Christian. Be intentional today. See, reach, give, tell, and love.

—— Ripple Effect ——

Each life creates a ripple effect. We are all connected by God's design, and He sees the entirety of every life past, present, and future. In my own heart, I believe God loves us so very much that He looks at circumstances that happen in this fallen world (illness, accidents, etc.) and says, "Right now is when bringing My child home will impact others for My glory and draw them to Me."

From the very beginning, the story of Joseph illustrates God's redeeming love. "You intended to harm me, but God intended it for good to accomplish what is now being done, the saving of many lives" (Genesis 50:20 NIV).

I once witnessed a family say goodbye to their sixteen-year-old son. I wept for their loss, and although I had only met Zach one time, he made an impression on me. He was engaging and kind; I could tell he was special. At the funeral, his mom shared his love for Jesus and others, and how Zach was not afraid to share his faith. Zach's family will never know on this side of eternity why Zach died so young.

Death is so deeply emotional and stunningly final. Since losing Mom to cancer and experiencing the sudden death of Lee, I have reconciled I will see them in Heaven and finally understand. I often remind myself that as children of God, our final destination is filled with awe and divine understanding, knowing all have been rescued.

My mom once was asked by a friend, "Jimi, why would God allow you to get cancer?"

After some thought, she answered, "Well, if one of my children, loved ones, or any lost soul grows closer or accepts Christ because of my journey, then it is worth it."

Her wisdom was gained through much study of the Scripture. In Acts 2, after Christ's death and resurrection, the day of Pentecost occurred, and thus began the Church. They worshiped together, struggled together, and took care of one another. They were willing to do whatever it took to spread the good news. "And the Lord added to their number daily those who were being saved" (Acts 2:47).

We are all witnesses to His saving grace, and we are called to be Jesus's hands and feet.

I believe if God had given Jimi, Lee, and Zachary a choice—a foreknowledge of their death and the ripple effect—each of them would have said, "Yes, Lord. The answer is yes!"

—— Heal Us ——

One morning as I was reading my Bible, I swiftly read over the familiar instructions written by Paul. "Be anxious for nothing, but in everything by prayer and supplication, with thanksgiving, let your requests be made known to God; and the peace of God, which surpasses all understanding, will guard your hearts and minds through Christ Jesus" (Philippians 4:6–7).

I felt the Holy Spirit whisper, "Go back." I read the verse again, slowly this time. Breaking it down, I asked myself the hard question: "Do I do these things?" It had been a hard week, and I thought about all the times I had been stressed and worried. Ugh! I had failed miserably at "Be anxious for nothing." Trying to make myself feel better, I exhaled and said, "Well, Mer, you pray and you're thankful."

The next word, however, stopped me dead in my tracks. Supplication? Not a word I use often, if ever. I looked up the definition and read aloud. "The action of asking or begging for something earnestly or humbly." While I was growing up, our parents always told us not to beg, whine, or ask for something more than once. I figured it counted for God too.

Then I wondered if I'd been missing a very important ingredient in my prayer life. "Do I plead with God to show me His will? Do I earnestly pray for my children, friends, and community? Do I beg God to bring peace to our country? Do I kneel in humility, asking the heavenly Father what I can do to bring Him glory?" The answers made me sad.

I'm certain our world, our families, and our own fragile hearts would benefit from doing "everything by prayer and supplication." I know I long for "the peace of God, which surpasses all understanding."

This revelation to Scripture changed my approach to prayer. Unfortunately, there's no going back to change things, but starting with the present, I'm going to ask God to fill me with His love for others, heal all hearts, and free all His people from the bondage of fear. "If My people, who are called by My name, will humble themselves and pray and seek My face and turn from their wicked ways, then I will hear from heaven, and I will forgive their sin and will heal their land" (2 Chronicles 7:14).

Just imagine: "heal their land." In the midst of all the confusion, hatred, tragedy, and violence, this is a gloriously beautiful thought. Let us pray.

Predictably Unpredictable

I like routine. I love a good solid plan, and I'm ultra predictable. One Valentine's Day, Jon took me to one of our favorite restaurants. Our church had given all the married couples a date idea to order each other's meal. We decided to give it a try.

Jon will eat anything and usually orders something different each time we go out. I get the same exact meal every time at certain restaurants. On this date, when I ordered Jon's meal, I chose something I thought he would enjoy, and I expected him to order my usual. When he ordered something much different than my standard fare, I smiled politely, but my brain screamed, *What in the world? Why would he do that?*

Don't we do the same with God? We ask Him to intervene in our lives, and we invite Him to direct our paths. Yet when His plan deviates from what we expect, we balk.

As we waited for the food, I took a deep breath and said to myself, *I'm going to eat it no matter what,* even though I knew I wasn't going to like it. Do you know what? When my meal arrived and I tasted my first bite, I was surprised at how delicious it was! The food was cooked just right and instantly became a favorite.

We want what we want, but God knows what's best. "And my God will meet all your needs according to the riches of His glory in Christ Jesus" (Philippians 4:19). I still like predictability; I'm simply learning to be more flexible, to expand my outside-the-box thinking.

God is predictably unpredictable. He is trustworthy but doesn't always show up in the way we think He should. The Bible says, "For My thoughts are not your thoughts, nor are your ways My ways" (Isaiah 55:8).

The next time things don't go as planned, remember the saying, "When things seem to be falling apart, they may be falling into place."

One Easter weekend, Katy asked if she could read the resurrection story to Jon and me. We waited as she opened her Bible, and then we listened to her read about the empty tomb and the disciple's journey down the road to Emmaus.

"Mer, why didn't the disciples recognize Jesus? Didn't they know Him?" she stopped to ask.

I thought, *Oh, no! This is one of those teachable moments I'm pretty sure I'm going to blow!* I hesitantly answered, "Well, um, maybe it's because the last time they saw Jesus, He was beaten, bloody, and all scratched up, and now He is raised back to life and clean."

Her question stayed with me for a while. "Why didn't they recognize Jesus?" I read the account again, pouring over the Gospel of John, where Mary Magdalene is weeping at the tomb and encounters Jesus. She thought He was the gardener at first, but when He spoke her name, she instantly knew it was her Lord (John 20:11–18).

In Luke, the two disciples walking the road to Emmaus had seven miles with Jesus, and they also didn't know it was the Master. Later while eating together, they finally realized who had been with them the entire time (Luke 24:13–35). Surely they hit the heel of their hands to their foreheads, saying, "Duh, we should have known it was Him!"

I thought, *Wow. It took Mary less than five minutes to realize it was Jesus, and it took the men seven miles and dinner.* (Sorry, gentlemen.) While grieving the loss of their teacher and friend, they must have been distracted by their circumstances, momentarily forgetting all of the promises and prophecies Jesus had proclaimed. Instead of running to the tomb on the third day with total expectancy of His resurrection, they were surprised He had done exactly what He'd told them He would do.

I also thought, *I'm no better than they are!* We get so caught up in the thick of things, the disappointments and sorrows, that we fail to remember and claim God's sovereignty, provision, and redemption. On our darkest days, Jesus is right beside us.

I've heard it said all my life that the devil is in the details. That's only partly true. Satan is in the details of our blame, guilt, shame, and woeful wallowing. These are the distractions He uses to take our eyes off the Deliverer.

But Jesus cares about our every heartache and tear. He is there to greet us at the tomb and walk with us down the road. We must keep our eyes open to His presence, which is the gift of Easter. He died and rose in victory so that we can live with hope-filled expectancy.

—— Two Buses ——

While living in a small town, I didn't get away with much as a teenager. And I didn't always appreciate it. As a parent, however, I usually knew what my kids were up to, and my appreciation of my tight-knit community grew.

The expression "It takes a village to raise a child" was proven true one high school prom season. Of the two buses rented to transport teens to the prom, one actually wasn't going to the prom. Parents spread the news, talked to one another, and encouraged their children to get on the "right" bus.

In life there also are two buses, and because God is a gentleman, He has given us the freedom to make a choice as to which one we board. He's also instructing us to make the right choice throughout His Word. "Enter by the narrow gate; for wide is the gate and broad is the way that leads to destruction, and there are many who go in by it. Because narrow is the gate and difficult is the way which leads to life, and there are few who find it" (Matthew 7:13–14).

My kids told me what seemed like a million times, "Mom, everybody else is doing it!" It certainly seems so, but the better way—though less popular and more difficult—actually leads to more freedom from sin, destruction, fear, and so much more. The path to abundant life appears to be the obvious choice. Yet the lure of instant, worldly gratification often skews our wisdom.

When standing at the crossroads, we must ask ourselves, "Will my choice glorify God, build my character, and lead others toward Christ?" If not, we'd be wise to go the other direction. Though the narrow way may look lonely at first, on this journey, "There is a friend who sticks closer than a brother" (Proverbs 18:24). And He is with us always, "even to the end of the age" (Matthew 28:20).

Jesus offers so much more than temporary pleasure. He wants to gift us with abundance and freedom. Climb aboard the bus that will get you safely home.

—— WORDS ——

"My darling, hateful words are like bullets: once they are released, you can't take them back. And when they hit their mark, they always leave a scar." That's how Momma answered my fourteen-year-old question about why someone in our family was getting a divorce. She knew it wasn't appropriate for me to hear the details of the adult situation at the time, but she wanted me to know how powerful words are.

It was the first and only time my mom gave me such advice. However, it made an impact then, and over the next thirty or so years, the lesson has come to mind time and again.

Scripture says, "Death and life are in the power of the tongue" (Proverbs 18:21). Also, "The words of the reckless pierce like swords, but the tongue of the wise brings healing" (Proverbs 12:18 NIV). James, the half-brother of Jesus, says, "No man can tame the tongue. It is a restless evil, full of deadly poison" (James 3:8).

That's powerful teaching! So, how can we keep from speaking ugly words to one another? God gave us the solution when, through Paul, Scripture tells us, "Casting down every argument and every high thing that exalts itself against the knowledge of God, bringing every though into captivity to the obedience of Christ" (2 Corinthians 10:5). And then there's "Whatever things are true, whatever things are noble, whatever things are just, whatever things are pure, whatever things are lovely, whatever things are of good report, if there is any virtue and if there is anything praiseworthy—meditate on these things." (Philippians 4:8).

Christ is the only way to bring our wayward minds and mouth muscles into submission. Hurtful thoughts and words toward others are careless and often rooted deep inside. "For the mouth speaks what the heart is full of" (Luke 6:45 NIV). My mom used to say, "Garbage in, garbage out."

Let's pray for our hearts, thoughts, and words every morning before we even greet our family, co-workers, and friends. We can fill our hearts and minds with the good things of God by reading His word and remembering to encourage others with words that affirm and lift. When Christ is in the forefront of our hearts and minds, we don't spew hateful words but only speak love.

—— DREAM ——

My family members and close friends know I dream frequently. I don't share my dreams with many people, but one a few years ago left a big impression.

I dreamed I was on an airplane and trying to sleep. People around me were shouting that the plane was going down and we were going to crash. I lifted my head and calmly told those around me, "Don't worry; it won't hurt when we hit the ground. But you want to make sure you have a relationship with Jesus. It's not too late."

Then I woke up. I remember wondering how many of the two hundred or more passengers knew Him as the Way, the Truth, and the Life.

It's scary to tell people they need a Savior, but God always opens the door for us to share our faith. He also gives us the courage. Sometimes we don't even have to say a word; our faith can shine on good days and even on days full of trial. My mom used to tell me, "Sweetheart, your life may be the only Bible someone will ever read, so let them see Jesus in your day-to-day walk, and they will want what you have."

Some days we can feel like we're on a collision course with anxiety and devastation. When fear presses in, speak the words of David: "Whenever I am afraid, I will trust in You" (Psalm 56:3). Faith dissolves fear, much like the sun burns away the morning mist.

The day will come when we'll each face the Creator and Judge. Will we be found faithful? Now, while we're still living, do we ask ourselves, "Am I sharing the good news of salvation or keeping it to myself?"

It's never too late to surrender our souls to Christ, no matter who we are and what we've done. The heavenly Pilot is waiting to welcome everyone to first class.

—— Who Are You? ——

Imagine meeting someone for the first time. A conversation begins, and before long the question pops up: "So, what do you do for a living?" Once the question is answered, this is likely how you are defined in each other's minds: banker, doctor, homemaker, construction supervisor, outside sales, teacher, pastor.

We subconsciously give ourselves titles. I am a widow, divorcee, orphan; I am unworthy, unloved, unclean, a failure. We think who we are consists of the roles we play or the things that have happened to us. But the labels we put on ourselves are not what God calls us.

God's Word is the ultimate truth, so let's look and see what it says about who we are. How we are defined by God is much different than how we sometimes define ourselves or how the world might define us.

We are God's "sons and daughters" (2 Corinthians 6:18), His "friend" (John 15:15), and God's "masterpiece" (Ephesians 2:10). We are "altogether beautiful" (Song of Solomon 4:7). My very favorite is that we are His "beloved" (Song of Solomon 6:3).

Are we going to believe the Word or the world? When Satan's lies invade our minds and we think of ourselves as less than lovely, we must not let the evil one's belittling take up space in our heads.

One of the hardest things for us to comprehend is the unconditional love of Christ. We are very hard on ourselves. And the rest of the world? Let's just say it can be ruthless. If Satan can't destroy us, he will try to distract us and tear us down with untruths.

Here's the challenge. Write down on one sheet of paper who we "think" we are, and on another write who God says we are. Now, burn the first piece, because who God says we are is the only thing that matters.

Be encouraged. He sees us through the precious blood of His only Son, and we are His beautiful and beloved children.

I rarely cook dinner. My mother-in-law cooks for the entire family every weekday evening. Yes, I am a blessed woman. This generous woman takes a task off my plate (pun intended) after a long workday and allows us to sit down together for a family meal. Plus, I actually love spending time with my in-laws.

One night as we finished eating and began to talk, I started gathering the plates. (The least I can do is wash the dishes!) Mimi suggested, "Why don't you sit and relax some more?"

I realized in that moment that I am a woman of action. I'm accustomed to finishing a task at work and then going directly to the next file, phone call, or crisis; I have programmed myself to keep moving. This developed trait was keeping me from relaxing and enjoying the moment. Past experience has taught me that the people we love and cherish may not be with us forever, yet I was missing out on creating memories.

This is reminiscent of another woman named Martha. She too was missing out on some really good stuff. In the Gospel of Luke, Martha and her sister, Mary, were hosts to Jesus and His disciples. Mary sat at the feet of Jesus and soaked up His every word while Martha was in the kitchen, focused on getting the meal prepared. When Martha complained about doing all the work, Jesus enlightened her. "Martha, Martha, you are worried and troubled about many things. But one thing is needed, and Mary has chosen that good part, which will not be taken away from her" (Luke 10:41–42).

Jesus knew He would not be with His friends for much longer, and while Mary was soaking up His wisdom and creating memories, Martha thought she was doing what "needed" to be done. In reality, the dishes would always be there to wash, and someone would always be there for her to serve. However, this special moment with Jesus would not always be there.

There are appropriate times for action, as well as times for being still and listening. Constant busyness, running from one task to the next, may cost precious moments and missed memories. Remember that distractions often destroy.

Sitting in the Word, communing with God, and carving out memories with loved ones are priceless.

When I was on a work trip once with Jon in Starkville, Mississippi, we were invited to dinner at the home of one of his old teammates, who became the head baseball coach for Mississippi State University. Jon and I both are directionally challenged, and so we used our GPS most of the trip. The Cohens live about fifteen miles on the outskirts of town, but we arrived without getting lost.

Heading back to the hotel was another story. It was dark and rainy, and there were tornado warnings in the area. We turned the wrong way upon leaving the neighborhood. A few miles later, we decided to put the hotel address into the GPS. Next thing we knew, the nice lady told us to turn down what we quickly realized was a dirt road. It narrowed dangerously, and we talked about turning around. However, with the rain, mud, and deep ditches on each side, that wasn't possible. We drove slowly forward. When we came to a rickety bridge, I was skeptical as we crossed, but we made it. Phew! Once it was practical to turn around, we had to decide: do we turn off the GPS and navigate ourselves, or do we keep following the voice?

I thought about Solomon's wise words. "But the path of the just is like the shining sun, that shines ever brighter unto the perfect day" (Proverbs 4:18). I prayed for some light. We didn't know what was ahead of us, and our surroundings looked a lot like a scene from the movie *Deliverance*. Utterly lost, with the rain pounding on the windshield, we dreaded the thought that the GPS was wrong. I felt a moment of panic; a trickle of fear ran down my spine.

We pushed ahead, deciding to follow the GPS, and made it safely to our hotel. My blood pressure finally returned to normal. I thought to myself, *That detour was a lot like life.*

We certainly don't know what's ahead. Hopefully it's easy travels, but most likely it's also detours, potholes, and dead ends. We will reach our final destination easier if we read the map (God's Word), trust Jesus's promises, and follow the leading of the Holy Spirit. "In all your ways acknowledge Him, and He shall direct your paths" (Proverbs 3:6).

Don't turn off the GPS: God's Plan of Salvation. Lay fears at the feet of the One who knows the path perfectly, and grow closer to Him while on the journey.

"I am the way, the truth, and the life. No one comes to the Father except through Me" (John 14:6). Jesus is the ultimate GPS, and following Him always leads to home.

───── WILDFIRES ─────

Dry conditions from seasonal drought, along with high winds, have destroyed thousands of acres in Florida, wreaking havoc on crops, homes, and lives. Fires can begin with a tiny spark or a controlled burn that gets out of control. The person innocently burning backyard trash or leaving a still-smoldering campfire unattended probably doesn't think about the potential for widespread harm.

Much like devastating wildfires, when our souls are parched due to lack of "water" (communion with God and reading His Word), we are more susceptible to sin. What we think of as small and harmless could become a roaring fire of destruction in our lives. Fortunately, the Creator knows us so well that He lovingly warns of the things He knows can hinder our relationship with Him and others.

James 3 reminds us that the tongue, while purposed for good (speaking, in this example), has the ability to cause tremendous pain to others, as well as lie. "It corrupts the whole body, sets the whole course of one's life on fire" (James 3:6 NIV). The eyes too can get us into trouble. Jesus gives the example, "But I tell you that anyone who looks at a woman lustfully has already committed adultery with her in his heart" (Matthew 5:28 NIV).

God's fire safety manual, the Bible, doesn't exaggerate. He knows us better than we know ourselves. In our world, think about the little white lie, the flirty glance, or the "just one drink" promise, and then recall the careers, marriages, and years of sobriety that have been wrecked. Of course, Satan wants us to believe a "little sin" is harmless." But Scripture sets us straight. Jesus says, "The thief does not come except to steal, and to kill, and to destroy. I have come that they may have life, and that they may have it more abundantly" (John 10:10).

Although what starts out as small may not seem so bad, it can expand and enslave or trap us without warning. God wants us to live in the freedom of His grace. "Jesus answered them, 'Most assuredly, I say to you, whoever commits sin is a slave of sin. And a slave does not abide in the house forever, but a son abides forever. Therefore, if the Son makes you free, you shall be free indeed'" (John 8:34–36).

Be quick to recognize a spark of sin that could turn into a wildfire. Act quickly and reach for the extinguisher; open the Bible, and turn to the ultimate Savior. Jesus drenches the soul with His love and forgiveness, and spiritual drought becomes only a distant memory.

God Revealed in Us

We wonder why bad things happen to good people. Even though we know God allows the natural consequences of our choices to unfold, often it's easy to feel like He's angry. The *why* comes in when we're living in a right relationship with Him and bad stuff happens.

There's a Bible story about a man who was blind since birth. Jesus's disciples saw the man and asked, "'Rabbi, who sinned, this man or his parents, that he was born blind?' Jesus answered, 'Neither this man nor his parents sinned, but that the works of God should be revealed in him'" (John 9:2–3). There have been times I've had similar questions. "What did I do to deserve this, God?" The Scripture in John teaches this is backward thinking. God sometimes allows situations so that He can be glorified. Doing the work of His Father, Jesus restores the blind man's sight, and many witnesses were awed.

We often look inward at our own situation or debilitation, not understanding why things are the way they are. From a small inconvenience to a terrible tragedy, it's very easy to forget life isn't all about us. We certainly may not have caused or deserve the challenges we face, but we are part of a bigger story—God's story.

Remember that we have a secure heritage and are assured earthly suffering is not in vain. "The Spirit Himself testifies with our spirit that we are God's children. Now if we are children, then we are heirs—heirs of God and co-heirs with Christ, if indeed we share in His sufferings in order that we may also share in His glory. I consider that our present sufferings are not worth comparing with the glory that will be revealed in us" (Romans 8:16–18 NIV).

Pain and misery are difficult. Yet, if we can grasp the truth that God never forsakes us but uses circumstances for the greater good of building His eternal kingdom, then the suffering may ease a bit. Joy may seem far right away now and trusting God's plan too hard, but His love is faithful. He will carry you until you feel strong enough to walk again and can proclaim, "To God be the glory."

The Bible story about the little boy with five loaves of bread and two small fish (John 6) is a good reminder our Lord is a miracle worker. But think about it: What if the boy had said, "I can't give you my food because it may not be good enough," and, "I may not have enough for myself." What if he was so worried about what other people might think of his gift that he hid it?

We know Jesus could have spoken an ample supply of food into existence. However, He wanted the boy to be a part of glorifying the Provider.

> He said, "Bring them here to Me." Then He commanded the multitudes to sit down on the grass. And He took the five loaves and the two fish, and looking up to heaven, He blessed and broke and gave the loaves to the disciples; and the disciples gave to the multitudes. So they all ate and were filled, and they took up twelve baskets full of the fragments that remained. (Matthew 14:18–20)

The boy's willingness to share what he had not only exalted Jesus right then and there but also lasted for generations to come. Imagine him telling his family and friends about his firsthand encounter with the Savior of the world. What an impact one child's selflessness had on the kingdom.

What are we holding back that could be used to glorify God and further His work? And *why* do we hold it back? What lie do we believe? That we'll be laughed at, be called a failure, or be rejected? Are we worried our ugly past eliminates us from serving Him?

The truth is that if our gift is time, talent, money, or resources, God will use it for His glory. Whatever is offered with an obedient and willing heart pleases Him, no matter how small or insignificant we may think it is. And just as Jesus told the disciples to gather up the remaining pieces of food, He has a plan for the leftovers in our lives. With Christ, nothing is wasted!

If we are willing, He will use us and our gifts, and He will not leave us, or our hands, empty. We are worthy, and we are useful. God is waiting to have it all.

One Sunday morning, my pastor opened with the question, "Is the amazing grace you experienced at the time of salvation still amazing to you?" It caught my attention, and I must admit I didn't hear much of his message after that. My thoughts were hijacked by how unfathomable it is that God's love for us is so great He would sacrifice His only Son for sinful mankind.

Scripture proclaims, "For God so loved the world that He gave His only begotten Son, that whoever believes in Him should not perish but have everlasting life" (John 3:16). When we forget the details of that sacrifice, our feelings of gratitude may wane, but it doesn't lessen the magnitude of the sacrifice.

Remember falling in love? The fast heart beats and wide smiles, with every thought and sighting of that person. The elation of being together. But as time went by and the relationship grew more comfortable, even though the frequent feelings of euphoria may have waned, the love didn't.

What about God's grace? New believers are often on fire and overwhelmed with the realization of Jesus's death and resurrection. As time goes by and spiritual maturity grows, the gratitude may grow complacent unless His grace and sacrifice are front and center. The brutal scenes from *The Passion of the Christ* evoke an emotional reaction, quicken our memories, and take us back to the moment we accepted Christ as Savior.

As a young person, I heard a story about an orphan boy who was adopted by a king. He was given new clothes and a steward of his own. Every morning, the steward watched as the boy dragged a box from behind his bedroom door, stood in front of the mirror, held in front of him the rags he used to wear, and cry. After several months, the steward finally asked the boy, "Why do you keep those ragged clothes in a box, and why do you hold them up in the mirror and cry?"

With tears in his eyes and a smile on his face, the boy said, "I never want to forget what the king did for me!"

We too have been adopted and redeemed. And though we do not need to rehearse our sin, we certainly should reminisce often that moment of the beautiful exchange when we surrendered to the Savior, and He took our sins and in turn extended His grace.

My Deepest Thanks

When I first felt an early tug in my heart to write this book, I resisted. The thought of being vulnerable back in 2015 didn't appeal to me, and the dread of reliving my grief loomed heavy. But through sharing bits and pieces of my story on Facebook with my sunrise photos, I discovered the world is full of hurting people who desire encouragement and hope.

I was also hesitant to put a spotlight on my story and the devastating death of Lee, because I worried it would overshadow the wonderful love I now share with Jon. But Jon urged me to believe that my story (in book form) is also part of God's plan, and to trust the divine timing and purpose of us.

My incredible husband is my biggest fan, and I could not ask for a more perfect life mate with whom to serve the Lord and walk through the midlife and senior years together. Thank you, Jon, for your all-in, amazing heart and the delight you bring to my life every single day.

As I prayed God's guidance, the words began to flow. I shared the pages with my daughter, Jimi, who was my partner in prayer over this project and my number one source of encouragement. As I sent Jimi the raw pieces of myself on paper, she lovingly returned honest and useful feedback. My other prayer warrior and book confidante was my mother-in-law, Joyce Shave, also known as Mimi. She was brutally forthright with her opinions (which I secretly love), and she never failed to offer support. Mimi called me often on Saturday mornings to ask, "Well, are you writing? You'd better get busy!"

I am so thankful for Jimi's soul-deep belief in me and Joyce's mothering love and cheerleading. Without these two faith-filled women and their constant validation, I'm not sure I would have been brave enough to keep on writing.

A window opened for me in September 2017 in a way other people might think was a door closing. I was given the opportunity to talk with a well-known Christian author and was excited to glean knowledge and guidance from her. She encouraged me to attend a writer's conference and offered some tips. Then she broke the news that my manuscript would most likely never get published traditionally. She shared that if I wasn't a known author, famous, or bizarre (like Octomom), no one would likely want to read my story. She was honest, and I was discouraged.

But God used that experience for good. That conversation prompted me to search the Internet for a Christian book coach, and I found Lee McCracken. Her tender heart and mine immediately melded. What a gift she is. God knew exactly who I needed to help me to the finish line. Thank you, Lee, for being not only a talented writer, editor, and coach but also a dear sister in Christ. Your heart for the things of God and others is inspiring.

I also want to thank Angie for proving that distance does not limit friendship. Ben, thank you for all of the advice over the years, and for being like a brother. Beth, you know everything about me and still love me, which is truly a gift. Bianca, my sixth sister, you encourage me daily, I am blessed to have you in my life. "RA!" Kara, your friendship, godly wisdom, and faithfulness inspire me to do likewise. Lindsay (Lou), "shame friend," you are one of a kind, and I love you. Lynn: wow, just wow; I would have to write another book to express how God has used you in my life. Thank you for being sensitive to His promptings; it changed our lives forever. Pam, your friendship and 6:00 a.m. Friday Starbucks dates are a highlight of my week. Tiffany, thank you for listening to me for hours upon hours of treadmill talk; you are wise beyond your years. Christy (you should have been a truck driver) and Laura, thank you for driving me to meet my book coach, because without you two, I probably would have ended up in Miami instead of North Carolina.

Dr. Linda and Dr. Judy, I can never thank you enough for your wisdom, love, and counsel. Thank you, Claudia (my soul sister) and George, for welcoming me into your home, giving me time to regroup and begin healing. Carolyn and Todd, thank you for making me leave my house and go to dinners with you (even if you did threaten to make me go in my pajamas if not dressed in ten minutes); you two never forgot about me. To the many others who encouraged, inspired, and loved me along the way: thank you.

When I think back over the years, my testimony of Jesus's saving grace in the midst of any storm is out of the fullness of joy I feel today. Thank you for reading my story and opening your heart to healing. May the Holy Spirit flood your soul with His peace.

Love,
Mer

About the Author

Meredith Shave is a wife, mother and grandmother who lives the hope of Jesus with every sunrise on her beloved Florida First Coast. With more than 20 years in the mortgage industry, she nurtures her creative side by writing and taking photographs at the beach. She also has a deep love of horses and finds joy in riding. Meredith was raised in the church and sang with her families performing group throughout her childhood. Her life's story is a testimony to God's redeeming grace.

Printed in the United States
By Bookmasters